The Me I Left Behind

MAGGIE'S STORY

TUCKAWAY BAY
BOOK FOUR

MADELEINE JAIMES

SAND DUNE BOOKS

Sand Dune Books by Maddie James

www.maddiejamesbooks.com

Copyright © 2025 Madeleine Jaimes

Author: Jaimes, Madeleine

Title: The Me I Left Behind / Madeleine Jaimes

Description: First edition, June 2025. Sand Dune Books

Identifiers: eBook ISBN: 9781622375660; Trade Paperback ISBN: 9781622375677; Hardback ISBN: 9781622375806

Subjects: Fiction / Women's Fiction | Friendships | Relationships| Family | Divorce | Beach Book

Editor: Wendee Mullikin, Purple Pen Wordsmithing, LLC

Cover Design by Author Journey Solutions

Published by Turquoise Morning, LLC., dba Jacobs Ink, LLC.

PO Box 20, New Holland, OH 43145.

Learn more about Madeleine Jaimes at www.maddiejamesbooks.com

Join the VIP Newsletter List at Newsletter – Maddie James Books

Author Note

This novel has a running theme of domestic and family violence—including emotional and physical abuse.

In the United States, domestic violence affects an estimated 10 million people annually—as many as one in four women and one in nine men. It comes in many forms and affects families in countless ways.

Many cases go unreported to health professionals or the authorities.

This novel also reflects the power of women friendships and the mother/daughter relationship.

The Me I Left Behind

The Tuckaway Bay books continue with Maggie's story. You first met Maggie in *Beach Therapy*. Now, dig deeper into her story in *The Me I Left Behind*—her life, her marriage, and all the secrets....

Maggie Oliver has everything—beautiful children, a lovely home, and financial security. Her husband, Max, often reminds her of that fact. So what if he has his share of discreet dalliances?

She'd agreed to the one-sided open marriage of her own free will, and with careful consideration. He would not give up his freedom. She needed the security he offered. Weighing the consequences, she vowed to make the arrangement work.

But when the baby came, and then two more, things changed. Max became less tolerant and increasingly abusive—emotionally and sometimes physically. Twenty years later, Maggie knows she is losing herself.

At what point did she leave herself behind? And why? She is determined to find out.

When she discovers her husband has a secret family in another country, her determination quickly unravels. Then a family tragedy strikes, changing everything, and Maggie's path to finding herself takes an unexpected turn.

One

June, Tuckaway Bay Beach

Thank God for friends with beach houses.

Maggie Oliver watched *the littles* play in the sand, a lazy sigh escaping her lips. It had been a while since she'd felt this relaxed—this much at peace. Her kids, too.

She supposed she should stop calling them *the littles*—which is what they'd called Jason and Chloe ever since Carol gave them the pet name years ago. They weren't little kids any longer. Jason was fourteen and Chloe almost seven.

Carol, who just turned eighteen, was working at the Sea Glass Inn Resort this summer for Zach and Lia—mostly at The Sandcastle restaurant but sometimes helping with housekeeping. It was a great experience for her and helped with upcoming college expenses. She'd be heading to Eastern Carolinas University in the fall. Maggie's alma mater.

Tilting her head back, she let the soft ocean breeze warm her face, the afternoon temperature mild for June. The waves were calm today, the Atlantic playing nice along the east coast barrier island. Life was better here. Not just good. Better.

No other way to put it.

Thank God for Tuckaway Bay.

The sea rolled endlessly behind the kids, the waves gently inching toward Chloe's sandcastle. Jason brought her water to bind the sand, running back and forth on his skinny legs. Those two had always played well together, although she sometimes worried Jason spent too much time with Chloe, and not enough time doing boy things with his friends.

He was protective of her, that was for certain.

Pushing up out of her beach chair, Maggie left her spot under the umbrella and ambled toward the kids. She wished Chloe had chosen a different spot to build because the tide would take her creation away, sooner rather than later, and Maggie would have to deal with the aftermath. While Chloe had come a long way over the past few months, she still had her moments. Earlier, Maggie had suggested she build further up the beach—but her daughter wasn't having it.

Live and learn, she guessed. Consequences.

"Look, Mommy. Two towers! One for the princess and one for the prince."

"It's beautiful, honey. You are so talented."

Chloe grinned. "Jason helped."

"He's a good big brother," she said, catching her son's eye. "Come here, you."

She grasped Jason's slim forearm and tugged him closer. Whispering in his ear, she said, "You are a very good big brother." She hugged him then, and as always of late, his body went stiff. *Don't hug me in public,* she'd been told more than once.

"Thanks, Mom." Then he grinned and took off with the water bucket.

Maggie studied Chloe's sandcastle again. "The prince and princess have their own towers?"

Chloe nodded. "So they won't fight."

Her words sucked the breath out of Maggie's lungs. Chloe looked up, her expression blank. No emotion. No question. Nothing going on behind those big brown eyes.

It was just a statement. *How it is.*

She held her daughter's gaze for another few seconds. Chloe's upturned face remained stone still—and suddenly, the thought hit her that perhaps her daughter was challenging her to say more....

But princes and princesses usually live together.

You and Daddy don't.

Well, Daddy is away, remember?

And when he's away, you don't fight.

So that's better?

Fighting makes everyone cry.

Or maybe Chloe was worried she'd said the wrong thing.

An overwhelming feeling of sadness overtook her, and Maggie had to turn away. The conversation in her head wasn't real, of course, but it could have been. She tried to cover her sob with a snort and a cough but wasn't sure she'd pulled it off.

"I'm going to get my toes wet," she said then, not looking at the kids.

Chloe said nothing. Jason gave her a wave.

They'd lost so much.

And all because she'd been too naïve, self-centered, gullible, and foolishly agreeable to stand up for herself, and for the children, for far too many years.

She *had* grown these past few months, certainly. She was stronger, smarter, more independent than even a year ago. But she blamed herself for not waking up to the reality of her marriage, of their situation, sooner.

Twenty. Long. Years.

Where was that girl she used to be?

The girl who could lose herself painting for hours?

The college graduate who wanted to travel before settling down, and chose a flight attendant job, instead of teaching, for the travel perks.

That carefree, boy crazy, back-seat-romping college co-ed who loved life, sex, choices, and freedom?

When had she lost that girl? Where had she left her behind?

SHE STARED OUT TO SEA, THINKING, WORRIED, THEN dropped her gaze as seafoam tickled her ankles, and a piece of seashell tumbled over her toes. She dragged her big toe into the sand, chasing the shell fragment, then bent and picked it up, washing off sand in the surf. It was the top of a scallop shell, pink and a little rosy on the edges. Her favorite shell.

A gift from the sea.

Smiling, she cupped it in her hand, then pivoted and headed back toward her chair and umbrella—glancing up at the Gull, the beach cottage Lia and Zach had graciously let her stay in for the summer. She waved at the littles as she passed, thinking about Carol.

They'd grown incredibly close since Christmas. She'd leaned on her too much, and perhaps that was unfair. But Carol knew more than the other kids and had experienced more of the chaos. Maggie saw no need whatsoever to drag all three children fully into the hellscape their father had created around them.

They were innocent. Practically clueless.

That's how it appeared then. Jason had known more than he'd let on, according to Carol—but ignored or simply refused to acknowledge. One or both. Maggie often wondered if all the secrecy and closed doors had bothered him. Until Max left, Chloe was a hard child to read on a normal day—shy, withdrawn, showing little emotion until she had a meltdown. The past months, however, she was coming out of her protective shell. Still, it was challenging to know how the mess had affected her.

Carol had assumed the role of Maggie's confidant and supporter, and together they unloaded and reflected on the issues with Max and contemplated what to do about it. As much as Maggie hated that, somehow, it was good for both of them.

While eighteen-year-old young women don't have the depth of knowledge or experience to understand the choices Maggie had made over the years, and why, Carol had needed her, too. Max had unceremoniously thrust her into the fray of their dysfunction. She had questions. Lots of questions.

The support was mutual.

Of course, Maggie could have found support elsewhere and often did. She had the girlfriends from college. And while they knew the situation with Max, and had for years, they'd not had the same experiences as Carol.

Alice was the mother hen of the group, the self-appointed fixer. She had a solution for most any situation. Too bad there wasn't an easy fix for Max's kind of crazy. Thing was, Alice had her own problems currently, with her pending divorce, and Maggie would not burden her with more.

Julia, her practical, no-nonsense attorney friend, gave practical, no-nonsense attorney advice as any lawyer would—unless she was giving Maggie shit for screwing up. Which often happened. But Julia... God, she owed her more than she could ever give back. She was getting her out of this mess so she could get on with her life.

And Lia, dear sweet Lia, always looked to the brighter side of life —though Maggie wasn't sure there was a bright side to anything related to Max Oliver. But she'd been her savior, offering them the Gull Cottage for the summer.

The twins, Wren and Willow, couldn't give advice, but were good listeners. That's how she framed it in her head, anyway. There were times she needed to talk or explode, and she'd go out to her backyard and shout at the sky, pretending she was talking to them. They never answered, of course, because wherever in the world those two women were living was a mystery.

Carol, however, was always there. For everything she'd been in the past, the spoiled bratty teenager to her, the darling daughter to her dad—she was neither of those things now.

She had, indeed, grown up too fast.

Back at her beach chair, Maggie plucked up her cell phone from where she'd stashed it under a book, shaded from the sun, and noticed a call notification.

She tapped on the call log. A missed international call from Australia. *Puzzling.* Max never called. All communication was through their attorneys.

The phone vibrated again in her hand. *Australia.*

"Hello?"

"G'day. Maggie Oliver?" The male voice spoke with a distinct Australian accent.

"Yes?"

"My name is Adam Barnett. I'm an officer with the Queensland Police Service. Your husband is Maxwell Oliver?"

What the hell kind of trouble is Max in now?

"Yes. That's right." Her heart rate kicked into overdrive. She would not bail him out of some stupid situation in fucking Australia. "Until the divorce is final."

His voice lowered. "I see. I'm afraid I have unfortunate news. Your husband...well he was...."

He rambled on, the words dipping in and out of his Australian dialect.

Two

Six months earlier

"Please stay longer, Maggie. There is no need for you to go."

Maggie plucked a pair of jeans from a clothes pile on her bed, loosely folding them. "You're sweet, Lia, but we need to get out of your hair. Christmas is over and we all agreed to leave after a couple of days so you and Zach can have a quiet New Year's holiday. Besides, he's tolerated us long enough, and Sea Glass Inn is still in recovery mode after the Christmas storm and all the related chaos."

"But you're not a problem, Mags."

Oh, but I am. I am always a problem. "Seriously? Drama follows me to every girlfriend getaway. You all don't need the Maggie shit show now."

Laughing, Lia stilled her hands. "Stop folding. Good gracious. Your family provided no more chaos than anyone else's."

"Oh? Whose daughter went off and told the world that Alice is gay? Who argued with Ella and made her run out into the storm? She could have gotten hurt." Pulling back, she reached for one of Jason's T-shirts on the bed.

"And whose daughter had a baby on the prep island in the restaurant kitchen? Whose ex-husband showed up unexpectedly with his new wife and stepdaughter? And Zach's not innocent in this, either. What about his fishing buddies crashing our holiday?"

Maggie met her gaze. "Exactly why the Oliver family needs to head home. Besides, I'm tired and sort of brain dead."

Julia sat on the edge of the bed. "Maggie, look. You seem a little tense. Don't let all the Carol stuff get to you. She's going to grow out of this crap sooner or later."

Staring at the pile of clothes on the bed, Maggie exhaled, then turned and sat beside Julia. "It's not just Carol." Pausing, she glanced at both girlfriends. "Well, she's involved, but this time she wasn't bringing the shit. It's Max."

"But he's still in Australia. Right?" Lia touched her arm.

She nodded. "Yes, but apparently his reach is far."

Shifting to face her, Julia asked, "What happened?"

Maggie pushed out another breath and briefly closed her eyes. She had to unload some of this, didn't she? She'd not wanted to get into it on Christmas Day, and then the day after, with all the storm cleanup. No one wanted to deal with her family shit then.

Especially her.

But now? Maybe.

"Maggie?" Julia prodded.

"All right." She stood quickly and paced a few steps. Abruptly, her insides felt like trembling jelly. "Let me just get it out, then we can talk."

"Sure," Lia said.

Julia agreed. "Of course."

Again, she took a deep breath. "Here's the gist of it. You know Max is working the holiday in Australia. Well, the kids and I had scheduled a video call with him for Christmas Eve at midnight Brisbane time, which was ten in the morning for us here. He didn't log on. About an hour later, Carol got back on the tablet and noticed that he had signed in—but apparently had forgotten to turn the thing off. The computer was in a bedroom and—"

"Oh no..." Lia gasped.

"Fucking shit. What did she see?" Julia stood too.

Maggie shook her head. "Not what you think."

"Then what?" Lia joined them.

"It was what she heard first—a baby crying. Then she saw Max get up to get the baby. And then him talking with a woman."

Both Lia and Julia stared for a moment.

"Wait. What?"

"I don't understand."

Turning, Maggie headed for the window and peered out over the ocean. "Evidently, Max is starting another family in Australia. It's his baby. His and this woman's."

"Oh, holy fuck." Julia came up behind her. "We will get his sorry ass, Mags. I swear. Just give me the word and I'll file divorce papers."

Maggie swiftly pivoted. "No. I don't know what to do yet. I don't know what I *want* to do."

"Of course, you don't." Julia paused, studying Maggie for a minute. Her voice lowered, she went on. "I don't mean right now, this minute. These things take time. But give me that time and we will make the sorry asshole pay."

Lia moved in and embraced Maggie from the side. "Oh, honey. Are you okay? What can I do for you right now?"

Her words overflowed with concern and Maggie's heart warmed. Turning, she gazed into Lia's eyes and soaked up her compassion. "I'm okay. I'm numb, actually, so I guess that's a form of okay. Who knows?"

"Have you talked to him?" Lia's eyes probed.

Maggie shook her head. "No. I've not. Carol has. He told her not to tell me, the bastard, and that he would call. Well, it's been three days...."

"Goddamn sonofabitch." Julia paced now, running a hand through her hair. "Tell me what you want me to do. I'll start researching the legalities in Australia and then we can—"

"Stop, Julia." Maggie grasped her forearm and met her gaze. "I can't go there yet. I just need to think."

Julia pushed out a breath. "Okay. I'm rushing you. But I will be doing some research behind the scenes."

Maggie nodded. *Let her work. It's what she does. And maybe it will keep her out of my hair for a while. Until I'm ready.*

"This is why you should stay, Maggie," Lia said. "It will give you time to unwind from this and all the other chaos, talk things through with us, and perhaps spend some quality time with the kids for a few more days."

"No."

"Why?" Lia stepped closer.

"Well, for one, I am not concerning either of you, or Alice, with my crap right now. You have families to be with," she said. "Besides, I'm not ready to talk this through, yet. And as for spending time with the kids? I can do that at home."

"Can you?" Julia asked. "You know what will happen. You'll get home and Carol and Jason will hook up with their friends, and you'll not see them until school starts in January."

She was probably right. "But this has been one hell of a holiday. With Max, and the storm, and Ella getting lost, and Belle's baby— Good God, Lia, you don't need me, my kids, or my problems hanging on, too."

"Then come stay with us, if that makes you more comfortable," Julia said. "Sam's place is small, but there is an extra bedroom. The littles can camp out in the family room. Carol can bunk with Hannah until she leaves for Albuquerque. Might be nice for both of them. It would be tight but—"

Maggie stopped Julia with a hug—which seemed to startle her friend. She spoke softly, but directly. "You both are lovely, and I thank you—but we should go. I have things to figure out."

"Can you do that at home? Alone?" Lia prodded once more. "Is that possible?"

She wasn't sure, to be honest. "I don't know."

"Maggie, please reconsider. It's only a few more days. Maybe until New Year's Eve?"

Returning to the pile of laundry on her bed, she folded a few more articles, her brain rolling over the question. "I don't know, Lia. Let me think about it. We'll stay tonight, at least. How about that?"

Lia smiled. "Perfect."

THE NOR'EASTER THAT BLEW OVER THE OUTER BANKS ON Christmas Eve and Christmas Day left them with mild temperatures and clear skies. Maggie pulled her legs up on the wooden beach chair and wrapped a blanket tighter around both her and Carol as they stared into the night.

"The stars are really bright tonight," she whispered. "Look, there's the big dipper."

"And the small one, too." Carol pointed. The two sat huddled together by the firepit at the back of the inn. Chloe was already asleep in bed, and Jason was up in their suite watching a movie. "I wish I knew the names of more stars and constellations. They are really pretty out here at the beach."

"Umhmm," Maggie murmured. "So easy to see. Hard to imagine people all over the world looking at the same thing we are looking at right now. Isn't it?" Times like this, Maggie realized how small their world really was. Her world, her life, her problems.

"Like Dad? Can he see these same stars?"

Maggie wasn't sure. "I don't know. Probably not right now. I don't know how that all works on the other side of the world."

Carol gazed upward. "I don't want to go home yet," she whispered. "Can we stay longer?"

"Don't you want to go home and see your friends?"

"Not really."

Maggie rotated toward her daughter, catching the uncertainty in her eyes. "You don't? I thought Sophie was texting you like crazy, wanting you to come home. Don't you want to see your best friend over the holidays? Didn't she mention a party?"

"Yeah, she did. But I'm not in the mood, really."

"You're sure?"

"Yes." Carol nodded. "I don't want to be where he was. I want to stay here with you and Jason and Chloe for a while longer and not think about him. My head is still kind of spinning around it all. It's like he's not here, but I know once we get home, it will feel like he is."

Maggie understood. Max permeated everything he touched. Whether or not he was there.

"I understand, honey. But we're going to have to go, eventually. We can't impose on Lia and Zach for too much longer."

Carol's head fell against her shoulder. "Please?"

Maggie sighed and wrapped the blanket tighter around them. "All right. Two more days. I want to be home before New Year's Eve. We have school to get ready for."

"Okay." Carol snuggled closer. "Thanks, Mom."

It wasn't like Carol to avoid her friends and want to be with family. Who was this child of hers right now? The Max incident seemed like a turning point for her.

And likely, would be for all of them.

"Sweetie, what was it your dad said about telling me?"

"He told me *not* to tell you. That he would talk to you. Did he?"

"No. I've had no word. You?"

Carol shook her head. "No." She inched her arms around Maggie's waist. "I'm not sure I want you to hear from him. My head tries to sort things out. My heart is really confused."

That statement hurt her own heart.

Carol went on. "I know you said there've been other women. But do you think this time, with this woman, it's different, Mom? They have a baby. Is Dad coming home, or what?"

Good question. "I don't know, sweetheart."

"But if he loves her and the baby, then what? What happens to us? Me and Jason and Chloe? What happens to you?"

"Sweetheart, let's not go there, yet." She paused, waiting to see if Carol said anything more. She didn't.

They sat for a few minutes, gazing up into the night. The rhythm of the waves provided a steady beat behind the silence, ticking off time.

Finally, Maggie said, "Julia will look into some legal things for me, here and in Australia." She wondered if Carol just wanted something to hang her hat on. "I don't know what is going to happen, honey, but there are obviously some things to figure out."

"I didn't think about that."

"I'm not sure I can stay married to him."

Carol twisted in the seat and sat up slightly, searching Maggie's face. "You mean divorce?"

Shit. Maybe too soon.

She shrugged. "Sweetheart, I don't know. Right now, I never want to see him again."

Carol blinked several times, then slowly nodded. "I get that. I don't either. What I don't get is how it all works afterward."

"After a divorce?"

"Yeah. With all of us." She stared. "I mean, you don't work. How will the bills get paid? Will Dad have to pay something? Child support? Will we have to move out of our house? What about school? I know it's expensive." She paused, glancing off, then back again. "College?"

"Oh, sweetheart." Panic gripped Maggie's heart. Obviously, this was worrying her. "That's a lot to digest. I don't know the answers to any of it, but I will say this—let us figure that out. Your dad and me. That's not for you to worry about."

"But I do worry. I have been. I don't know what is going to happen in the future."

"Do we ever, honey?"

Carol stared, and the look behind her eyes told Maggie she was frightened. "No. And that's scary."

"I know." Maggie squeezed her tighter. This uncertainty was going to be a problem. "I just don't have answers now, sweetheart. Negotiating with your dad might be difficult. But Julia—"

"She's a good lawyer, isn't she?"

"She is."

"She'll screw Dad over. Won't she?"

Hell, where was Carol's head? With a forefinger, she pushed back a strand of hair covering one of her eyes. "Honey, Julia will follow the law and do what's best—"

Carol grasped her hand. "No, Mom. Julia *needs* to screw him over. Look at all he's done! He's totally messed up all our lives. He's a fucking asshole!"

They locked gazes for a moment, then burst into laughter.

They hugged and giggled, and sank back down into the beach chair, wrapping themselves up again with the blanket. After a moment, they settled back into silence.

"Even though he's not here, it still feels like it. You know?" Carol murmured.

Maggie moved in her seat a little to look at her daughter. "He's thousands of miles away. He can't hurt us."

"Really?" Carol's eyes flared wider. "Mom, he hurts us all the time."

Her words stabbed Maggie's heart. "Carol, you and your dad were really close. It's bound to be confusing and hurtful."

"But he *still* hurt us. I love him. He's my dad. But he does things."

Anxiety bit into Maggie's chest. "What do you mean?"

Carol sat up straighter. "I mean, he's never hit me or Chloe. He *did* hit Jason once, that I know of, when you weren't home. I don't know if Jason ever told you. He smarted back about something, and Dad punched him in the mouth."

Maggie gasped. "Oh, no."

"Busted his lip."

Her mind raced. "When?"

"Last summer. Jason told you he got hit in the mouth with a baseball at practice."

She remembered that day. He'd not let her look at his mouth and waved her off. She'd thought it was one of those boy things, like no hugging in public. She'd had no clue Max had hit him.

"Oh, poor Jason," she whispered, looking away. Settling back into her seat, she watched the stars again. "But he's never hit you or Chloe?"

"No, he just yells at us when you're not there. Mostly, he yells at Chloe."

No wonder Jason was so protective of his little sister. Again, her brain stumbled over scenarios when she'd not been home, but Max was. "I tried not to leave you alone with him very often."

Carol nodded. "I know. But there were times he'd send you out for stuff."

That was true.

"And he'd get mad so easy about crap. Like, when Chloe spilled her juice."

"Did she?"

"Once."

"And?"

"He started yelling and threw a towel at her and made her clean it up. He scared her so much she cried, and she spilled it again, and then he stood over her yelling. He said it was your fault that you hadn't taught us not to spill or how to clean up, and all that. I tried to help."

"What did he do?"

"Pushed me away and called me a stupid-ass cunt."

"That fucking bastard." Her gaze never faltered from Carol's, and she saw the hurt in her eyes. Her heart ached for her. "I'm so sorry, honey. Why didn't you tell me?"

"The same reason Jason didn't. We were too scared to tell you."

"Oh, sweetie...."

"If we told you, then you'd say something to him, and then it would get worse. He'd come after you and then probably us again. So, we learned not to tell you."

Anxiety seized Maggie's heart. "This kind of thing has happened more than once?"

Carol looked away and ducked back down under the blanket. "Mom, let's not talk about it anymore. Not right now. Can we forget about it for the rest of the night? Please?"

Her child was shutting down. Her brave, bold young woman of almost eighteen years was suddenly reduced to an uncertain little girl. Just like Chloe.

They'd hashed this around too much tonight.

Shit. They were all going to need therapy. Weren't they?

"Mommy, can I see baby Grace today?"

Maggie met Chloe's gaze in the bathroom mirror as she brushed her hair. The child was obsessed with Belle's baby and asked to see her several times a day. "I will check to see if there is a good time. Okay? Remember, newborn babies sleep a lot and don't need a lot of new germs around them."

Chloe smiled. "But she is so cute!"

Maggie met her smile back. "She is, isn't she?" She kept brushing, pulling Chloe's hair up into a ponytail.

Her daughter nodded sharply.

Maggie had tried to keep things as normal as possible the past couple of days for all three of her kids. The littles deserved a fun break from school, especially after the scary storm. And Carol deserved some downtime from all the drama.

Honestly, she welcomed the change of pace from the hustle of daily life back in Rocky Mount. That hustle—school, sports, dance, cheer, and other activities—plus keeping the house up, groceries, managing Max's life, and all that.

With Max gone, though, she could relax a bit, perhaps.

Maybe.

Probably not.

Certain things were rooted into her routine after nearly twenty years, and managing Max, the kids, and the house was her full-time job. There was safety in that. Security, too. She'd grown into predictable routines.

Carol poked her head inside the bathroom door. "Hey, Mom. Julia and Sam are taking Hannah to the airport and asked me if I would like to ride with them. That okay with you?"

Turning, she smiled. "Sure. If you haven't packed yet, do that when you get back. Remember, we're leaving early tomorrow, and we are having dinner tonight at The Sandcastle with everyone."

"Yep. Sam said we'll be back in a couple of hours."

"Enjoy the time with Hannah. I'm glad you two are getting to know each other."

Carol shrugged. "She's cool."

Even though Hannah was a few years older than Carol, they

seemed to have some things to talk about the past couple of days. Maggie had noticed them walking on the beach together, chatting away one afternoon. And last evening, they'd hung out on the deck around the firepit drinking hot chocolate. Maggie wondered if Carol had told Hannah about her father.

Maybe it was good she had someone else to talk to, rather than herself.

"So, I'm off, Mom."

Maggie smiled and glanced at her again in the mirror. "I'll see you back here later. I think dinner is at six."

Carol gave her a quick salute and grin, then was off.

"Ouch, Mommy!" Chloe grabbed her ponytail.

"Oh, sorry. I didn't realize I was pulling."

Whirling away from her, Chloe said, "Let's go see baby Grace now!" She ran off into the other room before Maggie told her they still had to call Belle.

She waited a minute, holding the hairbrush, and stared into the mirror.

Honestly, they'd been sharing a two-bedroom suite for too long, and she was actually looking forward to getting home. Because once they got there, she had a lot of thinking to do—and some research, which reminded her she had some questions for Julia, later.

It was time she figured out what the hell was going on with her husband and this woman and her baby in Australia.

"Mommy!" Chloe ran back into the bathroom. "Baby Grace!"

"Alright, sweetheart." She set the hairbrush aside. "I'll call."

A few hours later, after a brief visit with Belle and Grace, they gathered at The Sandcastle for dinner with the others. The afternoon had gone by much too quickly.

Zach pointed to a long table. "Let's all sit over there. Order what you want," he said. "It's on the house."

"Oh, no." Sam pulled out a chair for Julia. "We'll gladly pay our share."

"Zach, are you sure? My kids can eat a lot." Maggie ushered her kids toward the table.

He smiled. "I'm positive. Let them eat!"

Lia moved in, too, and sat beside Julia. "There's not a snowball's chance in hell that Zach Allen is going to let any of you pay for dinner tonight," she said.

"Well, that is just too kind." Julia smiled at Lia.

"Are you sure?" Alice hustled closer and sat across from Lia. "Hi. It's just me. Ella and George opted to stay home."

"Are they okay?" Maggie had to wonder what kind of after-Christmas discussions had happened in the McBain household, since Alice officially—but not willingly—came out.

"They are both...prickly. Yes, that's a good word for it."

She stifled a laugh. Alice had rarely dealt with a prickly Ella or George before now, Maggie was certain. "I suppose prickly is under-standable given the circumstances?"

Alice shrugged. "Probably." She looked at Carol, then glanced off.

Maggie gave Carol a side eye. "Let's sit here, kids."

They found seats opposite Sam and Julia, with Jason sitting at the end of the table. Chloe sat between her and Carol.

"Looks like we're all here," Zach said. "Menus are on the table."

"Smaller group than on Christmas day," Sam noted.

Chloe tugged at Maggie's sleeve. "Baby Grace?"

Maggie glanced about, not seeing Belle. "Will baby Grace be joining us? Belle too? Chloe is obsessed." She grinned at Lia, then looked down at her daughter's questioning face.

Lia opened her menu. "She's tired, but might pop down after a while. Gracie was sleeping."

"Oh, shoot, Mommy," Chloe said. "I wanted to see that stinker."

Everyone laughed.

Chloe hid her face in her mom's side.

Julia teased, "I don't think I've ever heard Chloe talk that much ever."

Maggie hugged her child. "She is a quiet one, usually. But she really loves baby Grace."

Chloe looked up then and grinned. "Can we have a baby, Mommy?"

Maggie choked back a shocked cackle, made brief eye contact with Julia, then Lia, Alice, and finally Carol.

Carol's eyes twinkled. "Yeah, Mommy. Can we?"

Squaring her shoulders, Maggie said firmly to her oldest. "No, we cannot." Then turning to Chloe, she whispered, "Mommy's baby making days are over, sweetheart. You're my last baby."

At that, Chloe beamed and cuddled into her side again.

Maggie put her arm around her youngest and looked up at everyone staring back—then she eased out a slow, cleansing breath.

Alice leaned in, changing the subject. "It's too bad Grant and Ginger had to get back to Seattle so soon," she said. "I'm sure they would have liked more time with baby Grace, too."

Lia nodded. "Yes, of course. But Ginger had to get back to her other children for Christmas. Belle's fine about it. Grant knows his way here now."

"Oh, Lia..." Julia made a face and glanced at Zach. "Is that going to be difficult for you and Zach?"

"Not at all," Zach said, answering the question for Lia. "Actually, Grant and I got along quite well, and we plan to keep it that way. We're all adults here."

Maggie felt those words cut into her soul. She knew Zach meant nothing by it. He barely knew Max and wasn't sure what Lia had shared with him about this new turn of events in the Oliver world.

"I'm glad," she said softly. "Being adult can make a world of difference."

Lia caught her eye, questioning, and Maggie waved her off.

"Oh, look who's here!" Zach stood and headed for the door. Everyone's attention shot that way.

Belle approached the table with a baby carrier. "Hey everyone. Thought I'd come by for a few minutes."

"Oh!" Chloe jumped up.

Maggie snagged her arm. "Let her find a seat, sweetie."

But Belle could barely get seated before everyone crowded around her.

"Let's not all get too close, remember," Lia said, protectively. "Germs."

"Oh, Mom. It's fine." Belle tossed her mother a quick grin.

The restaurant door slapped shut again and everyone turned toward the sound.

Carol gasped.

"Well, well. If it's not Josh Sullivan," Zach said. "Fish stop biting?"

Belle slowly looked up.

Josh stepped across the room. Maggie recognized him. He was one of the anglers stranded at the hotel during the storm. An E.M.T., he had also helped deliver baby Grace during the power outage. They'd left Christmas day looking for another fishing charter, and Maggie had assumed they'd headed back to New Hampshire by now.

"I heard there was a newborn baby here. How's she doing?" Josh locked his gaze on Belle.

Belle's face brightened, smiling at him. "Hey. What are you doing here?"

Maggie caught Lia's eye momentarily. Lia blinked rapidly, then tossed a questioning glance back to Maggie.

"Thought I'd check in on my patient before heading back home to New Hampshire."

Zach snickered. "Grace or Belle?"

Lia elbowed him.

"Why, little Grace, of course. Goodness, she's grown!"

"It's only been a week, Josh," Belle said.

"Still, she's plumping up."

"Oh, she likes her milk." Belle shifted the baby in her arms. "Do you want to hold her?"

Josh grinned. "I do."

The server approached the table then, asking for their orders. Everyone scurried back to their seats, except for Josh and Belle and baby Grace, who sauntered off to a private booth to chat.

Carol leaned toward her mom. "Do you think there's something there?" she asked.

"I don't know. What do you think?"

Carol watched the couple for a few seconds, then nodded. "Definitely."

"I guess time will tell. Right?" Maggie said.

Their food came eventually, and they ate amidst chatter and stories and reminisces of the chaotic Christmas they'd just spent together. At some point, Josh and Belle slipped out, and it seemed no one noticed until long after they were gone.

"Do you think Belle and Josh are a thing?" Julia asked Lia.

Lia looked at Julia, surprise etched on her face. "A thing? Oh, good Lord, no. They just have a connection, you know, because of that night."

"Hmm." Julia gave her a snarky grin.

Maggie knew that grin of Julia's all too well. It meant, "Yeah, right."

"So," Maggie interrupted. "We will leave early in the morning. Until next summer, then? Are we back at Tequila Sunrise, last week of August?"

"Good by me," Julia said.

Alice tipped her iced tea glass. "I'm good for that week."

Lia nodded. "Plans are to open Tequila Sunrise for the season in late May, and we've already held the last week in August."

"Great!" Julia nudged Sam. "I'll be gone all week. Think you can survive without me?"

"It will be tough." He leaned in and kissed the tip of her nose. "But I will muddle through."

"I'm looking forward to it already," Maggie said. "Who knows what the next six months will bring?"

Get ready, Maggie.

Three

Max called the morning of New Year's Day.

Maggie chose not to answer.

Out of spite. Out of fear. Or just being goddamn stubborn. She refused to talk on his terms. When the time came, she wanted some sort of edge—even if it was simply being prepared for the call.

Today was not that day.

Pacing her kitchen, she watched a skiff of snow drift over the back deck. The kids were upstairs in their rooms, playing, sleeping, whatever. School started back tomorrow for the semester, so she had to make sure they got to bed early tonight. They'd had too many late nights over the holiday, and frankly, were all exhausted.

Herself, included.

"Mom!" Carol bounded down the stairway, her phone in hand. The look on her face told Maggie she was upset, concerned, something. She made it to the landing and pushed her phone toward her. "It's him," she mouthed, her hand over the microphone. "Dad."

Motherfucker!

Maggie stared at her daughter. "Jesus. What does he want?"

Carol shook her head. "What do you think? Just asked if you were home and said he wanted to talk to you."

With a sigh, she took Carol's phone. "We need to get new phone numbers." She waved Carol off, indicating she should go back upstairs, but her daughter just stood there. Waiting. Apparently not going anywhere.

Maggie put the phone to her ear. She refused to put him on speaker. "What do you want, Max?"

There was a brief pause, then he said, "We need to talk. Are the kids around?"

She looked at Carol, still standing there watching, listening. "No, the kids are all upstairs." Hell, Carol knew everything anyway, so why shield her from any of this now? Besides, her ass was making a permanent dent in the stair tread.

"Good. Mags, things have changed in my life, and...."

"Oh, fuck, Max. Spare me the sordid story. I know what you are going to say. You got some chick knocked up in Australia and now you think you want to play house with her. So, go screw yourself and your new pitiful life, too."

Again, silence from his end.

"Say something."

"You think you got this all figured out, don't you?"

"Jesus, Max. I don't have a damn thing figured out, and I won't until you stop changing the rules of the game. That's all this is, right? A fucking game?"

Max snickered.

She was in no mood for his fucking games. "So, tell me. Why call today? Is there some sort of symbolism in that? New year? New kid? New woman? New life? What a fucking idiot I have been. Of all things, I truly did not see this coming."

He laughed out loud. So loud, in fact, she pulled the phone away from her ear and looked at Carol, who apparently could also hear him.

"Glad I could still surprise you, sweetheart. I thought perhaps I'd gone stale on that."

She walked away from the stairs and Carol, and into the living room. Standing dead center in the room, between the piano and the massive wall of bookshelves, she stared out the picture window and into the street. "Max?"

"You don't know everything."

"I know enough."

"So, Carol told you."

She huffed. "Leave her alone. Do you hear me? She was upset. Devastated, really. Do you have any idea how traumatic something like that is for a kid? Especially for a child who adores you? No, you don't, because you don't fucking care."

"I love my daughter, Maggie."

"Right. So, you expected her to stay quiet and wait for you to call? Don't put that kind of pressure on our kids. Jesus, Max. It's been over a week. You could have called sooner."

He ignored that. "Do the other kids know?"

Other kids. Like, Carol was the only one who really mattered. "No."

"Good. Let me tell them."

"Over my dead body," she sneered.

"That would make things easier, don't you think?"

Anxiety raced through her like a jolt of electrical current. *Is that a threat?* She turned back to seek Carol's eyes, meeting her gaze. She still sat on the bottom step, her arms crossed over her chest, rocking a little. Maggie watched her pull in her lower lip with her teeth and bite. Nervous gestures.

"Of all the stupid shit, Max. This takes the cake."

"Settle down, Maggie. Get a grip."

She whirled back and paced again toward the window. "A grip? You want *me* to get a fucking grip? Jesus. Are you an adolescent? You're forty-six years old."

"I'm a grown man who can make his own decisions, Maggie."

"Well, goody for you. When do I get to grow up? Make my own decisions. Fuck around on you?" The second those words were out of her mouth, she panicked. She knew how he'd take them.

"You knew the deal."

"Yes, and I was too young and stupid to naïve to realize what I was getting into, what it would lead to."

"You enjoyed your perks. Right, honey?" His voice was softer, lower-pitched, seductive.

An immediate zip of sexual energy shot through her body, settling in her pelvis. *Shit.* She really didn't want to go there. Didn't even want to have this conversation. "Shut up, Max. I had no choice."

"You could have walked."

"How? You wouldn't let me."

"Goddamn, Mags, you've always had the power to make your own decisions. In fact, all you ever had to do was make one decision and your life would be your own."

"Oh yeah? What's that?"

"To leave."

"Excuse me?"

"You can leave anytime you want, but if you do, you'll lose more than you will gain."

That's right. She'd lose everything. Her kids, her home... *My kids.*

"If that's true, Max, then why in the hell do you even want me? Why are you tying me to this marriage with threats like that when you don't even want to be in it? I don't get it."

He laughed. "Damn, Mags. Don't *you* get it? You're convenient. You take care of things—the kids, the house, me... I don't want to train someone else."

His words literally stabbed her in the heart. "I'm the babysitter and housekeeper."

"Perhaps," he said. "With perks."

"And please tell me your definition of perks?" She knew what he was talking about, but wanted to hear him say it.

He chuckled again. "Well, me, for one. You get to fuck me regularly—when I'm home, that is. And there's the house, the money, and all that."

Closing her eyes, she tried to block out the noise unexpectedly crowding her head. Was Carol still in the room? She didn't want to look back and see. "Gee. Lucky me." Finally, she glanced back. Carol still sat there with her head in her hands. "But you didn't answer my question."

"I didn't?"

"No. Why are you tying me to this marriage now? Appears to me you already have someone in training."

"Eh. Time will tell."

"But why, Max?"

He paused, and she could hear his low growly chuckle again. "Because I can, Mags. Why else?"

Right. Fucker. And I fell for it.

She needed to switch the subject. "Max, what are your plans? I need to know. Are you staying there or coming home as planned by the end of the month? I'm not up for any more surprises."

Damn. She wished she hadn't said that. Sounded weak. She needed to be up for anything he could throw at her. Every. Single. Day.

Again, he chuckled, and she could absolutely envision the stupid smirk on his face.

"I'll call and let you know," he said. "I'm still working some things out here. Tell the kids hello."

He clicked off the phone.

Maggie stood there for a moment, the phone still to her ear.

Tell them hello? Not, I love you. I miss you. I'll see you soon. Happy New Year?

Just hello?

Carol stepped up, took the phone out of her hand, and put her arms around her.

"He's an ass, Mom. Let it go."

If only.

WITH CHLOE FINALLY TUCKED INTO BED, MAGGIE SOFTLY closed her bedroom door—leaving it open a crack so the light would peek through, like she always wanted—and stepped out into the upstairs hallway. Carol's door was closed, as was Jason's, and if they were still awake, at least they were quiet. They'd both showered early, after dinner, and had headed to their rooms not long after.

They'd be there for the night, she was certain. Jason sometimes played video games until he fell asleep. Carol was probably figuring out her wardrobe for tomorrow and texting with friends. They'd sleep soon enough, if they weren't already.

Heading downstairs, Maggie knew she'd rest very little tonight.

She had other things to deal with.

Max's office was off limits to her and the children. Always had been. When he was home, it stayed locked during the day, but open at night so he could go in and out, working or not. When he was out of town, he kept it locked up tighter than a drum.

She'd never questioned it, nor did the kids. By now, it seemed normal.

But was it really? What did Max have in there that he did not want anyone to see or know about? While she could guess, she knew she was relatively oblivious.

Clueless. Max could be involved in anything, really.

She knew very little about his business, his clients, and all that entailed.

The only time he allowed her into his office for any length of time was when she was planning his trip itineraries, which Max trusted her to do because of her years spent as a flight attendant. She knew the airports and kept up with the flight schedules and concourse changes, so she could get him to his destination and home again as efficiently as possible. Of course, he was always in the room with her, looking over her shoulder while she worked on his laptop.

Not this time.

Maggie stood staring at the walnut-stained door to the office. The room was situated just off the kitchen/family room area, down a short hallway. Her gaze dropped to the handle, and she jiggled it—locked, of course, as expected. Max had replaced the bedroom-door lock a few years back and had installed a coded keypad, plus a key lock.

She had to break through both—and no telling what she would come into contact with once she was inside.

Turning, she moved through the kitchen-family room area and headed to the garage, where she gathered up various tools from Max's tool bench.

While she figured the crowbar might make quick work of breaking in, she also assumed it would be loud and maybe cumbersome. She didn't want the door falling down on her, and she didn't want to disturb the kids while sleeping, either. And while bashing in the door with a crowbar might have felt remarkably satisfying, she couldn't risk it. So, she started with a thin screwdriver and attempted to pick the key lock, to see if she could get that one open first.

Nope.

What the hell kind of lock had he installed? The kids had locked themselves into their bedrooms, or the upstairs bathroom, many times, and the screwdriver trick always worked. What gives with this fucking lock?

Tossing the screwdriver aside, she stood back and studied the door.

Maybe she could remove the door handle altogether. She'd watched a few You Tube videos earlier in the day showing how. Running her fingers over the lock and the base, she felt for a set screw, or other screws, there. Finding none, she stood back and stared at the thing again.

Even if she could get the key lock open, she had to know the keypad code.

She could guess but was unlikely to guess correctly.

She supposed she could call a locksmith tomorrow to come when the kids were at school. She hated to involve anyone else in this, though. Or perhaps she could go for the hinges and try to remove the door that way. Otherwise, she was going to take a freaking drill and the crowbar to the lock—noise and caution be damned.

Try the hinges first.

After another quick tutorial video, she realized she'd made the right choice. The guy in the clip talked through step-by-step instructions, and in less than fifteen minutes, she had scooted the unhinged door open enough to slide through and was inside Max's office.

Waiting to flip on a light, she stepped away from the door, and slowly scanned the room looking for anything that might show he'd installed a live camera for security. Her gaze fixed on a small green light coming from the corner.

Maggie promptly dragged a chair over and stepped up on it. She jerked the device away from the wall, hopped down, and smashed the sucker with the crowbar.

Strangely satisfying.

"There," she mumbled. "Take that, Maxwell Oliver."

Scanning the room again, she searched for more devices. She found nothing, but did it matter? If Max monitored the feed from his phone, he'd know soon enough that she'd broken into his office.

She had about a day—perhaps twenty-five to thirty hours before he could get home—to do what she needed to do. Max couldn't get out of Brisbane for another four hours at the minimum, and the quickest route home once he was in the air was a twenty-five-hour-long trip. Lengthier, probably.

Too bad for him.

Time to get to work.

"Mom. Mom. Wake up."

Someone poked at her shoulder. *Carol?*

"What?"

"Wake up, Mom. What in the world are you doing in here?"

Pushing away from the pile of papers on Max's desk, Maggie swiped at her eyes and looked at Carol. Immediately, she panicked. "Shit! What time is it? I fell asleep."

"Obvs, Mom. Dad will kill you."

She glanced at her watch. Five-thirty. "The soonest he could even get here is around nine o'clock tonight—at the extreme earliest. I'll be finished by then."

"But what are you doing?"

Maggie studied her. "Why are you up at this hour?" Usually, their alarms went off at six.

"I went to sleep early and woke up early. I washed that pair of jeans you got me for Christmas so I could wear them today. They're scratchy."

"Oh. Okay."

"You still haven't answered my question." She glanced at the desk. "What is all this stuff?"

Maggie gave a shrug. "Files. Contracts. Shit papers. I don't know what half of it is or why he saved it."

"What are you looking for?"

"Anything." With a sigh, she sat back in Max's big leather chair and stared at Carol. "He already knows I'm in here."

Carol rounded the desk and leaned against it. "How?"

"Cameras. He has at least a couple. I found one but not the other one. Look."

She opened her phone and scrolled to a text from Max. He'd sent a video of her sitting at the desk going through the drawers. Carol took the phone. "Shit. Did you find the camera?"

"No." She shook her head. "I've looked everywhere."

"He can see us right now?"

"Maybe, but I suspect he's in the air. Read the message."

Carol clicked off the video and scrolled, reading the text aloud. "Whatever you are looking for, you won't find it. Get out of my fucking office or I'll take your head off when I get home."

Jerking up, she peered into Maggie's eyes. "I'm staying home today and helping you find whatever it is you need to find."

She hated to do that to Carol. "It's your first day back at school."

"Fuck school. This is more important."

"Language." But she knew Carol had almost as bad a potty mouth as she did. "I don't want him to blame you, honey. I'd rather he just be mad at me."

"Isn't that what you've been doing for years, Mom? Taking all the blame for everything us kids did wrong? Not this time. I'm staying and helping. Besides, this affects all of us."

Maggie blew out a breath. "The first thing we need to do is find the other fucking camera."

"Yes."

"And get the littles up and off to school." Standing, she stretched the kinks out of her back. How long had she slept hunched over his desk? At least a couple of hours.

"Right," Carol said. "Then we can dig in here."

She nodded. "I'm going to call Julia and get her advice."

"Good idea. She might know what we should and shouldn't do."

"I think she will say that we've already crossed the line."

Carol glanced about at the messy office. "Probably."

"Look," Maggie said. "Go get the littles up and keep them away from this room. Can you fix breakfast? I'll search for that damn camera."

"I can do that."

"Hopefully, I can locate and destroy it before I have to take the kids to school."

"I can drive them."

That wasn't their usual routine, but what would it matter? Chloe's school was one street over, and Jason's a few blocks further. She'd had her driver's license for over a year now. Surely, she could manage a ten-minute drop-off.

"Are you sure?"

She nodded and grinned. "I got this." Heading for the door, she paused and then turned back. Her gaze met Maggie's and held for several seconds. "I love you, Mom."

She left quickly, and Maggie was glad. Carol didn't need to see her cry right now.

Four

"I can be there in two hours."

Maggie pushed back her hair and sat again, hunched over Max's desk. Carol had just left, taking Maggie's car to drop the littles off at school. "Julia, I didn't call so you would come. I just want your advice. What can I look for to get something on Max?"

"Look. I'm almost dressed. And believe me, you're going to need my advice. Hold on."

Maggie heard shuffling and low talk in the background. It sounded like she was saying goodbye to Sam. Had she made a mistake pulling Julia into this, when she'd sent her a copy of the video Max texted earlier?

"Seriously, Julia. It's okay. I can handle it. Don't come. Stay with Sam."

Julia gave a mocking laugh. "Mags, it's not okay. You've committed a crime, and Max has it all on video."

"Crime? It's my own damn house!"

"True, but Max's office was locked, and you entered without his permission."

"I need permission to go into a room in my own house?"

Julia sighed. "Maggie, listen to me. You used force to get past the locks. It's illegal. It's breaking and entering."

"It's my own fucking house! Dammit!"

She pushed up and away from the desk, standing and whirling around, trying to find that damn elusive camera. Out of sheer frustration, she raked her arm over the desk and papers flew. Then twisting back, she set the phone aside and started pulling books off the shelf behind her.

"Maggie. *Maggie!* Listen to me." Julia shouted into the phone.

Maggie knotted up her fist and shoved it into the air, rotating from one corner of the room to another. "Max Oliver! If you are listening to me right now, I hate your fucking guts more than you even know."

"Maggie!"

She grabbed up the phone. "What!"

"Take a breath. I can't help you if you are upset like this. Now, find a place to sit for a minute, maybe away from the office, and let's talk this out while I drive."

"Carol will be back soon." Suddenly, she was exhausted. Leaning her backside against the desk, she glared at the shelf of books she'd just emptied. Almost. "Wait. Hold on a minute."

"What are you doing?"

She set the phone down again and moved closer to the shelf. Wires were sticking out of the back of a book she hadn't knocked over. She reached for it and realized it was tethered to some sort of an electrical box in the wall. She flipped the thing over in her hands.

"It's not a goddamn book," she murmured.

"What?" Julia questioned.

Maggie ran her hand over the spine. There. A small circle indentation. Black. Just like the book cover. The camera lens. *Fucking bastard.* She looked into it, peered into it with one eye, picturing in her head what Max was looking at, then drew back and stuck out her tongue. Ripping the cords from the book, she turned back to the phone and Julia.

"I found the other stupid camera," she shouted, then switched to speaker phone. "And I'm about to destroy it like I did the other one."

"How?"

"Crowbar."

"Shit, Maggie."

"Is that illegal too?"

"Probably."

She didn't care. The crowbar stood by the door, and she made quick work of obliterating the book thing with three solid jabs of the heavy tool. She snatched up the phone again. "Well, that's done."

"Great. Now listen to me."

Maggie sat again. "Fine. I'm listening. But Carol should be back any minute, so say what you need to say now if it's not something she should hear."

Julia exhaled from the other end. "Alright. Look. I'm going to tell you something you might not have considered."

"Besides the breaking and entering part?"

"Yes."

"What is it, Julia?"

"Max has video. You showed me that earlier. That means he has recorded it all, from the time you broke through the door until you pulled that fake book camera from the shelf. He has everything. Even you talking to me."

"I don't really care. So?"

"So, he can use it against you anytime he wants."

"Like?"

"Like in a divorce or custody case."

She still wasn't totally getting it. "Well, I suppose he could, but I haven't really done anything here but break in."

"You showed rage. You broke his cameras, yelled at him and said you hated him, rifled through his desk. Carol came in and you talked with her. He could nail you for making her an accomplice. He has all that, Mags. And he can twist it—or a talented lawyer can twist it—any number of ways."

"But that's why I need to find something on him—something dark and dirty—that I can hold over his head." *There has to be something.*

"Seriously, Mags. Max having another family in Australia is not enough? Go with that. It's your best bet."

"I feel like there is more, Julia. Like I need more. He keeps this office locked up for a reason. I want to know what it is. He used to go bat-shit crazy if I stepped inside while he was working and didn't lock the door."

Julia huffed. "Shit, Mags. He probably just goes in there and watches porn and jacks off."

"Illegal porn? What if he...?"

"Don't go there. Not yet. To be honest, I'm worried about something a little more immediate."

"Such as?"

"Him going to the police with the video."

"Like right now?"

"Yes."

Maggie shrugged and leaned back in Max's chair. "How? He's in the air, more than likely, so he can't access it until he gets on the ground."

"You think?"

"Pretty sure."

"Wi-Fi is available on most flights now, right?"

Dammit. She is right. "But phones still have to be in airplane mode, don't they?" She hadn't flown in so long she wasn't exactly certain.

"Does he have a laptop? Tablet?"

"Of course. Both."

"Well...?"

Maggie's chest tightened. "Shit."

Julia said nothing for a minute, which allowed Maggie to gather her thoughts. "But what if he didn't come home? What if he said, *fuck it* and deal with it from there? It is a long trip."

"It is. And you are right. We really don't know how Max is going to react. Do we?"

"No," Maggie said. "I have no clue. My first instinct was that he'd catch the first flight out because of what I did. Hell, maybe I even did it to provoke him, knowing he'd come home, and I'd have to confront him. But now? I'm not sure."

"Maggie, listen to me. Wherever Max is, he has the video. He can download it, and he can send it to the authorities here, telling them he is away on business and that there is an intruder in his house."

Why hadn't she thought of that? She'd been too hell-bent on trying to get one over on Max that she hadn't considered all the consequences. "Shit. What do I do now?"

"Don't let anyone in the house—I'm talking about law enforcement—unless they have a search warrant."

"And if they do?"

Julia exhaled again. "Stall them as long as possible. Tell them it's your house, your husband is away on business, the kids are at school, and you are there alone, and that no one has tried to break in."

"Maybe I should tell them Max is crazy as a fruit fly, and he makes shit up all the time? That it was me in the house all along?"

"No." Julia paused for a moment. "Less is more, Mags. The less you say, the better. And you don't want to accuse Max of anything. Even crazy. It sounds suspicious and could open a Pandora's Box full of more trouble for you."

"Alright. Got it."

"Let's just hope it won't go there."

Maggie wished that would be the case, but she was worried. "Should I clean up the office? Just in case they have a warrant and want to look?"

"Maybe. If they see a mess, and the broken door, they will question."

"What if I tell them that one of the kids locked themselves inside and I had to unhinge the door to get to them?"

"That might work. Except for the footage."

"Right. And if it doesn't?"

"Then say nothing. If they take you in, I'll be there in less than two hours as your attorney. Say nothing. Give them nothing, Maggie. Understand?"

"Yes. The kids?"

"I'll make sure they are okay."

"Fine. Right."

The front doorbell rang just then, startling Maggie. "Shit."

"What was that?" Julia asked.

"Doorbell." *Fuck, fuck, fuck....*

"Hold on, I'm pulling over."

Maggie waited.

"I'm back," Julia said. "Mags, listen to me. Look out the window. What do you see? Patrol car?"

Maggie rushed to the office window and pulled back the heavy draperies a little. A sliver of fear inched up her spine, circled around to her chest, and landed in her throat. Suddenly, she was cold. Very cold.

"Shit, yes, Julia. It's the cops. There's a car sitting out front on the street."

"Can you see anyone?"

"No. I can't see the porch from here."

"Alright. Listen to me. Keep this phone on. I'll stay quiet. Put it in your pocket or something. Go answer the door."

"I can't do this."

"Maggie, you can."

"I'll try."

"You will be fine."

The walk from the office to the front of the house took longer than any other time she'd ever walked it before. The bell sounded again, and she jumped. She took a breath and tugged open the heavy oak door.

Two officers stood on the porch looking back at her, their expressions blank.

"Officers? May I help you?"

"Are you Mrs. Oliver? Maggie Oliver?"

She nodded. "Yes, that's me."

"Carol Oliver's mother?"

Shit. What now? What has Carol done now? "Yes? Is everything okay?" Her hands started shaking.

One officer stepped closer. "Mrs. Oliver, your daughter was involved in a traffic accident a few minutes ago over on Winstead. We were in the area and assisted with the accident. If you would like to grab your personal things, a purse or such, and come with us, we can take you to the hospital."

Maggie clutched the phone still in her hand. "Hospital?"

Shit, my legs are going to give out.

"Ma'am." An officer grabbed her elbow. "Are you okay?"

"I... I don't know. Let me get my purse and keys." She turned into the house, then back again. *The littles!* "Was she alone?"

"Yes, ma'am."

Maggie blew out a breath. "Okay." *Jason and Chloe are at school. They are fine. But Carol? Oh. My. God.*

She gathered her things from an entry table, then closed the door behind her. "Is she hurt badly?"

"We have very little information. We know they took her to the E.R. The hospital is not far."

No, it wasn't. Thank God. "Alright. Fine." She glanced at the phone in her hand. "Oh, I was talking to a friend."

The officer nodded.

She put the phone to her ear. "Julia. Are you still there? Did you hear? Come to the hospital as soon as you can. Nash General."

She clicked off the phone, not waiting for her to respond.

"How long do I have to wait?"

Maggie sat on the edge of her chair, muttering to herself, her knees popping up and down as her legs shook. She glanced about the overflowing emergency waiting room—not a pleasant place—crowded with coughing, moaning, and crying people.

She'd rather be anywhere but there.

The officers left her almost as soon as they'd arrived, so she sat alone. Waiting. Julia had called once, and she told her she'd call her back as soon as she had news.

Glancing at the time on her phone, she realized she'd only been there about twenty minutes.

It felt like twenty hours.

She was mad with worry about Carol. Why wouldn't anyone give her any information?

She'd paced back and forth in front of the nurse's station until they'd asked her to sit. Apparently, being in their faces would not get her anywhere.

She was also worried about the house. About leaving the office in a mess. What if Max had contacted the police, and what if they entered the house when no one came to the door, and what if they found the unhinged door and the crowbar and the smashed cameras and the papers and books and shit all over the place?

And what if Max truly was on his way here? He'd kill her for letting Carol take the car and would blame her for Carol getting hurt.

Everything would be her fault. Everything.

But she supposed it was.

It always was.

Her stomach knotted, anxiety balled up underneath her breast-bone and pressed on her lungs, constricting her breathing. If she stood, she might pass out.

No, she couldn't do that. She had to be strong.

Anticipating all the unknowns was useless.

Focus on Carol now, everything else later.

She abruptly stood and glared again toward the sign-in desk and the staff sitting behind it.

A woman in scrubs stepped from behind the counter and into the waiting room. "Mrs. Oliver?"

She'd watched her earlier as she approached from a hallway behind the desk, reviewed some paperwork on a clipboard, then conferred with a nurse staring at a computer screen.

Maggie stepped forward. "Yes? I'm Maggie Oliver."

"Carol's mother?" She spoke with a slight accent—one Maggie couldn't put a finger on.

"Yes."

"Would you like to see her?"

"Of course! I've been waiting. How is she?"

The woman halted slightly and turned toward her. "No one has spoken with you yet?"

Maggie shook her head. "No! No one."

"I apologize for that. I'm Dr. Kendall." She pronounced it like "ken-doll" and Maggie almost snickered. "Let's keep walking and I'll fill you in."

Jamaican. She sounds Jamaican.

She and Max had vacationed on the island once when Carol was little.

Maggie strode alongside the fast-walking doctor.

"The accident caused the air bag to deploy, so Carol has suffered some facial trauma—some cuts and bruises, particularly around her eyes. She is complaining of a headache, which is normal given the circumstances, and says her neck hurts, so perhaps there is minor whiplash. We have examined her thoroughly, of course. She's lucky because air bags can cause a lot of damage, but she was wearing her seatbelt."

"And that helped?"

"Oh, yes."

"Good girl." Maggie sighed. "I'm glad she wore the seatbelt."

Dr. "Ken Doll" nodded. "Yes. Apparently, the other car ran the light. Carol was not at fault. But talk to the police about that later."

"She's not unconscious or anything. Is she?"

"Oh no. In fact, she's alert and quite vocal."

Maggie smiled, imagining she would be. "Are those her only injuries?"

The doctor stopped and turned. "She threw her right arm up before the air bag deployed, so there is a slight sprain. An X-ray showed no fracture. She'll go home with a sling. Other than the bruises and facial lacerations, she's fared well."

"That's a blessing."

"Yes." Dr. Kendall smiled. "We gave her a painkiller earlier and a sedative to relax her a bit, so she may be sleepy when you see her."

They rounded a corner. Immediately, Maggie heard Carol shouting. "I want to see my mother now!"

Maggie shot Dr. Kendall a look. "I guess the sedative wore off?"

She laughed. "Apparently. Or she needs something stronger."

Carol yelled again. "They told me she was here. Why hasn't

someone brought her to me yet?"

"Oh, dear." Maggie sprinted toward the ruckus and burst into the room. "Carol? Sweetheart!"

"Mom!"

"Oh, my poor baby."

"Mom...." Carol burst into tears, shaking. "It wasn't my fault. I swear it. I'm so sorry. I wrecked the car, and Dad is going to kill me!"

Maggie angled closer and sat on the edge of the bed. "Let me worry about your dad. Your job is to get better here. I'm just glad you are okay."

She pulled her closer. Carol sobbed into her chest.

"It's okay, sweetheart."

After a minute, she pulled back, sniffling. "Ouch. My neck hurts."

"I heard that. Your head too? And what about your arm?"

"They gave me pills. I think they are working."

"Good."

"I'm glad Chloe and Jason weren't in the car. That other car hit right behind my seat, where Chloe was sitting." Her eyes welled up again.

"Sweetheart, they are safe. And now you are, too."

Dr. Kendall stepped up. "So the shoulder pain has eased up somewhat?"

Carol nodded. "Can I go home?" She bounced a look from the doctor to Maggie and back again to the doctor. "Will you give me pills?"

"Soon. Yes." The doctor nodded, looking her over. "We'll talk about all that. You'll be here for another couple of hours."

"Can I sleep? I feel sleepy."

Maggie squeezed her hand. "That's probably the pain meds." She looked at Dr. Kendall. "Right?"

"Could be. Let me look at your eyes." She pulled a penlight from her pocket and leaned closer, shining the light into Carol's left eye, then the right. "Your pupils look normal and the neurological tests we did earlier did not show a concussion. I think you're fine to nap. The nurses will wake you when they check for vitals, anyway."

"Okay." Carol sat back. Maggie could tell she was getting groggy.

Standing, she faced the doctor again. "Thank you."

"My pleasure. I'll be in and out, and so will the nursing staff." She pulled the call button tethered to the bed away from the covers. "Call if you need anything."

"I will."

The doctor left. Maggie drifted to a chair in the corner and sat, watching Carol sleep. For a moment, she soaked up the calm atmosphere of the room, focusing on the steady drone of Carol's heartbeat on the monitor, and her even breathing.

She took a second to close her eyes and take a few deep breaths herself.

"Excuse me. Mrs. Oliver?"

She blinked, focusing on the man standing in the door. "Yes?"

"I'm Officer Daniels." He glanced at Carol. "Could you step outside for a minute?"

Maggie stood, inhaling deeply again as she did so, then letting out the breath slowly. "Yes. Is this about the accident?" Good God, if not that, then....

"Yes. Just a few details. This way." He turned, and she followed, giving one last glance at Carol.

He led her to a private nook down the hall. "Would you prefer to sit?"

She shook her head. "No. I'm fine. What do you know about the accident? It wasn't her fault, was it?"

"No. The other driver ran a light and hit just behind the driver's seat. Fortunately, neither vehicle was going fast, so the impact was less severe. I'm sure your car is totaled but you'll need to call your insurance, of course."

"I will."

"We took a statement from Carol earlier, on the scene. She was a little upset but speaking coherently enough that we got what we needed. Honestly, she was quite mad at the other driver, and we had to restrain her a little, to keep her from going after the older gentleman."

"Oh dear. Is he okay?"

"He was a little banged up, too, and slightly confused. We think he wasn't supposed to be driving. He said he was eighty-two."

"And Carol wanted to deck him, probably."

"Called him a senile old motherfucker, if I recall correctly."

Maggie whooshed out a breath. "Goodness. I apologize. I suppose I should find him and apologize."

The officer shrugged. "Honestly, he probably won't remember any of it tomorrow." He smiled and then tucked his clipboard under his arm. "An accident report will be available at the station by afternoon."

"Great," Maggie said. "I'll take care of that."

"The details of the other driver will be on the report. You'll probably need that for insurance."

"Of course."

"Well, that's all I need." He tipped his head. "I'll let you get back to your daughter."

"Thank you." She watched the officer walk away. "Wait."

He turned. "Yes?"

"My car?"

"Towed. Honestly not sure where it ended up, but all that may be on the report. I believe Thompson Wrecker Service did the tow. Check with them, too."

Fine. Great. Will do.

The phone in her purse vibrated. Reaching in to grab it, she noticed the caller—*Max?*

A nurse walked by and caught her eye, pointing to the sign on the wall.

No cell phones.

She gladly turned the phone off.

BY THE TIME JULIA CAME AN HOUR LATER, HESITANTLY poking her head inside the partially closed door, Maggie was a mess of nerves. Carol was asleep, and she had fought sleep herself. The few hours she'd dozed in Max's office earlier were not nearly enough.

Upon seeing Julia, however, she jerked herself alert and stood.

"Thank God you're here. I'm sorry I got you into this mess."

Julia glanced toward the bed. "Goodness, Maggie. I want to be here. Carol's sleeping, I see."

"Yes. We're waiting for discharge papers. Shouldn't be long."

Julia nodded. "How are you?"

"Nervous as a whore in church." She rubbed her hands up and down her arms. "My skin is crawling."

Julia reached in for a hug—something she rarely did. "We'll figure this out."

"I don't know what I am doing, Julia. What the fuck did I do last night? Why am I poking the beast?"

"Because the beast is far away, and you took a chance. You also wanted answers, or something." Julia sighed. "Hell, Mags, I'm sort of proud of you for taking a stand like you did."

"Even if it's breaking and entering?"

A smirk rolled across her friend's face. "Takes guts to do what you did. And as far as being illegal, we'll manage that. I had time to think while driving."

A breath burst out of Maggie's lungs.

Julia glanced again at Carol. "So, is she okay? By the way, I will take you two home."

"Good, because my car is probably totaled. I don't even know where it is."

"Probably impounded somewhere. Well, no worries." She paused, studying her. "I tried to call. Just got your voice mail."

Maggie glanced at Carol. "Yeah. I turned it off while in here." She gave Julia a direct look, pointed to her phone, and mouthed, *Max called.*

"Ah." Then she mouthed, *Did he leave a message?*

Maggie shrugged. *I haven't listened.*

"Okay. We'll catch up later."

"Definitely."

A couple of nurses shuffled into the room behind Julia. One went straight to Carol's bed, and the other to Maggie.

"Mrs. Oliver, I have the discharge instructions. Since we already have your insurance information, we'll just need to go over these quickly and get your signature. Then, as soon as we do a last vitals check, we can call for a wheelchair and get you both home."

"Oh, that would be lovely."

The nurse looked at Julia. "Is this your transportation?"

Laughing, Julia said, "Yes, that's me. Just call me Juber. That's short for Julia Uber."

Maggie chuckled and elbowed her friend. "You're crazy."

"Naw, that's you."

"Mom? Julia?"

Both women looked at Carol, now fully awake.

"Sweetheart. You're going home soon."

Groggy, Carol pushed up a little. "Good. I'm tired of being poked." She gave the nurse taking her blood pressure a foul look.

The nurse rolled her eyes. "You have any idea how often I hear that?"

"If we could just go over these last instructions?" The other nurse fluttered the papers again.

Maggie turned toward her. "Sure."

They made quick work of that while Julia chatted with Carol. Maggie couldn't hear everything that was said, but she could tell Carol was curious why Julia was there.

"I was on my way to Louisville and your mom called, told me what happened, so I stopped here to make sure you were okay."

Carol grinned. "Oh, wow. That's so nice of you."

Maggie caught Julia's brief glance and knew at once what the look on Julia's face said. *Who is this pleasant child?*

"So, as soon as we get the wheelchair," the nurse said, "Juber can drive around to the front entrance and park under the canopy. We will wheel Carol out."

Julia stood and nodded. "I'm sure I can find that. I'll head there now."

"Great. It shouldn't be long."

Carol sighed. "I'm so ready to be home in my bed."

Julia shot Maggie a quick look of...warning? An immediate sliver of panic shot through her gut. Were she and Julia on the same page? If Max came home tonight, should she—and the kids—even be there?

Five

When they arrived back at the house, Maggie pulled out deli meat, cheese and more, laying everything out on the kitchen island. They made sandwiches, opened a bag of chips, drank diet soda, and made small talk. After a few minutes, and eating only half a sandwich, Carol announced she was going to bed.

"You look exhausted, sweetheart." Maggie cupped her daughter's face in her hand. "I'll go up with you." She wanted to tuck her into bed and hold her close for a while, waiting for her to go to sleep. She used to do that when Carol was younger and not feeling well. That crazy mama bear instinct had kicked in wildly that afternoon.

She lingered for several minutes after Carol pulled the covers up to her neck, curled slightly onto her side, and gave a contented sigh. Maggie fiddled with a lock of hair flung across her forehead. Then, with a soft kiss on Carol's cheek, and a sigh of her own, she stood and headed back downstairs.

Julia looked up from her sandwich as she entered the kitchen. "Asleep?"

"Yes. Didn't take long."

"She needs it."

Maggie slid into the chair next to Julia. "I'm not sure of my next move, here."

Placing what was left of her sandwich on the plate, Julia faced her. "Of course you aren't. This is not an everyday situation. We need to consider all the angles before making any kind of move."

"I don't know how much time we have. You know. If he comes back. I hate to ask you, Julia... You've bailed me out of so much, and here I am again. But will you help me? Can we make a plan? I promise I won't keep doing this."

Julia studied her, then reached across the island for her hand. "Maggie, we're friends. More than that, sisters, even. Of course, I will help you. That's why I'm here. Right?"

"But this is all rather fucked up and—"

"Shut up." Julia placed a couple of fingers on her lips. "Just stop. We are going to figure this out."

Maggie met her stare and felt the sting of tears in her eyes. She and Julia had had their share of differences over the years. But she was still there for her. "Thank you," she murmured.

Julia smiled.

Then, standing, she lifted her plate and napkin from the island and headed for the sink. "We need to listen to that message Max left on your phone earlier. That may give us some direction. You haven't listened yet, have you?" She began putting away the cold items into the refrigerator.

"No. The phone's in my purse. I left it in the entry."

"Go grab it and we'll listen in here, just in case Max has more devices in his office."

"Goddamn I hope not." Maggie rolled her eyes and headed to the entry.

"We'll find out soon enough," Julia whispered.

After a minute, Maggie joined her again at the island and took out her phone. With a few taps and a couple of swipes, she logged into her voicemail.

"Put it on speaker, Mags."

"Oh, right." She did and laid the phone on the countertop.

Max: *Maggie! Goddamn it! What kind of fucking stunt are you* *trying to pull? Get the hell out of my office before I call the cops.* Several seconds passed, then his voice lowered. *Be careful, darling. There are eyes everywhere.*

The message ended.

Maggie stared at the phone.

Julia stayed silent, too.

"He's coming home."

"You think?"

"Pretty sure. He avoided saying anything specific on purpose, to keep me off guard. That's his M.O."

Julia nodded. "Could be." She glanced at her watch. "It's a little after noon. When do you think the earliest is he can get back?"

"No earlier than nine tonight, or shortly after."

"Then let's make that plan now. When do we pick up Jason and Chloe?"

She glanced at the kitchen clock. "Chloe gets out at two-forty-five, Jason at three. I usually make one trip. By the time I get Chloe, Jason is waiting at the pickup place."

"All right. That gives us a bit of time in the office. We need to look for more camera devices, but I'm betting there are none. Let me go in and give a quick scan—I took a seminar once on surveillance and equipment, so if there is anything, perhaps I can spot it."

"Okay."

They moved away from the island, then a thought struck Maggie. She halted and grasped Julia's arm. *Eyes everywhere.* "Do you think....? What he said about eyes...?"

Julia apparently caught her drift and started glancing about the room. "It's possible."

Damn him! A pang of anxiety, or something, jabbed into her gut. To think that he'd been watching her, them, all the time for perhaps, forever, was sickening. She clutched her stomach, hunching over a little. "I think I need to vomit."

Julia steadied her, bending closer, whispering in her ear. "If he has cameras all over the house, then he knows everything, anyway. Let's just do what we need to do then get the fuck out of here."

Maggie raised her head. "Leave?"

Julia led her to a chair in the great room and crouched in front of her. Still whispering, she said, "You cannot not stay here tonight."

"Oh. Yeah. But I need to talk to him."

Julia shook her head and whispered. "No. That's not a good idea right now."

"But—"

"Listen to me. I'll get a hotel room, a suite. We'll tell the kids it's my treat since I'm in town. Carol should be fine if she gets some good rest this afternoon. Maybe we can find a hotel with an indoor pool so the kids can swim. That might be fun."

"They would love it," Maggie said softly. "But I can't put anything on my credit card. Max will see."

Julia smiled. "Already thought of that. That's why I said it's my treat. We'll put it all on mine."

"Oh Julia, no."

"Not arguing with you, Maggie. This is what we are doing."

"Are you sure?"

"Positive."

"I'll pay you back. Somehow."

"Not necessary."

Maggie felt like letting her tears fall. She held them back earlier, but now... Once again, Julia was bailing her out of trouble. "Thank you."

With a sigh, Julia leaned forward and embraced her. Then a couple of seconds later, she stood and said louder, "I'm glad you're feeling better now, Mags. Just sit for a minute and I'll be right back."

She did that for Max's benefit, if he was listening, she guessed. Julia headed down the hall toward Max's office and returned a minute later with paper and a pen. She scribbled a note to her.

Write notes. No text. Phone bugged?

Maggie shrugged and wrote. *O.K.*

Julia took back the pen. *Office. Then Carol, get littles, and disappear.*

Maggie nodded again, fully understanding what she meant. They'd clear the office, get the kids, and then get the fuck out of Dodge.

"Okay, so let's make quick work of this." Julia scanned the room. "At first glance, I don't see any devices, but you never know." She headed to the window wall and took down a picture, ran her hand over the back of it, then replaced it. Rounding the room, she examined every piece of art on the wall. "Pretty sure the room is clear."

"So, it's okay to talk?"

"Yes."

"Great. Where do we start?"

"We could tackle this back wall of bookshelves, to see if he has any hidey-holes for stashing shit."

"Wow. This is sort of spy like." Maggie grinned.

Julia laughed. "You're getting a goddamned kick out of this, aren't you?"

"Most fun I've had in a while." But she knew this would not be fun. Dealing with Max and the aftermath was never fun. "I have to confess, that when I was crowbarring those devices and unhinging the door, I felt a strange feeling of satisfaction."

"I can certainly understand why, Mags."

"If I found something on him, something to hold over his head, I'd feel even more giddy."

Nudging her, Julia said, "Stop it. I can see hunger in your eyes. Don't linger over that thought right now, just concentrate on the tasks. Let's see what we can find." Julia pulled down three books. "I promise, we will find something. Anything unusual shout out or put aside."

"I can do that."

Maggie laid her hand on the shiny desk surface. "Maybe I should finish the desk."

Julia turned back. "Didn't you go through everything in there?"

"No." Maggie stepped closer. "I emptied a few drawers, that's it. One drawer was full of old planners, another with files of receipts. For taxes, I guess."

"Receipts?"

Maggie nodded. "Yes."

Snapping her fingers, Julia said, "Let's look at those first. Planners next. Two places where people's business happens and often gets recorded."

Maggie wondered if they had time to do that. "What if we put stuff in boxes and take with us to the hotel? That way we are not wasting time. I have some plastic totes in the garage."

She noted the half-worry expression on Julia's face. "I don't know if we should remove...."

"Geez, Julia. We're already up to our necks in it."

Nodding, Julia agreed. "True." She paused, peering into Maggie's eyes. "Alright, dammit."

"Good. Because we don't have time to really examine what's here, and I really want to nail him with something."

Smiling, Julia gave her a nudge. "I know. Let's clear the desk of any papers, binders, and the like, and then we can search the nooks and crannies."

They quickly tackled the desk, and the papers Maggie had scattered to the floor earlier that day, putting anything that looked even semi-important into the totes. While Maggie put the desk back together and arranged things on the top like Max had them—pen holder, a family picture taken years ago when Chloe was a baby, stack trays, a yellow legal pad, stapler and more—Julia removed items from the shelves behind Max's desk, examined them, and put them back. Maggie joined her, putting books in place. After several minutes, they stepped back, looking around the space.

"Looks clean enough," Julia said. "Let's load these totes into the back of my SUV."

"Okay." Maggie nodded. "Back in up to the garage. I'll open the door." She knew Max's Escalade was there, but there should be plenty of room to move around it, with her car gone.

"Good plan. I'll do that."

"I'll start moving the totes to the garage."

They busied themselves with that task for the next several minutes.

Julia closed the hatch door of her SUV. "Let's rehang that door before we go." She glanced at her cell phone. "We have time."

Maggie stared at her. "Why? He has me on video, Julia. Breaking in."

"I know. I just feel like if he calls the cops when he gets here—if he even comes—having the place look neat and tidy is a whole lot better than having it looked like it was ransacked."

With a sigh, Maggie glanced about the room again and nodded. "Okay. Let's do it."

But rehanging the door turned out to be more of a struggle than they thought, so in the end, they left it leaning up against the wall. Maggie returned the tools to the garage where she found them. Julia made a final sweep of the room, looking for anything they might have missed.

Within the next hour, they woke Carol and told her the plan. She and Maggie packed clothes and other items for the littles and themselves and stowed them into the SUV. By two-forty-five, they had picked up Chloe, and then Jason at three. By four o'clock, they'd settled into a suite with an adjoining room at a Hilton-branded hotel just off I-95.

"Sorry I couldn't find a place with an indoor pool, kids," Julia said, "but this might be just as good. Two big bedrooms— one for you kids, and one for your mom and me—and a sitting room and kitchenette to share in the middle. We have TVs in every room with anything you want to watch available to stream. Oh, and the Wi-Fi code is over on the refrigerator door."

The kids just stared at Julia.

Chloe was quiet the entire thirty-minute ride in the car. Maggie could hear Jason and Carol whispering in the back. She hoped to hell she wasn't telling him about Max—although maybe she should give him a heads up about what was probably getting ready to go down. But she didn't want Carol to tell him. She wanted to talk to Jason herself.

"Why can't we stay at our house?" Chloe cocked her head.

"Because of..." Maggie caught Julia's eye. "Bugs." She heaved a sigh and sat on the side of the bed. "Because I saw some nasty bugs in the kitchen this morning and called the exterminator and they are fumigating the house, which means we can't stay there. Fumes."

"What are funes?"

Maggie grinned. "Fumes, sweetie. That's the stuff that floats around in the air when people use chemicals, or like what comes out of the car. It's not healthy to breathe it."

"Oh." Chloe thought for a moment. "Will it hurt Cymba?"

Shit. I forgot about the cat. She glanced at Carol. "Cymba will be fine."

"Yeah," Carol said. "Cats lungs are different."

"Seriously?" Jason punched her arm. "You are so weird."

Carol glared.

"Look," Maggie started again. "Let's just make this a little adventure. We'll go out to eat tonight with Julia—how about Chinese?—and come back and watch movies and eat popcorn and all that stuff."

"I saw a sign downstairs that said there would be free ice cream tonight in the breakfast area."

Julia's face lit up. She looked from one kid to another. "Oh, that will be fun. Right? I love ice cream."

Jason rolled his eyes. "Sure." Then turning to Chloe, he said, "Let's go see if there are video games on the TV."

They headed into their bedroom.

Carol turned to mother. "Bugs? Really?"

Maggie threw up her hands. "It was just what came to mind."

"But we're not telling them the truth?"

Maggie frowned at Carol. "What do you mean? What truth? The one about your dad? Or the one about me breaking into his office? The one about our poor excuse of a marriage? Carol, look, don't start giving me grief about this. Okay?"

This time, Carol rolled her eyes. "Whatever. I'm taking a shower. I'm going out tonight."

Panic tightened Maggie's throat. "What? Where?"

"I have a date," Carol tossed over her shoulder. "And so much fun to have him pick me up at a hotel. Lovely."

Is my bitchy daughter back? "Carol, are you sure you are feeling up to it? I'm not sure that is a good idea—"

Twisting back at the door, Carol met her gaze. "I'm fine. The headache is gone. I slept all afternoon, and I want to go out. Tyler wants to take me to a movie."

Tyler? Had she mentioned him before? Maggie wracked her brain. "I don't think I know him."

"He's in my AP English class. You don't."

"Well, you'll need to introduce me, then."

Carol huffed. "Mom. This is all awkward anyway. What are you going to do, wait in the lobby with me until my date comes? Or have him come up to our hotel room door? It's all weird. Can't I just meet him out front?"

Maggie thought a minute. "How about if he joins us for Chinese? My treat." She had some cash so she could pay their share tonight. "That way we can all meet him."

"Mom. No. God."

Stepping closer to her daughter, Maggie clasped her hands. "But I'll feel more comfortable."

"We can't, Mom. The movie starts at seven and my curfew... There's no time for dinner with the family before that."

Maggie exhaled and glanced at Julia. *Let her go,* Julia mouthed, nodding.

"Okay. You're right. Awkward."

"Great." Carol headed into the bedroom.

Maggie stared at the door. "Shit."

Moving up behind her, Julia said, "She'll be fine. When is her curfew?"

"It's a school night, so ten."

"Good."

"Damn, this is all fucked up, Julia. My daughter is going out with a kid I don't even know."

Julia grasped her upper arms and turned her. "Times are different now, Mags. The world is bigger for kids today than it was for us back then."

"True." She searched Julia's eyes. "You look tired."

"I am. Somewhat. But we still have work to do."

"The totes?"

"Yeah." Julia nodded. "Stay here with the kids. I'll grab a bell cart, bring up those two totes, and put them in our bedroom while Carol is showering. We can go through them once the kids are asleep."

Several minutes later, Carol rushed out of the bedroom and headed for the door. "He's early!"

Maggie sprang up. "Sweetie. Come here. He will wait."

Carol halted, rotating back. "Mom!"

That Carol was jumping just because this boy showed up early reminded her of when she started seeing Max. She'd have crawled over hot coals naked for him and jumped to do his bidding on a nano-second's notice back then.

Was Carol doing the same thing? *Shit. I hope not.*

Slowly, she stepped toward her daughter, whispering. "Just give me a hug, you." Wrapping her arms around her, she planted a quick kiss on her temple and gave her a warm mom hug. "I love you. Be safe. You're sure you are feeling okay?"

Carol met her gaze. "I love you too, Mom. I'm fine. Be back at ten."

Then she was gone.

Maggie turned back to Julia with a sigh. "Chinese?"

Six

After dinner, Maggie and Julia started sifting through the totes in their bedroom, organizing piles of papers on the floor, while the littles watched a movie in their room. Maggie had no clue what most of the paperwork was for, or how important it was, but she kept pulling out the next one and stacking it.

Julia lowered a handful of papers to her lap. "I need to ask you something because we've not discussed it."

Maggie glanced her way. "What?"

"Do you want a divorce? Is this why we are doing this?"

She felt a little stunned at the question, to be honest. "Julia, yes. I want a divorce. Max has a lover and a baby in another country. I've lived with a lot over the years, but I can't live with that. I'm hoping you will help me. Can you?" She paused, searching Julia's eyes. "And if you can't, can you help me find an attorney?"

Julia stared. "I want to help you get out of this shithole life, Maggie. You and the kids. So, yes, I can represent you. But I have to say, you know, that we started down this road once before, and you backed out. I want to make sure that a divorce is what you want. If you do, great, and I'm all over it. But realize it's going to be a long road, and not an easy one. You need to be up for it."

She scanned the stacks of papers and planners and folders scattered around the room. Max's life in boxes, and none of it included her or the kids. But that's the way it had been for their entire marriage, right? Didn't she, they, deserve more?

"I want a divorce, Julia. I don't want to live like this any longer. I don't want the kids to, either. Please do your magic. Okay?"

Julia grinned. "I am quite good at my magic, you know."

Maggie laughed. "I'm counting on it."

JULIA PICKED UP HER STACK OF PAPERS. MAGGIE REACHED for and flipped through one of Max's planners, pausing when a yellow sticky note poked out between two pages. As soon as she read what was on the note, her heart thumped against her chest.

"Found something," she said. "Maybe."

"What?" Julia continued shuffling through a tote.

"A name and address. Something to hold over Max's head?"

"Oh?"

"Umhmm."

"And...?"

Maggie waved the note under her nose. "What do you think?"

Julia took it, reading. "Interesting. Don't let that get lost in the shuffle."

Maggie stared at the note for a few minutes, committing the woman's name and Brisbane address to memory, then stuck the note to the front of the planner and set it aside.

Her phone pinged from where she'd put it on the TV stand, a notification sound she didn't initially recognize. *The security alarm?*

She remembered when they had the home security system installed—that she'd had to choose a sound for the alarm notification. *Something you don't use for anything else*, the installer had suggested. *So you'll know immediately when you have an intruder.*

"Someone is in my house." She would not panic. Hell. Yes, she was.

"What?" Julia stood, watching her.

Maggie snatched up the phone, retrieved the text message, and hit the link to open the video. It showed the front door, with shadows, and someone entering. "Shit!"

"Is it Max?"

"I don't think so."

"Then who?"

Abruptly, her phone rang. *Armor Security Company.* "It's the security people," she told Julia. "Hello?"

"Mrs. Oliver?"

"Yes?"

"Are you home?"

"No. No one is home. Is someone in my house? I got an alert."

"It appears so, Mrs. Oliver. At eight-fourteen, someone entered the front door of your home, apparently with a key. They tried to turn off the system but were unsuccessful, so we sent the alert. I'll send you a text with a photo image from the inside entryway. Please take a look."

"Alright." She waited patiently for the link to come. "Finally," she breathed.

She clicked and saw who it was. *Fuck.* She forced out a breath. "I see the image. I know who it is. Please turn off the alarm."

"No need to send anyone over?"

"No. Thank you." Then, on second thought, she added. "Of course, if the alarm goes off again and is not reset, please investigate and alert me. I'm headed over there now. I appreciate your call."

"Will do, and my pleasure. Good night, Mrs. Oliver."

Maggie tossed her phone on the bed, ran her fingers through her hair, and stood there, shaking a little. "Can this day get any longer, or any more complicated?

"Is it Max?"

Maggie whirled back and flung her arms up. "Oh, hell no. It's Carol and that dickhead date of hers. Shit."

"Oh, hell."

"Right." Her brain rolled over a dozen scenarios.

"Wait," Julia said. "What time is Max coming?"

Maggie glanced at the clock on the nightstand. "I don't think he could get here this early, but I still need to get her out of there."

"Call her."

Why didn't I think of that? "Dammit. Of course." She snatched up her phone again and hit Carol's name on her call list and waited. "Dammit. Voice mail." She clicked off the phone and faced Julia. "May I borrow your SUV? I don't like asking, but...."

"I'm not so sure that is a good idea...."

Her brain spun. She had to get over there. "Then I'll call a cab."

"Maggie, let them be."

She swiveled back and glared. "Oh, hell no, Julia. Carol just went into the house with that boy, doing who knows what right now."

"Geez, Maggie. Let them do what kids do. Would you have wanted to have been interrupted by your mother at seventeen when you were with your boyfriend? They probably just want to make out and play around a little. Let them explore."

Good Lord, Mary Margaret Brennan, are you having sex with that boy?

A sudden flashback of her past—when she was seventeen and dating, and admittedly, already promiscuous—sped through her head. Her mother would have had a fucking heyday had she caught her in bed with a boy.

Yet, that didn't stop me from doing it.

She glared at Julia. "I realize they are going to do what they are going to do, but... If Max comes home and finds them fucking, he will absolutely kill that young man." She glanced at her watch. Eight-twenty. "But there is time if I move fast. Even if he took the first flight out, he couldn't get here by now."

Julia reached for her keys on the nightstand and tossed them her way. "I'll stay with the littles, so keep in touch. Let me know what is going on. But get in and out of that house—Carol too—as soon as fucking possible. Don't linger. You got that? Get our girl home, and that boy to wherever he needs to go, *and you,* back here safely."

SHE MADE THE THIRTY-MINUTE DRIVE IN TWENTY.

Not fast enough, she was sure. A teenage boy could probably do it twice in twenty minutes. Horny little motherfuckers.

Shit. And Carol. What the hell are you fucking thinking?

Not thinking. That's the fun of it. Right?

Approaching the house, she could see a dim light upstairs in Carol's room, facing the street. Dammit. Rushing to the front door, key in hand, she unlocked and opened it, the door swinging wide and inward. The alarm beeped softly once in warning, and she quickly typed in her code and re-set the alarm—just in case.

Bounding up the stairs, she shouted. "Carol! Goddamn it! Get dressed. Get out of the house now!"

She rushed across the second-floor landing to Carol's room and pushed the door. Locked.

"Carol!" She beat on the door.

"Mom! What?"

"Open up, Carol. Come to the fucking door now. Get dressed."

She heard shuffling and footsteps and mumbling behind the door. Finally, Carol unlocked and cracked it open a little. Her daughter appeared to be wearing Tyler's T-shirt. "Mom, what are you doing? This is so embarrasing."

"Saving your ass." She pushed the door open and caught a glimpse of Tyler's skinny behind as he pulled up his jeans. She noted the messy bed with tangled blankets and sheets. Quickly, she glanced away and glared at Carol. "Good fucking God, I hope you had a condom."

"Mom!"

"Listen to me. You need to get dressed and get him out of here. Your dad could be home any minute and if he finds you in this bedroom, half dressed, and with a boy in here..." She looked at Tyler again. "Well, we don't want to find out, but you can guaran-damn-tee that your boyfriend is going to get hurt."

"But M—"

The bedroom door slammed against the wall. "You sure as hell got that right. What the fuck is going on here?"

Maggie whirled back.

Carol, too. "Dad!"

Dammit! Maggie's brain raced. How...? What to do now? She

had to get the kids out of the house. Had to do... Something. "Max, what the hell are you doing here?"

He took a step toward her. "You can't tell me you didn't expect me, Mags."

She wanted to smack that cocky bastard grin off his face.

She lifted her chin, squared her shoulders. "I actually expected you a bit earlier. Nice to see you, Max. We have things to talk about."

"Yes, darling, we do."

He turned away and raked his gaze over his daughter. "Get. Dressed." Then, rotating to his left, he fixed a bead on Tyler. "And *you* get the fuck out of my daughter's bedroom, you little cocksucker." He took two steps toward him.

Maggie grabbed Max's arm, trying to stop him. "Go, Tyler."

Max flung his arm up and away from Maggie, releasing her grip on him. "Get off."

Tyler shuffled quickly to the other side of the room, where Carol was pulling on her sweater and jeans. She tossed Tyler his T-shirt. He shrugged into it.

"Go on, kids," she urged. "I'll talk to you later, Carol."

Max sneered. "Where are the other kids? They're not in their rooms."

"With a friend."

"And you let Carol stay here with this cunt-craving teenage ball of testosterone?"

Carol took a step. "She didn't know I was here, Dad. It's my fault."

He slowly swiveled and scowled. "I will talk to you later."

Maggie waved her arms, hoping Carol and Tyler would just go. Leave.

Max caught her arm by the wrist, twisted it, and held tight.

"You're a crap mother. You know that? How could you let her be alone with a boy in our house? You've got the hormones of a fucking rabbit, and you've passed them along to our daughter. Well, I'm going to fix that."

"Right. How?"

"I'm taking her to Australia."

Carol shouted. "No!" She pushed away from Tyler and closer to her dad. "You can't make me. I won't. I'll run away first."

"And I'll beat your ass from here to Brisbane." Max released Maggie and snatched Carol's arm, jerking her closer. Carol stumbled and cried out. "Ow!"

"Hey!" Tyler lurched forward.

Maggie grabbed him. "No. Don't."

"Dad, let go! You're hurting me!"

Something came over Maggie then, something she'd tamped down in the past, but couldn't hold back now. Seeing Max roughly handle Carol, like he had her all those years, broke the dam inside her.

She rushed forward, fists pummeling his body. She went straight for his face, head, and neck. Hitting, scratching, clawing. "Let her go! Let her go, Max, or I swear I will fucking kill you!"

He shoved Carol away.

Peripherally, she saw her fall to her knees. Tyler helped her up.

But what came next—even though she knew what to expect, her husband in prime form—was worse than anything before.

"You. Fucking. Cunt." He backhanded her across the face with a force that sent her sailing into the wall. At once, her jaw cracked and felt like it was coming off her face. Her head dented the sheet rock, sending plaster flying, and her body crumbled to the floor.

"Mom!" Carol screamed. "Dad! Stop!"

Maggie shook her spinning head and tried to focus on Carol, while attempting to pull up into a sitting position. Her vision was blurry, but she kept blinking and found her. Tyler held her back.

"Go," she uttered.

"Mom, no!"

"Tyler. Take her. Now."

The last thing she saw was Carol's eyes, and the boy she didn't really know, rushing her daughter away from the madness.

THE ONLY SENSATION SHE FELT AT THE MOMENT WAS relief.

Relief that the kids were out of the house. Relief that Chloe and Jason were safe.

Those things were all that mattered.

And oddly, relief that Max was here and dealing with her for what she'd done. The anticipation of his coming wrath would have driven her insane had he waited and let her stew on it for a while—wondering how he was going to punish her for breaking into this office.

From what she could tell, she was still in Carol's room, lying on her side, her left cheek pressed into the prickly carpet. After the kids had left, Max had struck her once more, this time square in the face, and she'd blacked out.

Her breathing was shallow, barely lifting her chest, and she measured every breath like it was her heartbeat. Maybe they were one and the same. With breath, there was a heartbeat. Without a heartbeat, there was no breath. One relied on the other. And right now, it seemed she had both things going for her.

But not much else.

She rapidly blinked her eyes open wide, staring across the bedroom floor. A pile of clothes over there. The legs of Carol's bed. A pair of sneakers. Cymba, their yellow house cat, poked her head out of the closet. Max sat in the chair at Carol's makeup table.

She breathed deeper and let the air out slowly.

"Time to wake up, Maggie. We need to talk."

He crossed the room and bent to grab her forearm, forcing her into a standing position.

"You're home. Early," she spit out.

He grinned. "Surprised you, huh?" He half-dragged, half-walked her over to the bed. Her head fell forward. Dizzy. "Sit."

"How." Still finding her words. Somewhere in the depths of her brain, though, she couldn't understand his being there, yet. Earlier than she'd expected. *To throw me fucking off course, that is why.*

"Charter jet services can work wonders in a pinch."

Ah. "Expensive."

"Oh, but so worth it to see your face, darling, when I walked through that door."

Element of surprise.

"Did you know the cops called me when Carol had the wreck? They called me first, sweetheart."

Shit. Why?

"How fucking stupid of you to let her take the kids to school while you were poking around in my things."

He paced away from the bed, grabbed the wooden chair he sat on earlier, and placed it in front of her. He sat, leaning forward, and glared into her eyes.

Lovely. Max at eye level. She hoped she could remain conscious. Alert.

Reaching out, he softly, seductively, ran a finger along her jawline.

She jerked her face away.

"Sorry I had to pop you one there, sweetheart, but you were getting out of line."

"Right. My fault." It was in her best interest to be compliant, at this point.

"You know it is, darling. My bad girl."

Don't start that shit.

"You do need to be punished. Don't you? I mean, this wasn't the punishment, you understand. Just the wake-up call." One corner of his mouth angled up in a half-grin. A heartless half-grin.

She jutted her chin up. "I'm awake."

"Good. Let's talk."

"Fine."

"Punishment later."

"Whatever." Her body gradually felt more aware, her brain sharper. The throbbing ache in her jaw was definitely a sign of being alive. She just wanted to keep it that way.

"So, did you find what were you looking for in my office, sweetheart?"

She glared back. *I'm not going there, Max.*

This was not the conversation she wanted to have. Not right now. What she wanted was to twist the narrative to something she needed to discuss—because this moment might be her only chance to get the upper hand.

If that were possible.

Besides, she wanted to keep him talking and not using his fists.

"I can't even believe you have another baby. What the shit?"

He chortled. "Seriously? You want to talk about the baby?" Sitting back in the chair, he shrugged. "Cute little bugger. You should see it."

It. Lovely. Maggie jerked her gaze away from his snarly, cocky attitude. She couldn't look at him any longer. "Right. Let's have a tea party," she muttered.

Max laughed. "Look, sweetheart. It's no big deal. Life goes on."

"Are you insane? Life goes on? What the fuck?"

He leaned forward again, peering into her eyes. "You get it. Right? Nothing needs to change. We can make this work, and the kids will never have to know. Of course, I realize Carol already knows, but she's practically an adult."

"What are you saying, Max?"

He smiled and touched her bottom lip. "I'm saying that life goes on just like it always has. You and the kids will stay here in the States. I'll come home now and again—just traveling and away more than usual. No one will suspect anything. And Lilly and the baby will live in Brisbane."

"Lilly?"

He blinked. "Yes. That's... her name."

Bingo. She thought about the sticky note. "Ah. Your mistress."

"Now, Maggie."

"So, she and it, AKA the baby, will live with you in Brisbane."

"Of course."

"While we, your family of twenty years, will live here in the states. And everything will be hunky-dory. Do I have that right?"

"Best plan of action, I think. Don't you?"

"Ridiculous." She pushed up off the bed and moved away from him, refusing to give in to a fleeting moment of dizziness. Crossing her arms over her chest, she hugged herself—*suddenly cold*—as she crossed the room and leaned against the window frame. Gazing out on the street, she said, "You can't have your cake and eat it, too."

"I can't?" He snickered. "I seemed to have managed so far."

She glared at him. He was right. And she'd let him, dammit. "Not this time. Because I won't let that happen."

"Right."

"You are a fucking asshole."

He chuckled.

God, how she'd hated that sound over the years.

"You're right. I am." His grin fell into a frown. Abruptly, he stood and followed her. "Don't fight this. I'm warning you. We can make this work, and no one will know. The beauty is that Lilly is half-way around the world."

"And no one *there* has to know, either. Obviously."

He ambled closer, that stupid cock-ass grin on his face. "Look, Mags. You have it good here. I'll send the money and pay the bills, like always. Nothing has to change. You all stay in the house, the kids go to their private schools, and you keep the fringe benefits of being my wife. Besides, you don't want to mess this up for the kids and their futures. I know you will do anything for those kids. And I mean, anything."

He paused, looking her over.

She felt like a piece of steak at the meat counter.

"Why, Max? Why play this game? Just let me go and you can have your family in Brisbane. I'll go on my merry way."

"With the kids, right?"

"Of course. You don't really have strong relationships with any of them. Not saying you can't see them, but...."

"No!" he barked. "Not happening."

Something out the window caught her eye. A patrol car? Pulling up to the house. *Shit.* Is that a good or bad thing?

"Carol has college coming up real soon. How could you pay for that without me?"

Bastard. "Scholarships? Student loans? Part-time job? How do you think people pay for things like that? I'll find a way."

He crowded closer. "You don't want to strap Carol with student loan debt."

No, she didn't. But she also didn't want to chain herself to Max for the rest of her life. Or Carol. Mostly, she wanted to separate the kids from depending on him too much because, frankly, with him having another family in Australia, how long could that last? At some point, she was going to have to tell the kids the truth.

Wait. Was that the thing she could hold over his head?

"On one condition, Max."

"What's that?"

"I'll go along with this two-family charade if, *and only if,* you tell the kids the truth. That you cheated on me, and often, and that you have another family in Brisbane. That's my condition. They deserve to know the reason their lives are turning upside down."

She could almost see the wheels turning in his head. If the kids knew, then who else? His family? The neighbors? "Not happening."

"Then I'll tell them."

His expression went blank. Stone cold. "And you know what will happen if you force my hand on this, Mags?"

Oh, she knew. *Punishment.*

In one swift motion, he grabbed her by the neck and shoved her up against the wall. "Back off. That's not happening. Things need to stay just the way they are with the kids. What they don't know won't hurt them."

His grip was tight, constricting her airway. Immediately, she went lightheaded. Couldn't. Breathe. Gasping...for breath.

"Fine." She half-choked out.

He squeezed tighter and held for a moment, the back of her head and neck pressed tightly against the wall, his gaze boring into hers. She knew her face was red, could feel heat in her cheeks. Her lungs screamed for air. Her legs weakened, and she knew the only thing holding her up was him pinning her to the wall by the neck.

Then, quickly, he released her, knocking her head back against the wall. She slid to the floor. Gasping repeatedly, grabbing her throat.

"You may have just saved your life."

"So... So, don't...tell the kids." She rested a hand on her throat, still leaning against the wall. Still trying to catch her breath. "But you can't...kill me. What would the kids...think of you, then?"

Max shook his head and stomped off. "There is an easy way,

Maggie. And a hard way. The one I proposed is the easy way. Quit making this difficult."

"Tell Lilly. About us."

He whirled back. "What?"

"Tell Lilly about us. Your family. Here. She needs...to know what she's getting into. I'll back off."

"She already knows."

"Really? Everything?"

He glared. Maggie held steadfast. He was lying. She refused to move even a fraction of an inch.

"I'll tell her, Max, if you don't."

Slowly, his face broke into a wide grin. "Like you could find her."

The doorbell rang downstairs, followed by a series of hard knocks on the front door, and shouting. Max twisted toward the sound. "Who the fucking hell?"

Maggie waited, saying nothing, until he rushed to the window and apparently spotted the patrol car. He turned back to look into her eyes. The seconds tripped by like silent heartbeats.

"Her name is Lilly Colling. She lives on Macleay Island. Do you want me to tell you her street address, too?"

Seven

Lilly Colling rushed out of her bathroom, plucked her earrings off the dresser, and paused briefly, looking out over the bay while poking the studs in her earlobes. The morning sun struck the crystal blue waters just right, sending up diamonds of sparkling light off the gentle waves. She savored the moment, then turned away and grabbed her heels.

Running a little behind.

Poppy is late, too.

She was due to show a house to a couple over on Karragarra Island at ten that morning, in roughly forty-five minutes. If she left in five, she'd have time to drive to the ferry, cross over to Karragarra, and meet the couple at the designated time. Since everything was within walking distance, she'd asked them to meet her at the ferry slip so they could stroll to the property together.

That was her usual M.O. when showing on the islands. A casual walk for a few blocks worked perfectly to set up the sale by the time they arrived at the property.

This home could go for a million plus, which, if she played her cards right and made the sale, would set her up nicely for the month. It could happen quickly, and she hoped it would.

While she hated rushing and feeling two-steps behind, she was going to cut herself some slack today. Some things just couldn't be helped. Sleeping in this morning was one of those things.

Sleep when the baby sleeps, they say. Advice heeded.

Slipping into her heels, she glanced once more at the quiet scene just off the deck and smiled. *Tomorrow.* Tomorrow morning she'd have a cuppa, the view, and a peaceful start to her day.

"Breathe, Lilly. Just breathe."

She took in a cleansing breath, then let it out slowly.

The rapid knock came on the door in the next instant, and before she answered it, she rushed across the hall to Leo's room, smiling down on the chubby, sleeping baby.

"You little sausage," she whispered. "Daddy will be so proud of you for sleeping in your own bed, in your own room."

She stepped back just as the knock came again, glancing toward the sound. She had to get moving.

Heels clicking the wooden steps, she navigated the stairs and opened the door at the downstairs entry.

Poppy stood on the other side, waiting.

She smiled and waved her inside. "Hi, Poppy. I'm running a bit slow this morning."

"G'day, Lilly. No worries." Poppy entered, grinning widely. The woman was always happy. "You had brekkie? I brought a couple of scones from the bakery."

Lilly eyed the pastries. What she wouldn't love right now was savoring one of those with tea sitting on the deck.

But no. Not today.

"Ah, no thanks, Poppy. I'm watching the carbs these days."

"Suit yourself." Poppy headed up the stairs to the main level. She took the stairs slowly, huffing a little. "I wish my knees were better," she said. "But no worries, I can chase after your little one when he gets moving."

"I'm not worried, Poppy." Lilly followed her, glancing at her watch. She could spare another minute or two.

"How's the bub this morning?" Poppy asked.

"Sleeping, thankfully."

"His nappy changed?"

"When he last fed at six o'clock, earlier. He's probably due, but I didn't want to wake him."

Poppy nodded, setting her bag on the countertop and smoothing her gray hair back with her palms. "Ah. Good." She read over the list of instructions Lilly had attached to the refrigerator with a fancy shell magnet last night.

"And he slept in his room, too. Victory!"

"Good news." Poppy swiped at her forehead and turned. "It's too hot for this early."

"Stinker of a day. Thank God for the coolers."

"Right-o."

Lilly gave her a smile and a few last comments. "Short day today. I'll be home late afternoon. I have two showings and need to spend some time in the office downtown."

"Are you stopping for lunch? You look thinner."

Lilly glanced down at herself. "Baby weight. It's still coming off."

Poppy simply nodded. Lilly didn't think she believed her. "Freya's in town and I'm taking lunch with her, so no worries. She always makes me eat."

"Hmpht." Poppy turned back to the refrigerator and opened the door. "Haven't seen that girl in no telling how long. She still over at Min Min Station?"

Lilly shook her head. "No. She and her husband run a cattle station not far out-of-town now, about a hundred kilometers. Big operation, though. She's in town on business."

"Ah. Say hello for me."

"Will do, Poppy.

"I can make dinner tonight for you and the Mister."

"Oh, no need." *You're the nanny, not the housekeeper and cook, Poppy.* She really should have a talk with her about doing too much. If she was going to cook and clean, in addition to caring for Leo, she needed to pay her more. The plump nanny was always thinking about food—but she knew there was a reason for that. "Mr. Oliver is in the states for a bit, so it's just me. I'll grab a salad or something on my way home."

Poppy eyed her again, up and down. "Oh? I thought he was going end of the month."

Lilly nodded. "Yes. Well, plans changed. Just a quick trip."

Again, Poppy gave her the once over, her gaze probing. Lilly knew what she was thinking. *Quick trip? How do you take a quick trip to the states?* Finally, Lilly glanced away.

"I'll leave a scone for you. For dessert," Poppy said.

"That would be lovely. Thanks." No use arguing. She glanced at the time. "I really have to go."

"Then shoo!" Poppy waved her arms. "I'm good here."

"I'll leave you to it."

"WELL, IF YOU AREN'T A SIGHT FOR SORE EYES."

Lilly looked up from her menu to see her childhood friend, Freya O'Brien, standing on the other side of the table, smiling widely. Instantly, she jumped up and tugged her friend into a giggly, girlie bear hug.

"You look so... Brisbane!" Freya exclaimed. "Relaxed and laid back."

Lilly laughed, putting Freya at arm's length. "Then you don't know my life. And you look as lovely as ever. I can't believe it's been two years."

It was true. Freya had kept that youthful look she'd always had—fresh-faced and freckled—which had always served her well, and even more so now that they were in their twenties. Lilly guessed all that sunshine and physical work were good for her.

They settled into their seats at the small table. "Well, work on the station never stops, and it's difficult to get away sometimes." Grinning, Freya reached for her hand across the table. "But I had some business in the city, so here I am. And here you are!"

"Yes!" Lilly squeezed her hand. "I hope you like the food here. This café is one of my favorites. I come here often."

Freya glanced about. "Sort of fancy for this bush girl, but I'm good at adapting."

Lilly laughed. "True. We both became experts in that at boarding school."

Her words sparked a flash of memory, the two of them as children playing in front of the sheep shearers' quarters at Min Min Station near Boulia where they grew up. They were very young then, and their families were poor as dirt. Her memory had them drawing lines in the dry sandy earth, playing hopscotch, a few years before their parents sent them off to boarding school. Those were happy times back then. Both their fathers were farmhands working at the station, shearing sheep, mustering cattle, and whatever else needed to be done. But after she'd gone to boarding school, she never saw her father again.

To this day, she could see his face as he waved from below, the bus carrying her and Freya away.

She'd learned later that he'd gone to prison and died there.

Her mother wouldn't talk about it.

"What are you thinking about?"

Lilly blinked and looked at her friend. Before speaking, she let go of a sigh. She guessed seeing Freya had stirred up the past. "The day we headed out to boarding school."

"Ah." Freya still held her hand and wove her fingers tighter around Lilly's. "That was a long time ago."

"I never really knew why we had to go."

"Or who paid for it," Freya said.

Lilly met her gaze. "I've wondered that over the years. When I was a kid, I didn't think about it. Just did what I was told. What was expected of me. But now...?"

"Now, there are a lot of questions." Freya held her gaze.

"You, too?"

She nodded. "So many questions."

Lilly drew her hand away and opened her menu. She stared at the selections, seeing the words, but not really.

Her thoughts drifted....

"You'll love your new school, Lilly," her mum had said. "There will be lots of girls and you'll make new friends and have so many adventures."

"But I have Freya. I don't need new friends. And I have adventures here."

Her mum stared down at her. "You don't know yet what you'll be missing, so keep your mind open. It will be good for you."

"But I want to stay here, with you and dad and Poppy."

She neatly folded her new school uniform and placed it in her backpack. "Poppy is moving to the city. She found work there."

"But you and Dad...."

"Me and your dad have work here. You're older now, Lilly. Boarding school will help you for later, so you won't have to struggle like your dad and me."

"But I love it here!"

"You have to go. I'm sorry. Freya is going, too."

She started to turn and run.

Her mum grabbed her arm and shook her. "Girl! Go and get out of this place. Make a better life for yourself. Forget us, me and your dad, and go."

The horror of her words had stayed with Lilly for years. In fact, she wasn't sure she had shaken them to this day. She wanted me to go. She didn't want me there.

Had Mum ever wanted me?

Freya's words penetrated her musing. "I think I'm going for a small bowl of wonton soup, then the Massaman Chicken Curry with coconut rice. And did you see they have milkshakes? Hand-dipped. I'll go for chocolate, myself. What about you?"

Lilly looked up. "What?"

Freya caught her gaze. "You were lost there for a moment."

"I know." She shook herself, trying to chase the memory away. "We'll talk later. Let's eat. What are you having?"

Freya chuckled. "I just told you. Soup, chicken curry, and a milkshake."

"All for lunch?" Lilly tossed her a silly grin and arched a brow. "You farm girls sure eat a lot."

"Wouldn't hurt you to put on a few pounds, Lilly. You're thin as a rail."

And there it is. "I told Poppy you'd make me eat."

"So, what looks good to you?"

"Salmon salad, I think."

"Bull crap." Freya said. "I'll order for you."

Their server appeared, almost as if on demand. Lilly let Freya order for her, knowing she could take anything she didn't eat for lunch, home with her for dinner. All good. Freya ordered double of everything she ordered for herself.

"Alright," Freya said, "Now, let's catch up. I'm dying to learn more about this man of yours and little Leo! I can't believe you have a baby, Lilly. Who would have thought?"

She smiled, thinking about the little bub she'd left sleeping this morning. "He's the apple of my eye, as they say. I love that boy so damn much, Frey. I can hardly believe it."

"Pictures?"

She nodded. "I have a few new ones I haven't sent you." She pulled out her phone, scrolled to her picture app, found baby Leo's folder, and opened it up. "Here. Scroll away."

Freya did. "Oh, that little stinkpot! And there's Poppy. She looks well?"

"She is." Lilly nodded. "She has a flat over in Stafford Heights and takes the bus and ferry over to Macleay when I'm working. I've cut back to part-time for a while, so it's not every day. She doesn't drive anymore because her eyesight is failing some, but she gets around well enough. At least that's what she says. I actually think she sold her car because she couldn't afford the gas, insurance, and maintenance on it. The busses and ferries can take her anywhere she wants to go, she says."

Freya sighed and handed Lilly back her phone. "I can understand downsizing. We've thought about it, but it's way too soon for us. We're still building and growing, to be honest. Scaling—isn't that what they say in the business world? Our station is quite large and difficult to manage sometimes, but Nate and me, we handle it."

"You have people though, right?"

"Of course. Some seasonal. A couple full-time. Reminds me of when our folks lived at Min Min. Those were good years, eh?"

Lilly nodded. "Good years."

The server came with their soups, setting them carefully in front of them. Lilly smiled up at the young woman, who had waited on her there in the past. "Thanks, Meg."

"My pleasure."

Freya chattered on. "So, tell me more about Max. I mean, this was so crazy quick for the two of you. Right?"

Lilly took a breath and let it out slowly, meeting Freya's gaze all the while. "It might have seemed quick, but we were seeing each other off and on for about a year before I got pregnant."

"Seriously?" Freya leaned forward. "How did you meet?"

"He was looking for an apartment to rent—something long-term, in a good area of town—someplace where he could entertain or meet with clients, but not too pricey."

"So, you were his agent?"

Lilly nodded. "Yes. He contacted me. We met, then had dinner that night and I showed him some properties online. We made a deal on a furnished condo downtown the next day, and he went back to the states after a few days."

"But when he returned?"

She gave Freya a sassy smile. "When he returned the next time, he called. And for months when he would be here, we'd get together and have dinner, explore Brisbane, and such. When I got pregnant, he was actually thrilled. I was horrified, of course. But he was so sweet, Freya. So loving and tender, caring for me and all that. I think he was extra attentive while he was here because he still had to be in the states most of the time."

"What does he do? For work, I mean."

"He has his own business. He does event planning for corporations—like golf outings, outdoor excursions, and the like. That's what he does in the U.S. He's expanding here in Australia because of some contacts he made in the states a couple of years ago—some guys from the rodeo business up in northern Queensland. You know, around Mount Isa where the big rodeo action is? He's been working on a contract with them...and also contacting stations for working guest stays." She caught Freya's eye then, and wondered... "Freya, if you're interested in making some extra income, Max might want to talk to you about setting up some guest stays at your farm. Scaling, right?"

Freya sat back and exhaled. "Ah, now. I'm not sure Nate would go for that, but I'll ask him. We've known stations that have gone that route and it's a bit dodgy, at times. Extra work to get people up to snuff, feeling comfortable enough to work with the animals, ride the horses, the insurance, and all that. I just don't know."

She shrugged. "It was a thought. No worries."

"So Max is out of town right now?"

"Yes." Lilly set her soup bowl aside. "He was supposed to be here for the month but had to pop back to the states. He actually wasn't here, in Brisbane, when he got the call—something about his daughter. He'd gone to Melbourne to check in with a potential client in the horse racing business and left from there."

Freya stared. "Daughter?"

Meg came with the chicken curry dishes and quickly left again.

Lilly picked up her fork. "This looks yummy. Good choice."

"Lilly?"

She looked up. "What?"

"Max has children? You never mentioned that before."

"Oh, yes. Sorry. A daughter."

"How lovely. A built-in family."

Lilly took a bite. "She's almost eighteen, so pretty much on her own."

Freya stayed quiet for a moment.

Lilly kept eating. The curry was quite good.

"Eighteen. That's just...."

She met Freya's gaze. "Yes, she's just seven years younger than me. Max is forty-six, Freya. He's divorced, so this will be his second marriage."

Freya looked a little stunned, Lilly thought, lips thinned out and eyes probing....

"Marriage?" she said. "Are you getting married?"

Lilly thrust out her left hand and showed her the diamond ring. "He proposed last weekend, right before he went to Melbourne."

———

GETTING HOME LATER THAN SHE'D PLANNED, LILLY walked with Poppy to the ferry slip, pushing baby Leo in his pram. While the sun wouldn't set for a few hours, she didn't want Poppy to feel uncomfortable on the walk.

"Are you sure you can get home alright? I know you are not fond of crowds."

Poppy waved her off. "Shew. I'm fine. The ferry isn't crowded heading into the city this time of day, and the bus ride isn't long. It's a short walk from there to my flat."

"I could come with you."

Poppy gave her a look—one that said she was stepping over the line. She'd seen that look often when Poppy cared for her when she was younger. "I am fine. Now, little Leo will be ready to feed again soon, so you get on with it."

Lilly leaned in to give her a gentle kiss on the cheek. "Be safe. See you on Thursday."

"Yes." Poppy nodded, then headed for the boat.

She took the long route back home, enjoying the sun and their leisurely stroll. By the time she made it back to her street, Leo started fussing. She hustled them both into the house and upstairs, where she quickly changed him, then took him out back to the deck with a bottle.

She'd wanted to breastfeed, but Max had talked her out of it. She was young, he said, and of course she wanted to keep her breasts firm and perky. Right? Not saggy and limp, like he'd said his ex-wife's had gotten after breastfeeding.

She thought back to that conversation. He'd played to her vulnerability—her body image—and she'd fallen smack into the center of that dysfunctional notion and agreed with him.

Of course she wanted to remain attractive to him. And she wanted to look nice while working. It was expected in her field. But did the drop of her breasts sully her value as a woman, or a wife, or even a top-selling real estate agent?

No, it didn't. And right now, what Max didn't know wouldn't hurt him.

Staring down into little Leo's face, she traced the edge of his cheek with her forefinger. Such a little miracle child. He fussed against her chest, obviously hungry and ready to eat. She glanced at the bottle, then unbuttoned the top two buttons of her shirt, lowered one shoulder and her bra cup, and positioned baby Leo closer to her breast. Guiding her nipple with two fingers, he eagerly latched on and began suckling. A contented sigh sneaked up on her then, and she let go of the long-held breath.

Smiling, her heartbeat kicked up, as she watched him gently suckle, his eyes closed, his expression intent on his feeding. How could she have passed up this beautiful experience?

Her cell phone vibrated on the small table next to her. She picked it up.

A text from Max: *Good time for a call?*

With one hand, she quickly texted back: *Yes.*

The phone rang. *Not wasting any time.* "Hello?"

"My little vixen. Damn good to hear your voice. How are you?"

"Good. How are things there?"

She heard a deep sigh come from the other end. "Challenging. But I'll muddle through."

Dare I ask? Had he opened the door? When he'd left, he'd been so vague. "I'm so sorry, sweetheart. Anything I can do?" *What happened?*

"No, no. Nothing to do."

"Is your daughter okay?" *Maybe that's a way in.* Sometimes he could be so secretive.

Another long exhale. "She was in a car accident, love. She's okay but banged up somewhat. Bruises and cuts mostly. Jacked up the car, though. I need to deal with the insurance people tomorrow. Seems the other jackass didn't have insurance."

"Oh no, Max."

"Yeah."

"But she's okay. Your daughter. What is her name again?" *Honestly, why don't you know her name by now, Lilly?*

81

Another pause. "Oh, it's Caroline."

"Pretty."

"We call her Carol."

This time, she paused. *We* call her Carol. *We.* "I see."

"I'll be home soon, love. Just need to deal with this car shit. The ex- isn't great at handling these kinds of things. Too flighty. She'd just make a mess of it, so I need to do it."

"I understand, Maxie."

He chuckled. "God, Lilly, you make me hard as a rock when you call me that."

"Then get home fast as you can, Maxie darling. I'm getting a bit bouncy here."

He growled from the other end, his voice lowering. "I may just skip the fucking insurance and catch a jet. How about if I call later, after you're in bed? Wear that sexy red piece I got for you before Leo came. You know the one. Be ready for video."

"Oh, Maxie, you are wicked."

His growl deepened. "You have no idea."

Eight

Four months later...

Standing at the bottom of the stairs, Maggie called up. "Carol! Tyler's here."

She paused briefly, listening, then turned toward the young man when she heard Carol's lethargic response. "Coming."

"She's usually ready to go. Must be running behind." It wasn't like her, making the boy wait. Typically, she was at the door, jittering about on pins and needles.

"It's okay, Mrs. Oliver."

Maggie had grown accustomed to Tyler being around the past few months, particularly after they'd gotten past that horrid night in January. He'd been skittish around her for weeks, and practically jumped out of his skin anytime they mentioned Max's name.

But didn't they all?

She didn't blame him. That was a tough night, to say the least— but all that was in the past. "What time is the movie?"

"We might miss it at this point." He fished his cell phone out of his jeans pocket and glanced at the time. "I think she's mad at me, Mrs. Oliver."

"Oh?" Carol being mad wasn't a good sign. *Poor kid.* "Don't you think it's about time you called me Maggie?"

His eyes widened, but he said nothing.

"Tyler?"

"My mother always taught me to say Mrs. and Mr."

Maggie nodded. "I see. Well. Come on into the kitchen, let's wait for her there. How about a pop or something?"

"Sure." Tyler glanced up the empty stairs. Still no Carol.

In the kitchen, Maggie pulled a canned drink out of the refrigerator. "Root beer okay? I have other flavors in the garage fridge."

"This is great. Thanks." He laid his cell phone face down on the kitchen island and sat on a tall bar stool.

Maggie leaned in, her elbows on the island, facing Tyler. "I respect what your mother has taught you, Tyler, but you've been around for a few months now, so calling me Maggie is fine with me. In fact, I prefer it, if you don't mind. Especially since Mr. Oliver and I are getting a divorce.

Tyler took a drink and nodded. "Okay."

"Good."

"Carol told me you all were splitting up."

He looked uncertain, like he questioned whether he should have mentioned that. Maggie studied him for a few seconds. "I'm glad she talked to you about it. That she has someone to talk to. Is she upset?"

He shook his head. "Doesn't seem to be—about the divorce, I mean. She's really mad at her dad, though." He paused, jerking his gaze away from hers. "Really mad."

I wonder how much he knows? "Yes, I know." She paused for a moment, then said, "Tyler, that night... I'm sorry you witnessed what you did, but I am thankful to you for getting Carol out of there. You were very brave."

He stared ahead, glancing briefly at her. "She was really upset that night. Worried about you."

"I'm sure she was." Maggie jerked a quick nod. "I'm sorry I haven't thanked you before now."

"I don't think any of us wanted to talk about it."

He met her gaze then, and Maggie understood. "I think you are right."

"I'm glad we tripped the house alarm, and then called 9-1-1, and that the cops came fast."

Yes, so am I. "You did the right thing."

What Tyler didn't know—what none of the kids knew—was that Max had slipped out the back before the police officers got inside and found her upstairs. He would have been jailed and charged, had they gotten to him, but Max was slick. Always was. He'd parked his rental car on the next block, apparently drove straight to his waiting charter jet, and was off to Los Angeles, and then Australia—where they couldn't touch him.

Bastard.

She'd contemplated pressing charges—but Julia warned her that nothing would come of it. If anything, they might use the threat of pressing charges as a bargaining chip in the custody settlement. An arrest warrant could keep him out of the states.

And honestly? Anything that would keep Max out of the country was fine with her.

There were so many times over the past months where she'd repeatedly replayed the scene in Carol's bedroom over in her head. Had he intended to kill her that night? If he had, it would have made his life easier. Right?

Tyler spoke again, halting her spinning thoughts. "I try to calm her down when she gets upset about him."

She didn't blame Carol for being mad at Max—but she had to get a grip on her anger, somehow. "I'm sure you are good at that."

"My parents split up when I was three."

"So, you've been through it." Maggie exhaled. "I'm sure it wasn't easy. Do you see both parents often?"

He nodded. "Yes. They live here, in town, and me and my brother, we go back and forth. It's all we know, really."

"I'm glad it's working for you, Tyler."

Maggie knew, in her head and in her heart, that joint custody would not be a good thing for the kids—but that idea would be off the table if Max stayed in Australia. Julia said she'd see to it. But if he came back to the states to stay, then she was going to have to worry about a different custody situation.

They'd not seen him since he'd left in January, after Carol's accident and the incident at the house. Jason and Chloe were clueless about what had happened that night. Max called twice in January, asking to talk to the kids, but there'd been nothing—no communication from him—since.

They asked why. She told them it was because of his work and the time differences. They bought it. She wanted to keep the details of Max's disappearance from them for the time being, hoping to maintain some sense of normalcy.

She, herself, had only heard from him through his attorney. Max had lawyered up after the incident in January—probably concerned about the pending assault charges. When his attorney had reached out to her, she'd referred him directly to Julia. She'd had no contact with Max after that.

It was like her husband had simply stepped off the stage.

While she expected that, given the circumstances, it also worried her. He was too quiet. Calm before the storm?

She supposed she needed to brace herself for anything.

"I don't think she's coming down."

Maggie sighed and met Tyler's gaze. "Is she mad at you, too?"

"Sorta. Yes."

"Want me to get her?"

"No." He shook his head. "Let's wait a minute."

Maggie had to chuckle inwardly. If Carol was mad, Tyler probably wasn't ready to face her, and she didn't blame him. "Sure. Do you want to talk about it?"

He took another long drink of his root beer, then set the empty can aside. "Apparently, I was looking at another girl. I mean, I guess I stared, or so she said, too long."

"Ah." Maggie stood, picking up his can and placing it in the recycling container. "The green-eyed monster reared its ugly head."

"I didn't realize looking was a crime."

Maggie had to laugh. The boy had a lot to learn.

Tyler looked surprised.

"Was this a girl she knows?"

He sniffed and ran a hand under his nose. "Yeah. Someone she doesn't like."

"Oh, well, that's not good. Is it? You ogling a girl she doesn't like?" She laughed, teasing him on one hand, but on the other, perhaps sending a message to the young man. *Ogling the enemy is a first-class offense.*

"I didn't know."

"Sorry, Tyler. Carol can be... How to say...?" *A little bitch?* "A lot to handle. I'm sure she'll come around."

"I don't know."

His cell phone pinged then, and seconds later, so did Maggie's. She and Tyler exchanged glances.

Tyler flipped his over and read the text while Maggie watched. He simply stared at the phone for several long seconds afterward.

Then she read her message.

Carol: *Mom. Tell him to go. I just broke up with him.*

Maggie lifted her gaze. Tyler still stared at his phone. "Tyler? You okay?"

He gave her a blank look. "She just broke up with me."

Her heart went out to the kid. "I'm sorry, Tyler."

"I don't understand."

"Me, either. Want me to talk to her?"

He rose, unsteadily, and drifted toward the front hallway. "No."

He said nothing more as he left. Maggie followed him to the door and watched him amble down the sidewalk, get in his car, and drive away. What in the hell had Carol actually said to him? Turning toward the stairs, she yelled up. "Carol!"

Immediately, the girl appeared, her hair and make-up done, wearing the new jeans and top they'd shopped for a few days ago. She scrolled through her phone as she skipped down the stairs. "Whew. Finally. He's gone?"

"Yes. What in the world...? He left in shock. That was terrible!"

"Mom. He was getting annoying." Carol halted at the bottom

step and made eye contact, obviously registering Maggie's disapproval. "What? He deserved it."

"Why did you make him come all the way over here and then not even come downstairs?"

"Because he pissed me off on the phone earlier."

"How?"

"He said I was acting like a spoiled brat."

Maggie arched a brow. "Were you?"

Carol's eyes widened and her mouth dropped open. "Mom! Whose side are you on?"

"Good God, Carol," she gasped. "I'm on no one's side. I don't even know what is going on."

Her daughter rolled her eyes and huffed. She reached for the car keys in a wooden bowl on the entry table. "I'm going out."

"No, you can't. I need the car tonight."

They shared one car. Max had bought an older model Toyota Camry with the insurance money from the wreck. He had agreed, reluctantly, because he didn't want to buy her anything, but Julia's strong nudge to his attorney was successful.

Pausing at the door, Carol slowly turned. "This is such shit. Dad promised me a car for my senior year and now nothing. He said he would pay if I picked one out. What the crap, Mom? I need a car. I'll be going off to college in the fall."

"You know we've talked about this. It's a divorce negotiation. Julia says it's best to wait."

The look on Carol's face nearly frightened her. "It's your divorce, Mom. You and Dad. That shouldn't have anything to do with me, or Dad getting me a car. He is still always going to be my dad, even if he is a jackass, even if he's not your husband. He has the money, and he has to provide for me. He's just dragging his damn feet, and Julia won't even bring it up."

Her poor child. She didn't get it. Did she? "Carol, the system doesn't work that way. You and Jason and Chloe are very much a part of all of this. I'm trying to fight for you too, so your needs will be met."

"Well, my needs right now are not being met. We need another car, Mom. Can't you drive Dad's SUV?"

Maggie shook her head. "You know I can't. He insured it only for himself."

"I really don't think that matters, Mom. It's insured, so it's good."

"But your dad said...."

"Jesus, Mom. Dad isn't always right, you know. He tells you what he wants you to think. He twists things to confuse you."

She was probably right. He'd been gaslighting her for far too long. "We'll figure something out, sweetheart. But tonight, I have my class."

Again, Carol gave her the eye roll. "Tonight?"

"Yes."

"Can't you skip?"

Maggie perched her hands on her hips and squared herself. "You know I can't. I need the class to help me get back into the work world. My resume sucks so I have to figure out how to present myself as employable. I have to find a job sooner or later, and right now, this class will help me do that."

Carol stared at her phone, texting someone. "Don't tell me I have to babysit."

"No. You don't. Jason and Chloe will be fine here. I'll only be gone a couple of hours."

"Good. You'll be home before me then."

"It's a school night," Maggie reminded her. "In by ten, please."

She nodded. "Sure. I texted Logan. He's picking me up."

Logan? Maggie watched her fingers fly over the keyboard again. "Who in the hell is Logan? My God, Carol. Did you have another guy waiting in the wings?"

Carol glanced up and smiled. "Maybe."

Shit. She is too much like me at that age. Dammit.

"He's here. Bye!"

A horn sounded loudly from the street. Maggie frowned and watched her daughter race across the lawn and climb into a newer model four-wheel-drive pickup truck. Memories of her own past raced through her head, strongly conflicting with the present reality.

"MOMMY, I NEED SOME STUFF FOR A PROJECT."

Butter knife in hand, Maggie glanced at Chloe. She plucked the toast from the toaster when it popped up. "What kind of stuff?"

"Art stuff. I have to make a poster thing. I can't remember what it's called. I have a paper in my backpack."

"Okay. When's it due?" She hoped not today. *Why do my kids wait so long to tell me these things?*

"I dunno."

Maggie finished buttering the toast, then placed the plate of toast on the island. "Carol! Jason! Breakfast." She made eggs that morning, with cheese and toast. Just how they liked them. Would Max be able to make breakfast like this for them when the time came? No, Max would throw them a box of tarts or donuts.

Not coming to that, Maggie. Don't think about it.

Carol rushed into the kitchen. "I'm late. Can we go?"

Behind her, Jason drifted in, scratching his head, and sat. "I'm not ready."

"Well, I am!" Carol nudged him and Jason nearly fell off his seat.

"Hey."

"Stop you two. Sit down and eat. Carol, we'll go when everyone is ready," Maggie said.

Carol grabbed two toasts, put a spoonful of eggs and cheese between them, and squished the sandwich flat. "But I'm already late."

"I don't recall you saying you had to be at school early for any reason."

"I didn't."

"Then...."

A horn beeped in their driveway. Carol quickly wrapped her sandwich in a paper towel and darted toward the window. "It's Logan." She whirled back. "I'll ride to school with him, Mom. Okay?"

The girl was practically out the front door before she'd said she could. "Fine, I guess," she muttered.

Jason sleepily looked at her. "You know he's not in school. Right?"

A zip of anxiety punched at Maggie's heart. "What?"

"He dropped out last year."

Shit. Shit-shit-shit.

"No, I didn't know that." She paused, thinking. What would she have done at Carol's age? "You don't think she's skipping school, do you?"

Jason shrugged. "I dunno. Can I have cereal? I don't feel like eggs."

"Sure." *Whatever.*

With a sigh, she studied him as he got up and stumbled toward the cabinet for the cereal, opened the door, and stared at the boxes. At least it wasn't the refrigerator.

"Were you up late playing video games?"

He shrugged, his back still to her. "I need a shower. I'll eat after."

"What about the cereal?"

"Not the kind I like."

"Oh."

He turned and ambled out of the room again, yawning. Not looking at her. He'd been quiet lately. Too quiet. And exhausted all the time. Was he sleeping at all?

"Can I have his eggs?"

"What?" She looked at Chloe, who was on her third piece of toast. "Sure."

She scraped Jason's eggs onto her plate and took a big bite. "The paper's in my bag, Mommy."

"Oh?"

"The art thing."

That's right. "Okay. I'll get it. I have to go downtown this morning, anyway."

A GIDDY SENSATION CREPT UP FROM SOMEWHERE DEEP IN her tummy and curled upward, warming her chest. Maggie felt a keen surge of happiness roll over her as her fingertips gently caressed the row of pastel chalks lined up in the box on the store shelf in front of her.

To her left sat a display of paint brushes, so she wandered closer. She picked up a long-handled brush with a natural bristle, smoothing the fine hairs between her forefinger and thumb. Down the aisle, she saw the display of acrylic and oil paints, and more.

Beyond those were aisles of various types of art media.

She let go of a long breath. It felt like she'd been holding that breath for a couple of decades—and she felt free.

Normally she would have picked up supplies at the local drugstore, or the big box store a few blocks away, but she'd had to go to the florist downtown to order flowers for a funeral, and knew the art supply store was next door. She'd rarely been there—had passed it by many times and glanced inside via the large glass-pane windows. Her heart always did a little twitter-pat when she did so.

She loved color. Loved paints. Adored watching the pigment spread across a page in a sketchbook, soak into watercolor paper, or slide off the brush onto a canvas. She loved the chaos of color on a palette, dried up oils and fresh acrylics alike. When she was younger, she wasn't so great at cleaning up her painting messes and often left the oils to harden and dry on the wooden palette. As she'd matured in her art, after she'd started taking classes in college, she got better at cleaning up—palettes, brushes, whatever... But nothing said art to her as much as the leftover drips and spatters on tables and floors and aprons and old shirts and even the walls.

To her, messy was good.

Probably why Max disapproved of her painting *hobby*, as he called it.

Not thinking about him now. She was enjoying this too much to ruin it.

Ambling down the aisle, she let her fingertips glide over the tubes of paint, losing herself in the sensation of freedom. To be free and relaxed enough to let the muse flow from within and embark on a creative adventure.

But her mind did wander to Max.

The messiness of it all was what had ticked him off years ago.

She'd set up a studio after they'd moved into their new house, when she was pregnant with Carol and not working, and taking a couple of art classes at the local community college. The lighting there was perfect, and she had plenty of space for storage and her easels. She'd taken the curtains down to tease the outside into the room, and worked with the windows open, until it got too cold for her to do so.

Max complained about the smells, about the windows being open, about her not cleaning up "properly" as he would say, meaning he wanted her to clean and put away every brush, any media she was using, every night, so that the room was fresh and tidy, neat and clean, just in case someone came by.

"I can shut the door, Max," she'd told him. "It's not a big deal. Painting is messy and sometimes projects can't be disturbed for a while."

A few days later, while she was out running errands and grocery shopping, he'd brought a moving crew in to pack everything into boxes. He told her he'd stored them in a storage unit across town until they had a better space for her. To her knowledge, those boxes were still there, somewhere—if they indeed still rented that storage unit.

She should find out.

The following day, Max set up his home office in that same room. That was the first time he'd shut her out with locks on the door.

"May I help you find something?"

Shaking herself from the memory, she looked up into the face of a tall man standing beside her, looking down and smiling. He had dark hair, blue eyes with crinkles at the outer corners, and a kind face. He also sported a slightly scruffy beard, which she'd always thought sexy. She guessed him to be about her age, maybe even younger. Glancing lower to his chest, she noticed the store logo on the artist's work apron he wore.

"Oh. Hi. You work here?"

He smiled. A nice, wide smile that nearly covered the lower half of his face. "I do. What can I help you find?"

She dug into her bag for Chloe's paper. "I... My daughter has this project for school. I need supplies, a variety, I guess. I probably should have brought her with me, but I was downtown now, so..." *I'm babbling. Rambling.* "The instructions are vague, so I was just looking around to see what struck me and...."

He took the paper out of her hand. "Ah. The second-grade selfie project. Mrs. Anderson's class."

She nodded. "How did you know?"

"She does this every year. And my daughter, Anna, is also in her class."

"Really?" Maggie took another look. *Should I know you?* "I'm Maggie Oliver, by the way. My daughter is Chloe."

He shifted the paper to his left hand and put out his right one. "Andy Ryan. Nice to meet you."

"And you." She took his hand. Warm. Quickly, she dropped it. "So, the project? It says mixed media, so I'm assuming we can use whatever we like. I was wondering about a canvas, or perhaps a heavy paper? What do you suggest?"

He nodded. "Kids seem to like to add on, and keep adding on, so I'd suggest something substantial—and also something they can easily handle. But really, anything could work. Poster board. Cardboard. And it doesn't have to be flat. It could be 3-D."

"I'm not sure where to start."

"Well, what does your daughter want? The project is about her. I think it's important that she pick the media to express herself. Don't you?"

That was an excellent idea, of course. And one she should have thought of.

"You're right. How late are you open? I could drop back by with her after school today."

He grinned again. "We're open until five."

"Great." Maggie glanced again at the paints and brushes.

"Those are great brushes," he said. "A new company for us, but I've been very pleased with the quality."

"They are very nice." She ran her fingers over the tips of a few standing upright in a container.

"Do you paint?"

With a sigh, Maggie dropped her hand and faced him. "I used to."

He caught her gaze and held it for a few heartbeats. "That's a shame," he finally said.

She nodded. "Yes. It is." *Not getting into that discussion.*

Brushing past him, she took a few steps down the aisle, then rotated to face him again. He had turned toward her, too. "I'll be back later with my daughter. Thanks for your help."

"My pleasure."

Nine

Pulling up to the curb at the middle school, Maggie waved at Jason, motioning for him to get in the car. She watched as he stood with a group of boys—a couple of them she didn't recognize—as they jostled about, pushing and shoving each other playfully.

At least she thought it was playful.

As Jason glanced her way, one kid pointed, then punched him hard in the shoulder. Jason stumbled, going down half-way on one knee. The gang of boys laughed.

The anger that immediately boiled up inside her was nearly all-consuming, and she wanted to shove the car into park, jump out, run over to that mob of stupid adolescent testosterone-fueled nonsense, and give them each a piece of her mama bear mind.

But she didn't.

She gripped the steering wheel tighter, gritted her teeth, and counted to twenty while Jason ambled across the school lawn toward the car. She rolled down the passenger side window and could hear the shouts and jeers from the group of boys.

Jason jerked at the latch and plopped into the front seat, not looking at her.

"Are you okay?"

"Drive."

She didn't say a word, didn't look at him either, and pulled out of the school parking lot.

Forget the art supplies. Another day.

No, she couldn't forget the art supplies. Chloe needed them. But did she need them *tonight*? What did that paper say? When was the project due?

Stopping at a traffic light, she reached into her bag on the console and pushed items aside. *Where is the fucking paper?* Not there. "Dammit." Had she left it at the store?

"Don't cuss, Mom," Chloe called out from the back seat.

"Yeah, Mom," Jason echoed. "Language."

She looked at him, trying to assess his demeanor. He was easily embarrassed, but this looked more like humiliation. The boy who punched him had pointed at the car—or was it at her? What had he said to Jason? *Am I making a mountain out of a mole hill?* Lately, she wasn't sure which Jason she was going to get—the amenable, loving, big brother to Chloe, or the lethargic, musing, and maybe depressed adolescent teenager.

A horn honked behind her. She glanced in the rearview mirror, then at the light. Green. She pressed the accelerator.

"I need to go downtown for a few minutes," she said to Jason. "Chloe needs art supplies. Okay with you?"

Pulling his headphones out of his pocket, he plugged them into his phone, then put them in his ears, dismissing her. "Fine."

Turning at the next light, she headed downtown and found a parking place not too far from the art store. She turned to Chloe. "Let's go, pumpkin." Tapping Jason's knee, she added, "You coming or staying?"

He made eye contact then. "Staying."

Fine. "We won't be long."

His eyes closed and his head dropped back against the headrest.

As she and Chloe entered the store, she glanced at the enormous clock on the wall. Three-twenty-seven. Plenty of time.

"Wow, Mommy. This is a great store." Chloe's eyes widened as they stepped into the aisle she'd visited earlier.

"I know. Look at all the colors," she said. "I just love the colors."

"Me, too." Chloe ran forward, straight for the rows of paint tubes. "Can we get these?"

"Those are oil paints, sweetheart. I think, perhaps, you should start with acrylics. Those are over here."

"Okay." Chloe joined her. "Are these good? I need paintbrushes, too."

"You really want to use paint? Not markers or pencils or crayons?"

"No." She looked at Maggie. "I really want to paint, Mommy."

Her heart swelled. *Me, too.* She did not know Chloe was so interested in art. Oh, she'd always loved the little crafty projects they did around the house, but it hadn't dawned on her that her baby girl might have inherited her love for all things artsy. That notion thrilled her to no end. "Maybe we'll get enough supplies for both of us."

Footsteps sounded behind them, and Maggie turned. A college-age girl, wearing the same artist's apron as the man this afternoon, approached. "May I help you?"

The paper. "Oh, yes. I was here this afternoon and spoke with a gentleman about my daughter's school project, and I think I left the paper with the instructions with him. Do you know if he is still here?"

"That would be Mr. Ryan, and no, he is gone for the day. I think he may have left this for you, though." She reached into her apron pocket. "Mrs. Anderson's second grade selfie project?"

"That's it. Oh, thank you." Maggie took the paper. "No, wait. This isn't ours. It has a list clipped to it, and something else."

The young woman leaned in. "Yes. Mr. Ryan attached a list of supplies for you. Just some suggestions, he said. Looks like he added a class schedule, too."

Classes? They do classes here? She quickly scanned the list and dates. *Watercolor for Beginners. Mastering Oils. Pen and Ink Landscapes. Acrylics Refresher.* The list went on.

"That was very nice of him. Please tell him thanks."

"I will. Now, can I help at all with finding supplies?" She looked directly at Chloe.

Chloe beamed. "Yes! I want paint. Lots of paint. Did he put paint on that list?"

"I believe he did. Let's go look at all the kinds we have." She glanced back again at Maggie. "I'm really good with kids. Do you mind? I'm an art major. I want to teach younger kids."

Maggie smiled and suddenly felt the sting of tears. A very long time ago, she'd wanted that, too. "Of course. Thank you."

The two girls meandered down the aisle.

Maggie smiled at how happy Chloe looked, then glanced again at the paper in her hand, scanning the list of classes.

THE FIRST THING MAGGIE NOTICED AS SHE TURNED DOWN their street were two pickup trucks at her house. One was Logan's, parked on the street. The other truck was angled in the driveway, blocking her from getting to the garage. Both things pissed her off.

She turned into her driveway, pulling in behind the mystery truck. She stared at the house momentarily while trying to get a grip on her anger.

"Somebody's gonna get into trouble," Jason sing-songed.

Maggie rotated toward him. "Whose truck is that? You know? Does Logan have friends?" Unless Maggie was home, boys were not allowed in the house with Carol. Alone. That was the rule.

"Nope. No clue."

"Mommy, let's go inside. I want to paint."

She cracked her door open. "Jason, stay here with Chloe."

"Sure." He grinned then, apparently eager to watch the drama unfold.

Stepping out of the car, she looked toward the house as the front door opened. An older gentleman moved onto the porch, chatting with Carol—who caught her eye and waved frantically. Logan followed.

"What the hell?" Maggie slammed the car door and sprinted for the porch.

"Mom! He's here for a house inspection. Did you call him?"

The man approached with an outstretched hand. "I'm Matthew Riley," he said. "I'm with Final Look Home Inspection."

Maggie shook his hand. "Home inspection? I don't understand." She glanced at the kids. Carol looked frustrated. Logan stood there looking a little sheepish.

The inspector gave her a puzzled look. "This is the Oliver residence. Correct? Max and Maggie Oliver."

"Yes. I'm Maggie Oliver."

He glanced over the paperwork on a clipboard. "We had an appointment scheduled for four o'clock this afternoon to do a pre-inspection on the house."

"Pre... What? Authorized by who?"

He glanced at the paper again. "Mr. Oliver, I believe."

"What? Why?"

"Sometimes people do inspections before the sale, so they can see what needs to be fixed before it goes on the market."

Maggie watched Carol's eyes fly wide open and felt hers do the same. "On the market? What sale?"

"Mom, what's going on?"

"I'm not sure." She turned to the gentleman. "Do you mind... May I see that?" She gestured toward the clipboard.

He shrugged. "Sure."

She took it and scanned the information on the sheet. The person requesting the inspection was indeed Max. He'd listed his address in Brisbane and a phone number. Not his cell phone number. *Goddamned motherfucker.* "Carol, do you have your phone? Mine is in the car."

"Yes." She moved around the inspector.

"Take a picture of this page, please."

The inspector stepped forward, reaching for the clipboard. "Now, wait. I'm not sure...."

Maggie jerked the clipboard out of his reach. "Look. It's my house and my information on this page. I have a right." She thrust the clipboard out, away from the inspector.

Carol quickly snapped several pictures of the form. "Got it."

"Great. Send me those." She handed over the paperwork and peered at the man. "No inspection today, Mr. Riley."

He cocked his head. "Now, I'm going to get into trouble if I don't

101

get this done today. We have a tight schedule and lots of business—I just can't pop in here on a moment's notice."

"We're not getting an inspection. I'm sorry for your trouble." Maggie held eye contact with him for several seconds. "Max Oliver doesn't live here anymore, and this is not his house."

"But he's already paid."

"Then deal with him, not me. Not my problem." She glanced toward his truck. "Now, please move your vehicle so I can get mine in my garage. I'd appreciate it."

"But what do I tell Mr. Oliver?"

Maggie chuckled and looked him square in the eye. "Look. I realize this is an inconvenience... And I don't want you to get into trouble... But if Mr. Oliver asks about the inspection, tell him I said to stick it up his slimy, shitty ass."

Matthew Riley stared back, looking rather dumbfounded.

"Yes, ma'am."

He was on his way within seconds.

"MOM WAS SUCH A BADASS, JASON. YOU SHOULD HAVE SEEN her."

Maggie set two large pizza boxes on the kitchen island and glanced at Jason. He didn't seem too impressed with his mother's confrontation skills—or lack thereof.

"Not a badass," she said. "Just confused and frustrated. You all know how I get a potty mouth when I'm upset or angry."

"You must have been both," Jason said. "I heard you from the car."

"You are correct." She flipped back the lids on both pizzas. "One cheese and one extra-supreme with jalapenos. And here's some garlic dipping sauce, too. Sorry you're not getting tuna casserole tonight, but I don't feel like cooking."

Chloe dragged the cheese pizza box toward her and her sister, and they both picked up a slice.

"God, Mom, we'll do pizza anytime." Carol snickered.

"Yeah, but it's expensive." Maggie glanced at her. "Where did Logan rush off to?"

"He works some evenings."

"I see." She'd not yet approached her with the news Jason had dropped earlier, that Logan wasn't in school—or the fact that she wasn't supposed to have boys in the house if she was alone. "Too bad. The pizza is good."

Carol kept eating, not responding.

"One of these days, soon, sweetie, I'd like for Logan to stay for dinner. Just so I can get to know him. Can we do that?"

Her daughter chewed her pizza...and probably also chewed over Maggie's words in her head. "Sure." She shrugged. "I'll have to check. You know, his work schedule."

"Sure." *Is that it? Work? Or something else?* She hated to be suspicious, but Carol always seemed so vague about him.

"I'll get drinks from the garage fridge," Jason said. *Did he sense the tension in the room, too?* "What does everyone want?"

"Diet whatever," Carol called out.

"Same," Maggie added.

Chloe took a bite of pizza and mumbled. "Orange please."

Jason nodded, retrieved the drinks, and quickly returned.

Grabbing a roll of paper towels and a stack of paper plates from under the counter, Maggie set them on the island. "Here. Use these. We're using the fancy napkins and Sunday china tonight." She ripped off several squares of paper towels.

"Did you call Julia, Mom?" Carol took a towel and swiped her mouth.

"Left a message. She'll call back soon, I imagine."

"Great."

Turning toward her, Maggie said, "Tell me what the guy said when he was here. Did you let him look at anything?"

Carol reached for another piece of pizza, then sat back. "He came to the door, said who he was, and that he was here for the house inspection—like he told you."

"Then what?"

"He asked if either of us were over eighteen—me or Logan—and

Logan told him he was nineteen. The guy said he couldn't do the inspection unless there was someone over the age of eighteen in the house."

Maggie nodded. *Interesting.* Probably standard procedure. "And...?"

"And then he asked a few questions, like how many rooms, was there a basement, how old was the furnace, did we care if he got on the roof, and stuff like that."

"What did you say?"

"I told him what I could, but that he needed to wait for you. It wasn't too long until you pulled into the driveway, so I sent him outside."

Maggie sighed. "Good. So he didn't go anywhere in the house?"

Carol shook her head. "No."

"Great."

Carol made eye contact with her. "Mom, Logan and I were not in the house alone. We know the rules. The guy was already parked in the driveway when we pulled up and I just assumed you had called him. At first, I thought he was a repair guy or something."

Maggie gave her a smile. "I understand. It's okay, sweetheart."

They all stayed silent for a minute. The kids continued eating. Maggie stared off, thinking and wondering what Max was up to.

Then Jason piped up. "Mom. What is going on? What is this inspection about, anyway? I don't get it."

She faced him. "Frankly, I don't either."

"Does it have anything to do with Dad?"

She waited a few seconds, wondering if she should be honest about that. The thought had niggled at her brain ever since the inspector left. "Probably. More than likely."

"Does it have anything to do with why he has been in Australia for so long? Is he staying there now?"

She met Jason's questioning gaze and held it for several seconds. Then pivoting, she glanced at Chloe, who was busy with the cheese pizza, and then at Carol, who sat quietly looking back.

With a sigh, she focused on Jason again. "There are some things we need to talk about. Yes, this probably has something to do with your dad."

Abruptly, Jason stood up and pushed his paper plate filled with pizza away from him. "Are you splitting up? Is he selling the house? Where the hell are we going to live, Mom?"

"Jason. Stop." She glanced at Chloe, who seemed oblivious. "I don't know what is happening with the house. That's why I called Julia, so...."

"Julia?"

Shit. She'd stuck her foot in it. "Yes. She's helping me deal with some...things."

"But she's a lawyer, right? Why do you need a lawyer?" Jason's voice rose. "Please tell us what is going on? Because I'm tired of not knowing."

So, is this why he's been moody lately? She glanced again at Carol, who nodded.

"See? Carol knows something," Jason shouted. "Why do you tell her stuff and not me? I can deal with stuff, Mom. I want to know."

She responded slowly. "I know you do, Jason. And until now I wanted to keep things as normal as possible for all of you, but—"

"Normal! Nothing is normal. Dad isn't here, he never calls anymore, feels like we have no money, and now this inspector... Something is not right."

Her cell phone rang on the counter. Maggie ignored it, moving around the island. "Jason, we need to talk. Just you and me. Okay?"

He shook his head. "No. Tell all of us at the same time."

Her phone pinged with a notification. *Voice mail.*

Again, she scanned the room—from Jason to Carol, then to Chloe, who was still happily eating, or perhaps ignoring.

She couldn't avoid this any longer. Could she? She'd not said much because she feared her family would fall apart. Well, it was happening anyway, wasn't it? Carol was tinkering with boys, Jason was moody and apparently having trouble with friends, and little Chloe was eating herself silly.

Her phone rang again. Once more, she ignored it.

"Alright, Jason. We will talk. All of us. Just let me get my head wrapped around a few things and answer that damn phone. It's probably Julia. Eat your pizza and go play some video games or watch TV for a while." She glanced at Carol. "I suppose it is time to get this out in the open."

Turning, she picked up her phone and checked the call list. "I'm going to my room to call Julia back. Hopefully she has some...news."

She started to say "good news" then realized that was highly unlikely.

It was Max they were dealing with here. Right?

Ten

Julia answered on the first ring. "Mags. Hey. Got your message."

"Do you have a clue what that was today? I mean, I have my suspicions, but I'm hoping you have facts." Maggie shut the bedroom door behind her and wandered toward the window.

"I'm getting a handle on it. How are you doing?"

"I've had better days—and worse, obviously—but I'm good. Did you find out anything?"

"Are you home?"

Now she was worried. "I am. What's going on, Julia?"

There was a slight pause from the other end. "Mags, I spoke with Max's attorney earlier in the day, before you called. I got back in touch with him after I received your message. He came clean with some information—apparently Max is hot on selling the house, for some unknown reason—but admittedly, the lawyer was clueless about the inspector. He's going to get back to me after he talks with Max."

"It's the middle of the night there, so that means we're waiting."

"Approaching morning, I think. Might hear nothing for a few hours."

Maggie stared out at the street. "Maybe it's a good thing Max acted without consulting his attorney. He thinks he's invincible, so perhaps we have that going for us."

Julia laughed. "He's not goddamned invincible. I can assure you of that."

Maggie sighed, watching some kids playing in the yard across the street. Suddenly, she wished her kids were young again like that, and their days were carefree and easy.

Those days are gone. Their innocence is about to be undone.

"We have several things to talk about, Mags, and I don't want to discuss any of it over the phone. I don't trust that son-of-a-bitch. Can we meet halfway in the morning? Say ten o'clock? Where would be a good place?"

"Yes. I can leave after I drop the kids at school. Julia, is it bad news?"

Another pause. "Not necessarily. I officially told the attorney that we are filing for divorce, so to be ready. I've flung the possibility around before now, but it's time. We're just getting started, of course, but I want you to consider all the angles. Too much for a phone call."

"Well, okay. Let me think. There's really not much midway between Tuckaway Bay and here—just a bunch of small towns."

"Maybe that's better, to be honest. Surely, we can find one with a restaurant or at least a gas station. I'll look and text you later."

"Sure."

"Talk soon."

"Julia?"

"Yes?"

"Am I screwed?"

"Not if I can help it."

SHE KNOCKED ON CAROL'S BEDROOM DOOR AND EASED IT open. Carol sat on her bed, propped up with pillows, looking at her tablet.

"Let's go chat," Maggie said. "With Jason and Chloe."

Carol set the tablet aside. "How much are you going to say?"

With a shrug, Maggie whispered, "I have no clue. I guess I'm winging it."

Meeting her at the door, Carol slipped a hand in hers. "Mom... I'll help if you need me."

Oh, this girl. She could be a pain in the ass, or the sweetest child ever, but she loved her to pieces either way.

Maggie tugged Carol into her arms and held her tight. "I'm sorry you've had to shoulder some of this with me. But I'm also very grateful to have you to lean on, occasionally. And you know you have me. Right?"

Pulling back, Carol searched her eyes. "Mom. I love you. I know we fight sometimes, but I love you."

"I know that." Maggie smiled and touched her cheek. "I love you too, sweetie. Now, let's go do this."

"I'll get Chloe."

"Thank you."

Maggie rapped on Jason's door. She knew better than to go in without him saying it was okay. He didn't respond immediately, so she knocked again. "Jason?"

"Yeah."

"Can you come out, please?"

She waited a few long seconds. Carol and Chloe headed downstairs. Finally, Jason came to the door.

"We're all heading downstairs. Let's have that talk."

The look in his eyes told her he was curious, frightened, and maybe heartbroken already. She knew exactly how that felt. She wanted to hug him, hold him like he was her little baby boy, and stroke his cheek with feathery touches—but that would not happen.

Jason brushed her arm as he passed.

She followed him down the stairs.

ALL THREE SAT TOGETHER ON THE SOFA, CHLOE IN THE middle, Carol and Jason like bookends.

Jason put his arm around his little sister, creating a protective cocoon for Chloe. Maggie's heart warmed as Chloe looked up and searched her big brother's eyes. Carol leaned closer to them, too, but stared at the floor, her hands clasped in front of her.

Maggie couldn't say who she was worried about more—she was concerned about all three equally, but in different ways. Pulling up a side chair, she parked herself in front of them so she could see all three faces at once.

"Just get it over with, Mom," Jason said.

Maggie inhaled deeply, then let the breath go, easing out some of her anxiety with it. She hoped, anyway. "Alright. Let me just say some things and then you can ask questions."

"Sure, Mom," Carol said.

Chloe stared ahead, biting her lip.

"I spoke with Julia, who talked with your dad's attorney earlier this evening."

"Wait," Jason interrupted. "Dad has an attorney, too?"

"Well, yes." Suddenly, she realized she'd probably jumped the gun a little, had gotten ahead of herself. "Just hold that thought for a minute, can you? I'll get there in a minute."

Jason leaned back and sighed, looking away.

She continued. "Apparently, the inspector was here today because your dad wants to sell the house. He didn't tell me that, of course, so it was a surprise to me."

"But why?" Jason asked. "Why does he want to sell the house? Are we getting a new one?"

She breathed in and out again. Slowly. "No. We are not getting a new house. I believe your father wants to sell because he either wants the money, or he wants to punish me."

"No. Dad has money." Jason's face screwed up, questioning. "What did you do to him, Mom?"

"She didn't do a damn thing, Jason. It's all Dad."

He twisted to look at her. "How do you know that?"

Maggie leaned forward. "Kids. Stop. Listen to me. Please? Just listen for a minute."

Jason closed his eyes, as if he were trying to block it all out.

Chloe's arms snaked around Jason's waist.

Bracing herself, Maggie started in again, knowing she didn't want to stop until she'd said everything she wanted to say. "Kids, your father and I haven't gotten along for a long time. There are a lot of reasons for that, and I will not go into them right now. Maybe when you are older. What you need to know is that we are getting a divorce. That's one reason your dad has been spending the past few months in Australia. It's true he started a new business in Brisbane, and needs to be there right now, but it's also because he and I do not want to live together any longer."

Jason stared. "So, it's not just work. It's an official divorce."

"Yes."

"Then, you lied." His stare was intense.

"I wasn't ready to talk to you kids about it yet. And as the adult here, that was my prerogative."

Jason ignored that. "What about us? Me, Carol, and Chloe? Don't we get a say? What happens to us?"

"Of course, you do." She let go of another sigh. *This is going to get difficult before it gets easier.* "In a way. Look. I'm going to be as honest with you as I can be. I don't know a lot yet. Julia is handling the divorce, and part of that is custody. And yes, your dad has an attorney, too, to handle his end of things. That's the way it works. To answer your question, Jason, I don't know exactly what will happen. Sometimes in a divorce, the kids live with one parent full-time and visit the other on weekends and holidays. Sometimes there is joint custody, where the kids spend, say, a week at one parent's house, then a week at the other. But I think you all know that already."

"We do, Mom. Friends..." Carol offered.

"That sort of sucks, doesn't it?" Jason said. "What about school and stuff?"

Geez, she hadn't expected to go there yet. "While I don't want this to happen, if your dad doesn't pay for private school, then you'll have to go to the public school. I won't be able to afford it."

Jason glared. "Well, if you'd worked before now, maybe you could afford it."

"Your dad didn't want me to work, Jason."

"Right."

"I'm telling you the truth." She studied him. Obviously, he was tearing himself up inside, rolling over all this information. Yet, she knew he'd been moody and stewing on something for a while now, so perhaps getting it out in the open was a good thing.

He glanced off, apparently thinking. "What if Dad doesn't live in the same school district, or he wants us to go to a different school than you do? How does that work? We can't go to two schools."

"No, you can't." She reached for his hand, but he pulled away. Instead, she touched his knee. "Jason, these are legit questions. All that has to be worked out between your dad and me and the lawyers. The thing is, as long as he is living in Australia, which is a different country, the judge will probably say that you should live full time with me, and you can visit him on vacations."

"Geez, Mom. Whatever you did to piss him off, you sure weren't thinking of us, were you? You've totally screwed up our lives."

Of all the things she had mentally prepared herself for, Jason's words—him blaming her—were not among them. She choked back a sob and looked away.

Carol scooted to the edge of the couch, leaning toward her brother. "Jason! That's total bullshit. Mom didn't do anything. You know how Dad treats her. You know how he treats us. Whenever he can get a dig in, he does. If he wants to slap us around, he does that too. And Mom has had enough of it. You got that? So just shut the fuck up."

"Carol..." Maggie grasped her arm.

"No, Mom. He needs to know the truth."

Jason sat, staring at the wall. "The truth? Right. No one is telling the truth here."

Maggie shifted in her seat so she could catch Jason's eye. "Jason, listen to me. I'll admit I've kept things from you kids, a lot of things over the years, but I did that to protect you. In fact, everything I've ever done since you've been alive is to protect you."

"Sure. Right."

"Jason!" Carol reached out and punched his arm. "Stop. You don't have a clue, do you? God, Mom, just tell him or I will."

To be honest, Maggie wasn't sure which thing Carol wanted her to tell. The part about the night in January when Max beat the shit out of her? Or the part where he'd knocked up some random woman in Brisbane? Or that Jason had a sibling he didn't know about.

Carol glared. "All right, then I'll say it."

Jason stood and took a step away. "I don't want to hear it."

"Oh yes, you do." She reached across Chloe and grabbed his arm.

He jerked back and glared.

"Carol..." Maggie warned.

She ignored her. "Dad hit Mom, hard. I was there. I saw it. He wanted to hurt me, too."

"What are you talking about?" He scowled.

"Do you remember when Julia was here in January, and you and Chloe stayed with her in the hotel? Well, Dad came back home that night and attacked Mom—because she was protecting me. Dad was mad because Tyler was in the house, and grabbed me hard, shaking me. Mom went after him, and he hit her more than once. He hit her so hard, he knocked her out, Jason. *And he choked her.* Mom told Tyler to get me out of the house. We tripped the alarm and called 9-1-1, and the cops came, but Dad slipped out of the house and left. Mom spent the night in the E.R."

Jason glared, looking first at Carol, then Maggie. "What did you do, Mom?"

"What do you *mean*, Jason?" she said.

"You must have really done something bad to make him hit you like that."

Carol interjected. "She didn't do a damn thing! Don't you get it?"

Suddenly, Maggie realized what a dangerous example Max had set for the kids, whether or not they realized it. Jason, in particular. In his adolescent mind, Max was—probably always had been—punishing her for something she apparently had done wrong.

If the kids did something wrong, something he didn't like, they got punished.

Therefore, if Max punished her in that horrible way, then she must have deserved it.

Shit.

She took a step closer to her son. "Jason, your father is a mean-spirited, controlling asshole of a man. He is mentally and physically abusive to me, and to all of you, whether or not you realize that. And my only fault in all of this, even though I tried to protect you as much as a could, is that I didn't see it, stop it, sooner. But now I can, and I will. And all of us—you, Carol, Chloe, and me—are going to stick together so we can stay together because, frankly, I can't lose you."

She sniffled briefly, still focused on him. "And yes, I made him mad. I found out something over Christmas that changed things."

"Christmas? We were at Tuckaway Bay then."

"Right. Remember when your dad missed the call on Christmas Eve?"

"You said he texted and something came up."

"Yes."

Carol sighed and pushed closer. "Jason, I tried him again later on Mom's tablet. He had logged on but forgot to sign off. I saw him in a bedroom with another woman and a baby."

Jason's eyes widened.

Maggie moved closer. He took a step back.

"Jason," she whispered. "Your dad is living with another woman in Australia, and they have a child together. And after we got home from Tuckaway Bay, I broke into his locked office and searched for more information. Whatever I could find. Turned out he had cameras in there and saw me. That's why he came back. And that's how I ended up in the E.R." She stared, held his gaze.

Jason stood unmoving, barely breathing, it seemed. "Dad has another kid?"

"Unfortunately, yes."

Maggie blinked away tears and glanced at the couch. At some point, Chloe had gotten up and moved to the coffee table, where she'd taken out a coloring book and crayons. *Oh, my sweet baby....*

Jason sat, his head hanging. "I don't want to move to Australia, Mom. I don't even want to visit him in Australia. I don't have to. Do I?"

Thank God he's softening somewhat. "That's what Julia and I are working on. I don't want any of you to be with him. He's not good for you, for any of us. I want you with me and I will fight to make sure that happens. But your dad...."

Maggie glanced at each of her kids again.

Chloe kept coloring. Staring at her paper. Silently scribbling hard and fast.

Carol just sat there, looking sort of numb. This had taken its toll on her, hadn't it? Was she thinking about how her life was unraveling? How everything she'd ever had—everything Max had given her, provided for her, awarded to her—was going to stop? He'd always doted on her so....

"I'm with Jason. I really don't want to be with him. But Dad has connections," Carol said. "And that sucks. Will a judge make us?"

"I pray not. Julia will do her best. She's an excellent attorney," Maggie said.

"I'm almost eighteen, though. I can choose, right? Have a say?"

Maggie nodded. "I don't know the exact age. Maybe Jason can choose, too."

"Me, too?" Chloe begged. "Mommy, I get to choose, too. I choose you!"

Her heart literally felt like it was snapping into pieces.

I don't know what my own life is going to look like. How can I help these kids feel secure in all this? How will they know, and trust, that I can keep them safe? Fed? Warm and happy?

She knew in her heart she would fight tooth and nail for custody, but Carol was right. Max had power. Connections. And around there that was everything—white male, good-old-boy network power, which was abundant in this southern state. Plus, Max played golf with the judge.

"Mommy?" Chloe looked up from her coloring book, searching Maggie's eyes. She pressed so hard on her crayon that it broke, flipping off the coffee table. "Who will tuck me in? Daddy doesn't know how." Big fat tears made a slow progression down her cheeks, and her baby girl started crying, mumbling. "I don't like when Daddy throws things. Will I still go to my school? Will you take me? I don't like riding the bus with other kids. They're mean and icky."

That's when Maggie's soul cracked. Fully and completely. Splintered.

She quickly swept Chloe into a tight hug, her chest tight and aching, unable to stop her sobs. Jason and Carol rushed in to join them.

LONG AFTER THE CHILDREN WERE IN BED, MAGGIE STARED out her bedroom window again, observing the dance of leaves and branches swaying in the breeze, backlit by the streetlamps. It was all sort of mesmerizing, and calming, and in some strange way, had soothed some of her anxiety.

They'd all turned in early. The *olders*—Jason and Carol, she no longer wanted to include Jason as a *little*—had isolated themselves in their rooms. She didn't know if they were sleeping, but it didn't matter. Hopefully, they were dealing with things, rolling them over in their minds like she was doing.

Chloe was a different matter. Maggie stayed with her until she finally fell asleep. It took three books, four songs, some tears, and a couple of whispered prayers before her girl finally went to sleep in her arms. Maggie left both of their bedroom doors cracked, so she could hear if Chloe called out.

The look on the kids' faces earlier, when reality struck, was painful. That's when Maggie knew that their truth had set in—and they understood that life was going to change. That they might no longer live in the house they had lived in all their lives. They would no longer have their father at home when he wasn't traveling. They might never see him again at all. Money would be tight, and Mommy would have to work. And they would have to do what millions of other kids of divorced parents routinely do—juggle visitation schedules.

They didn't like any of it.

Her heart hurt just thinking about it.

That was when Maggie realized her kids had grown up privileged.

But it wasn't their fault, was it?

Max *had* provided for them—gave her enough money every

month to meet their needs. Apparently, his company had done well, although he never shared exactly what he was worth, or how much money he made. All of that business detail, he kept to himself.

Plus, his family suffered from generational wealth.

Suffered. Yes. Max's family was dysfunctional in ways her own family had never dreamed.

Yet, she'd been an eager participant because he met her needs, too. Checked all the boxes—security, financial and otherwise, and a sense of feeling safe, a sense of belonging.

Physically. Sexually.

Even if she wasn't. Safe.

Emotionally. Physically.

How had she totally misinterpreted what Max had done for her? How had she allowed him to control her life, their lives, in the way he had?

It really is *my fault. Isn't it?* She'd allowed Max's shit to happen.

And for what? Security? Money? A beautiful home? Private schools?

Love.

She'd done it all—*endured it all*—for love. Hadn't she?

At least in the beginning.

She just wished she hadn't lost herself somewhere along the way—and understood why she'd let it happen. Why was it okay to give over her life to Max? Had she grown tired, worn down, and caved to his demands? Or did she just get lazy and accept the life he allowed her to live?

Eleven

The day Maggie's mother threw her brother's piggy bank against the wall, shattering the glass and sending pennies flying, was the day she realized her mother was crazy.

Maggie actually remembered thinking those words. She was five years old. Does a five-year-old know what the word crazy means? She couldn't be sure.

But to this day, she remembered thinking it.

My mother is crazy.

And it wouldn't be the last time she thought it.

Looking back, she realized her mother had various stressors in her life. She was unhappy in her marriage and had fought depression for years. She'd endured a traumatic childhood, mostly in her earlier years, when her mother, Maggie's grandmother, had abandoned the family. This left her and two younger siblings under the care of an alcoholic father.

The odds were stacked against her. She had no positive parental role models growing up.

There was more.

Maggie was certain her mother had affairs. Her father, too, which only heightened the tension between them. Their all-night fights were not her favorite lullabies. There was a time when her mom became very thin, and everyone was sure she was anorexic—or taking pills.

But the worse thing—the very worse—was how she could cut you to your core, take you to your knees, with her words. And in doing so, made you feel like the worse piece of shit ever.

Maggie had to wonder how her mother's madness had affected her own life.

She'd attempted therapy for a while, to cope with the notion of the maternal control Maggie permanently felt, her mother's disapproval of everything she did, the choices she made—the fact that even her own basic instinct told her she needed her mother's approval for everything, even though she knew disapproval was more than likely forthcoming.

Even though her parents now lived in California, Maggie still felt the emotional vise grip.

Once, when Maggie shared in conversation—hoping to get some motherly advice—that she was concerned how Max disciplined the kids, the words flew. They'd argued loud and long, even dragging her father into the fight. Her mom shouted she should be happy for her situation, that Max had money, that he provided well for them all, and then finally, that she should just *shut the fuck up* and quit complaining.

She wasn't complaining. She was asking for advice.

"There could be worse things in life than having a controlling husband," her mother told her.

Maggie knew though, that there *were* worse things.

Like a controlling mother.

1992

Staring at the wall of tubes and brushes in the grocery store aisle, Mary Margaret Brennan wondered which one was best for her. The red tube was supposed to make your fine lashes thicker. The white tube promised ultra-long lashes to frame your eyes. But the fat pink tube claimed super-sexy, lush lashes that would practically change your life.

She'd been pondering that for weeks, every time she came to the store.

"Mary Margaret. I've got no time to waste here. We need to go."

She turned toward her mother. "I have babysitting money. Can I get some?" She pointed to the mascara.

Her mother's face crinkled into an irritated frown. "Hell no. You're barely thirteen. Mascara is for older women with thinning eyelashes."

Mary Margaret stared. That was not true, and she knew it. All the girls in her class wore mascara. They'd started last year in seventh grade. And besides, her mother wasn't that old, and she wore it, too. She'd seen the tubes in her makeup drawer in the bathroom. She'd even tried to sneak some once and nearly got caught.

"But I have money, and all the other girls...."

"I don't raise all the other girls," her mom snapped. Then she sighed, leaning on the handle of the grocery cart. "I forgot milk. Go grab a gallon and then we're leaving. I'll think about it, but you'll have to ask your father."

She was off then, pushing the cart in front of her, the boxy shoulder pads of her equally boxy jacket bouncing along with her hurried steps. Always in a hurry.

She stared at the makeup display again. Why ask her dad? What do men know about mascara, anyway? Made no sense.

1993

"Go back and change. You're not wearing that."

"Mom! It's fine!"

She'd been planning this outfit for days. Her friend, Deni—short for Denise—asked her to go to the high school basketball game with her family. Tonight. She'd laid out jeans and different tops, finally deciding on a T-shirt, an oversized blouse tied at the waist, some bangle jewelry and her hiking boots.

Everything matched, the colors were magnificent, and she felt awesome.

Even Jack, her older brother, complimented her when she'd left the bathroom earlier.

"Good God, Mary Margaret. That top doesn't go with those jeans. It's too blousy and silky. And the T-shirt clashes and is too low-cut. Are you trying to show off what little boobs you have? Hell's bells."

"No, Mom. I'm not. I—"

"And don't you know better than to put two patterns together like that? A print and a solid is what you want. Not a print and a print. That's stupid. Plus, that bandana scarf on your head is ridiculous. Take it off."

"But the colors are perfect for each other and they all match...."

Her mother glared. "No daughter of mine is going to leave this house looking like a tramp, or like you went shopping at the Goodwill. Now, find something else to wear. Go."

Tramp? Mary Margaret looked down at herself. *It's not trampy, is it?* It's what the popular girls wear.

She glanced at the kitchen clock. Deni's parents were supposed to be there soon.

"But Mom. I don't have time!"

"Change or don't go. I don't care."

A car horn honked in the driveway. "They're here."

Her mother stared at her, hands on hips. "Well?"

"I... I guess I won't go."

She turned away.

Her mother went to the back door, opened it and waved, then yelled. "She'll be right out."

"Mom! Why did you say that?"

Her mother rushed forward, closing the distance between them, her voice raised. "Just go. You love your little slutty outfit so much, wear it. You'll get some attention all right. Isn't that what you're after? I'm sure all the boys are going to look at you now. Of course, the girls will just laugh. I hope to hell you do not embarrass me in front of my friends. Now go, get on out to the car. Don't make them wait. That's rude."

Mary Margaret felt the sting of tears but sniffled and pretended they weren't there. *Fake it, Mary Margaret.* She'd learned a long time ago to fake things and sometimes the feelings just go away.

Be who you want to be, not who you are.

Heading out the door, she tugged the bandana from her head and stuffed it into her back pocket. With every step she took toward the car, her stomach knotted.

1994

She's angry.

And if she knew anything, Mary Margaret knew how to watch her step when her mother was *out-of-sorts.*

They stood at the kitchen sink doing dishes, her mom hand-washing them, while she dried and put them away. The dishwasher was broken. Mom had been pissed for a week because her dad hadn't gotten around to fixing it.

The water sloshed in the sink, her mother's hands frantically swiping over the plate, turning it over and washing on both sides. She placed the plate under the hot water flowing from the faucet, then handed the wet plate over.

Mary Margaret took it and dried it off, adding it to the stack.

Her mother stopped washing. She stood, looking down. Staring down. The dirty gray dishwater swirled in the sink while random bubbles spun along for the ride. Her mother's hands gripped the side of the countertop and Mary Margaret could see the tiny red veins on her knuckles, just under the thin skin turning white with her grip.

At once, her mother called out in anguish, pushing away from the sink, flinging water, drying her hands on a tea towel, and throwing it across the room.

When she turned and looked at her—when Mary Margaret met her gaze and looked deep into her eyes—she saw the turmoil.

The question. Frustration. Anger.

"Mom, what's wrong?" She kept her voice low, quiet. *When Mom is in a mood, keep things low key.*

Her mother twisted away, pacing back and forth in a tight circle. Her agitation was not unusual—Mary Margaret had seen her this way before—but today she seemed distressed. She did not know why.

Pointing her finger, her mother took one big step toward Mary Margaret.

"I'm going to tell you this, and you better listen to me. When you get a chance to get away from here, do it. Leave. Don't think about me, or your daddy, or Jack. Don't think about none of us. Just get out of this damn town. Out of this fucking house. You understand?"

Her mother exhaled then, as if letting go of a seriously enormous burden.

The thing was, it felt like it landed on Mary Margaret's shoulders. *She's telling me to leave? I'm only fifteen!*

Her therapist had asked her once, "Do you see any correlation between the two—your mother and Max?"

It took a minute for Maggie to understand what she meant back then. Today, she could see it plain as day. "I'm not sure," she'd told her. "Say more."

"Both crave control. They want, need, to control you. Different reasons, but it's still control."

"How so?"

The therapist uncrossed her legs and leaned forward. "When you were a little girl, it was easier for your mother to control you. You knew only what you knew, and that she was the one in charge. But as you grew older, as your world and experiences and social circles grew wider, you started deciding for yourself. Your mother felt her control slipping, so she fought to hold on to it any way she could. Unfortunately, she did that by making you feel inferior and inadequate."

"I see." *I think.*

"Why would she do that?"

"So you would continue to need her, perhaps. Or maybe because that's what she, herself, experienced growing up."

Maggie knew her mother's upbringing was chaotic. "Or, maybe... Not to contradict you, at all, but my mother grew up not knowing where her next meal was coming from, if her dad would come home from the bar or not...and she was passed around from family member to family member over the years. She had no control over her life."

"And then...?"

"And then, once she got married and had me, she tried to control everything in her life."

The therapist nodded slightly. "Why do you think that?"

"Because maybe then, she thought she would be happy."

"Was she?"

Maggie shook her head. "No, because happiness doesn't work that way, does it? Life doesn't work like that, either."

The therapist smiled. "Yes. That's right."

"Simple, but complicated."

"Yes, in some respects." The woman studied her for a moment. "Max used the same tactics, you know. Belittling you. Isolating you from others. Keeping you in the house and seeing to his needs, rather than out in the work world. He made you feel inferior and full of self-doubt. He counteracted that by making you feel like he was taking care of you—he made himself your provider, keeper, savior. Am I correct?"

She was. "Why have I not seen this before?"

"Because you were too busy complying with, and pleasing, everyone else—even your kids—and not yourself."

"You think so?"

"I do. Maggie, you'll bend over backwards and do whatever you can to please him—whether or not you realize it."

"Or keep him off my fucking back."

"Perhaps that, too. But you are a pleaser."

Maggie sighed. "Fine. Maybe I am."

"Just think about it."

She did. For an entire week, until their next session.

"You're right," she told the therapist the next time. "What do I do about it?"

"One thing at a time. Let's start with your mother. Can you eliminate her toxicity from your life?"

"What do you mean?"

"Can you divorce her? Completely exclude her? Cut off all ties?"

Divorce? Maggie's response was quick. "No. Because divorcing my mother means divorcing my father, and I'm not ready to do that."

While she sometimes blamed her father—he'd done very little to protect her and her brother from their mother's wrath when they were younger—she also knew her dad often took the brunt of her craziness, too.

Probably why he drank.

She'll never forget that day with the therapist—when she realized she'd traded one controlling person in her life for another. It all made sense, but she also felt completely powerless.

How could she change things? What could she do about it now?

Am I moving forward, away from all that? Making the decisions I need to make?

She'd escaped a controlling mother and fell into the arms of a controlling husband—*from the frying pan into the fire*—with only her college years and a few more years of freedom in between.

But oh, those were good years.

And for the first time in a very long time, Mary Margaret Brennan Oliver wanted those years back.

Twelve

At fifteen minutes before nine o'clock, the morning after she'd told the kids everything she knew about Max, Maggie sat in a diner off the highway about an hour east of Rocky Mount. She'd left right after dropping the kids off at school and had to be back no later than two-thirty to get a decent spot in Chloe's school pickup line.

Julia dropped her a GPS pin the night before, sharing the location and the name of the place. She had about an hour's drive too, coming inland from Tuckaway Bay.

The eatery was one of those old-fashioned diners inside a silver and red trolley car. Maggie had always thought those cute and nostalgic. This one had a soda fountain with red bar stools on one side, and tables along a long wall of windows on the opposite side.

The server was cheerful, leading her to a table at the end—Maggie had asked for some place less busy—and she quickly set her up with menus, coffee, and a large glass of ice water.

The drive and the wait for Julia gave her some time to reflect—on her life, on her kids' lives, and on what their futures might look like. Her mind rolled over some things she'd not thought about for some time—her mother, the therapy sessions she'd gone through about a decade earlier, and how it all connected with Max somehow. Not to mention her lack of ability to cope with all that.

Should she seek out therapy again? What about the kids? They were all going through some shit.

But she was going to do better, now. With or without counseling. She would put herself on a new track and improve the trajectory of all their lives. Just as soon as they finished with this damn divorce.

She paused at that thought, staring off into the parking lot. Why wait? They all needed that change now.

"Hey. You made it."

"Planned to all along." Smiling, she stood and gave her a hug. "Thank you."

Julia grasped her hands and peered into her eyes. "We'll get through this, Maggie. Max will not know what hit him."

"I hope so."

They sat, and their efficient server—Angie—was there with more coffee and water.

"Have a look at the menu," she said. "I'll be back in a few."

"Can you leave a pot of coffee on the table?" Julia asked. "We might be here for a couple of hours."

Angie smiled. "Of course. Be right back."

"I'm glad the place isn't too crowded," Maggie said.

"It could pick up at lunch time, maybe." Julia looked over the menu.

Maggie opened hers. "So, how is Sam? Hannah?"

Looking up, Julia smiled. "Sam is wonderful. How did I live my life without that man? I'm not sure. He's just...perfect for me."

"I'm sure he's glad to have you, too," Maggie said. "I have to admit, though, I never in my wildest dreams would have paired you with an older fisherman."

Julia laughed. "Remember that he had a different life for decades. Being a Navy SEAL can make you want to retire to fishing and domestic life. Or so he says...."

"And Hannah? Carol mentions her occasionally. I think they still talk."

"She's great. She's landed an internship at a medical facility in New Mexico. And yes, she mentioned Carol texted her the other day."

"I'm glad Carol has someone else to talk to."

Julia touched Maggie's hand. "I'm sure Hannah won't steer her wrong. She takes her counseling degree seriously."

Maggie smiled. "Please tell her thanks."

"I will." Julia looked back at the menu. "Let's order. It's on me. I'm starving."

"Oh no. I can pick it up. I have cash." She didn't use credit cards for things she didn't want Max to know she was buying—like lunch with her attorney.

"Save it." Julia smiled. "I'll put it on your bill—you know, the one Max is going to pay in the end."

Maggie laughed and grabbed her menu. "I like the sound of that."

"In fact, Maggie," Julia added, "It's probably not a bad idea for you to save back as much cash as you can, if that's possible. I don't know how you and Max work the finances."

"Why?"

"In case he cuts you off."

"Oh, he wouldn't." *Would he?*

"He might. I've seen it happen, going both ways, depending on which spouse is the major breadwinner. People worry about not having a partner to contribute to the expenses, so they start the money-grab. And in a way, that's what I'm telling you to do, but it's okay, because Max is a motherfucking asshole."

Maggie laughed, then turned serious. "But he wouldn't do that, would he? That would put the kids in jeopardy."

Julia gave a shrug. "Divorce does crazy things to people."

So does marriage.

She'd not had to worry about money for a long time, so she was just used to having it. What if she didn't? She met Julia's searching gaze. "I have a credit card for household supplies, groceries, things for the kids, gas, and all that. And we have a joint checking account. Max puts the money in, and I take out a monthly allowance to have cash around the house should I need it, for incidentals, kids' allowances, their activities, and such."

"Max agreed to a set amount for the month?"

"Yes. A thousand dollars."

"How long have you been doing that?"

Maggie thought for a moment. "He raised the amount over the years as the kids got older, but the thousand has been for a couple of years, or maybe three. He started doing that when Carol started school."

Julia nodded. "So, the pattern has been established for what? A dozen years?"

"Yes."

"That's a good thing. A plus for you."

"Great."

"Try to save as much of that as possible," Julia cautioned. "If you can."

Maggie exhaled. "Right. I will do that. I have saved some already. I try to keep a few hundred put back."

Julia gave her a nod, then opened her menu. "Let's see what they have here."

"Sure. I only had coffee earlier, so am ready for some protein."

They perused the menu and ordered—Maggie, a breakfast combo with eggs and sausage and hash browns, and Julia a yogurt parfait and an oatmeal cookie—and they settled down to business.

Julia pulled a yellow legal pad out of her bag.

Maggie noticed a lot of notes and scribbles on the page.

"All that for me?" she asked. "Looks intimidating."

Julia flipped over a few top papers and found a clean sheet. "Just some notes while I was on the phone with Max's new attorney."

"New?"

"Yeah." Julia looked up. "He switched firms, apparently. This new guy is out of Raleigh. His name is Jonathon Murray, just in case he contacts you for any reason. He shouldn't because I've instructed him not to, but you never know. He, or one of his assistants, could try to catch you off guard."

"Goodness. Is this case going to be that difficult?"

Julia sighed. "Mags, it's going to be high profile—that is if the media ever gets hold of it. I'm trying to avoid that."

"Good. I don't want that for the kids."

They paused when Angie brought the pot of coffee.

Julia leaned over the table. "So, if anyone, and I mean anyone—friends or foe or unknown—asks questions about Max, your marriage, your pending divorce, your kids, or anything related, your response is what?"

Maggie shrugged. "I don't know. What?"

"No comment. That's all. Let me hear you say it."

"No comment."

"Great. Say it and then get away from them. Don't trust anyone right now. I have some idea of what Max is capable of, but I also know we may not have scratched the surface of Max's intent. Be cautious."

Maggie sat back, suddenly not very hungry. "I shouldn't have ordered that big breakfast."

"You okay?" Julia looked concerned.

Not really. No. "I'm fine. Let's get on with it."

Julia held her gaze for a moment. "Alright. So, I had the call with this Jonathan Murray yesterday."

"You said he knew Max was interested in selling the house, but didn't know about the inspection."

"That's right. I told him Max was jumping the gun and requested he back off until we've met with a judge."

"Wait a minute." Maggie shifted in her seat. "We've not filed yet. I don't remember signing anything. Is that putting the cart before the horse?"

"No, we've not filed, but I want to soon. I know what you want, and I know what you need to demand, so I've drawn up preliminary documents for you to look over."

"Today?"

"That's up to you. You can keep and review, or we can go over them now."

"If we have time, let's do that."

Julia reached into her briefcase and pulled out a file folder. She sat it to her right on the table. "Alright, but first, I want to share a few things I learned yesterday."

Maggie braced herself. Max was thousands of miles away, yet his presence in the conversation was palpable.

"Max wants to sell the house. You've built up quite a bit of equity in the years you've owned it, and the property in that subdivision has substantially increased."

She nodded. "I imagine it has. Ours was one of the first houses built there. So, if we sold, we'd split the equity. Right?"

"Normally."

"But this isn't normal, is it?"

"No." Julia flipped the papers over to the top again on her legal pad. "Max will push the envelope on everything. He insists on selling the house, and that the proceeds go directly to him, because he is the sole owner."

"Wait. What?"

"I did some research, Maggie. Your name is not on the title, deed, or the mortgage."

"But it is marital property, right? Don't I have some say in whether or not the house sells? Am I not entitled to any of the proceeds?"

"That's generally the way it works. Even if your name isn't listed, you've been married for twenty years, you've established a residence there, made a home for your children and maintained it for Max. Those are pluses in your column. But Max can request whatever he wants to request. He likely won't get it, but a judge could agree, and that's what he's betting on."

"Shit."

"He is also making the case that instead of you getting proceeds from the sale, he will buy you a two-bedroom condo,"

Pushing back, Maggie stared out the window. *What the hell?* "I don't want a fucking condo, and I don't want him to buy it for me, either. I'll buy and choose my own place. Besides, I need more room for the kids."

"That's the other thing."

Maggie froze. Icy tremors tripped up her spine. "What does that mean?"

"He's suing for full custody, claiming you are an unfit mother, citing a history of mental illness."

"Excuse me?"

Julia took a breath. "He claims you've been on antidepressants for years and that there is mental illness in the family. Apparently, he says your mother was hospitalized for depression."

"Fuck." Maggie's stomach turned over. "You know he's only doing this, making the case for wanting them, because he doesn't want them to think he's abandoning them."

"Maybe so. And we can certainly play that up." Julia reached for her hand. "But let's address his claim."

"Well, I take antidepressants, yes. Who wouldn't, given the circumstances?"

"Anything else?"

Maggie's thoughts rolled over her recent recollections. "I saw a therapist years ago because of my mother issues. Max knew that. Do you think he's talking about that, too?"

"I don't know." Julia exhaled and glanced over her notes. "Maybe. You never talked much about your family, Mags. Is he right? Is your mom mentally ill?"

My mother is crazy.

Just get out of this damn town. Out of this fucking house.

Mary Margaret Brennan! I'd kill myself right here and now, put a gun in my goddamn mouth and pull the fucking trigger, but I don't want you to feel guilty for the rest of your life.

"Mom spent time in a facility," she told Julia. "She threatened suicide, waving a gun around, and my dad called the cops. She willingly agreed to commit herself. But seeking help with mental health is not a bad thing. Is it?"

I am not like my mother.

Julia squeezed her hand tighter. "No, but let's see how Max and his attorney spin it. Right now, let's worry more about some of the other things."

She would have a difficult time doing that, but would try. "Like...?"

"Like, the condo thing. He wants to move the kids to Australia.

Therefore, all you need, according to him, is the condo. His attorney even suggested Max was being generous with the two-bedroom unit."

"Well, how fucking special."

"Of course, we will not agree to any of that."

"No." Her stomach was still queasy though...that he could even think about taking her kids. And this mental health issue? How far would he take that? The last thing she wanted was to rehash her dysfunctional relationship with her mother.

"Him having custody of the kids would be traumatic for them, Julia. Please play that up. Chloe is not prepared emotionally for anything like this. And Jason? I'm not sure he is, either. Carol will outright rebel, refuse, and tell him to go to hell."

"You're right. I will definitely play up the trauma angle, but since Carol is heading off to college in a few months, her issue is moot—except for Max footing the bill. Jason's input will be considered down the road. And like you, I worry mostly about Chloe. Just don't mention the custody issue to them. I will make sure this does not happen."

"Too late. We talked last night, so they know about the pending divorce, and why. Jason was having a hard time, so I had to tell him everything. Chloe was...." She sniffled. "They had lots of questions, and I told them what I could. They needed some assurance that I would not let Max take them. But I won't say anything more until things are final."

"Oh, Mags. How did that go?"

"Rough." She sniffed and wiped her nose with a napkin. "But things were better this morning."

Angie swept up to the table with a tray, setting both breakfasts in front of the women. "Enjoy, darlings. Let me know if you need anything else."

Maggie took one look at her eggs, sausage, biscuits and gravy, and rushed off to find a restroom.

———

WHEN SHE RETURNED, MAGGIE NOTICED JULIA HAD ASKED Angie to take her breakfast away—which was a shame, since an hour earlier, she'd been craving a good country breakfast.

But not now.

"I had her bring tea. That okay?" Julia said.

"Perfect. I'm sorry about that."

"It's okay, Mags. This shit is going to get worse before it gets better. We just don't need to get ahead of ourselves."

"I can't stand the thought of Max getting custody of the kids."

Julia shook her head. "That will not happen. We'll present to the judge that he abandoned his kids here, because he has a new family in Australia. He will argue that he wants his family intact. While he has broken no laws, his ethics and morals are questionable, and we will double down on that. The other thing is the domestic violence charges that were never filed. I know we discussed that, but I didn't push it. Technically, we could get a prosecutor to file charges against Max within two years of the event. It's a misdemeanor, but could mean jail time if he's found liable. Getting those charges filed while he is in the U.S. for the divorce hearing could be a plus. I'm sure he wouldn't expect it."

Maggie exhaled, feeling a little better. "Let's do that."

"Great. I agree. I'll get in touch with the right people, and we'll go from there."

"Okay. So, should we go over the divorce papers now?"

Julia reached for the file. "We should." She opened the folder, handed Maggie a copy, and kept one for herself. "North Carolina is a no-fault divorce state, but we can claim fault for an absolute divorce and seek separation support and maybe alimony. I'm suggesting we claim marital misconduct due to abandonment, illicit sexual behavior, and cruel and barbarous treatment endangering your life. In North Carolina, you also have to be separated at least for a year—living apart —before the divorce is granted. This is April, almost May, so you're nearly five months in. Under no circumstances is Max to come home and stay in that house overnight. You can't let that happen. Call a locksmith and get the locks changed as soon as possible. We don't want anything to trigger a reset on that length of time."

Maggie nodded. "Gotcha."

"If you look further, you'll see that I'm asking for equitable property distribution, spousal support, and full custody. Max will pay health insurance for you for two years—allowing you enough time to find employment with benefits—and for the kids until they are out of college. He will pay for their private schools and college expenses."

Maggie sighed. "Sounds like a lot."

"You and the children deserve a lot."

"There's more, nitty-gritty details we can get into." She glanced at the time.

Maggie figured there was. "What time is it?"

"Nearly eleven."

"I have time. Let's get it done." She was ready to nail Max Oliver's hide to the wall.

THE DRIVE BACK TO ROCKY MOUNT PROVIDED THE SPACE she needed to let her mind drift while cruising the highway. She contemplated taking the longer way home, ditching the main road and traveling the narrow back roads, but then thought better of it. While she had plenty of time before making the school pickups—she didn't want to risk any delays or unexpected detours.

Still, she had an hour to process all that she and Julia had discussed. And after her chaotic and emotional day yesterday, she needed that time. Letting her mind simply go blank—not thinking of anything in particular at all—was a welcome change.

It all boiled down to one thing: the children were her priority.

Her uppermost goal was to see that they were loved, safe, protected, emotionally secure, and had their needs met. They were all going to lower their standards somewhat, as this fight with Max rolled on, and she was going to have to soften that blow to make things easier for them.

Plus, she had her marching orders from Julia:

Change the locks on the house.

Keep Max out, no overnight stays.

"No comment" to anyone who asks about Max or the divorce.

No conversations with Max. Period.

Keep life stress-free for the kids.

Keep her own nose clean—meaning nothing to suggest she was a less than stellar mother, wife, general good person, and upstanding citizen.

A lot to live up to. Hopefully, some of her past transgressions would not come back to haunt her.

Her phone rang and Carol's name popped up on the navigation screen on her dashboard.

She pressed to answer. "Sweetheart? Everything okay?"

"I'm fine, Mom. But you're not home."

Does that mean she is? "No, I'm not honey. Why?"

"Well, I'm here and—"

Maggie interrupted. "Carol, why are you home from school this time of day?"

"We had early release today, Mom. I'm here and so is Logan and...."

Maggie jumped in again. Two things abruptly hit her. "Wait. Did the littles have early release too?" *Shit.* Were they waiting for her? Was she suddenly failing in the stellar mom category?

"Just high school."

"Good." Her shoulders suddenly relaxed. "I met Julia for breakfast at a diner between home and the beach. On my way back now. But what's this about Logan?"

"I'm trying, Mom. I really am. I know Logan is not supposed to be here if you are not home—but I thought you would be. He picked me up from school and we got a pizza and wings for lunch and came over here to eat them before he goes to work. But when you weren't here, I called you."

She really was trying. Wasn't she?

"Mom?"

"It's fine, sweetheart. You can't eat wings and pizza in the driveway. Go on in and don't trip the alarm. Remember your code? I'll be home after I run a few errands."

"Okay, thanks! See you soon, Mom."

"Save me a piece of pizza. Looking forward to chatting with Logan."

There was a slight pause. "Oh, he has to be at work by two today."

"Okay. Another time. And Carol?"

"Yes?"

"Stay downstairs."

"Right."

Who am I kidding?

1996

"Did you have sex with that boy?"

Mary Margaret stared across the room at her mother sitting on the sofa. They were all in the family room—Jack, her mom, and her aunt Phoebe—watching *The Price is Right*. Thank God her dad was still at work.

"I don't know what you are talking about," she said, still looking at the TV.

"That boy you've been seeing. Have you had sex with him? You're late."

She rolled her eyes. "Mom, I'm always late. My periods are weird."

"You're over a week late."

She finally turned and met her mother's gaze. "Do we have to talk about this right now?"

"Yes, we do. I want witnesses."

"Oh, fucking hell, Mom!"

Her mother jumped up. "Don't you take that tone with me, Mary Margaret Brennan. You're not allowed to cuss."

She'd had about enough. Slowly, she kicked the footstool in the recliner and sat straight up. Looking square into her mother's face, she yelled, *"Fuck. Fuck. Fuck. Fuck. Fuck!"*

Aunt Phoebe laughed out loud. Jack hid his smile.

"You goddamned little slut."

"Well, you always call me that, so guess I should just be one."

"Are you pregnant?"

"No. I'm not pregnant. I'm late."

"Have you had sex with that boy, Mary Margaret?"

For once, she felt like she had the upper hand. *I have information that you want, and I don't have to give it to you. That's for me to know and you to find out.* "Do you want me to lie or tell the truth?"

Her mother scowled, and Mary Margaret thought she might pop her eyeballs out of their sockets. "You need to break up with that boy before he gets into your pants and knocks you up."

Mary Margaret glared. "I'm taking a walk."

"You better be home before dark."

"Jesus, Mom, I'm sixteen and it's summer." She headed for the kitchen.

Her mom yelled after her. "Going to go have sex with that boy? Go on, slut. That's what sluts do. Spread their legs for any boy that comes along."

"Mom," Jack said, "That was harsh."

Mary Margaret stood in the kitchen, stone still. She'd not spread her legs for any boy yet, but maybe she just might. And maybe it would be tonight. *My body, my choice!* Whirling back, she rushed back into the family room and met her mother's stare.

"That boy has a name. It's Kevin. He is my boyfriend. And if I want to spread my legs for him, I goddamn will. And it's none of your fucking business!"

Thirteen

"All right, Chloe," Maggie said, staring down at the selfie art project instructions the next morning. "Your project is due on Monday, so we should probably get started today when you get home from school."

"Goodie!" Chloe mumbled between bites, then looked up at her mother and smiled.

Maggie grinned back and watched her daughter happily gobble up her pancakes—with extra syrup and butter—and sausage. Heaving a sigh, Maggie focused again on the project paper, then glanced at the box of supplies they'd picked up the day before yesterday. "Do you think we have everything we need?"

"Maybe..." Chloe swiped syrup from her chin with a napkin. "We have paint and brushes and the big thing to paint on."

"The canvas. That's what it's called."

"Canvas. Yeah, I forgot." Chloe cocked her head. "Did we get glitter?"

Maggie drew in her lower lip. "Glitter?"

Chloe beamed. "Yeah, because I sparkle."

She had to laugh out loud. Her baby girl was growing in so many ways since Max had stepped out of their lives. She loved her little personality.

"Then I'll pick up glitter after I drop you and Jason off this morning." She glanced down the hallway toward Max's office. "You know, I was thinking... Let's turn Daddy's office into our art studio. What do you think?"

"Yay!" Chloe shoved her pancakes away. "You mean I can go in there?"

That panged her heart a little, but she pushed the feeling away. "Yes, you can." She rounded the island and gave Chloe a hug. "I'll get some things today to get us started, and we can work on your project in there tonight."

"Oh, goodie, Mommy."

Carol rushed into the kitchen. "Oh, my God. I'm late. He is going to kill me."

Maggie shot a look at her. "Sweetheart. Slow down. Who is going to kill you?"

"Logan." She sighed.

"Good grief. Get something to eat, please," Maggie told her. Why is she so agitated?

"I'll grab a granola bar at school. I don't want to keep him waiting."

A horn blasted from the driveway.

"Impatient, isn't he?"

Carol sighed. "He worked all night, overtime. He gets testy when he's tired."

The horn again.

Maggie frowned. "Will you tell him not to do that, please? We have older neighbors who sleep in, you know."

Carol exhaled. "Okay. It's just that he's tired."

"Well then, he should go home and go to bed, and I'll take you to school."

Her daughter's eyes flashed bigger. "But this is practically the only time I get to see him! He works so much. This week is mandatory overtime."

"The boy should be in school."

Carol glared. "He can't, Mom. You don't understand."

Maggie shook her head. "No, I don't."

"Sorry. Gotta run."

Then she was gone.

Maggie stared after her for a few seconds. There was more she wanted to say, but she supposed that had to wait.

"Wow," Chloe said. "That was fast."

And a little unnerving. "Yeah. Okay, go brush those teeth and tell Jason to get down here. We're leaving in fifteen minutes." The entire scene left her a bit unsettled. It wasn't the first time she'd noticed Carol being jumpy around Logan, and to be totally honest with herself, she didn't like it.

Too much like Max in our early days.

She didn't want to think about that.

An hour later, Maggie stepped into the art supply store, list in hand. She was out for glitter, of course, but she'd also made a supply list for herself. Taking a cart, she moved into the store, meandering down the aisles, getting lost in the smells and visual sensations of nearly everything she encountered.

She located glitter. Lots of glitter. So many colors, and she likely overdid her selections in that department. But if Chloe was happy, then that was all she cared about.

She selected a couple of canvases of different sizes for herself, along with a container of gesso and brushes for priming, and a set of acrylic paints. She also needed brushes for painting, brush cleaner, and some pencils for sketching.

Oh, and a palette.

It had been so long since she'd done any of this, she wasn't sure if the tools or techniques had changed over the years—but she could always rely on her past knowledge and experience. Right?

She placed her items in the cart and headed toward the back of the store, where she'd noticed a display of easels earlier. She perused the display... *Where in the heck is my old easel?* Was it in storage, like Max had said years ago?

Where *was* that storage unit, anyway? Did they still have it?

Suddenly, she didn't want to buy a new easel. She wanted *her* easel. The one with splattered paint and the leg she'd had to hobble together with duct tape. And her own palette—with blobs and layers of paint, bursting with color and probably crackling with age, by now.

She should hold off getting anything new until she located the storage unit, wherever that might be. Maybe she could find some information in Max's paperwork?

Or she could simply call around town until she found the place where Max had an account.

You really should have been more on top of these kinds of things, Maggie.

"Is there something I can help you find?"

Deep in thought, Maggie swiveled and caught the eye of the man she'd talked to several days ago. There he was again, wearing his artist's apron and that broad smile. "Oh! Hello."

"In the market for an easel?"

She glanced at the display. "Perhaps."

"You looked lost in thought."

"I was, sort of, thinking about where my old easel was—I think it's in storage—and that I should probably check there before buying." She paused, noticing his intent gaze as she spoke. "But that's probably not what you want to hear."

He crossed his arms and grinned even wider, if that was possible. "Oh, I don't know. While I would love it if you bought an easel from me, I also understand locating the one you already have. I'm sure it's much loved and appropriately aged."

"Ha!" That made her smile. "Right. I'm not sure I can even find it. It's in storage...someplace."

"Moved a lot?"

She didn't immediately respond, not wanting to get into specifics about why the easel was missing. "No. Just needed the space in the house. Oh, and by the way, thank you for the suggested list of supplies for the selfie project. I think we bought everything on your list."

"Except for glitter, I see."

Maggie looked at her cart and laughed. "Yes. Except for glitter. I received those instructions this morning."

"Kids." He leaned in and counted the glitter bottles. "I think ten sparkling colors should cover it, though. Well, done."

"As Chloe said to me this morning, 'I sparkle' so...."

He chuckled at that. "By the way, I'm Andy, in case you've forgotten. I own this place."

The owner? Interesting. "Well, it's a fine place, Andy. I'm Maggie...in case you've forgotten." She put out her hand and he shook it. The touch was brief, but she noticed the warmth in his palm, and that his hand nearly surrounded hers. How long had it been since a man had actually held her hand?

Don't go there, Mags.

He glanced over the other items in her cart. "If I recall, you mentioned the other day that you haven't painted for a while. You know we do classes here."

She nodded. "You attached a list."

"Want to join one today? It's watercolor. I see you are into acrylics, so that might not be your medium, but...."

"I actually don't know what I'm into these days, but I thought acrylics might be a good place to start. I'm long overdue dusting off my skills..." Maggie glanced up at the big clock on the wall. "But I'm not sure I have time today. Maybe another—"

He touched her arm, and her immediate reaction was to jerk slightly.

Making quick eye contact, he dropped his hand and turned. "I was just going to say come over and take a peek. This way."

With a sharp exhale, Maggie followed him to the far corner. Her reaction a few seconds earlier, when he touched her elbow, was unnerving. Why had she jerked away like that? It wasn't a threatening touch. In fact, it was rather friendly.

A quick flashback crossed her mind—a split-second moment of Max grabbing that same arm several months ago. *Shit.* He'd done a number on her, hadn't he?

Let it go, Maggie.

In the class area, she saw several women sitting around a large table, painting a watercolor still life. Andy moved from person to person, looking over their shoulders, and providing quiet guidance.

He looked taller as he paused behind the artists. Everyone seemed to take his tips and advice to heart, laughing and agreeing with him. Andy Ryan seemed to have a calm demeanor and relaxed approach to his teaching.

What a nice man.

What might it be like being with an easy-going guy like that?

Forget it, Mags.

He moved to the front of the room, then turned and smiled, catching her eye. Maggie gave him a quick wave, hoping to signal it was time for her to leave. She headed for the checkout counter and placed her items there.

The young woman rang up her purchases. Maggie inserted her credit card into the chip reader.

"I'm sorry, but this is coming up declined."

Maggie stared, puzzled. "Excuse me?"

"The card has been declined."

That had never happened to her before. "Declined? I don't understand."

"It means you can't use the card." The girl sighed.

"Why?"

She rolled her eyes. "Either you've hit your limit, haven't paid your bill, or the card has been canceled."

"No, no. None of that. Can you try again?" Maggie glanced about. Where was the friendly young woman who helped her and Chloe the other day? This girl appeared annoyed.

"Sure. Remove the card."

She did.

The girl did her thing.

Maggie inserted and waited again.

"Same. Declined. You have another way to pay?"

Self-conscious and confused, Maggie tugged the card out of the reader and slipped it back into her wallet. Julia's words from yesterday rolled around in her head. *In case he cuts you off.* Dammit! Should she try her debit card? No. She wasn't supposed to use it for purchases like this. Max would be suspicious. Plus, she wasn't sure she could take any more embarrassment if that didn't go through either. "I might have enough cash. How much again?"

"One-hundred-forty-six dollars and sixty-nine cents."

Maggie checked her wallet. *Shit.* Only three twenties and some ones. She forced a sigh. "Okay, sorry. Let me pay for two glitters now —the purple one and the green one—and I'll come back later for the rest. Can I do that?"

"Sure." The bothered clerk set everything but the two glitters on a counter behind her, then quickly rang up the two bottles. "Eighteen-ninety-six."

She handed her a twenty.

The girl took it, counted out her change, and handed over the money and her purchase.

"Thanks. Sorry for the card issue. I'll be back later."

"Sure. No problem."

Wrong. There is a problem. A big fucking problem.

Settled into her car, Maggie stared out the windshield, wrapping her brain around what had just happened. Humiliation crept up her neck and heated her cheeks. "Did Max fucking cancel my credit card?"

Immediately, she texted Julia.

Maggie: *My credit card won't work. Declined.*

Julia: *What?*

Maggie: *So embarrassed. I didn't know what to do.*

Julia: *Call the number on the card. Ask why.*

Maggie: *Okay.*

Julia: *Then call me.*

Maggie: *Will do.*

Inhaling deep, she fished the card out of her wallet again, found the number on the back, and called. After several transfers and over twenty minutes on hold, she finally spoke with a human who looked up the card information, and then simply said, "Mrs. Oliver, the person responsible for the account canceled the card. Is there anything else I can do for you before we disconnect?"

"No. Wait." Maggie pleaded. "Give me a name, please. Who canceled it?"

"I'm sorry. I can't do that."

"Excuse me? I've had this card for years. My husband is the account holder." She paused, perhaps for emphasis...or maybe because she was in shock. "Did my husband fucking cancel this account?"

The silence on the other end went on a lot longer than she would have liked.

"Are you there?"

"Mrs. Oliver, that *card* was canceled. Not the account. You should probably talk to your husband."

Well, fuck a goddamn duck.

She ended that call and dialed Julia, who quickly picked up. "What did you find out?"

"Max fucking canceled my card."

"What happened?"

"I don't know, Julia. I was buying some art supplies for Chloe's art project and the store wouldn't take the card. That was so embarrassing. I felt like a criminal."

"Bastard. I was afraid he might pull something like this. I spoke to his attorney yesterday about the house issue again, and he said Max was livid. My guess is he's pulling this stunt in retaliation." A breath whistled through Julia's lips. "I'll put in another call to Murray and see what the hell is going on. Max is digging his own grave."

"I'm sure he doesn't see it that way."

"What did the credit card people say?"

"Only that he had canceled the card, not the account. Seems pretty obvious he's cutting me off. Shit. Should I check the joint account?"

"Yes. Get online when you get home and see what's what."

Maggie paused, again feeling somewhat ashamed and inadequate. "Julia, I don't know how. Max always took care of that."

"Shit, Mags. Then how do you know how much money you have in the account?"

"I don't. Max never gave me the credentials to access the account." *Oh fucking shit.* She'd really screwed herself, hadn't she? By not being involved? And here she'd been all these years thinking he was simply taking care of her. No. It was all just another form of control, the therapist was right. "I have a debit card. I withdraw a thousand dollars a month. That's how Max told me to do it."

"Well, you need to find out if the debit card works and if you are still on that account. And I mean ASAP."

"Alright. I will. What do you suggest?"

"Is there a local branch?"

"Yes. That's where I withdraw the cash every month."

"Good. Go there and get the balance. Have them print the current month's statement. Make sure it has a balance amount on it." She paused. Maggie could hear her even breathing. "And maybe if you're feeling brave, draw out as much money as you can."

Shit is starting to hit the fan. Isn't it? Twisting the key in the ignition, she glanced into the rearview mirror. "I'm heading there now. I'll let you know."

"Be safe, Mags."

"Always."

The bank was only a few blocks away. By the time she'd entered the building and made her way to the counter, she'd worked herself into heart palpitations and sweaty palms. Ridiculous. Max had always taken care of the banking and bills—but doing something like this shouldn't make her so apprehensive. How on earth had she allowed this to happen?

"Good morning. How may I help you?" The young gentleman behind the plexiglass smiled and pushed his glasses up with a forefinger.

Maggie pulled her debit card out of her wallet and slid it under the barrier. "I need a current balance on this account, please—preferably a printout of the deposits and expenses to date for the month. Can you do that?"

He nodded and smiled. "Yes, of course." He slid the card toward him and started typing information into his computer. He'd pause, glance down at the card again, then back to the screen and start typing. Finally, he looked at her and said, "I'll be right back."

She figured he was going to go get the printout. But when he came back, he had the branch manager in tow. The woman was about her age, she guessed. She wore a black business suit with a red blouse and equally red heels. "Mrs. Oliver? I'm Sandra Martindale. Would you mind stepping into my office, please?"

"Is there a problem? With the printout? I don't mean to cause any trouble." Her hands were shaking.

She smiled. "It's no trouble. We'll have that for you in a minute if we can. But there's something I would like to discuss with you, if I may." She gestured toward a wall of office windows to her left. "I'm just over here."

She rounded the short counter. Maggie met her in front of the office with Ms. Martindale's name on it.

"Please have a seat."

Maggie entered the small office. Sandra closed the door, motioned to a seat in front of her desk, and sat behind it.

"Something is up, isn't it?" Maggie settled into the leather chair. "Just tell me."

The bank manager sighed. "Mrs. Oliver...."

"Call me Maggie, please."

"Alright, Maggie. Your husband has had an account with us for over twenty years. You've been an authorized account user for nearly that same length of time—that is, until this morning."

Maggie fixed her gaze on the woman. "I don't understand."

Again, the banker exhaled, this time with more force. "Maggie, I'm telling you this as a courtesy because I've seen you come in here every month for years and withdraw a specific amount of money. You're like clockwork."

"Yes. And...?"

"This morning, your husband removed you as an authorized user. You can no longer withdraw money. You no longer have access to this account. I'm sorry, I have to keep your card."

"What?" She felt frozen. "He can do that? I thought it was a joint account."

"No. The account is his. You only had signer privileges. He has always had the ability to revoke your privileges at any time."

"I see." Those heart palpitations from earlier were now full-blown, erratic tremors bouncing around inside her chest.

Sandra stayed silent for a moment.

Maggie let her brain roll over Sandra's revelation and what it literally meant.

"So, I have no money. Great."

"Mrs. Oliver... Maggie. I'm very sorry."

She met her gaze. "Can I still get that printout?"

"No. Again, I apologize. My hands are tied."

Maggie was suddenly too uneasy to sit. She stood and fiddled with her zipper on her shoulder bag. "What if my attorney requests it?"

"I may need to take that higher up. But if I may...."

Maggie took a couple of steps toward the exit, then halted. Beyond her initial shock now, she was getting angry. "If you may, what?" she snapped.

Sandra joined her at the door. "I wish I could say this is the first time I've seen this kind of thing, but it's not. I don't know what you are going through right now, Maggie, divorce or something else, but I advise you get an attorney involved, if you haven't already."

"I have. And she will be in touch soon."

Sandra Martindale gave her a sympathetic look as she stepped out, which only made Maggie want to slap her. Hard.

Of course, she wouldn't. It wasn't the banker's fault. No use taking her frustrations out on an innocent party.

But fuck her. And her goddamn sympathy.

AFTER SHE'D LEFT THE BANK, MAGGIE SPENT A FEW HOURS contemplating their current situation. Make no mistake, this was a family situation, not just hers, because having no money was going to affect them all.

Unfortunately, she'd not come up with any immediate solutions.

Her mind rolled around the day's events, and how she might solve this current problem while she made dinner for the kids. The tuna casserole she'd teased about a few days ago was their dinner that night, along with cornbread and salad. They had ice cream in the freezer for dessert, if anyone wanted.

There would be complaints, she was certain, but no one ever died from tuna casserole. Right?

Cooking relaxed her, especially when Max wasn't around. She rather enjoyed it, to be honest. All the years she'd kept the house, did the laundry, cooked, and cleaned—she really hadn't minded it all that much. In fact, she'd rather enjoyed being "domestic." She didn't have to worry about getting off to work in the morning, scheduling work priorities around her family's schedules, and the like. She'd witnessed her friends' chaotic lives, balancing work and home life—and she'd never had to do that.

To be honest, she'd never wanted to.

But today, she'd felt so inadequate when the card wouldn't work, and the prissy girl behind the counter made her feel like she'd just committed a crime, or something. Humiliation didn't begin to cover how she'd felt. At the bank, her emotions took a completely different turn—she felt the woman's pity for her, which only angered her. Sandra Martindale had strived for empathy, she assumed, but it wasn't received that way. At that moment in the bank office, Maggie hadn't needed her patronizing words or condescending attitude.

Maggie Oliver doesn't need anyone's pity. Goddamn it.

She hoped they'd sort this out soon, but she wasn't holding her breath.

Julia was on top of the legal aspects, although she'd warned Maggie her efforts would be limited until the filing—which she was working on. Once in process, they'd stand a better chance of getting a judge's compliance.

Bottom line was, for the time being, Max could do whatever he goddamn pleased.

"But not without consequences," Julia advised. "Especially if he is hiding assets or moving funds to make it appear his net worth is less than it actually is. It's risky on his part."

"How so?"

"A judge could lean heavier on your side once things get rolling, if they determine Max was malicious in his intent to keep funds away from you and the kids."

"But he would risk that, wouldn't he?"

"Damn straight. I'm heading to the county clerk's office in Rocky Mount in the morning to get the ball rolling. I'll swing by your house first. Okay?"

"That's perfect. Thanks, Julia."

Fourteen

"Okay, kids. Listen up. I need everyone's help after we finish dinner."

The casserole and cornbread sat cooling on the stovetop.

Fortunately, she had a pantry full of staples and a stocked freezer. She was actually very good at making the food budget stretch, and had always prided herself on her cooking skills, so they should be fine for a couple of weeks in the food department—although she only had forty-nine dollars in her wallet, and another few hundred stashed away in her jewelry box upstairs. Still, that should be enough to get them through for a while, but she was going to have to figure out something else soon.

There were still too many unknowns. Would Max continue paying for the utilities? Insurance? What about the school tuition? Her car payment?

She'd talk more to Julia tomorrow.

"Tuna casserole, Mom?" Groaning, Jason stepped into the kitchen. "Ugh. I could smell it all the way upstairs."

"Yum!" Chloe jumped up onto a bar stool, her eyes wide. "I love it!"

"Well, you can't please everyone. Can you, Mom?" Carol grinned and nudged Maggie. "How long do you need us? Logan doesn't have to work tonight, so we were thinking about catching a move."

"Maybe an hour?"

"I have time to help before I go."

"Don't be late though," Maggie warned. "It's a school night."

"Of course."

The kids found their seats on the opposite side of the kitchen island from where Maggie stood. She placed the casserole in the center, along with a big serving spoon. "We have salad and cornbread, too."

"Yum!"

Carol laughed. "Chloe, you're eating like a little piggie lately. You better watch it!"

"Watch what?"

Jason nudged his little sister. "Watch your butt get bigger."

Chloe punched her brother. "Jason! My butt isn't big. It's little."

"Not if you keep eating like a pig."

"That's not true. Right, Mommy?"

Maggie enjoyed their banter—but she gave Jason a quick side-eye. "Only if you eat like a hog."

It was all in good fun, she knew, but the last thing she wanted was to contribute to an eating disorder for her child.

Are you going to let her eat like that, Mary Margaret? Good gracious, she's shoveling it in like a little orphan child who hasn't eaten in days.

She suffered through enough of that herself, as a child.

Girls like you should never eat cookies, Mary Margaret. Or pancakes. Or ice cream.

Go away, Mother.

God only knew how many times she'd been told she was getting chubby.

And of course, Max hated it when she'd put on a few pounds. He would belittle her until she'd starve herself for a few days to get them off.

They all laughed. She grinned again at their easy-going banter. *Not thinking about Max right now. Or my mother.* She gave each child a small side salad, then set a basket of cornbread beside the casserole.

"Mommy," Chloe said. "Can you dip me some?"

"Of course." She did and then sat at the end of the island. When Max wasn't home, she and the kids always ate at the island. When he was there, though, he insisted on having dinner in the dining room. Suddenly, she was glad those days were gone. The intimacy and casualness of eating with her kids in the kitchen was much nicer.

"So, Carol, to answer your question. I want to clear some things out of your dad's office and store them in the garage. That room is going to become my art studio." She glanced at Chloe. "Oh, and Chloe's, too."

Her little girl beamed. "I'm an artist."

"Yes, you are. And we have a school project to work on this week." She glanced at the others. "We can all use it for projects. Plenty of room there to store stuff on the shelves."

Jason huffed. "Dad will have a fit."

"Dad won't even know," Carol interjected. "It's not like he's coming back here, or anything."

Maggie shook her head. "No, he's not."

"Mom..." Carol paused, apparently thinking. "You know that for sure, right? I mean, could he come back?"

She took a second to make eye contact with each child. Carol just sat there, the question hanging in the air. Jason's glance skidded off hers. Chloe held her gaze with big, wide eyes. "He'll not be back. And you should know that I'm filing for divorce tomorrow. Julia is coming in the morning. She advised that your dad not stay here if he comes to town. He'll have to stay elsewhere. Tomorrow, a locksmith is coming to change the locks on the doors, so we'll have new keys."

"What about the security system?" Jason asked, suddenly rotating back to look at her. "And the garage door opener?"

She met his gaze. He really didn't want him here, did he? "Good questions, Jason." And ones she'd not thought of. "We may need to make some changes there, too. I'll check into it."

"But if we change the locks," Carol said, "then his keys won't work and he can't get in anyway, right? So the security system should be good?" She glanced away.

"Probably..." She'd talk to the locksmith about that. "I am concerned about the garage door, though. If he has his clicker, then he's inside."

"Right. But his car is in the garage and the clicker is in it, so he can't get to the garage door."

"There is the keypad, although we rarely use it."

Jason thought about that. "I think he has the app on his phone, too. There probably is a way to change the frequency, or something. I'll look online."

Maggie smiled. "That would be great, Jason." She studied her son, who was actually eating his casserole. "And speaking of phones, Jason, no communication with him. Okay? Has he texted or called you lately?"

"Not since early February." He looked at Carol. "You heard from him?"

"That's about the last time he called me, too."

Maggie wondered if they were both telling her the truth. "Well, let me know if he calls or texts, okay?" She let go of a breath and then said more quietly. "Look, you all. I know it's not a great thing to tell you *not* to be in contact with your dad, but it would just make things so much simpler if you wouldn't. I know him. We all know him. And right now, he's angry and he'll try to manipulate us into getting what he wants."

"And what does he want?" Jason peered into her eyes.

What he always wants. Having his cake and eating it too. "Basically, Jason, he wants it all. Us, his family in Australia, everything. But I do not agree with that, so here we are."

After a moment, Carol asked, "He actually said that, Mom? That he wants both families?"

"He did."

Jason mumbled. "That's some kind of fucked up."

Maggie didn't know if she'd ever heard her boy drop the F-bomb before. "It is. But enough of all that. Let's talk about something else."

Chloe picked up a table knife and started buttering a piece of cornbread. "Let's talk about my selfie project! I get to paint and use glitter!"

Maggie smiled. *Indeed you do, darling.*

Carol's phone buzzed. She read the text, then turned her phone over.

Waiting a moment, Maggie said, "Everything okay?"

"It's just Sophie."

"Oh? I've not seen her around lately. How is she?" Ever since Logan came into the picture, Maggie had noticed her girlfriends were not hanging around as much. "You and Sophie have been friends a long time. She okay?" *Are you two okay?*

Carol tossed a shrug. "She's fine. She wants me to come over tonight. I'll tell her I'm helping you."

But Maggie noticed she didn't pick up the phone and text back. "Sweetheart, if you want to go to Sophie's, that's fine."

"No. I'm good, Mom. Besides... Logan."

"Oh, right."

Chloe jumped down from her seat. "Done! Let's paint!"

Looking down at her plate, Maggie realized she'd not taken a bite of her dinner, yet. In all honesty, she wasn't hungry. "Let's clear some shelves first."

"Aren't you going to eat, Mom?" Carol asked.

She smiled at her. It was nice when someone noticed such things. "I will later. You two join us when you're ready." She put out her hand for Chloe.

THE DOOR TO MAX'S OFFICE HAD REMAINED OPEN SINCE January. Maggie stood and stared at the thing, silently marveling that none of the kids had mentioned going into the room. She supposed it was because the notion was ingrained in them, the space was hands off —no kids allowed.

Even with the door wide open.

"Well, none of that now," she whispered, stepping over the threshold.

The first thing she did after entering the room was tear down the heavy draperies hanging in the large window. Dust flew as the brocade fabric fell to the floor in a heap. Maggie stood back, a rather cathartic feeling rushing over her, and stared out the sun-streaked windows to the front yard.

The room faced the street and east. She'd put lighter curtains up soon—something airy and gauzy perhaps—to let in the sun and provide a bit of privacy. But for now, she wanted the depressing ugliness gone.

The morning sun would warm the space and allow in tons of light.

"Exactly what this room needs," she muttered. There wasn't a lot she could do about the equally dark wood bookshelves and Max's massive mahogany desk at the moment, but she had plans to paint the walls and shelves as soon as she could spare the cash to do so.

"I wonder if there is paint in the garage?"

"Who are you talking to, Mommy?"

"Oh, just myself." She glanced about the room. "What do you think? Can you work in here tonight?" *Honestly, I can't wait to find my easel and get my stuff set up here, too.* In all honesty, she was probably just as excited as Chloe.

"Yes!" Chloe grinned wide, her eyes echoing her pretty smile. "I'll get the supplies. You buy glitter?"

"I did. It's in the box. Have Jason bring it in, won't you?"

The desk top had long been cleared, since the day after she and Julia had raided the office back in January. The desk drawers were empty, too. Maggie had already taken all the kids' pictures down that Max had on the shelves and stored them in an upstairs closet. Some of his personal items, like a golf trophy and some sales awards and other trinkets he'd gathered over the years, she'd put in a box in the garage. One day she'd gladly hand it over to him.

Or not.

Julia had taken the totes they'd filled with Max's stuff home with her after the night he came back. Maybe she should send her a message to bring those with her in the morning—unless, of course, she needed them for her case.

"Here's Chloe's box, Mom." Jason put it on the desk. "Wow. I didn't realize how big this room was."

"You were probably very little the last time you were in here."

Carol popped into the room, too. "This is amazing. Just pulling those drapes down makes all the difference in the world." She glanced about. "What do you want us to do?"

Maggie stared at the shelves. "We need empty boxes from the garage."

"I'll go get them," Jason said.

"Thanks." She eyeballed the shelves. "Let's see if we can clear some low space tonight. Then Chloe can arrange her art supplies on one of those shelves. Tomorrow I can tackle the cabinets underneath. Let's start there."

"This might take us a few days."

Maggie nodded, crossing her arms over her chest. "Yes. But well worth it, don't you think? We'll just do a little every day."

"Oh, by the way, I have more time tonight." Carol reached for a couple of books. "Logan got called into work, so I'm not going anywhere."

Turning, Maggie looked at her. "Oh, I'm sorry, honey. Why don't you go to Sophie's then?"

Carol took down a few more books and stacked them on the cabinet. "No, that's okay. I'll stay here with you."

Something wasn't right. Maggie took a couple of steps closer to her daughter. "Sweetheart, this won't take too long tonight. Go see Sophie."

"But I enjoy spending time with you, Mom."

She had to admit, those words warmed her heart. Maggie took a few steps toward her and gave her a hug. "There's nothing I like more than to be with you and the littles."

Carol gave her a tentative smile.

She patted her shoulders. "You go see Sophie. It's fine with me."

A few seconds ticked by. Carol's gaze skipped over hers, back and forth. Finally, she said, "No. Logan wants me to stay home. He doesn't like it when I go somewhere without him."

Maggie faced her more fully. "Carol, it's Sophie. You've been friends for years. Why wouldn't he want you to visit her?"

She shrugged and looked away. "He says he likes to keep our circle small."

"Excuse me?" Maggie wanted to be certain that what she thought she'd heard was actually what Carol had said. "What does that mean?"

Blowing out a breath, Carol's gaze was steady. "Just that he... Mom, it's okay. Logan only trusts a few people, so we only see certain friends."

"But Carol... That's ridiculous."

A stabbing pain abruptly hit Maggie in the gut—like someone had punched her in the abdomen with a hammer. *Stop, Maggie. Take a pause.* Her first instinct was to react, to tell her daughter to quit being a fool—shouting the words until they penetrated her brain.

Are you crazy? Don't let that boy ruin your life!

Tell the sonofabitch to go fuck himself!

You're smarter than this, Carol. Don't let him suck you in.

Oh, God. He's just like your asshole father.

And you're acting just like me.

She'd be the first to admit that she had previously ignored niggling things about this Logan situation—things that had made her uneasy —but had yet to bring up with Carol.

Maybe it was time?

She peered deeper into Carol's questioning eyes. Was she reaching out for help? The last thing she wanted to say was the wrong thing. No way in hell would she say the kinds of things her mother would have said. She wanted no reason for Carol to turn away from her— and run smack into Logan's arms.

They'd come so far in their relationship—she couldn't screw it up now.

"I see," she said. Maggie leaned in for another hug, then whispered, "Let's talk more later, honey, okay?"

Pulling back slightly, she searched her eyes.

Carol gave her a quick nod. "Sure."

"Mommy! Let's paint!"

Her hand idly traveled from Carol's shoulder to her hand. Maggie squeezed it once, then swiveled toward Chloe with a smile. "Yes, of course. Let's get you started. We need the canvas and a pencil first, so you can draw your selfie. Can you find the pencils in the box?"

"Yep." Chloe happily busied herself with the items, taking out one at a time.

Maggie glanced back at Carol, who had turned away now, and was slowly stacking books.

Jason came in from the garage carrying empty boxes.

CHLOE WAS DOWN FOR THE COUNT AFTER A COUPLE OF hours of drawing and erasing and re-drawing and erasing some more, followed by painting and glittering. After which, she claimed she would finish another day...and could she please have some more tuna casserole before her bath?

Maggie supposed it was better than ice cream. Maybe.

She'd be damned if she'd let her girl go to bed hungry. She'd done that enough herself, as a child and as an adult. Besides, Chloe's weight was just fine. She was a growing child, after all.

Both Jason and Carol had gone to their rooms early, too, but Maggie suspected Carol was still up. She'd heard her showering in the bathroom she shared with Chloe earlier. Softly rapping on her door, she cracked it open slightly and saw the glow of her bedside lamp.

"Still up, honey?"

"Yeah."

Maggie moved into the room, shutting the door behind her. Carol sat cross-legged in the middle of the bed with a shoe box in her lap and a couple dozen photographs scattered about on the bed in front of her. When Carol lifted her gaze, Maggie saw her tears.

"Oh, sweetheart..." she whispered, sitting beside her. "What's wrong?"

"This." She shoved several photographs towards her, sending them flying. "What's wrong with my asshole father?"

Maggie sifted through the pictures. All of them were photos of Max and Carol. Many she'd never seen before and wondered who had taken them. At least she didn't remember doing it. Carol was very young in most of them, under the age of five or six, Maggie guessed. There were a few when Carol was older, too—at soccer practice, her piano recital when she was twelve, pictures of her and Max fishing in the mountains.

She studied Carol. "Were these in his office?"

Carol wiped her eyes with the corner of her bedsheet. "In the cabinet below the shelves. There's one for Jason too. But not Chloe."

That didn't surprise her. Max hadn't doted on Chloe like he did Carol—and even Jason when he was younger. He'd always resented Maggie getting pregnant the last time. He'd insisted she get an abortion, but Maggie had refused.

That wasn't a pleasant time in their marriage.

"He adored you, sweetheart," Maggie whispered. "Still does."

"Funny fucking way of showing it lately." She scooped up the photos and crammed them into the box. "Here. I don't want them. Just a stupid reminder of the person I thought he was."

Maggie wondered if someday she would want them. She took the box and set it aside. "I'll keep them for you. Just in case."

Carol plopped back against her pillows. "You know, I can understand him being an asshole. Even when I liked him, he was still an asshole."

"Sweetheart, you had him wrapped around your little finger. He doted on you."

Carol stared ahead. "I loved him, Mom. I don't think I can love him anymore. I'm not sure he ever loved me."

That cracked Maggie's heart a bit. "Your dad loves in a strange way, and to be honest, I'm not sure he's capable of loving the same way that you and I do. Or most people, for that matter. His entire family is not a very loving family. You've seen that."

"Not for a long time. We've not been to Grammy and Grandpa Oliver's since I was little. I don't think Chloe has ever seen them. Has she?"

"No. That's because your dad and Grandpa had a falling out— something about a trust fund."

"They have a lot of money, don't they?"

Maggie exhaled. "Oh yes. And your dad learned at an early age how to manipulate people with their money. But let's discuss that another time. You look tired."

Carol yawned and stretched. "I am a little, but my brain is spinning, so I know I won't sleep for a while."

"Can I get you something warm? A cup of tea?"

"No." She drew her knees up and hugged them. "Mom, what I don't understand is how Dad could simply dismiss us. All of us. Shove us aside like we're some bad decision he made and now he's moving on." She paused for a moment. "And then he tells you he wants us all? Isn't that like, illegal or something?"

"I suppose not, unless he would marry the woman in Australia, and we did not get a divorce. But that will not happen."

"So he throws us away."

Maggie scooted closer. "Maybe he's tired of playing the game. He was never cut out to be a husband, a family person, honey. When I got pregnant, that forced him into a situation he never wanted."

Carol stared at the ceiling. "I don't understand."

She took a breath. "Max was a flirt, a player I think they say these days. He traveled and had women all over the world. I suppose I was one of them." Hearing herself say those words, Maggie felt a little ashamed.

"You were a flight attendant then."

"Yes."

"Did you have to quit your job when you got pregnant?"

She shook her head. "Not at first. The company I worked for grounded flight attendants at the start of the second trimester. But after a couple of months, your dad told me we'd get married, so I quit."

"That's when dad made you the deal, huh?" She looked at Maggie. "Honestly, why did you take it, Mom? You could have gone off and had me on your own."

"Yes. But I felt vulnerable and very pregnant. Plus, unemployed. Honestly, I was scared."

"Women raise children alone all the time."

Yes, they do. But she hadn't wanted to. "I wasn't sure where else to turn. Besides, I loved him and thought he'd change his mind about things. Eventually."

Carol searched her eyes. "You loved him then?"

Maggie breathed easily and smiled. "I sometimes think I still do." The last thing she wanted was for Carol to think she was not conceived out of love.

"Oh, Mom...."

She reached for Carol's hand. "It's okay. Back then, I felt I had no choice. I'd made my bed, so it was time to lie in it."

"Nans and Pops would have helped."

Sure. Right. "Sweetheart, Nans and Pops could not help. Besides, Nans and I never really got along. Me coming home to stay at twenty-four with a baby wouldn't have been pleasant for anyone—and definitely not a suitable environment for you."

"Nans can be a little bitchy."

"Right." Her parents might live in California now, and Maggie was grateful for that fact, but her mother's reach was far if she wanted it to be. "But sweetheart, I want to ask you about something else. Can we talk about Logan?"

Carol pushed up, her back straight against the headboard. "Sure. I wondered when that would come up."

Maggie twisted around to face her. "It's just that I don't know him very well. He has spent little time around us, just pops in and out, or you run out to meet him in the driveway. I wish I knew him better. I would feel more comfortable."

"Why? He's my boyfriend, Mom. I know him. You don't have to."

"I think I do, Carol. I want to know that he's going to be good to you. Good for you. Treat you right. Keep you safe. Not do stupid, dangerous things in that big, loud truck." Memories of her own past came flooding back.

Carol huffed and rose off the bed, crossing the room. She grabbed a hoody off her vanity chair and shrugged into it. "You don't have to worry about any of that, Mom. Logan is older and responsible, plus he's very protective of me."

"Possessive, you mean?"

Carol glowered. "Protective, is what I said."

"He likes to keep your circle small. You said that, too. Honey, that's exactly what your dad did to me. Kept me home and away from my friends. He wouldn't let me go back to work after you were born."

Laughing, Carol sat and pulled on her tennis shoes. "Mom, seriously? Logan works hard and he's tired when he gets off work. He doesn't want to hang out with my friends and honestly, I don't either. All I need is him. I'm past all the high school shit."

"But what about Sophie...?"

Carol shrugged off that notion. "Sophie is too needy, Mom. She bugs the shit out of me. We're not really friends anymore." She headed for the door.

"Where are you going?"

Carol glanced back. "Out. Logan gets off work at ten. I'll meet him out front."

Maggie pushed off the bed and followed her. "But it's a school night, and it's already late."

"I'm not going anywhere. We'll just talk in his truck in the driveway. Besides, I'm not going to school tomorrow. It's Senior Skip Day. Unofficially."

"You're skipping?"

Carol glanced over her shoulder at the top of the stairs. "Maybe." She bounced down a few steps.

"I thought you were past all that high school shit."

Pausing, her daughter glanced over her shoulder, then continued down the stairs.

Fifteen

The next morning, Maggie turned into her driveway after dropping the kids off at school, noticing Julia's SUV parked in front of the house. She pushed the button on her garage door opener, pulled into the two-car garage beside Max's Escalade, then met Julia outside the house.

"Is that Max's vehicle?" Julia asked, peering inside.

"It is. He doesn't like long-term parking at the airport. Good thing, huh? That bill would be astronomical by now."

Julia snorted. "Hmm."

Maggie knew that look. Wheels were turning inside her friend's head. Coupled with that "hmm" comment meant Julia was pondering something.

"You have the keys?" Julia moved into the garage and tried the passenger side door. Locked.

"Sure. There's a set inside. Why?"

"Glove box. Make and model, registration, and so on..." Julia replied. "Details for later. Assets. Come on, let's go inside and talk."

Maggie led the way between the cars and into the mudroom door. She punched the garage door button as they both went inside and moved on into the kitchen.

Julia plopped her paper-heavy leather bag on the granite island top. "Been thinking. The two-hour drive is good for that. I have some news and some thoughts. But first," she pulled a file folder out of the bag, "I have papers for you to sign. This will get us started." She slid the paper-clipped stack toward her.

"Is this the same as we discussed?"

"Pretty much. I also tried to get my two cents in about selling the house, or anything else, but we will see how that goes."

"What about him paying utilities? The kids' tuition?"

"I made sure to include that he maintains all support as it was until the divorce is final."

"Good."

"Look it over, Mags. Sign when you are ready." She stood. "I'm heading to the little girl's room."

"There's a powder room off the living room," Maggie said. "You know where. Right?"

"Yep. Be right back."

Maggie flipped through the stack of papers, lingering over some of the newer additions. While she knew she should probably read it all word-for-word, she trusted her friend to no end. Of course, she needed to understand the exact terms of the filing, but she wouldn't take time right now to scour the documents. Later.

Bedtime reading, probably.

Julia hustled back into the room. "Well?"

"It's all fine. Let me find a pen."

"Here." Julia plucked one from her bag.

Maggie signed in all the places Julia had marked, then handed the paperwork back to her. "Let's do it."

"Great." She put it all back in the file folder. "Ride along with me. You can point me in the direction of the county clerk's office."

"Sure. We'll be back by one, right? The locksmith is coming then to change the locks."

"Oh good. This won't take long."

"Great." Maggie paused, watching Julia slide the pen into its little holster inside her bag. "But I'm just curious. What were you thinking earlier about Max's Escalade?"

Julia laughed. "You really want to know?"

"If it's that funny, I do." What *is* she thinking?

"If Max tries to screw you over with the house, we need to hold that Escalade hostage. Did he buy it or lease?"

Why the fuck didn't I think of that? "I'm sure he bought it. But seriously, Julia? That's brilliant." Her brain was spinning. She *did* need money. "Could we sell it?"

"Probably not. I'm sure it's in his name. Right?"

"Oh, I'm positive about that. The registration is probably in the glove box. But the title? Do you think it's in the papers you have?"

"Maybe. I've not gone through everything yet. But we should check around here, too." Julia exhaled, staring out the window. "Since we can't sell it... If we only had someplace to stash it. Like I said. Hold it hostage."

"What good would that do?"

Julia gave a shrug. "That Cadillac SUV is worth a lot of money. I'm sure we could use it as a bargaining chip. Especially if it's paid for."

"Pretty sure it is. But why would we need to hide it? If the locks are changed, he can't get to it, anyway."

"At least we can honestly say it's not on the premises. Maybe you thought he took it the last time he was here? Maybe it's in long-term parking after all?"

Maggie wondered if they should go down that road, though. "I'm not sure I want to fuck with him, Julia. He's good at playing games. Me? Not so much."

Julia laughed again. "Sweetheart, playing games and fucking with people's heads is *my* forte. Let me worry about that. I won't let him get anywhere near you or the kids."

"I *can't* get the kids involved."

Julia nodded. "I know. Are they okay?"

"They are *just* okay. Not fantastic, to be sure—but okay." She didn't want to get into the Carol story of last night. Not yet, anyway. Thank God, the girl had come in at a decent hour—but she was off again early that morning. Maggie had no clue if she was in school or skipping. The only thing she knew for certain was that Logan had honked that damn horn too early.

"Good. That's something." She reached for the handle of her bag and turned. "Tell me more in the car. Ready?"

Maggie smiled. "Definitely."

"Good. Then let's go. The sooner we get these papers filed, the better."

SHE STAYED IN THE CAR WHILE JULIA FILED THE PETITION.

When she returned, Maggie asked her about the next steps.

"The papers need to be served to Max. Since he is in Australia, there are some extra hoops to jump through. If they can catch him in the states, say if he returns for work, they can simply hand them to him. If not, they'll work through the Australian law and courts. I gave them all the information I had about where Max was, his business, and the like. They are going to let me know what comes next, but it's going to take a while. In the meantime, we wait."

"No." Maggie shook her head. "I can't just sit around and wait. I have things to do."

"Like?"

"Figure out how I'm going to live without money, and maybe a home."

"I don't think it will come to that, Mags, but if they can't find him to serve him, he could push it until then. I will reach out to his attorney this afternoon to let him know we have filed."

"Good."

Julia studied her. "So, how *are* you sitting for money?"

Her head fell back against the headrest and Maggie closed her eyes. "Not good. The one credit card I have is kaput, as you know. The bank has cut me off, too. As you also know. I have maybe a few hundred dollars stashed back. That's it."

Nodding, Julia screwed up her mouth, apparently thinking. "My fear is that it's going to take time for Max to get served, and in the interim, he's going to do whatever he damn well wants to do. Let me think about this."

"Sure. I will, too."

"Back to your house now?"

"Maybe." Something still nagged at her from earlier. "Just thinking, but... What if we had a place to stash Max's SUV?"

Julia twisted back, staring. "Do you?"

"I'm not sure."

"What are you thinking?"

Was her idea stupid? Might as well put it out there. "Max has a storage unit somewhere. Not sure how big or if the Escalade would fit in it, though. When he took down my art studio and made it his office, he said he put everything in storage. Now, that could have been a lie. I don't know. But I've been thinking about that a lot lately because Chloe and I are turning the office into a studio again, and I want my easel. But I have no clue where the storage facility is."

Julia smiled. "Wait. Hold that thought."

"What?"

She reached into the back floorboard and hoisted her leather bag up between the seats. "I found some old invoices from a couple of storage facilities in Rocky Mount. That definitely piqued my curiosity. I pulled that file and brought it with me and had planned to ask you about them today."

She flipped through the papers and pulled out two tattered invoices. "They're several years old, and I haven't called to see if they are still in business, but I thought we could investigate."

"Makes me wonder why Max needed two storage units?"

Julia agreed. "Absolutely. Here. You call one and I'll call the other."

"Right now?"

She shrugged. "Why not?"

Maggie took the top invoice. "Looks like this one is out off of I-95 near the intersection of Sandy Cross Road."

She punched in the numbers.

A man answered. "Smart Self Storage. This is Ron Smart."

"Hi. This is Maggie Oliver. My husband has a unit there, but he's out of town right now and I can't get in touch with him. Can you tell me the number of the unit, please?"

"Name again?"

"The account would be under Max Oliver."

"Just a minute."

Maggie waited, glancing at Julia, who had her phone to her ear.

"Did you say Oliver?"

"Yes."

"We have no account under that name."

Maggie frowned. "Oh, I'm sure it was there. I actually have an old invoice."

"Maybe he had one here years ago, but not now. The business changed hands. Anything not accounted for after the sale, we sold at auction, especially if he stopped paying the bill. Sorry."

"Thanks." Maggie ended the call. *Well, there goes my easel....*

She looked at Julia, who was staring out the window. "Yes, ma'am," she heard her say.

Maggie waited, listening.

"Yes, that's it. Perfect," Julia continued. "We'll be there soon. Thanks so much."

Grinning widely, she faced Maggie. "Bingo!"

"You found it?"

"Yep. Two Gals Storage on Sunset Drive. Pop it into your GPS." Julia twisted the key in the ignition.

She was almost giddy inside. Hell, she was fucking giddy all over.

Twenty minutes later, they pulled up to the office of Two Gals and went inside. Maggie stepped up to the counter.

"Hi. We called earlier. Max Oliver's unit? I'm his wife."

The woman behind the counter nodded. According to the embroidered name on her denim shirt, her name was Louise. "Of course. May I see your I.D.?"

Maggie handed over her driver's license. The woman took a quick glance and gave it back. "Unit forty-two. It's down the row to your left, near the end. You need a key? I understand your husband is out of the country."

"Yes," Maggie said. "On both counts."

Louise fished a key and a slip of paper out of an envelope. "Just sign here that you're accessing the unit today."

Maggie glanced at Julia, who nodded back. She took that nod as an okay to sign.

She did, and Louise handed over the key. "That's his spare so don't lose it. I'll need it back before you leave."

"I can't keep it? I might need to come back in a day or two."

Louise hesitated. "I suppose it will be okay, since he's not available. To be honest, I've worked here for eight years, and I've never seen Mr. Oliver come in, so I doubt he'll need the spare. We have a universal key if we need it."

Julia stepped up to the counter. "So, Max never comes by?"

"Unless he comes at night. Some people do. We keep it well lit."

That was intriguing. Maggie leaned closer to Louise. "Can you tell me how long he's had this unit? I'm looking for something we stored years ago and just wondering."

Louise flipped the key envelope over. "Looks like this account was opened in July 2002." She looked at Maggie. "Wow, that's quite a long time."

"Yes." *It certainly is.*

"How does he pay?" Julia asked.

Louise cocked a brow and frowned, and Maggie was uncertain if Louise would respond.

"Just curious, if he doesn't come in," she added.

Louise pointed to a line on the envelope. "Says here by credit card. Automatic withdrawal."

Convenient. "Well, thanks. I appreciate your help. We'll check back in before we leave." Maggie glanced at Julia. "Ready?"

They drove to the storage unit, opened the heavy-duty padlock, and lifted the garage-type door. It rolled back and sunlight streamed inside, creating rays illuminated with dust motes.

Both women stood in the doorway, looking into the unit.

"Wow," Julia said after a minute. "Super dusty."

"I don't know where to start," Maggie added.

The unit was definitely not big enough to stash an Escalade, but it was big enough to store a row of large plastic boxes with labels neatly stacked along one side, and on the other, two filing cabinets, a desk, and a floor-to-ceiling utility shelf filled with banker's boxes and other items.

"What is this?" Julia stepped further into the unit. "No one has definitely been here for a while, but my guess is that at some point, this was a makeshift office."

Maggie wandered deeper, past the desk and utility shelf to the corner. "And possibly, an impromptu place to spend the night."

"What?" Julia caught up with her. "Why the fuck would Max need a cot and pillows and a sleeping bag in here?"

"No clue. Weird."

Julia turned back to the desk. "No weirder than the 2002 desktop calendar and Franklin Covey planner—both of which I am taking with me, I might add—and..." She reached for an item on the desk, turning it over. "Oh, hell."

Maggie pivoted back. "What is it?"

"A picture." Julia handed it to her.

Maggie took it and stared at the smudged image in the frame. She brushed away dust as she focused on the couple. A wedding picture. "Well. That's definitely Max. Quite a bit younger, but it's him."

Julia leaned in closer. "But that blonde bride is definitely not you."

No, it wasn't. That took a moment to settle into her brain. *Fuck!* "The asshole is also married to someone else?"

"Or he was married to someone else before you?" Julia took the picture from Maggie and set it back on the desk.

"I don't know. Maybe. Looks like it."

"Maggie, this unit is a treasure trove of information, and we need to go through it."

Maggie checked the time. "It's almost noon. I should head home soon. The locksmith."

"Right," Julia said. "Keep the key. I'll spend the night. We'll come back in the morning with the Escalade and load up stuff. We can use both vehicles."

Maggie shook her head. "I can't drive the Escalade. No insurance for me."

"What the hell, Maggie?"

"It's Max!"

"Jesus, he is a fucking sonofabitch!"

Maggie held her gaze. "Yes, he is."

"Okay, fine. We'll figure that out tonight. Probably no reason to load up stuff anyway, since no one has obviously been here for years, and you have the key now. But let's take twenty minutes to get a handle on what's here and maybe take a few things with us."

"Fine. You take the desk. I want to get a look at those plastic totes." She wandered toward the stacks. "One thing is for certain, I don't see an easel or any of my art supplies."

"Maybe somewhere else? Who knows how many of these storage units Max has. Maybe even under different names?"

Shaking her head, Maggie figured that probably was true. "Unbelievable."

"Maggie?"

"Hmm?"

"Are you okay?"

Rotating back, she made eye contact with Julia and held it. "I don't even know anymore."

SHE TOOK PICTURES OF THE LABELS ON EVERY TOTE, wanting to leave nothing to memory. Every one of the plastic containers was blue, the labels—made with a label maker—neatly printed in uppercase letters, and affixed tear the top of one end, about two inches down. There were five columns, each column three totes high. Fifteen in all.

"This is so very odd," Maggie finally said aloud. "Max was never this organized."

She glanced back at Julia, who was going through the desk.

"Oh? What do the labels say?"

Maggie perused the collection again. "That's interesting, too. Various things, mostly personal and household items." She rattled off a few things. "Winter clothes. Summer clothes. Kitchen utensils.

Christmas decorations. Books. Nothing really unusual, it's just that I never pictured Max keeping or saving things like this, let alone organizing them. He did none of that around the house."

Julia looked up. "No, because he had you to do it."

"Shit. Truth."

"Did you look inside any of them?"

"Not yet."

"Well, do."

Maggie ambled toward the last column and took down the tote on top. "Okay, this one is curious," she said. "Miscellaneous 2002." She moved it to the ground and popped open the lid. "Interesting." She crouched and pulled out a school yearbook.

"What?"

"High school yearbooks from 1992 to 1996. Decatur, Georgia."

"Georgia?"

"Yeah. Max is from Raleigh. He went to high school and college in North Carolina. As far as I know, he never lived in Georgia."

Julia rose and left the desk, looking over Maggie's shoulder. "What else is in there?"

"Looks like a couple of scrapbooks, a box of newspaper clippings and old photographs, and some awards, like 4-H ribbons and scout badges."

"Scouts?"

"Yes."

"Boy or girl?"

Maggie blinked and lifted two badges. "Girl Scouts." She looked up, meeting Julia's gaze. "Why would Max have Girl Scout badges?"

Julia straightened and stared at the other containers. She went to the ones marked winter and summer clothes, unsnapped both lids, and pulled out a handful of clothing. "Maggie, these are women's clothes."

Standing, Maggie stared at the items. "I don't understand."

"These aren't Max's things, Maggie. They belong to someone else."

"But who?"

Julia stepped closer. "The woman in the picture?"

Suddenly, Maggie's throat started closing up, anxiety racing across her chest. "Julia, goddamn it. What the fuck has Max done? Who is this woman and why is Max holding onto all of her things?"

"Since 2002, no less."

She shuddered. "If we find a fucking body carved up in one of these totes, I'm going to lose it."

"By now there would only be bones, I'm sure."

"Julia!"

"Sorry." Julia faced her. "Look. There are several things rolling around in my head, but I don't want to jump to conclusions. I need a few more facts, first."

"Like?"

She crossed the room again to the desk. "Like what might be inside this fireproof lock box. There is no key to be found." Julia picked it up and showed Maggie.

It was a small box, perhaps ten inches long and four or five inches wide, but she supposed it was large enough to hold some important paperwork.

Maggie pulled her phone from her hip pocket and glanced at the time. "I'm tired of fucking around. Take it with us and let's let the locksmith have a go at it."

"Good thinking, Mags."

Maggie realized it felt good making decisions—even small ones. "And I'll take this tote, too, with all the women's memorabilia. Surely, we might find some clues there."

"We'll tackle the rest tomorrow."

Sixteen

Her phone alarm sounded softly, nudging Lilly awake. She silenced it with a quick tap, then yawned and stretched. Waking slowly was her preferred way to start the day.

She rolled closer into Max's side and nestled her chin on his bare chest. It was early still, the sun just rising across the bay—sending threads of sunbeams peeking through the mango trees off the deck. Everything was quiet, including the baby. A good time, perhaps, to bring up something that had been on her mind for a while.

"Max, are you awake?" she whispered.

He sniffed and rubbed his nose. "Barely. What is it, love?"

"Just thinking..." She let a few more quiet minutes drift by. This seemed as good a time as any, even though he was half asleep. He'd been gone so much lately and was so preoccupied in the evenings. "Your business is growing fast. Maybe it's time to secure a lease on a downtown office? I saw a few nice ones listed this week, and I could check them out for you."

"Hmm. I don't know." He yawned and ran a hand up her back.

"And if so," she continued, "why not save some cash and let the downtown condo go? You could move in here. I have plenty of room. Most of your things are here, anyway. What do you think?"

She snuggled closer and planted a soft kiss on his collarbone. "Leo would love having you here all the time," she added. "Me, too."

He lay unresponsive for a moment, eyes closed. "Leo..." he began, "is only six months old. He doesn't know yet what he loves and what he doesn't."

"Oh, I disagree." She pushed up on one elbow. "Have you seen how his eyes light up when you come home?"

His lips curled up slightly at the corners. He had noticed.

"The condo lease was for two years. Not sure I can get out of it," he said.

"I can help with that." She skimmed her fingertips over his chest. "There are always ways."

"Naw." He rolled toward her abruptly and wrapped his arms around her. "I need the condo for client meetings, and..." His lips found hers and he nibbled. "You know there will be times you will want to get rid of me, so I'll need a place to go to."

She pulled back slightly, his tone and words setting off a minor alarm in her head. "What do you mean? I don't want to get rid of you."

Chuckling, he wrapped his arms tighter around her. "Easy, darling. All couples need time away from each other, you know. It makes things spicier when we get back together. We do fine with you having your space and me having mine."

"But you travel so much, Max, and we have *that* time alone." *And all too often lately, I might add.*

"*You* have that time alone, sweetheart. I'm working then. I need a down time when I get back."

Can't down time happen with me? Though she supposed what he said was true. Not knowing exactly what "down time" meant to him was a problem.

At least for her.

She had to admit, she *did* like her privacy, her alone time, occasionally. But with Max gone so much the past few months, her alone time had recently felt...excessive.

"It's just that you're gone so much...."

He slid her a snarly look, his eyes piercing—like he was displeased with her but didn't really want to say so. "And you knew that when we got together, love. I travel to make us money. It's work. Little Leo also needs a college fund."

That was also true. Max was a hard worker. And she'd be hard-pressed to call that a bad thing. "I just thought I'd mention it because you talked about leasing office space recently. I assumed you wouldn't need the condo, then."

"Not ready to let the condo go yet, Lil." His words were stern. "Don't assume."

"Right-o." She untangled herself from his arms and sat on the edge of the bed. To say she was slightly agitated, would be correct. "With all the new contracts you've signed recently, it just seemed like the timing was right. That's all I'm saying. You talked about hiring staff, too."

"Talked about it. Yes. But I need more contracts to feel comfortable making that change. I can work out of the condo for the time being."

He rolled away from her, in the opposite direction, and stood. She watched him stroll across the room and look out over the bay, standing there fully naked and framed by the floor-to-ceiling windows.

"I understand that Max, but when it becomes inconvenient for you to—"

"Lil!" he barked, his head turning only slightly toward her. "Enough."

Subject closed.

Conversation over.

She took a deep breath, in through her nose and out through her mouth. Counting to five, she rose and slipped into her bathrobe, then padded off toward the bathroom. She paused at the dresser, where Max had left his phone charging, when she saw the face light up.

No sound. *Must be on 'do not disturb.'*

"You have a call." She stopped and focused on the name. "Jason somebody. Early for business calls, eh?" She reached for the device, intending to unplug and hand it to him.

Max abruptly lunged toward her, his brows furrowed. Snatching the phone from her grasp, he pressed the answer button and put it to his ear, turning his back to her. "Jason?"

Lilly watched his shoulder muscles tense up and ripple, tighten and relax, as he spoke.

"Okay. Glad you called. Yes, it's early here. Let's talk later today."

He paused again, still listening.

"I'll call you. Text me a good time."

He ended the call and pivoted back, staring at her, his expression contorted with anger—a bit unnerving for her liking. He took a swift step forward, grasped her chin with one hand, and squeezed.

"Ouch. Max!" Her first instinct was to jerk away.

He gripped tighter. His gaze seared into hers, his face inches away. "Don't ever touch my fucking phone again. Got that?"

Lilly stood stone still. Frozen.

He'd never raised his voice like that.

Had never looked at her in that way.

"Got it?" He yanked her chin.

Had never *touched* her like this. "Yes, Max," she said softly.

He released her and headed into the bathroom. She stood there for a couple of minutes, unmoving, gathering herself. Shaking. Listening to him putter about in there and then start the shower.

A rush of emotion swept over her as the sting of tears threatened.

I will not cry.

Leo fussed from the other room and, as if on demand, her milk let down, dampening her robe. "Shit. Not now." She rushed off to the baby's room, grabbing a couple of folded cloth nappies to stuff inside her robe, then lifted the cranky boy into her arms.

Within seconds, she burst into tears.

MAX LEFT FOR A MEETING BEFORE SHE'D MADE HIS COFFEE.

Leo had occupied the minutes while he was showering and dressing, so she hadn't had time to prepare the coffeemaker. He had a client meeting at nine—one Lilly didn't know about.

One he'd not deemed important enough to share with her, obviously.

"I'll get coffee downtown," he barked.

"I'm sorry, Max. I'll grind the beans tonight for tomorrow morning, and—"

"No." He caught her eye while she was fussing with Leo. "I want my beans freshly ground. In the morning. I don't know why you can't get that right."

"Leo needed—"

"Get your act together, Lilly."

She didn't finish her sentence. Max wandered off.

How dare he!

Appalled and frustrated, Lilly was honestly anxious at his tone.

Leo had needed changing first thing, before she could even get to the kitchen, and it was a messy job, at best. Then, once dry, he'd wailed to be fed and wasn't at all pleased with the bottle she'd offered. Frustrated, Lilly tried to soothe him best she could, coaxing him to take the formula, but she was certain her frustration was carrying over to the unhappy child.

Max was not pleased with any of that.

If she'd only been able to pump yesterday, like normal—or like she did when Max wasn't home—she could have substituted breast milk for the formula, and Max wouldn't have known. And her breasts wouldn't have been so full and leaky....

If Max was going to be home more, she might have to wean Leo off the breast.

But that was the least of her concern, at the moment.

The morning coffee routine was difficult for Lilly to latch onto, even after all these months. She enjoyed a cup of tea in the mornings —and had no understanding of this obsession with the bitter brew. Max never recognized her lack of interest in his coffee habit. Tea was easy to brew quickly. Making his coffee was a laborious process when one hadn't even a marginal interest in the outcome.

But she'd attempted to accommodate. She'd purchased the specific coffee grinder and coffeemaker he'd said he wanted, and his favorite coffee beans, and had gifted them to him for Christmas.

He'd not once used them himself. He expected her to make the coffee for him.

That hadn't been her plan. But when he'd handed the items back to her, and said, "How sweet of you, Lilly, to gift me with fresh coffee every morning. I can't wait until you make the first pot," she knew she was mistaken.

She'd considered correcting his thinking—but then he'd flashed that sexy grin of his and tackled her to the floor by the Christmas tree and made love to her until she was silly with pleasure.

The next morning, she mastered the coffee grinder.

Mistake. Huge mistake.

Put it out of your mind, Lilly. Time to get ready for work.

Poppy arrived a couple of hours later, and Lilly still had not showered or dressed yet when she answered the door.

"Goodness, girl. You look a mess."

"It's been a bloody hell of a morning, Poppy." She bounced a cranky Leo on her hip. She'd been agitated with Max, of course, and everything else, and had apparently passed that on to Leo.

Poppy set her bag and sunhat on a side table by the door and reached for the child. "Give me the boy. You go take a minute, and then we'll talk."

Lilly exhaled and handed Leo over. "You're sure?"

Poppy shooed her off. "Get on with it. Take a long shower. This bub and I will be fine."

"Bless you," Lilly whispered.

She padded off up the stairs and into her bathroom, where she showered and had a good cry. The warm water did wonders to settle her brain and her heart. But deep inside, she had questions she didn't know if she could answer.

Questions she didn't know if she wanted answered.

By the time she'd dressed, Poppy had Leo in his baby seat in the kitchen, happily chewing on a biscuit. She'd brought her breast pump from Leo's room, where she kept it in the closet when Max was home, and headed to a chair at the table to pump.

Poppy was at the stove. "I'm making eggs and sausages and grilled tomatoes."

"Oh, I'm not too hungry."

The older woman tossed her the side-eye. "I didn't ask you if you were hungry."

A not-so-subtle message. Poppy wanted her to eat.

"Fine. I'll have some. Right after I pump."

"Good. There are no breast milk bottles in the refrigerator. Only that stinky formula. I swear, I think that gives him gas."

Lilly nodded. "I know. Max is home, so I switched, but I shouldn't have."

Again, Poppy glanced at her from the stove. "Man needs to stay out of woman's business."

"I know."

She'd made the mistake of telling Poppy a while back Max didn't want her to breastfeed Leo. Poppy hadn't taken too well to Max after that. And if she knew how he'd treated her today, she wouldn't have liked that, either.

They'd both seen enough abuse of women—physically and emotionally—living on the station in the outback. Poppy had left her partner because of it years ago, and moved to the city. She wouldn't stand for it now, either. Lilly had also seen her fair share of violence between her parents, and others, too.

So, she wouldn't say a word about any of it to Poppy.

"The man and you argue this morning?"

Well, shit. "No, Poppy. Leo was just fussy, and I was aggravated."

"Hmpht."

She didn't believe her. Whatever.

"You working today?"

"I canceled my showings. I'll reschedule. Wanted to check with you first to see if you can come tomorrow or Friday."

Poppy turned. "You know I can come whenever you need me, Lilly. Just say."

She knew that. "Tomorrow then. Can you come early? I just wanted to make sure you didn't have plans."

"Plans?" The woman's face lit up as she turned toward her. "You and that baby are my plans, you know. You are my life."

Lilly's heart just about jumped out of her chest. If she wasn't attached to the breast pump, she'd have bounced up to hug Poppy. "You've been my friend for a very long time. Thank you, dear Poppy."

"I'll be here at eight."

"Good."

Poppy dished up the eggs and sausages, then looked at Lilly. "More than friends. Family."

Lilly smiled. "Yes. That's right."

"Now, you finish up there and eat this. I'll fix you a cuppa, too. Then we talk."

Lilly looked up into her friend's soft gray eyes. She'd been looking into those wise eyes for most of her life. "Thank you, Poppy," she whispered. "You're a gem."

Poppy lifted Leo out of his seat and started singing to him as she ambled toward the sliding glass doors leading to the deck.

They spent the rest of the morning chit-chatting about this and that. Lilly didn't let the conversation turn to Max, no matter how much Poppy wanted to talk about him and kept nudging her in that direction. It was too fresh for Lilly. There were too many things she needed to ponder, consider, sort out.

Tomorrow. Maybe tomorrow.

At around one o'clock that afternoon, Lilly suggested Poppy head home. There would be fewer people on the passenger ferry that time of day. "Besides..." she'd told her, "you're coming earlier than normal tomorrow and you deserve a restful evening."

They'd put Leo in his pram and strolled along, chatting softly while the baby napped. Lilly was glad to get out of the house. The weather was mild for May, getting cooler every day. All she'd needed was a light sweater, and Leo was fine wrapped in his blanket.

She turned to Poppy. "I'm glad you brought your jacket with you. The ferry might be chilly."

Poppy waved her off. "I'll be fine. I like the breeze and enjoy the sun when I can."

Smiling, Lilly hooked her arm in Poppy's. "You be careful."

"I am always."

They ambled along, enjoying the twenty-minute walk. Lilly knew that when the weather turned even cooler, she'd want to drive to the terminal to pick Poppy up and take her back. While the temperatures in Brisbane and the islands were subtropical, they would have their share of chilly days in the upcoming winter months.

But they'd talk about that in a few weeks.

Perhaps, even, she'd ask Poppy to move in with her for the winter. She had plenty of space. And Max had no interest in doing so.

They lingered at the ferry slip until the boat came, then Lilly gave Poppy a hug and she watched her toddle off down the ramp to get on board. She waved and turned for home, grateful Leo was still sleeping, and for the pleasant walk.

The exercise did wonders for her mood.

As she approached her home, she noticed a utility vehicle parked across the street in a place where no one usually parked. She pointed the pram toward the house and headed up her driveway.

A stocky young man wearing jeans, some sort of novelty T-shirt, and boots left the ute. "G'day, there. Miss Colling, isn't it?"

She turned. *This man knows my name?* He stood behind her, a few feet back, waving a large envelope in his hand—she presumed to catch her attention.

"Yes?"

"Just a minute of your time, please. I'm looking for a Mr. Max Oliver? He lives here, right?"

Actually, he doesn't. Just ask him. "And you are...?"

He shrugged, smiling, his longish bangs hanging over his forehead, where she could barely see his eyes. A bit unnerving, actually. "Doesn't matter my name. Is he at home?"

"Max Oliver does not live here," she told him.

He grinned wider. "That's odd. I thought I saw him leaving earlier this morning. He's the bub's dad, right-o?"

Lilly sucked in a breath and turned, pushing Leo closer to the front door. "I need to get the baby inside. Good day."

He rushed up beside her. "Wait."

Lilly stopped and glowered. "You do not want to push me, Mr... What did you say your name was?"

"I didn't."

"Then we have no business here." She moved forward, her heart skipping beats as she pushed the pram. She wanted him gone before she had to pull out her keys and unlock the door.

"I'll wait then."

Lilly whipped around. "Long wait, I'd say. I do not expect him. But if you must, please do so in your ute."

One corner of his mouth turned up in a mocking grin. He bowed and gestured, like he was tipping his hat to her. "G'day, ma'am."

He left to go to his vehicle. She quickly unlocked the front door and pushed Leo inside, rapidly closing and locking it again behind her.

Her back against the door, she inhaled a deep, cleansing breath and then let it out slowly. Then again. After a moment, she lifted Leo out of the pram and headed up the stairs.

THE MAN HAD AN EXCEPTIONALLY LONG WAIT—MAX didn't come home. Lilly could only assume he had stayed at the condo.

So be it.

He didn't call or text her.

She didn't call or text him.

This had happened once before. She'd angered him for some reason she'd now forgotten, and he'd stayed at the condo for two nights. Her punishment for not being a good girl?

Well, bullcrap. She'd have none of that. She might only be in her twenties, but she'd lived enough life to know that she didn't want to be bossed around, or manipulated, by a man. Especially one who professed to love her.

She'd seen enough of that at Min Min Station growing up—but she didn't have to live that kind of life—and she wouldn't.

When she'd gone to bed, the ute was still parked across the street. When she got up, it was gone. Admittedly, she was relieved, because if he were still there come morning, she'd have to call the police before Poppy arrived.

No way would she leave Poppy and Leo alone with that man outside.

Fortunately, she didn't have to worry.

Now, as she stood leaning against the railing on the ferry, crossing over to Brisbane, she let her mind wander over the past twenty-four hours. The man in the ute had unnerved her, to be certain, but even more, Max's actions earlier in the day had caused the tide to turn inside her.

She no longer wished to be the woman hanging on a string, waiting for him to come home and dangle pretties before her, enticing her...luring her...into his arms and his bed.

His anger had soured that. Her fear of him had soured that, as well.

And if that was the way it would be with him? If that was his expectation of what their life would look like together? Then she wanted none of it.

She'd rather raise Leo on her own—and she had the means to do so—than accept a part-time, half-committed relationship with his father.

She wanted it all, or she wanted nothing.

And perhaps today was the day to find out exactly which way it would be.

Max's condo was close to the real estate office, so she headed that way. Her plan was simple—wake him, tell him her expectations, and gauge his reactions.

At his building, she took the elevator up to the third floor, strolled down the hall and around the corner to his unit, and knocked on the door.

The time was almost nine. Most days, he didn't schedule meetings until lunch, using his mornings to make calls.

He didn't come to the door.

She knocked again.

Suddenly, she wondered if there was a reason he'd never given her a key.

That thought niggled at her as the door jerked open.

A woman stood framed in the doorway. She wore a man's white

collared shirt and nothing else, or so it seemed. Her long, dark blond hair fell over one shoulder, and she blinked several times at Lilly with big brown eyes smudged with eyeliner.

And all Lilly could think of in that instant was that she looked like someone she'd seen once in a movie.

But this wasn't a movie.

"Yes?" the woman said.

"I have an appointment with Max Oliver." Lilly lied. "Nine o'clock."

"Oh. Come on in." She waved her into the condo. The condo that she had picked out for Max, all those months ago. Shit. Over a year ago.

"Please excuse me." The blonde sauntered off, her long legs crossing the living area toward the bedroom.

Lilly heard her speak as she moved inside the bedroom, "Sugar, your appointment is here."

Unbelievable.

She stood in the center of the large living area, facing the bedroom, waiting, and watching the door the woman had disappeared into. She felt no emotion...was surprisingly calm. And vowed to stay that way until she walked out that door again.

"I don't have a nine o'clock appointment, darling," she heard Max say.

They chattered on, their voices lowered, and then finally, Max, wearing jeans and a T-shirt, pushed open the bedroom door and stepped into the living room.

He halted. "Lilly?" His expression morphed from shock to annoyance.

"Good day, Max."

"What are you doing here?" He glanced back at the bedroom, then to her again.

"Unfinished business."

He cocked his head and stepped closer. "Excuse me?"

Lilly held her calm demeanor as he approached. "Two things." She lifted her chin. "One, you will never, ever touch me—or shall I say manhandle me?—again, like you did yesterday. Nor will you ever raise your voice to me—or my child—again." She hadn't intended to bring Leo into this, but suddenly, standing there looking at him, she realized if he could treat her with such disrespect, what kind of father would he be to her little boy?

You are doing the right thing, Lilly.

Max just stood there, waiting for her to finish. Frowning.

"And, two. Someone is looking for you. A man. He came to my house yesterday evening. He need not show up there again or I am calling the police—so fix whatever it is you need to fix, so he does not come back."

He touched her forearm. "Lilly...."

She took two steps in the reverse, his hand falling. "Who is she?" Lilly nodded toward the bedroom.

He shrugged. "I don't even remember her name."

Lilly huffed and stepped away. "Goddamn bloody hell, Max!" She headed toward the exit. When her fingers found the doorknob and twisted, Max leaned against the door with force.

"Listen to me, Lilly."

She glowered, her gaze meeting his. "No."

"You have my son. We are connected, whether or not you want to be."

Like hell, you bastard. "There are courts for that."

"We're not married, so we can work this out. C'mon, Lilly. I'll move in with you. We can do all the things you want. I'll take care of you and Leo. You'll want for nothing. The only thing I ask is that I occasionally partake of a few liaisons of the sexual variety outside of our relationship. Harmless fun, really. Stress relief."

Down time. Right-o.

To be honest, she couldn't quite believe what she was hearing. "You mean that really works on women?"

He laughed, pushing away from the door. "Some women. It worked on my ex."

"For a time, apparently." Lilly didn't mince words. "Well, it won't work on me. I don't need to be taken care of, Max. I have a job, money, a home, everything I need. And if I want sex? I can find it. I don't need you for that, either. So, if you are proposing a deal here, my response is this—bloody fucking hell no."

She twisted and pulled the doorknob and stepped out into the hallway.

Fucking wanker.

Seventeen

The locksmith made quick work of the lockbox, popping open the lid within a few minutes. "That was easy," he said, handing the box back to Julia.

Maggie watched her hold the box, staring down at it. She wondered if she had a premonition, of sorts, of something good or bad that would emerge from the dusty thing. Julia held onto it for a few seconds longer before looking at Maggie. "Let's open it in the kitchen."

"Sure." She looked at the locksmith. "Please add that to my bill."

He waved her off. "Didn't take any time. That one's on the house."

"Well, I thank you."

He handed her the paper invoice. Maggie gave it a quick peek, noticing the amount. "I have cash upstairs. I'll be right back."

She could hear Julia and the guy talking as she took the stairs. Getting the locks changed was a priority, she knew that, but the cost was going to deplete her meager savings. Still, she counted out three one-hundred-dollar bills, stuffed two more back in the jewelry box, and headed back downstairs.

She paid him. He left, and Maggie and Julia stood staring at each other.

"Let's do this before I have to leave for kid pickup."

They headed into the kitchen. Julia set the box on the island. "I don't know why I feel kind of anxious about this."

Maggie exhaled, deep and long. "I know. Me, too. It's probably nothing. Right?"

"And it could be everything."

"It could be the thing that I've been looking for—to get something damning on Max. Do you think?" That thought gripped her heart a little.

"We'll never know if we don't open it."

"All right." She grasped the box and flipped back the lid.

Both women peered over the meager contents.

"That's a marriage license," Julia said, picking it up to look closer.

Maggie plucked up the paper underneath it. "And this is a death certificate."

"And those," Julia added, pointing back into the box, "are wedding rings."

They locked gazes.

"You first," Maggie said. "Whose names are on the marriage certificate?" Like, she didn't know Max was one of them already.

Julia gripped the paper. "Maxwell David Oliver and Caroline Susan McDowell, married May 22, 2001." She quickly met Maggie's gaze. "Well, that's official. At least we know the woman's name now. And the death certificate?"

Maggie took a sharp breath. "Same. Caroline Susan McDowell Oliver. Date of death, June 18, 2002."

"Shit. That's just a little over a year later."

Why does that date, June 18, sound familiar? It would come to her, eventually.

Maggie felt a little dizzy and braced herself against a chair. "So, Max was married before he married me, and her name was Caroline? That motherfucker!" Maggie pushed away from the island and paced a few steps away, and back again. "He never told me. He never once said he'd ever been married before. I mean, it's not like it would have mattered to me, or anything. People get married. People die. People remarry. Why did he keep it a secret?"

"Million-dollar question." Julia took a beat, then moved closer to Maggie. "People usually keep secrets when they don't want other people to know things. What I want to know is, what is that *thing* about this marriage that Max didn't want you to know?"

"There has to be more."

"Yes. I agree."

Maggie headed into the family room and grabbed her tablet from the coffee table. "I'm going to do a search. I need to know how she died."

"Are you sure you want to dig into that now?" Julia followed her and sat beside her on the sofa. "We have to pick up the kids in an hour."

Maggie pulled up the browser on her tablet. "Yes. I'm tired of being in the dark. I'm tired of a lot of things, actually—a dead wife here, a lover, and bonus kid there—and I want to get it all behind me. But right now, I need to know what happened to *this* woman." She typed her name into the browser, then scanned the results. "Shit."

"What?"

"There's a lot of stuff here."

Julia took the tablet. "Let me look at it first."

Maggie grabbed it back. "No. You've been taking care of me for way too long. I will not fall apart by whatever I find." She softened her voice then. "Sorry, not trying to be bossy, but I need to do this. Why don't you look in that tote?"

Julia gave her a grin. "Perfect. I'll go do that."

Maggie watched her head into Max's old office, where they had stashed the "miscellaneous" tote, and she returned her attention to the tablet. There were pages of information about a Caroline McDowell from Decatur, Georgia—her family, her life, and her death—and the more she read, the more Maggie felt like she was stepping into a crime novel.

About twenty minutes later, Julia headed back into the family room. Maggie looked up.

"I think we need to go back to the storage unit before we pick up the kids. It's close to the schools, isn't it?"

"Not far." Maggie glanced at the time. "We have time. What's up?"

"Going through that tote of Caroline's personal things... I don't know why but it just felt too...odd, I think is the word. I can't get past why Max kept all these things."

Maggie agreed. Something had been niggling at her, as well. "What strikes me is the organization of the totes, the labeling, and so forth. That wasn't Max. He wouldn't sort through clothes and label the boxes like that, just to store them away."

Julia stared off. "It's kind of like she had already packed them up before she died. Right?"

"Exactly." Maggie bit her lip. "Like, perhaps, she was packing things up to move?"

"Or leave him?" Julia added. "Shit. I don't want to read too much into this because we are just speculating here... But maybe Caroline wasn't so happy in the marriage and was preparing to divorce him?"

Maggie forced out a breath. "Perhaps. Which only adds to the other reason it feels so odd."

"What is that?"

She locked gazes with Julia. "I've read enough about Caroline's death to know that Max wasn't an innocent bystander."

Julia's eyes widened. "You think Max killed her?"

Maggie shook her head. "I don't know. Maybe. But not intentionally."

"But if he knew she was planning to leave him...."

"I don't know, Julia. I think he was at fault, and it was all covered up. Caroline died in a boating accident. Max was driving the boat, it was just the two of them, and he was drunk. Some people at the lake saw them arguing before they left the marina."

"Sounds like a lawsuit to me."

"That's what I thought. It appears her family in Georgia challenged the decision that Max was not negligent, and has sued for pain and suffering, and so on. Then I found an article where Caroline's parents abruptly dropped everything against him."

"They settled."

"Sounds like."

"Max's family has money. Right?"

"They are a very established North Carolina family, old money for sure. His grandfather was a Duke board trustee for years. His father is the CEO of the university medical center."

"Ah," Julia said. "Generational wealth and the southern good ol' boy network can get you everywhere."

"Exactly. And since the accident happened here, in North Carolina, with North Carolina judges presiding, and all that, well... The Olivers definitely had the upper hand. The McDowell charges were dropped after a few years, right before they were headed into trial. That was 2005, about the time Max and I got married—also the same time Max and his father had a major falling out."

Julia stared. It was almost like Maggie could see the cogs clicking in her head. "So, family upheaval, a lawsuit settlement, plus a marriage with a baby on the way—all at once. Triple threat, some might say."

"Yes. Seems so."

"The plot thickens."

Julia moved across the room to grab her purse and keys. "Let's talk more on the way to the storage facility."

"Right."

They hashed and rehashed what they knew for the twenty-minute drive back to Two Gals Storage. Julia drove straight to the unit. They both jumped out of her SUV and Maggie unlocked the door, flinging it open.

It rolled back with a bang and then rocked back to settle into place. The thud it made echoed loudly in the storage unit.

Empty.

Both women stood there, staring into the void.

"Son-of-a-bitch," Maggie murmured. "He has eyes everywhere."

———

THEY DIDN'T DISCUSS THE EMPTY STORAGE UNIT UNTIL much later in the evening.

After picking the kids up from school, they ordered Chinese take-out, compliments of Julia, and then started moving things out of the office while Chloe finished her selfie art project.

Every time Maggie looked at Carol, she thought about the woman Max had married. He was the one who had mentioned the name Caroline when they'd discussed baby names. He'd told her then that it reminded him of "the Carolinas," meaning the state where they lived—and subsequently, a Carolina state of mind, easy and laid back.

Now, she knew differently.

And fuck him, their daughter possessed nothing close to an easy-going, laid back, state of mind. *That backfired, didn't it, Max?*

While Max's previous marriage was a bit of a shocker, she was more concerned about what came after—and wondered how all that had affected Max over the years. Could the death of this woman have been the reason for his detachment? His desire for control? His anger? His inability to care about people? To love?

Or was he simply built that way?

She might never know.

She was glad for the pause in the action, so to speak, and to spend a little time with the kids. While they were doing mindless tasks, filling boxes with books and dragging items to the garage, her mind wandered aimlessly over all she'd learned the past few hours.

"You know, earlier," Maggie said to Julia, "when we found the death certificate and marriage license, I had a strange feeling about the date of Caroline's death. There's something familiar about it, but I can't put my finger on it."

"Oh? Tell me more." Julia moved a box of books to a corner of the room.

Maggie shrugged. "Not sure. It's no one's birthday I know of, or any other significant day, but June 18 is something... I just need to think about it longer, probably."

"Well, if you remember, let me know. Okay?"

"Sure."

Julia reached for something behind the desk. "So, now that the kids are all upstairs, and hopefully down for the count until morning, how about if we open this bottle of wine I found in your kitchen and ponder some next steps?"

"I'll get the glasses."

When Maggie returned from the kitchen, she found Julia sitting cross-legged on the desk, opening the Bordeaux. She approached and set the glasses on the desktop, then joined Julia, facing her. "Max's favorite. Let's drink to the slimy sucker."

Julia laughed. "You drink. I have this diet pop over here. Remember? I'm the alcoholic in the room."

"And I'm just the woman who lost her way somehow. But you know what? I'm determined to find my way back."

Julia popped the top on her canned soda and poured some into her wineglass. "I have no doubt that you will, Maggie Oliver. In fact, I see you getting stronger every day."

Smiling, she squared her shoulders. "You know what? I feel stronger."

"Awesome."

Maggie took a sip of the wine. "Yum...."

Julia ran her hand over the top of the desk. "You know, this is a very nice desk."

"It's mahogany, I think. Heavy sucker."

"Expensive sucker, too." Julia threw her legs over the side and hopped down. "And it's in excellent condition."

Maggie shrugged. "Max took care of things. Besides, no kids were allowed in here to ding it up."

Julia smiled. "Right. Let's sell it."

Laughing, Maggie shouted. "You're crazy."

"I'm not. Max will never know. We can sell it on social media."

"But I don't know how to do that and besides, Max and I are connected everywhere."

Grinning, Julia took a tour around the desk, still looking it over. "I bet you could get seven hundred for it. Maybe a thousand even."

"Seriously?"

"I could do it for you. I could post it in the marketplace. They could pay me, pick up here, and then I'll pay you."

"I do need cash."

"Yes, you do." Julia glanced toward the office door. "And you have a lot of crap in the garage, too. You could do a cash only, one day, flash garage sale."

"I don't think the homeowner's association allows for random garage sales."

"Then we'll use the marketplace again. Or eBay."

Maggie thought about that. "I wonder what a set of Bentley golf clubs would bring? Used, of course. They are in the back of the Escalade."

Julia's eyes grew wide. "Probably enough to get you through this thing and then some. I think we may just have solved your money problems."

A quick breath whooshed out of Maggie's mouth. "Well, that would be a good way to end this day."

"Right?"

"I'm pouring more wine."

Julia looked past her, focused on something.

"What is it?"

"Not sure." She headed for the window. "Someone just parked in front of your house. Looks like the car is still running because the lights are on. Wait...."

"What?"

"They're putting something in your yard. A sign, maybe?"

Maggie jumped up. "What the fuck?"

Both women headed for the front door. By the time they got outside, the car was gone. But the "For Sale" sign tucked in between her mailbox and her driveway was not.

"Fucking cocksucking bastard," Maggie hissed. "He's put the house up for sale."

"It says 'Coming Soon' though, so it's not officially listed yet." Julia hooked her arm in hers and led her toward the door. "He's just scaring you. Come on. You have wine to drink, and darlin' it's been one hell of a day already, so you deserve it. Don't let this throw you. I'll get on it first thing in the morning."

"You know it's retaliation for today, right?" Maggie felt the anger rising inside her for the first time today.

"Of course. That's the way he rolls."

"I want to roll his fucking head."

They entered the house and shut the door behind them. "No head rolling. Let's just sell his fucking golf clubs."

"And anything else I can get my hands on," Maggie added.

THE NEXT MORNING, MAGGIE DELIBERATED OVER MAKING breakfast, but made no moves toward preparing anything, while waiting for the kids to come downstairs. Julia was up too, sitting on the family room sofa, her nose in her laptop. She'd been there since before Maggie got up, apparently, and had already made a full pot of coffee.

"Thanks for the coffee. Much needed this morning." Maggie yawned, covering her mouth with the back of her hand. "You're up early."

"Doing a bit of research," Julia said.

"Oh? For...?"

"This and that. The McDowell case. The autopsy report. The value of those golf clubs. Louise at the storage unit. You know, stuff like that."

An interesting list, to be sure. Maggie smiled and let her be. Her friend was in her element and would likely have answers before noon.

The kids straggled down on their own time frame, so she was glad she'd waited to make breakfast. No use cooking things they didn't want.

Chloe came first, asking for chocolate pops cereal and a banana. Frowning, Maggie said, "We're fresh out of chocolate pops, sweetie. How about some granola instead?"

"Okay, fine." Chloe sighed.

Maggie grinned, watching her settle into her seat. "This granola is my favorite."

"Mom," Chloe said, dismissing the cereal discussion. "I have to take the selfie project into school today, so it's ready for Monday. Don't forget you have to come for selfie show-and-tell then."

That's right. There were so many things going on, she couldn't forget about Chloe's art debut. "I won't forget, sweetheart. I can't wait to see you to show your art to the world!"

"I have to talk about it too, why I drew myself the way I did."

"You're going to be great. I'm excited." She turned to the magnetic calendar on the refrigerator and added a reminder for Monday. "Got it inked in right here."

She glanced at Chloe, who beamed.

Jason stumbled into the kitchen, complete with bedhead and still wearing the sweatpants and a T-shirt he'd worn to bed.

"Can I have coffee? It smells good."

"Coffee?"

"To wake me up."

Maggie stared at him and thought, what the hell? He looked like he could use a caffeine jolt.

"How about if I make you a coffee drink with protein powder and some cocoa—sort of a mocha thing. You want it hot or cold?"

"Hot. I stayed up too late last night."

Maggie eyed him while pulling the blender closer. It wasn't like him to actually confess something he wasn't supposed to be doing. "Why?"

He hesitated. "Playing video games with a friend."

She stayed silent for a moment and went about her task. She pulled down the cocoa and protein powder from the cabinet, then measured and added them to the blender. "Well, tonight, to bed early. Okay?"

"Yeah."

She added some sugar and hot coffee, whirred the contents for about thirty seconds, and asked Jason again. "You sure you don't want this over ice? I could make a frappe."

"Hot, please."

Carol skipped into the room. "Oh, that looks good. Could I have one? But cold, please."

"Of course." She eyed Carol. "No makeup? You feel okay?"

Her daughter straddled a bar stool and leaned into the island. "I'm fine. It's just a half-day today because we have graduation practice in the afternoon. God, I can't believe graduation is only a week away. I dressed down today. Besides, Logan says I'm prettier without makeup."

Those were words she'd never expected coming out of her daughter's mouth. Maggie tossed a quick glance at Julia, who caught her eye, and then back to Carol. "I think you are beautiful either way. It's just that I don't think I've ever seen you not wear makeup to school."

Carol shrugged. "Logan says he thinks makeup makes a girl look trampy."

Logan says, Logan says... What the fuck?

1992

She chose the red tube.

It was the least expensive one. She only had so much money. Mary Margaret figured if she liked it, if her eyelashes looked good with mascara, she could save up more money for the ultra-pink tube later on.

The lighting was better in the bathroom than in her room, so she lingered extra-long in there, until she got the hang of how to apply the dark tint to her lashes. She had a magnifying mirror, too. A hand-held one that she used to see up close and then looked into the big mirror to see the overall effect.

She liked it. Except for the smudges underneath her eyes. Avoiding the smudges was the hardest part, but a cotton swab helped.

Her thin, short lashes actually looked longer. Would the kids at school notice? Would anyone say anything to her? Or would she just look...prettier?

"The bus!" Her mom yelled from the kitchen.

Mary Margaret rushed out of the bathroom, stashed the red tube in her underwear drawer, grabbed her backpack, and sprinted toward the front door. At the mirror in the entryway, she stopped, looking once more at her eyes.

She smiled again. Perfect.

Jack pushed past her, gave her a thumbs up, and headed for the road.

Her mother rounded the corner, took one look at her, and gasped. "What the goddamn hell did you do to your eyes? Good God, Mary Margaret, you look like a slut."

The shock of her mother's words rippled over her. *Slut?* She wasn't exactly sure what that meant. "It's just mascara, Mom."

"Did your dad say?"

"Yes. I asked him."

"Well, you didn't ask me if you could wear it to school. That looks awful."

Jack yelled from the driveway. "Come on, Mary Margaret!"

"Go wash it off."

"I can't. I'll be late and you'll have to take me to school."

Her mother huffed. "Such an embarrassment. Go to school looking like a goddamned slut. See if I care, Mary Margaret Brennan. Just go."

She ran from the house. Ran past Jack and as soon as the bus door opened, trotted up the steps. She took the first empty seat, scooted all the way to the window, and buried her head in her hands.

By the time she got to school, she prayed she had all the mascara rubbed off her lashes. But when she went to the bathroom, she realized all she'd done was smear it and make her eyes red.

Sue Martin stepped up beside her, staring at her reflection in the mirror, and grinned wide. "Oh, Mary Margaret. Soooo pretty." She giggled and skipped back to a group of girls behind her.

She watched them in the mirror, staring, mocking. A sickening thud landed on her stomach, like a punch to the belly with a dodge ball.

She wanted to cry. Wouldn't.

Then she heard their words. *White trash. Slut. Ho. Tramp.*

She wanted to go home. Couldn't.

"Here." Deni came up beside her, looking at her reflection in the mirror. She carefully wiped away some smudges under her eyes with a paper towel, giving the other girls a backward glance. "Don't listen to them, Mary Margaret," she whispered. "You're beautiful."

Eighteen

"Mom? You hear me?"

Maggie shivered, shaking off the old memory. She'd not conjured up that piece of her past in an exceptionally long time. "I'm sorry. What?"

"Logan is taking me to school this morning. I don't need a ride."

"Oh, right. Sure." The remembrance had shaken her a little, leaving her a bit discombobulated.

"So," Julia called out from the family room. "This boyfriend, Carol. I need details. What's his name? Logan?"

"Hey, Aunt Julia." Carol looked into the family room. "I didn't see you there. I'm glad you stayed over."

Julia looked up from her laptop and smiled. "And here I am sitting here, thinking I'm invisible."

"Naw." Carol smiled. "I like when you're around. You're never invisible."

"And this boyfriend?" Julia prodded. "Details, girl."

Maggie watched Carol blush and grin. "Well. He's nineteen, really tall, dark hair. Super cute."

"Nineteen? Older guy." Julia winked. "Where's he going to school?"

Jason snickered.

Carol stuck out her tongue at him. Maggie noticed her expression fall. "Oh, he's not. He works at the engine plant over in Whitakers. Nights mostly, so he swings by in the mornings to see me before school."

"Goodness. You'll miss him then when you go off to ECU in the fall."

Carol froze, looking away from Julia. Maggie watched her fiddle with her cell phone. "Maybe. Not sure of my plans yet, to be honest."

Those words cut rather deep. "Excuse me?" Maggie said. "You're going to ECU. It's where we go."

"No big deal, Mom. I might just go to the community college."

"That's not up for discussion, Carol."

The look her daughter aimed at her then was obvious disapproval. "Oh, we will definitely discuss."

"Well." Julia interrupted, not missing a beat. "I can't wait to officially meet him."

"Ditto," Maggie muttered. "Officially." She was amazed, actually, at the information Julia had extracted in just a few seconds.

Carol glared. "Mom, I forgot. Did you know there is a For Sale sign in our yard? What the fuck?" Obviously, she felt the need to change the subject.

Maggie shot her a warning look. "Language. Little ears."

"But what?"

"I don't know. It happened last night."

Julia set her laptop aside and stood. "I'm on it. I've already left a message with the agent, so I hope to get a call back later this morning. I've also left a message with Max's attorney. I don't think your dad can do this, but...."

Carol interrupted. "But dad is an asshole. Who knows what he'll do?"

Jason piped up. "Dad is not an asshole."

"He is, Jason. Stop defending him."

"He's just trying to make sure he gets what is legally his."

Maggie's heart literally jerked, and she gasped, locking eyes with her son.

Julia stepped into the kitchen, also looking straight at Jason. Maggie waved her off, though. She didn't want Julia stepping into this.

A horn honked from the driveway, breaking her concentration. To say it was an unwelcome intrusion was an understatement. Suddenly, Maggie's anger at Max and frustration with Jason turned elsewhere. "Goddamn it, Carol! Tell him not to do that. I have asked repeatedly."

"Of. Course." She headed for the door. "Abso-fucking-lutely, Mother."

Shit. "Do I need to pick you up from graduation practice?" she called out after her. "Do I need to be there?"

Carol waved her off with a flick of her hand. "No to everything. See you later."

Maggie watched her go, heard the front door slam, and then after a minute, the pickup truck roared out of the driveway.

"That girl is going to be the death of me," she murmured. "My best friend one day and my nemesis the next."

Julia touched her arm. "Let it go." She nodded toward Jason, as if to say, *we have more fish to fry here.*

Maggie centered herself again, taking a deep breath and releasing it slowly. "Jason, talk to me."

He stood up. "I gotta get ready for school."

"Jason. Stop." Maggie rounded the island. He halted, but didn't look at her. Maggie crouched a little to look into his face. "Look at me."

He slowly lifted his chin.

She peered into his eyes. "What do you mean he wants what is legally his?"

Jason let go of a sigh and blurted out, "He just wants what is his, Mom. His name is on the house, and he bought it with his own money. You didn't help. He should be able to sell it if he wants to. You paid nothing. It's his. We just live here. Besides, he's going to buy something else."

You never paid for anything. Wrong. I paid for it with my freedom, my life.

Maggie glanced at Julia, then back at her son. "Jason, I want you to think carefully before you answer me. How did you know that only your dad's name is on the house? I've never told you that."

He stood frozen before her, their gazes locked. Finally, he took a breath and said, "I talked to him. He told me."

"When?" Maggie shouted. "When did you talk to him, Jason?"

She wanted to shake him—wanted to scream and rant. But she pulled everything she possessed inside her together to avoid that kind of scenario. "Jason?"

"We text sometimes."

"I asked you not to."

He cocked his head. "See? Dad said you would try to keep me away from him."

"Jason, you don't understand. This is complicated. You have to do what I ask. Do you understand me? There are things you don't know, and you are going to have to trust me."

He huffed. "Right."

"Did you actually talk to him or just text?"

"We talked once."

"When?"

"Last night. Late."

"And that's why you didn't sleep."

He nodded. "I called him."

"Why?"

Maggie could see the emotion welling up in his eyes, on his face. "Because I'm confused, Mom! Dad texts me things, and I don't know what is right or wrong. He tells me things about you, and you and Carol say things about him, and all I want to know is the truth."

"The fucking bastard." Maggie pivoted away, running her hands through her hair. "That motherfucker."

Julia interjected. "Language. Little ears."

She glanced at Chloe, who was preoccupied with her food, peeling her second banana and dipping it into her granola. "Right." She turned back to Jason. "Give me your phone."

He shook his head. "Mom, I need my phone."

"I'll get you a new one as soon as I can. But right now, I need for you to go upstairs and get your goddamn phone."

"You taking Carol's, too?"

"Probably. You both are due new phones, anyway." She glanced at Julia, who nodded. How she could afford them, she didn't know. "We need to keep a tight circle here. I don't trust your father and I especially don't like that he is confusing you, Jason. That's unfair to you, especially if he is lying."

"Are you lying?"

She stood still, stunned. "Jason, I told you days ago I would not lie to you." She paused, studying his facial expressions. "And you can't lie to me, either. Got it?"

He nodded. "Yes."

"Good."

"My phone is crap. I do need a new one."

"Alright. Go get it, please, and I'll take care of it."

Julia stepped forward. "And Jason, don't delete anything. Okay? I know you probably don't want your mom to read your dad's messages, but it's important that you keep them."

He twisted and glared at Julia, his eyes narrowed. "Why? So you can use them against him in court?"

She took a step closer. "If there are things there that can be used against him in court, things you don't want your mom to see, then Jason, it's important not to delete them. And all the more reason for your mom to protect you. Your dad is twisting things to his advantage and frankly, it's unfair to you and everyone else."

Maggie wished Julia hadn't gone there—she didn't want Jason to get on the defensive any more than he was—but what's done was done.

"I don't want to talk about it." He eyed his mom. "I need a shower. I'll bring it down later."

"No." Maggie stood firm. "I'll come up with you now and get it."

The look on his face told her all she needed to know. He was pissed. Confused. Annoyed. Maybe even a little defeated. Not a good place for a fourteen-year-old boy to be, and that worried her.

"Fine," he said. "Take it. Just take fucking everything."

WHEN MAGGIE RETURNED HOME AFTER THE SCHOOL DROP-off, she found Julia huddled over her laptop at the kitchen island, her leather briefcase spilling open with papers, her yellow legal pad full of scribbles, and several wadded-up pieces of paper littering the counter.

"You've been busy," Maggie said.

"I'll have more to do when I get home." She looked up. "I'm going to leave in an hour, if it's okay with you."

"Sure. I know you need to get back."

"I want to make sure you are okay, though, Mags, and I have a few things I think we should discuss."

Maggie noted Julia was making a list on the legal pad. She leaned in, reading over her shoulder. "What's this?"

"Just things I want to make sure I mention."

MAGGIE GAVE JULIA A NOD. "ALRIGHT. HAVE AT IT." She had to admit she was curious about some things on the list. *House. Attorney. Storage. Sell things. Kids.*

"Have a seat. I will belabor nothing. I just want you to know what I know... What I'm getting a sense of...."

Where was she going with this? "You're alarming me, to be honest. Just spill it."

Julia sighed and nodded. "I spoke with the agent about the house. It's listed as coming soon, so it's not officially on the market and people can't request a showing yet—but they can request a viewing as soon as it goes on the market."

"How long is it on 'coming soon' status?"

"The agent said a few weeks. I've asked her to keep me in the loop."

"Did you explain the situation?"

"Vaguely," Julia said. "Max is her client, so I don't want to over-step boundaries. My gut says he's going to hold it on there for a while. Probably just to annoy you."

She figured that was right. "But I don't have to worry about show-ings, or inspections, or moving, and all that right now. Correct?"

"No, you don't. And if anyone shows up, tell them to contact the agent. If that doesn't work, call me."

Maggie thought about that. "Sure. What about the attorney?"

"He was in a meeting. I left another message. I'm sure he's avoiding me."

"Typical."

Julia agreed. "Yes."

"And the McDowell case? Caroline's death? Anything there?"

She shook her head and stacked some papers, sliding them into her briefcase. "I found a few things I want to dive into this afternoon. I'm also going to make some calls on my way home. I will keep you posted."

"Thanks, Julia. You've done a lot already this morning. I hope you know how much I appreciate it."

Julia gave her a nod and a quick grin. "I do." She picked up her phone. "While you were gone, I took pictures of the desk and the golf clubs. I hope you don't mind. I'll see what I can do to get those sold and I'll be in touch. If you can, look around the house for anything else to sell. I'm happy to help."

"Are you sure, Julia? This is a lot."

She smiled. "It's fine. The thought of selling Max's clubs brings me great pleasure."

Maggie laughed. "Me too. Honestly." She glanced at Julia's list again. "There's one more thing you wanted to discuss?

Julia made direct eye contact. "Yeah. The kids."

Turning, and with a deep exhale, Maggie went to the sofa in the family room. "Come sit down. This is not a standing discussion."

Julia came with her and sat. "You know what I am going to say, right?"

"That my kids are a mess?"

"Well, that's not exactly how I was going to put it."

Maggie leaned forward, not looking at Julia but staring at the dark television set. "I know my kids, Julia. Chloe has had issues since she was young because Max basically dismissed her. Jason is an adolescent boy trying to figure out what kind of man he is going to be, and Max's insufficient role model, past and present, isn't helping. He's always been my buddy, but right now, he's questioning everything—and that includes my role in all this mess. Carol? She's not sure whether I'm her friend or her foe at the moment, mostly because she's being pulled in two directions—family and boyfriend. Plus, she's getting ready to launch from the nest, and with all this family drama going on, I'm sure that will not be a simple transition."

"Well," Julia said, "I think that pretty much sums it up."

"I'm on top of it. I promise."

"I just want to make sure. Don't ignore any warning signs, and if you can't help them, then find someone they can talk to. In fact, the judge might suggest counseling, so be thinking."

"I will."

"And don't forget to talk to Carol about college. That was an interesting twist."

Maggie glanced off, thinking. "I know. I don't think I'm going to push it with her right now. It's not the right time."

Julia nodded. "You've noticed Chloe's food obsession?"

"Goodness, yes." She rose and stepped toward the TV, then turned. "Max ignored her from the start and Chloe made herself invisible. If she called attention to herself in any way, good or bad, Max would get annoyed and either belittle her or shout at her. I think the food thing right now is her way of being invisible—kind of like she's sinking into the food, so she won't have to deal with what's going on around her. But honestly, Julia, I've seen her shine lately, too. That art project she worked on last night? I swear it brought out the real Chloe."

Smiling, Julia said, "She takes after you."

"I'd love to get back into my art one of these days soon."

"You should." Julia stood also and crossed the room. "It might be good therapy."

She'd considered that. "It might. Getting Chloe's art supplies whetted my appetite again. There are classes at the store. I might take one down the road—a refresher. But not yet."

"If you can carve out the time, I think you should do that as soon as you want to. Don't forget to take care of yourself, Maggie. You can't take care of all the others unless you are healthy yourself."

How well she knew that. She was proud of herself for recognizing that sometimes it was okay to put herself first.

Her own mother was the poster child for not taking care of herself. Had she worked on being healthy herself—mentally and physically—things might have turned out differently for them in the past, and well, even in the present. They may have even been able to salvage a relationship. But she'd long given up on the idea that she and her mother could have a healthy relationship in the future.

"I've been rehashing a lot of my past lately, things I screwed up, things I let go, things I wish I'd said or done... I've been recalling some issues I had with my mother and trying not to make the same mistakes with my children. The memories, the flashbacks, are vivid—some I hadn't thought about in years."

Julia reached for her and gave her a hug. "Are you okay?"

The significance of that didn't go unnoticed. Hugs from Julia were a rare thing. "I'm good. I finally feel I'm dealing with all that."

"Mags, from what you've shared about your mother over the years, I don't think you are anywhere close to being like her."

"God, Julia. I hope not."

Julia flashed a grin. "Have I told you lately how proud I am of you? Seriously, Mags, you've grown leaps and bounds in the past few months, even amid all this absurdity."

Those words meant more to her than anything. "I'm trying, Julia. I've considered therapy again—but honestly? The thought of laying down paint on a canvas is really what I think will pull me back together. Maybe that and a prolonged stay at the beach." She grinned.

"Talk to Lia about that. I'm sure she can accommodate."

"Just let me get through graduation."

"When is that happening again?"

Maggie glanced at the calendar on the fridge. "Next week."

"I'll be back then."

"Deni! Wait up. My college letter came yesterday. Did you get yours?"

Deni Albright turned away from Mary Margaret and opened her locker. "Yes. Mom opened it." She glanced over her shoulder and rolled her eyes. "Mothers."

"Yeah."

Mary Margaret looked again at the letter. "It says my roommate assignment will come in another letter. I sure hope they didn't screw up. I can't wait for us to room together."

Deni pulled out several books and stuffed them in her backpack. "Oh? I had a dorm assignment, actually." She faced her and bit her lip. "Mary Margaret, Mom wants me to get to know some new people, so she thought it best if we not room together. She changed my application, and took your name off, before she sent it in."

She stood there, stunned, staring after Deni. They'd planned this forever. *What the fuck?* "I don't understand."

Deni smiled. "No biggie. Right? We'll still see each other. But there actually is something else I need to tell you."

"What?"

"It's about your mom. Something she said to mine."

Mary Margaret's heart felt like it dropped—with a palpable thud —a couple of inches lower in her chest. "What did my mom do now?"

"Be prepared for her to get you to ditch the art major. She told my mom that neither of us have a talent for it, so why the hell were we majoring in art, anyway? She was trying to recruit my mom into getting us to change majors."

Mary Margaret couldn't utter a word. Art was her first love, her passion. It was the one thing that she was super good at—or so she had thought. No talent? Her goal was to be an art teacher, not a Grand Master Painter. Although she wouldn't put something like that past her mother, why in the hell had she done that? "She's not said a word to me."

Which was true.

"Well, it's what she told my mom."

"Right."

216

"I gotta go. See you at lunch?"

She nodded at Deni, but really didn't even see her walk away. "Sure."

Pulling the college acceptance letter back out of its envelope, she re-read the first paragraph.

WE ARE PLEASED TO INFORM YOU OF YOUR ACCEPTANCE TO attend Eastern Carolinas University beginning the fall semester, 1997, major undeclared. Your dormitory and roommate assignments are forthcoming.

"MRS. SHEPHERD CALLED TODAY. SHE SAID YOU'VE NOT been to your art class in three weeks."

She'd wondered when that subject would come up. "That sounds about right."

"We've paid for those advanced lessons, so you need to go. Besides, you said you needed the extra push for college. Right?"

Mary Margaret went back to making her sandwich, smearing mustard, then mayonnaise on the bread. "I quit. Not going."

Her mother quickly crossed the kitchen. "You insisted you should take those classes."

"Not important now."

"Why?"

"Undeclared, right?"

"Excuse me?" her mother said.

"Because I'm not majoring in art, Mom. You win." She'd actually contacted the college and changed her major to business education. Knowing her mother thought she sucked at being an artist would only cloud her entire college career and probably her future if she stayed with art.

It took several seconds for her mother to respond—for it to sink in what she had meant. "What are you going to major in then?"

Mary Margaret met and held her gaze. "I thought maybe I'd major in spreading my legs for the boys."

Her mother glared.

Mary Margaret didn't budge.

After a minute, she said, "Well, you need to call her then—Mrs. Shepherd—and tell her you won't be back. At least we'll save the cash."

She broke eye contact and turned, methodically placing the mustard and mayo and deli meat back in the refrigerator. "You call her."

"Oh no, young lady. That's your responsibility."

She laughed. "Really? Not." She headed to the family room with her sandwich.

"Mary Margaret!"

Ignore her. Let her fucking figure it out. I'm done.

Maggie heard the front door slam shut. She glanced at the clock. Ten. Home just in time. Curfew discussion avoided. She expected Carol would run upstairs to her room, and she'd likely not see her again until morning.

Okay by her.

The day was long enough already. The last thing she wanted was to start an argument with her teenage daughter.

But Carol joined her in the family room, sitting beside her on the sofa. "Hey, Mom."

"Hi, honey. How was graduation practice?"

Carol shrugged, looking down. "Okay. Kind of sad."

"Oh?" Maggie turned toward her. "What's wrong?"

Carol scooted closer and laid her head on Maggie's shoulders. "I hung out with a bunch of my friends after practice. We went to Luigi's, you know that pizza place? It just hit me, Mom. Everyone is going to be going their separate ways soon. I know I said I was over high school shit—I really meant the drama—but I realized today I might never see many of my friends again after we graduate."

Maggie thought back to her own classmates. "I hate to say this, sweetheart, but that's probably true." She put her arms around her girl and held her tighter. "I wish it weren't, but...."

"It's all gone by fast."

"And it will only go faster. Enjoy every minute while you can." They sat quietly for a minute. "I love you, you know."

Carol snaked her arms around her waist. "I love you too, Mom."

Maggie played with a lock of Carol's hair, savoring every second of closeness. She'd already decided earlier, after rehashing her own college entry experience, that she would not interfere. "Honey, about college. It's totally your decision. I will not—"

"Right." Carol eased off her shoulder and faced her. "Mom, I told Logan I'm going to ECU as planned. It is my decision. Not his, although I respect how he feels. I thought about it today when I was hanging out. I even talked with Sophie, and then later, Hannah. I know you wanted to discuss it, but really, we don't have to."

She searched Carol's eyes. "You're sure?"

"Positive."

"And what did Logan say?"

"He said he still loves me, no matter what. He wants me to go to college because he thinks I'm smart. He didn't have the chance to go."

"Oh?"

"You know, he's really smart, too, Mom. He should have stayed in school, and he knows it."

"Why didn't he?"

Carol released a sigh. "His dad died last year. His family needs the money coming in."

"Oh, sweetheart. I'm so sorry."

"He works hard, Mom. And I know I need to have him in for dinner. It's just that he works so much and he's a little shy. He's sure you will not like him."

Maggie reached for Carol's hand. "Tell him he's welcome here anytime. Maybe we need to start over."

Nineteen

"And that's why I painted myself like I did." Chloe smiled and her classmates clapped. The Monday morning selfie art project show-and-tell had gone off without a hitch.

Maggie wasn't sure she'd ever seen her child grin so broadly. When her teacher, Mrs. Anderson, gave her the nudge that it was time for the next student to share, Chloe ran across the room and into Maggie's arms.

"I'm so proud of you," Maggie whispered into her ear. "You are a beautiful artist."

Chloe hugged her tight. "I love you so much, Mommy."

Her heart swelled bigger than her chest wall. Could people actually see that? "Oh, sweet girl, I love you too. More than anything."

Chloe tilted her head and looked into Maggie's eyes. "Thank you for the glitter. That rocked."

"It absolutely did."

Maggie stood and held Chloe's hand, waiting for the next classmate to share. She glanced across the room and saw Andy Ryan, from the art supply store, looking her way. He stood behind a little girl Chloe's age, his hands resting on her shoulders. She remembered his daughter was in Chloe's class, too.

He smiled and gave Maggie a thumbs up.

She gave him a tentative smile back.

After the show-and-tell was over, Maggie kissed Chloe goodbye at the classroom door and headed toward the exit. In the parking lot, she was about to lift her car door handle when someone called out to her. "Hello, there."

She turned. "Oh. Hi."

He stepped closer. "I'm Andy. From the art supply store."

"Yes, of course. I remember you."

"Maggie, right?"

It felt good that he remembered her name. "Yes, that's me." Pausing for a moment, she added, "Your daughter's presentation was quite fun and unique. Who would have thought she'd selfie herself as a unicorn?"

"Oh, my Anna is definitely one of a kind." He laughed and shrugged. "But honestly, your Chloe literally shined."

Maggie leaned toward him. "You mean sparkled."

"Right."

"Blame it on the glitter."

"Definitely."

Stepping back, she studied him for a moment. "Thanks for your help with the supplies. I really appreciate it."

"No problem." He toed some gravel on the parking lot. "I hope to see you in one of my classes soon?"

It was a question and also a statement. Maggie wasn't sure how to take it. "I would love to but honestly, the timing is not good right now. Maybe in a couple of months."

He nodded. "I understand." He glanced at his watch. "Speaking of timing, I have about an hour before opening the shop. Are you up for a cup of coffee? We can talk art and easels and stuff. Glitter, too. Us second-grade selfie parents should stick together."

"I suppose so." She shouldn't. And yet, she wanted to, somehow. "Oh, I don't know."

"My treat."

Shit. Did he know about the credit card fiasco? About leaving most of her purchases behind—the ones she never went back to get? Surely not. She was reading into things that weren't there.

She was unexpectedly embarrassed.

"That's unnecessary," she quipped. "I have money."

He blinked, stepping back. "I didn't mean to imply—"

"Sorry. And I didn't mean to be rude." She touched his arm. "You know what? I could use a coffee about right now, but I want to make sure we're on the same page first."

A corner of his mouth turned up in a half-grin. "I get it. You're not emotionally ready to jump into a relationship." He leaned closer, his voice lowered. "Love at first sight is overrated, anyway."

Maggie snorted a laugh. "Ha. I didn't expect that."

"I'm glad I could make you laugh."

"But it's kind of true, you know?" She slanted her head, watching him. "I just don't want to get off on the wrong foot—avoid any misunderstandings. Coffee as friends would be great. I'd actually like to hear more about your studio and classes. Plus, we second-grade parents *do* need to stick together, as you said. But anything else is...."

"Bad timing." He caught her gaze. Simultaneously, his right eyebrow shot up in question.

She nodded. "Exactly. Sorry to say."

He took a deep breath and looked down the street. "I get that, too. Hey. There's a little coffee shop called Ma Malone's on the next corner. Hole-in-the-wall but super-strong java. Meet you there in five minutes?"

She grinned. "Alright. Who can resist super-strong java?"

But when she parked in front of the coffee shop a few minutes later, anxiety gripped her. She sat there, staring at the lettering on the door.

This was not the time to start something she couldn't finish. There was too much going on in her life—not fair to her or to anyone else. She couldn't focus on pleasing another person—she had kids to focus on. Because she's a people pleaser, right? That's what the old therapist had said years ago.

Was that still the case? Honestly, she didn't know.

Have I finally learned my lesson?

She drummed her fingers on the steering wheel. "I should just go," she whispered.

Why in the hell did I even agree to this? While it seemed safe at the time—Andy had made it feel safe—the idea sounded extremely ridiculous and a little risky.

She liked him, true, and would also like to get to know him better —but she was not on the hunt for a new man in her life. Didn't know if she'd ever want to be attached to another man, again. She'd sort of grown numb to the idea of it, to be honest.

Take care of yourself, so you can take care of the others.

Julia's words rang in her head. But does taking care of oneself equate to having coffee with a handsome man she barely knew? She wasn't sure that it did.

She couldn't just walk away, however. That would be rude. And if anything, she wouldn't mind nurturing this relationship for the sake of art—his classes and such. Besides, she loved shopping at his store and didn't want to stop doing that.

Friends. They could be friends.

She got out and stepped onto the sidewalk. Andy caught up with her at the door and opened it for her.

They made eye contact. "I thought for a minute there you were going to ditch me," he said.

Maggie took a breath. "I think I almost did."

He smiled, and it warmed her heart a little. "It's just coffee, Maggie."

JUST COFFEE WAS EXACTLY WHAT SHE NEEDED.

Conversation with someone other than her girlfriends, or her children, was very welcome. She'd learned about Andy's daughter, Anna, and his ex-wife, Kate, who lived in Rocky Mount, too. They shared joint custody, and Andy swore it was the best thing for Anna.

Maggie revealed little about Max—just that they were divorcing and that he was currently living out of the country. She figured she could leave the details for another time—if there would be another time.

They chatted about second-grade girls and other random topics. Then he invited her, again, to an acrylics class on Thursday. She didn't commit, but said she'd think about it.

Forty-five minutes later, they went their separate ways.

Maggie eased out a very lengthy sigh once she got in the car. She took a minute to herself, thinking over the past hour.

"Nice," she murmured. "That was nice."

But it was time to get on with her day. Grasping her cell, she quickly texted Julia.

Maggie: *I'm stopping by the storage place this morning.*

Julia: *Sure you want to go by yourself?*

Maggie: *I'll be fine. Yes.*

Julia: *I bet Louise knows things.*

Maggie: *I wonder if they have cameras.*

Julia: *Ask to see the footage.*

Maggie: *What if she refuses? Wants a court order?*

Julia: *Tell her your lawyer will be in touch.*

Maggie: *Gotcha. Will get back with you.*

She sat there a moment longer, holding her phone and staring at the messages. Should she mention her coffee chat to Julia?

No. I'll keep that to myself.

She headed on over to Sunset Drive.

Louise jerked her head up from her work as Maggie stepped inside the cramped office.

"Can I help you?" she asked.

She didn't appear to recognize her, but Maggie wondered if that was true. If not, the woman possessed a damn good poker face.

"I hope so." She crowded up against the desk, getting as close as possible to Ms. Louise. "I was here on Friday. Came by my unit to get some things and guess what?"

Louise's eyebrows shot up. "I have no idea. Find a rat inside?"

She had to laugh at that. "I could smell one, to be sure, but find one? No. In fact, my unit was empty."

She had to hand it to Louise. She held that deadpan facial expression like a champ. "Oh? Empty?"

"Yes. And the day before, it wasn't. Someone took all the contents. Or moved them."

Louise blinked. "Unit number?"

"Forty-two." Louise, the gatekeeper—which was how Maggie was referring to her in her head—flipped through a file of envelopes and plucked one out of the stack. "Oh."

"Yeah. Oh." Maggie leaned over the desk. "Max Oliver's unit. I'm his wife. Remember?"

Louise looked up.

Maggie held her stare.

"You say things are missing?"

"Everything is gone. I was here on Thursday, and it was all there. Friday morning, everything was gone. So, I'd like to see your security camera footage for Thursday night."

Louise laughed. "We don't have cameras."

She leaned in. "Seriously?" She looked up at the office corner. "Then what is that?"

Louise didn't even look up. Instead, she methodically placed the unit envelope back in the stack, then met Maggie's gaze with a hard stare.

"I guess I'll just have to call the police, report this as burglary, or something," Maggie said, pushing away from the counter. She glanced about, as if taking mental notes. At least that's how she hoped it would appear to Louise. "And contact my lawyer, who was here with me and saw all the items in the unit on Thursday, so she can file changes for negligence against your company. No cameras? Faulty security? Broken locks? What is my husband paying you for, anyway? Of course, I might choose to not go the legal route and just post some bad reviews, write a letter to the editor, call the Better Business Bureau...."

Louise put up a hand. "Stop. I'll save you the trouble."

Maggie smiled. "Oh?"

"I know where the things are."

"You do?" This was getting interesting.

"Yes."

"And...?"

"I moved them."

That came from left field. "Why would you do that?"

"Because your husband paid me to."

Maggie's curiosity piqued. Again, she asked, "Why?"

The gatekeeper grumbled. "I found a note in his envelope that said he should be contacted if anyone besides him wanted to access the unit. I didn't see it until after you left. I texted him and he called, wanting to know who was here. I told him it was you, his wife. Then he said he'd pay me five hundred dollars to move everything to a new unit."

"Wow." Max was desperate. "So you did?"

She nodded. "Look, I don't make much money here and I've got two kids to feed. My old man ran off with another woman five years ago. That was a lot of money."

"I understand. So, which unit are the things in now?"

Again, she exhaled long. "I can't tell you that. Strict orders from your husband. He might be an ass—and I suspect he is—but he said if you came back, I was to call the police. Now, I won't do that, but you'll have to not do all those things you said earlier."

Maggie got it. Louise was playing the game, just like women have done for ages. "Look. I'm leaving. But I may very well be back, and if I am, be prepared to hand over the key. I'll deal with my husband."

Louise ran her tongue over her lower lip. "Sure."

She headed back to her car, unsure whether to feel relieved or frustrated or thankful that at least, they knew where the stuff was. Before she headed home, she dialed Julia.

She picked up the call quickly. "Mags?"

"Julia, you were right. It was Louise."

"I freaking knew it."

"But she was doing Max's bidding."

Julia paused. "That's interesting."

"Yeah. So, here's the deal..." She chattered on, telling Julia what had happened. In the end, they opted to sit on the information, especially since the things in the unit weren't going anywhere. At least

227

they knew where everything was, and they knew Max was still keeping tabs on things.

"Not the time to let our guard down, Maggie."

ON THURSDAY MORNING, MAGGIE BUSIED HERSELF IN THE kitchen, thinking over the events of the past few days, realizing that it had been a fast but quiet week. Julia had sold the desk and the golf clubs, and she now had money in her pocket. Knowing that made her feel all-the-more secure. She'd taken some of that money and invested in new phones for Jason, Carol, and herself, opening her own account at the phone store. That was an accomplishment because she had no credit history. But they worked with her and made it happen.

Was she on her way to independence? Yes, ma'am!

The kids were surprised and happy. Jason even hugged her. They all agreed to a "no contact rule" with their dad. "I'll jerk those phones so fast your heads will spin," she'd told them. "And you'll never see them again."

She was pretty sure neither Jason nor Carol would risk it.

Max hadn't surfaced since the storage unit fiasco—which could be a good or a bad thing—but at the moment, she'd take the lull in the action. She was nervous about Carol's graduation next week, though. Would he show up?

They were all settling into their new normal.

She set out a fourth plate on the kitchen island for breakfast. Today was pancake day, she'd decided, with scrambled eggs and sausages for anyone who wanted them. She'd set out the butter and syrup—maple and blueberry—along with ketchup because she knew her kids wouldn't eat eggs without ketchup.

How that paired with the maple syrup, she didn't know. And didn't ask.

Carol came down first, sitting in her usual place. "Four plates?"

Maggie faced her. "Yes. Text Logan and tell him I want him to come inside and eat breakfast with us."

"Oh, Mom, he probably won't want to. He's usually dirty and tired from work, and besides, he's...."

"Shy. I know. But there's no better time than the present. And besides, he can wash up here and get his tummy full before he has to go to sleep for the day."

Carol breathed heavily. "He *is* usually hungry. And his mom has to leave for work before he gets home."

"Then it's settled. Text him, please."

"Alright."

Maggie watched her fingers fly over the phone keyboard.

"Done." Carol looked at her and smiled. "Thanks, Mom."

Maggie grinned back.

The other two kids came rushing in. "Pancakes!" Chloe said. "My favorite!"

"And blueberry syrup," Carol added.

"Yum!"

"Got coffee, Mom?" Jason stumbled to his seat.

"Of course. Coming up."

Carol's phone pinged. She turned it over and read the text, then looked up at Maggie. "He's coming. Almost here. And he said thanks!"

Maggie grinned. She loved seeing her daughter happy. "I'm looking forward to spending a little time with him other than a fly-by."

"I know." Carol nodded. "Me, too."

"Sausage patties and scrambled eggs are ready." Maggie placed platters of both on the island. "Pancakes coming up."

"Goody!" Chloe called out.

Maggie had to laugh about her enthusiasm for food. She wasn't concerned about her eating habits, right now. She hadn't gained weight, and she was eating healthy foods mostly. Besides, she was a growing child. Let her enjoy.

"I'll help you, Chloe," Carol said, filling her little sister's plate.

"Hey, leave some for me!" Jason said.

"Kids, there's plenty. I have more over here on the griddle."

The doorbell rang and Carol looked up. "I didn't even hear his truck." She ran off to open the front door.

Maggie turned back, flipping pancakes. Since Logan was here now, she'd need to put a few more on. Grasping the large measuring cup full of batter, she poured two more cakes onto the flat griddle.

Footsteps sounded behind her, and she turned with a smile. "Hi Logan. It's—"

She made eye contact with the person standing on the other side of the kitchen, slightly behind Jason and Chloe. Her heart jerked, and her hand went to her chest.

The measuring cup of batter slipped from her hand, crashing to the floor.

"Max..." she whispered.

"I'm sorry, Mom." Carol rushed toward her. "He just came on in."

"Dad!" Jason jumped up and gave him a hug. Max didn't fully reciprocate.

Chloe's eyes flashed wide, and she shoved her eggs away. Turning slowly, she looked at her father, then slid off her chair and rounded the island to Maggie.

MAGGIE GRASPED CHLOE'S SLIM SHOULDERS, TUGGING HER closer.

Her child turned, burying her face in her tummy.

Maggie circled her little body with her arms.

"You need to leave, Max," she said calmly and directly. *I will not let this escalate into a scene.*

He simply stared at her, a stupid Cheshire cat grin on his face. "We have some things to discuss."

Maggie glanced from Carol to Jason, trying to gauge their reactions. "We talk through our attorneys. You are not supposed to be here."

Jason took a step forward. "Mom, it's fine. Let him stay. We haven't seen him in months."

She shook her head. "No, Jason. He can't be here."

Max ignored Jason and lowered his gaze to look at Chloe. "There's my baby girl. Come see Daddy, won't you?"

Chloe clutched Maggie's hips tighter. Maggie rubbed her shoulders.

"You changed the locks," Max added.

"On the advice of my attorney. Yes, I did."

Max huffed and cocked his head. "Julia? Huh. I suppose she's doing this pro bono? You women, always sticking together...."

Carol interrupted. "She's good to Mom, Dad."

He eyed his oldest child. "And you! I didn't even get a hug." He spread his arms, urging her to come closer.

Carol moved in the opposite direction, sidling up to Maggie. "I don't want to hug you, Dad. The last time you hurt me, jerked my arm and called me names. Why are you even here?"

"Do you think I would miss my oldest child's high school graduation? I'm so proud of you."

She narrowed her gaze. "I don't want you to come. I don't even want you here right now. I don't trust you."

"Sweetheart, that was a terrible night. So many things were happening. I was out of line."

Maggie snorted. "Out of line? Max, you were out of control. And I want you to leave now, before that happens again."

"Not happening." He locked his gaze with hers for several heartbeats, then jerked away and smiled again at Carol. "I brought you a present, sweetheart. For all your hard work."

Maggie could sense Carol's hesitation. Glancing sideways, she caught the uncertain expression on her face.

"I don't need anything," Carol said. "Mom takes care of me just fine."

Max reached into his jacket pocket and pulled out an envelope. "Here. These are yours. If those dates don't work, just call the airline and change them. Let me know if I need to pay the difference. Come see me in Australia when you're ready. Bring a friend. We'll have fun exploring the Outback."

Maggie noted the name of the airline on the outside of the envelope. *Like hell she would let her go to Australia!*

"Cool!" Jason exclaimed. "Take me with you!"

Max gave him a quick glance, then settled again on Carol.

Her lips thinned out and Maggie was sure she was clenching her jaw to keep from reacting. Carol grappled for Maggie's hand and squeezed it.

Suddenly, Chloe screamed and pointed. "Pancakes!"

Maggie turned to the smoking griddle. "Shit!" She turned it off and quickly scraped up the burned pancakes with a spatula. Flustered, she tossed it all in the sink, then turned back to Max.

"Go, please. The kids need to eat breakfast and get to school."

"They can wait."

"Max, look," Maggie said. "Let's find another time to talk, just you and me. You are upsetting the kids."

"I'm not upset," Jason said. "I think he should stay." He turned a smiling face toward his dad.

Max held eye contact with Maggie, dismissing Jason, once again. "You don't want to talk about things in front of the kids? Why is that, Maggie? You have things to hide?"

"I have nothing to hide, Max. You, on the other hand...."

She stood firm, staring him down. Her brain rolled through any number of things he could accuse her of... But what the hell? She had more on him.

Max frowned. "I'm trying to figure you out. Something's different about you."

If that were true, then she knew exactly what it was. She wasn't up for his bullshit any longer.

"Time to go, Max."

"Wait. Dad," Jason said. "If Carol doesn't want to go, can I come? And can you go upstairs with me for a minute? I want to show you this new video game. I'm really good at it and—"

Abruptly, Max coiled back and backhanded Jason across the face. "Won't you just shut the fuck up, you whiney screwup kid!"

Jason pitched to his right with the blow, then staggered into the back of the family room sofa.

"Get *the fuck* out of my house now!" Maggie yelled.

"Jason!" Carol screamed and ran to him, pushing past Max.

Chloe started wailing, her tears wetting Maggie's shirt. Her little arms clutched tighter around the hips.

"What's going on?" Logan burst into the room. "Is everything okay? The front door was open and..." He looked around, a questioning expression on his face.

"No. It's not," Maggie warned. "Get help." Her brain suddenly flashed back to the night in January, with Carol and Tyler.

"Logan!" Carol shouted. "Be careful. He's my dad."

"Who the fuck are you?" Max glared at him.

Logan stood his ground. "The guy who might take you down if you lay a hand on anyone in this room."

Max laughed.

"I'm calling 9-1-1," Carol said, then spoke into her phone. "Yes! We have an intruder at 358 Calvin Way. Please hurry!"

Twisting away from Logan, he glared at his daughter. "Now, why in the fuck did you go and do that?"

"Mr. Oliver. You need to leave." Logan put a hand on his shoulder.

Max whirled back and swung.

Carol screamed.

Logan ducked.

Max stumbled when the force of his swing didn't make contact. "You little fucker."

"I hear sirens," Jason said.

"Great," Maggie said, taunting Max. "Now we can have an official witness to the madness and since you are in town, I can finally file those assault charges against you from January."

Max gave her a look that could kill. "No need to rush things, darling. I'll be back to finish what I started here."

"I believe that's a threat. Did you all hear that, kids?"

Max glared, then turned and headed for the front of the house.

"Thank God," Maggie breathed. "Carol, come take Chloe."

She peeled her youngest off her and handed her over to Carol, then raced into the entryway. Max jogged down the driveway. She slammed the door shut and locked it, before he reconsidered and returned.

The sirens grew louder. They'd be there soon.

She quickly texted Julia, asking how soon she could get a restraining order.

Back in the kitchen, she rushed to hug the kids. All four of them, at the same time. Logan included.

"Thank God he's gone," she whispered. To Logan, she said, "I'm sorry about all that, but am grateful you came when you did."

"You saved us, Logan," Carol whispered. She looked up into his eyes and gave him a sweet kiss on the lips.

Maggie's heart swelled. She turned to Jason, inspecting his jaw. "Are you okay?"

He shrugged, his eyes lowered.

"I'm so sorry, buddy."

Carol agreed. "Me too. He's an asshole, Jason. We told you that."

He finally looked at Maggie, his eyes misty. "I know. I'm sorry, Mom. I just wanted him to notice me."

"Oh, Jason." She bear-hugged him, holding him close. "*I* see you, every single day, and you are an awesome, incredible young man."

Jason buried his face in her shoulder.

After a moment, Chloe tugged on her shirt. "Mommy?"

Maggie released Jason and redirected her attention. "You okay, honey?"

Chloe nodded. "Got any more pancakes?"

She smiled. "We certainly do. And just so you know, I'm declaring this an official skip day. We'll all stay home. Maybe watch movies and eat pancakes all day. Logan? Can you still stick around for breakfast? Or as long as you like?"

He nodded and grinned. "I can."

Carol gave him a hug.

"Good. I feel like having my family close today."

Twenty

Carol handed Maggie her cap, gown, and diploma, flashed a tearful smile, then tucked her arm into Logan's.

They all stood outside the football stadium—Maggie, Jason, and Chloe, along with Julia, Lia, and Alice—after the graduation ceremony had wrapped up. Families mingled and lingered, taking pictures and praising accomplishments. Some were relieved their kids made it, Maggie figured. Others dreaded the next steps in their children's lives.

Max didn't show up. Julia had told her earlier in the week she didn't think he would risk it, and apparently, she was right. She'd not seen nor spoken to him since he'd come to the house the week prior. She knew Julia was in negotiations with Max's attorney and wouldn't say much until she had firm news to share. Maggie had been so busy helping Carol get ready for graduation, she didn't mind.

Max had requested the Escalade, saying he needed it when he was working locally. She and Julia discussed, and Maggie gave over the keys.

Score one for Maggie. It was only the beginning.

She hadn't mentioned him to Carol at all, and she didn't plan to unless her daughter brought him up—which was doubtful.

"Can we go now, Mom? It's hot." Jason wiped sweat off his upper lip.

"Wait for me by the car. I parked in the shade."

"Me too, Mommy." Chloe looked up and grinned, then slipped her hand into Jason's. "I'll go with Jason."

Maggie nodded. "Keep an eye on her. Okay?"

"Sure." He turned to his big sister then. "And congrats. You made it, dork."

Carol stuck out her tongue. "Like I wouldn't?"

He grinned and nudged Chloe. "Come on."

As they left, Carol gave Maggie a hug. "Bye, Mom. We're leaving, too. I'll touch base before we head to Project Graduation. Will you make breakfast in the morning?"

"Of course." Maggie sniffled and dabbed at a tear in the corner of her eye. "Your favorite."

"Waffles and those spicy link sausages?"

"You bet, sweetheart."

"I love you!"

The couple sprinted toward Logan's truck and, in seconds, were off to do high school graduation things.

"Wow. Our girl has grown up." Julia eased an arm around Maggie's waist. "You okay?"

"Yeah," she said, "how the heck did that happen?"

Lia reached for her hand. "She's grown up in so many ways. That girl has matured over the past six months."

"She had to," Maggie said. "Sometimes I am grateful that she's grown out of that rebellious shit—and other times, I grieve the loss of her innocence, so damn quick."

Alice leaned closer, whispering. "And that boyfriend of hers? He seems to be a very nice young man and kind of hot. Isn't he?"

"Super cute—according to Carol. I'll just leave it at that," Julia remarked.

Lia laughed. "Alice. I thought you were into women."

"Eh." Alice shrugged. "I can go either way."

Maggie smiled at that. Alice being casual about her sexuality was interesting. Her past few months were complicated, to say the least, since her rather involuntary coming out over the Christmas holiday at Tuckaway Bay.

Yawning, Lia stretched her arms. "I just have to say it. That was a really long ceremony."

"I wouldn't have minded it so much if the seats were a little softer," Alice added. "Those bleachers were wicked."

"There's only one cure for that," Maggie said.

"And that is?"

"Tequila on my deck. Or wine. Your choice." She looked at Julia. "Except for you."

Julia laughed. "No problem. I'll own being the resident alcoholic. I bring my own bottle these days."

THEY MADE ALL THE FIXINGS FOR MEXICAN FOOD WHEN they got back to Maggie's, to go with the margaritas. She had shopped earlier in the day, keeping the tequila theme in mind.

They spread all the food across the kitchen island, buffet style—spicy beef, grilled chicken strips, refried beans, Spanish rice, chopped lettuce, peppers of all kinds, green and red chili sauce, mild and hot salsa, Mexican corn, shredded cheese and queso, sour cream, guacamole, chips, tortillas, and more. Everyone helped themselves, making whatever they pleased—tacos, burritos, nachos, taco salad. Whatever.

While Maggie made margaritas on-the-rocks-with-salt for the drinking girls, Julia made a spicy non-alcoholic frozen version with margarita mix, lime, and a hint of jalapeno, and shared with the kids.

Jason was impressed. Chloe wrinkled her nose and asked for ice cream.

Later, with the kitchen cleaned up and Jason and Chloe off to their rooms, the four women headed to the backyard deck overlooking the golf course and settled into comfortable chairs. Maggie brought a platter of nachos with her and set it in the center of the patio table.

"Ooh, these pillows are so soft. Much better than the stadium bleachers," Alice exclaimed.

"I'm really glad you all came for graduation." Suddenly, Maggie realized how tired she was, and propped her feet up on a wicker footstool. *Long day.* "I didn't expect you to, so that was a pleasant surprise —and honestly? I am more than ready for some girlfriend time."

"I'll second that emotion." Julia tipped her drink glass.

"Me, too," Alice said.

Lia sighed. "Gosh. I wish Wren and Willow were here."

"Yeah. Weed." Alice took a drink of her margarita. "But tequila is nice, too."

They all laughed.

"Willow could sniff out a weed dealer a mile away. Couldn't she?" Maggie said. "I wonder where in the hell those girls are. It's been way too long."

Alice put her feet up, too. "What's it been? A couple of years?"

"They've missed two August beach weeks," Lia said.

"Holy shit." Julia set up, reaching for a tortilla chip. "I guess I was too tied up with my own crap for a while to realize."

"I'll second *that* emotion," Maggie echoed, and tipped her glass toward Julia. "And my shit has kept you busy for the past few months."

"Wouldn't have it any other way, Mags."

She tossed Julia a heartfelt grin.

"I wish we could get them to come to Tequila Sunrise this year," Alice said. "That beach house is not the same without them."

Lia nodded. "True. Let's see what the next couple of months bring. Gosh, I can't believe it's June already."

Maggie thought about that for a moment. So much happened this past year. What would next year bring? Obviously, it was going to be a different one for her and the kids. Would they set out on fresh adventures? Or face more challenges?

She didn't want to dwell on it.

Time to switch direction. Not going there tonight. "Speaking of weed, I wonder about those cannabis drinks. Have any of you tried them?" She looked at Julia. "Are they addicting? Just curious if you could try those."

"Good question. And my answer is that I have no earthly idea."

"Might be something to look into." Maggie swirled the lime in her drink.

"Perhaps."

They all sat for a moment, soaking up the silence.

"Hey," Alice said. "Remember last summer when Julia got really pissed at us for smoking pot on the back deck at the Gull Cottage? Maggie, you were super stoned."

Maggie sat up. "And you, Miss Goody-Two-Shoes, were just as guilty—and as high—I might add." She glanced at Julia. "And yes, I made you mad. More than once that week, I think. I'm sorry."

Julia waved her off. "Forgotten. Old news."

Alice leaned forward. "Well, I guess it's going to be up to me to bring up the elephant in the room."

Maggie cocked her head. "Elephant?" She literally didn't know what Alice was talking about.

"Max! He didn't show. Do we know why?"

"I'm just thankful he didn't." Maggie laid her head back. "After the episode last week, I don't care to see him again. I mean, I didn't realize how much I truly despised that man until I turned around and saw him standing in my kitchen."

"That had to be unnerving," Lia told her.

"It was scary, coming totally from left field." She stared off for a few seconds, looking over the backyard. "Man, I wish Willow were here. I could use a toke off a big fat doobie right now."

Lia burst out laughing. "You sound like you just stepped out of the 70s."

"Um, the 90s maybe? We weren't even born in the 70s."

"Sidebar convo!" Alice interjected. "But what about Max?"

"I don't even have a clue, nor do I care," Maggie said. "I'm just happy he didn't spoil my daughter's graduation."

"I can fill in the blanks," Julia said, looking at Maggie. If you want to go there. I didn't want to say anything earlier, with all the graduation hype, but I have some news if you want to hear it now. Or we can wait until later."

Maggie took a gulp of her margarita and leaned toward Julia. "These people," she waved her arm. "These *women*, all of you, are my emotional support people. Share away, please?" She reached out her hands. Alice took one, and Lia grasped the other.

Julia smiled. "There's good news, actually. So far, anyway."

"Shoot me straight, Jules." Her head was getting a little dizzy. *Margaritas, do your stuff.*

"Alright. First, Max agreed to 'no contact' with you or the children until there is a settlement about custody and the divorce is final. He realizes I am poised to file charges and a restraining order against him for January, and for last week, should he violate the verbal agreement. So, you shouldn't have to worry about him coming to the house."

Maggie blew out a sigh. "Great. What else?"

"He's backing off on selling the house for now, so the sign can come down—but he still wants to keep that on the table for down the road. That buys you time."

Maggie thought that was fine. "I hate to think about moving from this house, but I know selling it is likely inevitable. I can't afford it. But you are right, this buys time."

Julia nodded. "Yes. And we agreed to let him have the Escalade, as you know. That's a plus in your column for being reasonable. He also wants to come at some point and get clothing and other personal items. We will work out those details. You and the kids cannot be here when it happens, but I will be."

"What about custody?"

Julia smiled. "It's still an item. We want full custody. So does Max. It's truly unreasonable for the judge to move in his favor."

"I can't believe he thinks he can do the work he does, traveling and everything, and raise kids, too. Idiot."

Julia nodded. "That's one factor. He is ready to play hardball, though."

"Such as?"

"He suggested, through his lawyer, of course, that he wants psychological evaluations done on all three children, and on you. He cited the history of mental illness in the family again and suggested that the children do not want to be with you. That the children have suffered from your instability over the years. I told him evaluations were fine, as long as he paid for them, and as long as a professional of our choosing also evaluated him."

Maggie felt a little tug at her heart. She didn't want to put her kids through any kind of testing. Not that what they might say about her was a concern, but that it might be traumatic for them. "What did he say?"

"He didn't budge on the kids. Refused evaluation for himself."

"Shit."

"He is going to keep pushing it—until I pull the right cards."

Maggie leaned closer. "But we have those cards. Right?"

A wicked grin broke over Julia's face. "You bet your sweet ass. We were on a video conference call this morning. Max, his attorney, and me. I told them you were busy with graduation details, which was understood. I requested a laundry list of things regarding custody, school, college, and sports expenses, plus health insurance, and the like. I requested supervised visitation once a month, if he was in the country. I specifically said the children were not to leave the country without your permission."

"And what did he say to that?"

"Oh, he laughed."

"Bastard."

"But not for long. You should have seen his face when I told him, and the attorney, that should he not agree with our demands, and drop his silly notions of mental illness and psychological examinations, then I would have no other recourse but to bring up the Carolyn Oliver wrongful death lawsuit and his negligent drunken behavior which lead to her death, in addition to the assaults on you and Carol and Jason. And that if he persisted, we would make sure all the above was public knowledge and that his concubine in Australia would learn all about it."

"You really said concubine?" Maggie asked.

Julia laughed. "No. I just call her that in my head."

I can go with that. "And what did he say?"

"He got angry, of course. Said a whole slew of things, which I, of course, recorded. Max's attorney quickly ended the call. Then, about an hour before graduation, I got an email from the attorney. I'll forward it to you later tonight, Mags."

"What did it say?"

"That Max would drop the mental health issues and the psych evals—but only if we agree to never bring up the wrongful death incident and not file assault charges. He still wants to fight for full custody."

Maggie stared at Julia. "He is an ass."

"Of the biggest kind."

"Don't agree to that." Maggie rose from her seat and stepped away from the group, thinking. Twisting back, she said quickly, "I will fight for my kids, and I will not let up. I don't care anymore what he tries to do to me. He can bring up my mother's mental illness and my depression all he wants. I can certainly justify my depression. He can slam me to the curb if he wants. But I will never, *ever*, give up fighting for my kids. I want them with me. I want them safe and secure and loved. I will work three jobs if I have to, and I will take care of them every, single, damn, day. And that is something he cannot do."

She forcibly exhaled, instantly feeling a huge sense of relief.

Alice, Lia, and Julia stared back at her, smiling.

"We're proud of you, Maggie," Lia said.

"Mom?"

Maggie turned toward the house and saw Carol standing in the doorway, Logan behind her. "Sweetheart. What are you doing here?"

"I wanted to change clothes."

Maggie nodded, swiping tears from her cheeks.

"Mom?" Carol whispered. "Are you okay?"

She nodded. "I'm fine. More than fine, actually. In fact, I'm fabulous."

Carol rushed into her arms. "I love you so much," she whispered. "It's going to be okay."

WAFFLES AND SPICY SAUSAGES WERE ON THE MENU FOR brunch. After the tequila night, no one wanted to get up early to cook or eat—except maybe Julia. Maggie took control of the waffle machine while Alice cooked the sausages. Lia and Julia salvaged leftover Mexican ingredients to make a couple of Southwest style breakfast casseroles.

"If Sam were here," Julia said, "he'd be digging into this enchilada egg dish about now."

"Please take some home to him," Maggie said. "My God, we have plenty."

"You also have growing kids."

"True."

Logan and Carol cuddled together on the family room sofa, sleeping. It had been a long night for them at Project Graduation. Maggie heard them come in about five o'clock that morning and decided not to wake them until the food was ready.

But Jason and Chloe were up already. Julia showed Jason how to make the fake frozen margaritas in the blender. Chloe just sat at the kitchen island saying, "Yum!" to every new dish added to the brunch buffet.

"Jason, when you're finished there, see if you can wake your sister and Logan, and let's eat."

He did, and for the next several minutes, chatter filled the kitchen while everyone filled their plates and then headed for the deck.

Once everyone found a seat, Alice set a champagne bottle and a pitcher of orange juice on the deck table. "Mimosas anyone?"

"Seriously Alice? After all the tequila last night?" Julia shot her a look.

"Now, don't go getting all *goody-two-shoes* on me, Julia. Really, now."

"Oh, gracious yes. Me," Maggie said. "I'll get a corkscrew." She set her breakfast food aside and headed back into the kitchen. She checked the drawer where she usually kept her corkscrew, but didn't see it. "Crap."

She pulled open another drawer.

"We also need glasses." Julia joined her.

"Okay." She moved some things around in the messy junk drawer. "I can't find the damn corkscrew." Then her hand pushed aside a stack of plain postcards, held together with a rubber band. Immediately, something gripped her heart, and her breath caught. "Shit. I remember now."

"I bet the corkscrew is still in Max's office. Oh, I mean your studio."

Maggie slowly lifted the cards and removed the rubber band.

"Maggie? Did you hear me?"

"Sure. Yeah. Studio."

Julia stepped closer. "I'll get it. What are you doing?"

She shuffled through the cards. There were over twenty of them. All with the same message. All dated and postmarked June 18.

Maggie looked at Julia. "I'd almost forgotten about these."

"What are they?"

"Postcards. They come addressed to me every year. On June 18. The day Caroline died."

Julia held her gaze for several seconds, then read the top card. "*Be careful.* That's all it says."

"That's what they all say."

"But who...?"

"I don't know. I never knew. I just stuck them in the drawer here. I never even told Max."

Julia sat. "Shit, Mags. Someone has been sending you a warning."

"To be careful I don't end up like Caroline?" Suddenly, she didn't want to dwell on that any longer. She took the cards from Julia. "Let it be. We will say nothing about this right now." She peered into Julia's eyes. "You hear me? Not a word. We'll talk about it another time."

Julia was reluctant, Maggie could tell, but she agreed. "Fine."

Maggie nudged her elbow. "For now, we have breakfast to eat. Mimosas to drink."

"Right." Julia jerked a nod. "Take the glasses. I'll get the corkscrew."

With no further discussion, they retrieved the items and headed back to the deck. Alice played bartender, making mimosas. Maggie sat back and absorbed the banter and cheerful faces.

Nothing is going to ruin this day for me, or for anyone else.

After a while, Lia set her plate aside. "I have something to say, if it's okay with everyone."

Maggie shrugged. "Sure. Everything alright?"

She smiled. "Yes. I just wanted to say how proud I am of all of you. Carol, congrats on graduation and going to ECU in the fall. You know we all love that place, so it's great you are going, too."

"And," Alice added. "You'll get to see my Ella there this fall."

Carol nodded. "Right."

Lia continued, "You worked hard, and I'm sure it wasn't easy these past few months. And Jason? You are such a good brother to your sisters and a big help to your mom. I'm proud of you, too."

Jason smiled and looked a little embarrassed.

"And Chloe!" Lia added. "My goodness. I saw your selfie project —your mom sent us a video—you are quite the artist!"

Chloe beamed, her eyes bright. "I know! I sparkle."

They all laughed.

Lia made eye contact with Maggie. "But you, my dear, I'm most proud of. In fact, we all are." She glanced at Alice and Julia. "I'll not say a lot right now but just know that we see you. We've watched the struggle, and we see how far you have come. We are proud of you, Maggie Oliver."

Maggie almost had to choke back tears.

"But enough of that. I have one more thing—a gift for all of you. You, Maggie, and the kids. I hope you will accept it."

Maggie shook her head. "Oh, Lia. You do not need to do that."

"Please come stay at the Gull Cottage for the summer. It's booked next week but I've cleared it starting the middle of June through the end of August. It's yours. Rent free. Our treat—Zach and me. For you and the kids. I figure everyone needs a getaway sometimes. Right?"

"Oh, Lia. We couldn't." Maggie glanced at Carol, who was looking at Logan, and then at Jason and Chloe. "Or could we?"

Jason furiously nodded. "That's actually perfect timing, Mom. Our last day of school is next week. Right Chloe?" He elbowed her.

"Beach? Yes!"

But she figured Carol might be the sticking point. She met her gaze. "What do you think, honey? I know you would be away from Logan, and he has to work, so...."

Carol looked at Logan again. He nodded.

"Mom, Logan got laid off from his job. He and his mom had a talk this week about that. She wants him to get his GED this summer and then apply to ECU."

Maggie grinned. "Well, that's excellent news, Logan! Congrats on making that decision."

The young man beamed. "Thank you, ma'am. I mean, Maggie. My mom hated when I dropped out of school, so she's happy."

Alice piped up. "There is an adult education program in Tuckaway Bay. You can work on your GED there. I know the person who runs it. But—" She glanced at Maggie. "I may be overstepping here."

Logan stopped her. "I appreciate that, but I'll stay here with my mom for the summer and take my classes in Rocky Mount. I don't need much to get the certificate. But since I'm not working, I can drive to the beach on weekends, maybe?" He looked at Carol, then Maggie. "If I am invited?"

"Of course, Logan." Maggie watched them both, Carol and Logan, as they gazed into each other's eyes. She also glanced from Julia to Alice, and then Lia. "I hear the beach is excellent therapy."

"Best ever," Lia said.

"I can attest to that," Julia added.

After a minute, she finally nodded. "Well, kids. Looks like we're going to the beach."

Jason jumped up. "Tuckaway Bay, here we come!"

Twenty-One

JUNE, TUCKAWAY BAY BEACH

AN ARRAY OF PINKS DRIFTED JUST ABOVE THE HORIZON, teasing at the yellows flaring from the circumference of the sun, while lavender beams pushed through the haze and into the early morning light. The sun lifted gradually, painfully slow, and Maggie wished it would slow down even more.

She took a quick picture of the sunrise with her phone—but knew the colors wouldn't be the same as looking at it with her raw vision. She loaded her brush with a bit more yellow and skillfully slid it along the surface of the canvas—blending the color with a little orange.

Standing back, she viewed her work from a short distance. It wasn't bad, but not the best. *Practice, Maggie. Keep at it. You'll get better.*

She stepped away, bringing her brushes and palette with her, then padded on bare feet across the porch and back into the cottage. After putting the palette in the freezer, she cleaned her brushes and set them aside to dry.

A good morning's work. That made her happy.

Moving back to the porch, she stood against the rail and gazed out over the beach. The sun climbed steadily in the eastern sky, and the colors she'd used a few minutes earlier were lost now, no longer visible.

That's okay. There will be another one tomorrow. Same sun. Different colors.

Breathing deep, Maggie closed her eyes and savored the quiet, the waves, the seagulls calling out to each other. She always imagined the gulls telling each other about snacks left on the beach. *There's bread over here*, one would say. *Pizza on the deck there. An ice cream cone on the path.* She laughed to herself, just thinking about it.

Scanning the beach, she spotted Sam, Julia's boyfriend, casting a line into the surf near the edge of the resort. He was there most mornings, sometimes with Julia. Today he was alone.

The kids would be up soon, although Jason and Chloe were sleeping later each day as the weeks rolled on. Carol would head to The Sandcastle in about an hour for her breakfast shift.

Glancing again at her painting, she remembered the day they left Rocky Mount. She'd stopped by the art supply store, wanting to pick up supplies to take with her—unsure what materials she would find in Tuckaway Bay—and had hoped to see Andy while she was there.

She did not—but asked about him when she checked out, and learned he'd taken the morning off. Her bad luck. Glancing at the counter, she noticed a stack of flyers with the fall class schedule.

Feeling brave, she asked the young girl behind the counter—the nice one, not the crabby one—if she could leave a note for him. Taking a flyer, she perused the class times and then circled the water-color class. Thursday mornings, at ten o'clock, starting in September.

She scribbled her note: *Andy, please add me to the roster for this class. Thanks. See you in September. Maggie Oliver.*

Then she added her phone number for good measure.

Later that day, he texted.

Andy: *Got your note, Maggie. I've added you to the class list.*

Maggie: *Thanks! I appreciate it.*

There was a brief pause before the next text, and then....

Andy: *Coffee again soon?*

Maggie: *I can't, sorry. At the beach for the summer. See you in the fall.*

He didn't respond.

AFTER A QUICK BREAKFAST, THEY CARTED OFF SAND TOYS, beach towels, chairs, and their big beach umbrella to their daily spot —halfway between the cottage and the surf. Mid-morning was a good time to claim their place, although Maggie knew that as more vacationers invaded the Sea Glass Inn resort in July, they might have to settle in earlier.

But today, the beach was blessedly uncrowded. Sam was still fishing, although she knew it was about time for him to pack up and head home. She'd given him a wave earlier, and he'd given the requisite nod back.

I wonder if he'd teach Jason to fish one of these mornings? I'll have to ask him.

Settling into her chair, Maggie closed her eyes and listened to the kids' chatter, while Chloe played in the wet sand and Jason dodged waves at the shoreline.

Picking up her book, she intended to read, but knew she'd likely doze off, or let her mind drift....

Lately, peace and solitude often coaxed her brain into reflection— and she supposed that was a good thing. She needed time and quiet to process all that had happened over the past six months—and what was to come, she suspected.

She'd done some things right. Hadn't she? In all the years of their marriage? As a wife? Mother? She'd not always been the total screwup Max told her she was.

One look at the kids told her she'd not screwed up there, even though she'd sometimes wondered.

But her marriage? She would not blame herself any longer. That was on Max. She'd been gullible, yes, and naïve, but also perhaps lovestruck. And perhaps a little addicted to the sexual power Max had over her.

That was the really fucked up part, though—she'd put him up on a goddamn pedestal, hoping he'd do the same for her in return. Why? Because she'd needed to feel loved—and wanted and cared for and adored. All the things she never, truly, got from Max.

From anyone, really. Even her family. Especially her mother, whom she could never seem to please. But that subject was beach therapy for another day and time.

She'd kept Max up on that pedestal, even when she'd had to fake it. Isn't that what she'd done all those years—fake it? She'd played the game because, on some level, she mistakenly thought he might actually care.

Might love her.

And love *just might* be the thing she had over all the other women.

Somewhere along the line, she'd confused his promise of security, his insatiable appetite for her body, for love.

Foolish.

She and Max had shared an intense, satisfying, and sometimes over-the-top sex life. Max was aggressive, pursuing her when he wanted her. Possessive of her body and jealous if other men looked at her. Maggie learned to play that up over the years. She'd dress sexy enough to please him while they were out, and alluring enough to catch the eyes of other men. Other men looking at her, or flirting with her, would ramp up Max's temper, and his libido, and by the time they got home, the sex they shared would be explosive.

Exhaustingly, naughtily, explosive.

And she had to admit, she had loved it.

He'd had her—and he'd had any other woman he'd ever wanted.

When he wanted. How he wanted.

She knew that early on and had agreed. It was transactional, in a way. That sounded cold and impersonal, but wasn't that really how it was? She was pregnant back then, after all, with his child. Carol. While she'd *wanted* his love and affection, she'd *needed* his promise of security.

As the years rolled on, the kids needed the security, too—and even though she'd wanted to leave him, she couldn't.

Until Christmas—when she found out about the family in Australia.

To be honest, she had to wonder about this woman—this Lilly who had given Max a bonus child. What was it that drew Max to her? What was she like? Was she young, old, thin, or thick? Was she blond or brunette, or maybe even a redhead?

Did she give blow jobs? Like to be bound and cuffed? Consent to a little risqué public display of affection, occasionally?

What did she have that Max wanted so damn much that he gave her a baby for?

She'd never know.

It didn't really matter.

Because when she'd found out about his second little family— that's when she'd known the end was near. When he assaulted her and Carol, she knew then the end had come.

Pushing up out of her beach chair, Maggie exhaled long, as if purging all those thoughts from her body, and meandered toward the kids. Poor Chloe, the tide would take her sandcastle away, sooner rather than later, she feared.

She chatted with Chloe for a moment, then strolled off to the surf and stared out at the sea. She dropped her gaze as sea foam tickled her ankles, and a piece of seashell tumbled over her toes. Dragging her big toe into the sand, she chased the shell fragment, then bent and picked it up, washing off the sand in the surf.

It was a shell fragment, the top of a scallop, pink and a little rosy on the edges. Her favorite shell. A gift from the sea.

Smiling, she cupped it in her left hand, then pivoted and headed back toward her chair and umbrella—glancing up at the Gull Cottage. She waved at Jason and Chloe as she passed and noticed that Julia had joined Sam down the way.

At the umbrella, she picked up her cell phone from where she'd hidden it under her book and noticed a missed call.

A tap on the call log showed an international call—from Australia. Odd.

It wouldn't be Max. She'd not spoken to him since his surprise visit in May, which was their agreement. He would stay away. She'd refrain from pressing charges. For now. All communication was through their attorneys until the divorce was final.

Suddenly, the phone vibrated again. *Australia.*

"Hello?"

"G'day. Maggie Oliver?" The male voice spoke with a distinct Australian accent.

"Yes?"

"My name is Adam Barnett. I'm an officer with the Queensland Police Service. Your husband is Max Oliver?"

What the hell kind of trouble is Max in now?

"Yes. That's right." Her heart kicked into overdrive. She would not bail him out of some stupid situation in fucking Australia. "Until the divorce is final."

His voice lowered. "I see. I'm afraid I have unfortunate news. Your husband...well he was...."

He rambled on, the words dipping in and out of his Australian dialect.

Maggie couldn't grasp it all at first—unsure whether she just couldn't hear him, wasn't hearing correctly, or if her brain could not comprehend. *Accident. Ravine. Air lift.* The rest of his speech fell into an abyss of incoherent sentences and misplaced phrases.

Deceased.

A sharp pain pierced her left palm, and she looked down at it—blood. She was still holding the shell fragment, and she'd squeezed it so tight she'd cut herself.

Deceased?

For a moment, her world was quiet. Still. Frozen in time.

"Mrs. Oliver?" the man on the phone queried.

Then abruptly, her world spun, and all the breath left her lungs, exited her body, squeezing her chest against her backbone. Lights sparked behind her eyes. She looked at Chloe, still playing with water and sand. Paying no attention to her. She glanced at the cottage and saw Carol step off the porch.

"Oh, God. No." Maggie fell to her knees in the sand. Had she screamed the words? Or were they only in her head?

Jason ran to her. "Mom?"

Peripherally, she saw Chloe sitting there, watching, staring.

Sam rushed up, calling her name. "Maggie! What is it?" He crouched in front of her, examining her left palm. "You're bleeding."

Julia shouted. "What happened? Mags?"

"Shell," she said. "I'm. Okay."

"Mom!" Carol's voice came from behind Sam. "What's happening? Are you okay?"

"I... I..." She met Carol's gaze. How could she tell her?

How could she tell any of them? That their father....

She searched for Jason's eyes.

"Oh, God... I'm so...sorry." She whispered the words, almost choking them out... Couldn't hold back her tears any longer. She wasn't crying for her. Or for Max. She was crying for them.

Carol sat beside her. "I'm here, Mom. What is it?"

She held out the phone. "Australia."

The look on Carol's face told her she understood that something was wrong. Carol took the phone and put it to her ear. "Hello? Is anyone there?"

Maggie watched her facial expression. Her girl remained surprisingly deadpan.

"Yes," she said. "I understand. No, no. That was my mother. I'm Max Oliver's daughter." Carol held her gaze while she listened for another minute or so.

Maggie wasn't sure anything could break that connection.

Carol lowered the phone and looked at Jason. "It was...about Dad."

"Oh, God," Julia uttered, and hugged Maggie.

"What's happening?" Jason said. "Carol?"

Tears dripped over her lower lids. "He's gone, Jason," she whispered.

He moved closer. "What? Where?"

She tossed the phone and embraced him, throwing her arms around his neck. "He's...gone. He...died."

Maggie's heart burned, ached.

Chloe's little hand found hers.

THE DAY MAX TOLD HER THEY WOULD HAVE A ONE-SIDED, open marriage, meaning *he* was free to do as he wished but not her, was not the day worst day of Maggie's life. She'd accepted that reality and had adapted.

Nor was it the day she'd learned he had a second family in Australia. That was difficult, but didn't destroy her. By then, she was nearly oblivious to his indiscretions—although his having another child had proven somewhat challenging to accept.

The day she'd told her children their father had left them. That their lives were about to change forever. That day, her heart had shattered. For them. The kids. Not her. And she'd cursed every fiber of his cowardly ass for hurting them.

But just like Maggie, the children had coped and adjusted.

All of those days were not good days.

The day her kids learned their father had died, however—that he was truly never coming back—that was the day that burned a hole in her heart.

Her kids were confused. Conflicted. Wondering whether they should be sad, angry, or relieved.

They loved him, and they didn't.

They needed him, and they didn't.

They missed him. And they didn't.

They didn't want him to die...just maybe go away and leave them alone.

To be honest, that's how Maggie felt, too. *Should I be sad and upset? Or feel relieved and celebrate? What a terrible thought.*

He didn't have to die. She just wanted him to let her—*let them*—go.

"I DIDN'T EXPECT SOMETHING LIKE THIS WOULD AFFECT ME so," she said later, the evening that they learned Max had died. Lia and

Julia and Alice had been by her side—had been there for all of them—since they'd gotten the news.

The women claimed the front porch of the Gull Cottage. She'd offered margaritas, but no one was interested. Maybe she'd have a glass of wine later. To be honest, Maggie felt at loose ends, unsure which way to turn. For a while, they sat in relative silence, while she simply let her mind waft over this sudden and new reality.

She was worried about the kids.

Logan drove in from Rocky Mount as soon as Carol called him. Her oldest child was holding up extremely well, she thought, but Logan's coming had done wonders to boost her spirits. Ella came with Alice, too, which was also nice. The older kids, including Jason, had taken up residence on the back deck of the cottage. She was glad. Jason needed to spend more time with the older ones. Lia ordered pizza from The Sandcastle.

Chloe, who had been mostly silent, showed little visible response or emotion to the news. That worried Maggie. She was out for ice cream with Sam and Zach now, and no doubt they would spoil her. She wondered if she'd open up to either of them but doubted it.

I need to spend extra time with all three before bed.

Oddly, she couldn't stop thinking about Lilly, Max's mystery lover. Did she know what happened? Had the police contacted her? Did Max have her contact information on him, as well as hers? How very...cozy.

This Lilly... She could be just as innocent as she was years ago. Naïve, gullible, needy, perhaps? Or, Maggie supposed, she could be just the opposite. Independent, self-assured, capable of supporting herself.

And if either were the case, then how was she dealing with Max's death?

What did she know at this point? About the accident? About his family in the states. His wife and kids. Did she even know anything at all?

While her heart ached for her own children, and for herself—she *had* spent over twenty years with the man—but her heart also ached for Lilly, and her child.

"Maggie?" Lia asked. "Are you okay over there?"

She dragged her gaze away from the beach and slowly angled toward the other women. "Sure. I'm fine. Just thinking."

"Definitely lost in thought, there."

She was, but probably not about what they were thinking.

"I know." She turned to Julia. "My brain can't handle a lot of details today, but what does this mean for us now? The kids and me."

"We need to see if he has a will and go from there."

Alice shifted in her chair. "Oh, good grief. Surely, he had a will?"

"You never know," Julia said. "Sometimes people get so busy with life, they don't think about death. I'll contact Max's attorney tomorrow and see what I can find out."

Maggie was a little concerned. Not once had Max mentioned a will. Then she realized. "I don't have a will. I'm betting Max didn't either."

Julia blew out a breath. "Well, we need to fix that for you ASAP. In the meantime, I'll dig into North Carolina law regarding the death of a spouse, and what all that entails, with or without a will. I also want to see how separation affects things."

"Fuck. Is this going to be complicated?"

Julia leaned forward, reaching for Maggie's hand. "Stop guessing about anything until we know more. Have some details. I promise you will be okay, no matter what."

She believed her. Truly, she did. But still... "Obviously, I don't need to worry about the kids or the house right now. Do I? Maybe money? Remember, I am not on his accounts."

"The will, or lack of one, should make things clear." She peered into her eyes. "Maggie, listen to me. Today is not the day to worry. Just absorb what has happened and let me be concerned with the details."

"Tomorrow, or the next," Maggie said. "No hurry, I guess."

"Right."

She wasn't sure Julia was being straight with her. She stared off over the beach again. "How do I get him home?"

Julia stood. "You're worrying about things that can wait."

She could sense her frustration rising. "Look. If there is something

I need to do, I need to take care of it. Stop coddling me. Okay? I should call that officer back." She rose and turned toward the cottage door. She'd left her phone in the bedroom, she thought.

"Wait, Maggie. I already called."

She glared at Julia. "What?"

"I borrowed your phone earlier and made a call back to the officer and got the details. It will be days before the officials can process the body and ready it to transport back to the states—seven to ten days, likely. We can coordinate all that with a funeral home in Rocky Mount."

"Did you find out anything more about the accident?"

Julia nodded. "Yes, some things. It was a helicopter crash. Apparently, it went down in the Northern Territory of the Outback. Very remote. Took days to get to him and the pilot, who also died. Likely, Max didn't pass away in the crash, but succumbed much later from his broken legs and loss of blood. He lingered there a while, apparently, and was probably in a lot of pain."

"Shit," Alice said.

"Oh, that's terrible," Lia echoed.

Maggie didn't want to ponder that. She straightened her shoulders. "I should call his parents. My God, I didn't even think to do that."

Alice intervened. "Maggie, I'll do that. Listen to Julia."

"No. I have to." She turned back to the house. "Good Lord, I haven't spoken to them in years. I don't think Max had either. I'm not fond of them, to be honest. Nor them of me."

She caught Julia's gaze as she stood facing her. Finally, Julia said, "Give me the name of the funeral home you want to use in Rocky Mount. I'll call Max's attorney, and he can share the details with them. You don't need to put that on yourself right now."

Maggie sat in the nearest empty chair. "Just pick one. I don't care. I'm braindead."

Lia hugged her shoulders. "Just let it all settle tonight, Maggie. Let Julia do her lawyer thing on your behalf, and you let things happen as they will. There's really nothing more for you to do tonight but take care of yourself."

Maybe. And maybe not. She felt like there were probably some things she should *do*. "I don't know if I can."

"Be here for the kids. That's good for now."

Yes, yes. I will do that, of course. But there is more. More that I have to do—not for the kids, but for myself. Things I need to know.

Julia leaned toward her. "I can see if Melinda, my therapist, can schedule a call with you."

No. I don't want therapy. I want answers. "Thanks, Julia, but no. Not now. Maybe later."

Julia nodded. "Okay."

"There's something else I have to do first."

Alice touched her hand. "What is it, Maggie?"

I think I need to go to Australia.

She thought about telling her—telling them all—but didn't want them to talk her out of it. Besides, this was something she knew she had to do for herself. And probably by herself.

Unless she could talk Carol into going with her?

That thought warmed her heart somehow, even at the end of this horribly, tragic day.

Maggie clasped Alice's hand. "Nothing for you to worry about, Alice. Just something I need to handle on my own."

Twenty-Two

Lilly looked into her rearview mirror to check on Leo, who was blessedly asleep in the backseat. She had adjusted the mirror in such a way so she could peek at him easily while driving, rather than turn around. While that rendered her rearview mirror practically useless, she felt better being able to see him. She'd learned to effectively use her side mirrors ever since Leo was born.

Glancing at Poppy seated to her left, she smiled as the older woman's head bobbed with each dip in the road. Lilly wasn't surprised. She'd started yawning not long after they'd left Poppy's apartment. The morning sun warmed her side of the car, too, which would lull anyone back to sleep.

The wheels of her Mazda droned against the pavement, providing a backdrop beat to the thoughts rolling through her head. Lilly flexed her fingers and then gripped the steering wheel, as if holding on tighter would keep herself in check. The past weeks had been a bit of a nightmare, and it was time to get out of town for a few days. Her emotional self needed rest, and her physical body craved safety and security.

She'd been uneasy after her encounter with Max at his condo—the morning she'd discovered the other woman there. Uneasy enough to hurry home and make sure all the doors and windows to the house were secure. After the day he'd grabbed her face in the bedroom, and the subtle threats he'd tossed at her the following day, she didn't want to feel vulnerable.

But she *felt* vulnerable. And she would not sit around and wait for him to embolden himself to take more serious action. The locksmith came that day—she'd called and gladly paid extra for a rush job. He changed all the locks and installed a new security system with cameras.

Max badgered her by phone and text for days, wanting her to meet him so they could talk. When she didn't respond to his texts, he started calling, leaving messages and demanding she call him back. When that didn't get the action he apparently wanted, the gifts started arriving—roses, chocolates, her favorite wine, lingerie....

That's when her vulnerability quickly morphed from concern into panic.

Max's next move, she felt certain, would be to arrive at her doorstep.

And she was right.

He showed up early, pounding on the downstairs door and demanding she let him in to see Leo, shouting threats, and cursing the fact that his keys wouldn't work, nor his security code. She called the local police. He left before they arrived, but she gave the officers all of Max's information—how and where to find him, his phone number, and his business.

That's when she left... Heading to the bush to visit Freya. She convinced Poppy to come with her.

They all needed a break, she'd argued.

Poppy had said no originally, oblivious to all that was going on. "You need time with your friend. Go visit Freya and have fun. I'll rest at my place while you're gone. Dibble-dabble in this and that. Unless you want me to house sit for you."

"Oh no. I don't want you at my place. I want you to come with me."

Poppy still hesitated. But when Lilly finally told her the reason—told her more about what Max had done—Poppy agreed and was happy to do so.

"That man needs to be dragged by a team of horses into the Outback and left to die over a nest of brown snakes."

Lilly laughed. "I think that's a bit harsh, isn't it?"

"Humph. They did that in the old days."

"Maybe in the movies, Poppy."

But whatever got Poppy to come with her, Lilly was grateful. She wasn't sure what Max was capable of, and if he thought Leo could be at her apartment for any reason, she wanted to avoid a scene if he showed up there. She also wanted to keep Poppy safe, and didn't know what she would do if anything happened to her.

Lilly was frightened, she had to admit. Frightened of Max, and his behavior, and of what he might do next.

How in the bloody hell did I get here?

She'd ignored the red flags. Hadn't she?

NEARLY AN HOUR LATER, POPPY YAWNED AND STRETCHED, angling her body toward Lilly. "Are we close?"

"I think so. Freya said the farm is an hour out of Brisbane, and we've been driving for about that long, so we should start watching for the station sign."

"Good."

"She is looking forward to seeing us. I wouldn't be surprised if she's put on a spread for us."

"I could use some tucker about now," Poppy said, laughing.

Lilly had to chuckle as well. Poppy and her food fetish.

"What's the name of her farm again?"

"Ballymore Station."

"Sounds Irish."

"I believe it is. There's some history there, I think. Maybe Freya will share with us."

Poppy nodded, watching the side of the road. "On my side or yours?"

"Should be yours."

"Then there it is," she said, pointing, then reading the sign. "Bally-more, Cattle and Sheep Station, Freya and Nate O'Brien. Well."

Lilly pulled off the road and crossed the stock grid at the entrance. She glanced in the back again at Leo, who was fussing and squirming a little. "Well?"

"I like her husband already."

"That so, eh?"

Poppy grinned. "Her name's on the sign and he put her first. Dare say you don't see that a lot in these parts. Bloody blokes."

Lilly grinned and traveled down the farm road. Ever since Poppy had left her husband back at Min Min, she'd been down on blokes. "The house looks to be set back a ways here."

"Probably around that curve."

And it was. Lilly pulled up to a very large old home, settled between outbuildings, a veggie patch, and a couple of barns. She noticed a sheep shearing shed and shearers' quarters out back of it. A smaller house set off to the side in a grove of trees. She shut off the car engine and rolled down her window, sitting for a minute, just breathing.

"Smells like home," she whispered. "Like Min Min."

"Smells like shit," Poppy countered, then cackled. "Sheep shit."

Lilly nudged her arm. "You love it, and you know it. Let's get Leo."

She had barely lifted the boy out of the back seat when Freya trotted out of the house toward them. "Poppy!" Her arms encircled the woman, and she hugged her tight. "It's been too damn long. What's it been? Years, I know."

"Decade or two, maybe." Poppy held her gaze. Lilly thought she might have seen the glimmer of a tear in Poppy's eyes. "You look great, Freya. Just great."

"And so do you." She kissed Poppy's cheek, then turned to Lilly. "And this handsome young man has to be Leo!"

Lilly grinned. She'd not had the opportunity to show Leo off to friends much since he'd been born, so this was rather nice. And she was very proud of her boy. "He's a bit of a chunky sausage but cuddly to hold."

"Yes!" Freya's eyes grew wide. "Give him to me while you get your things, then follow me to the house." She glanced off toward the shed. "Wait. There's Nate."

She waved to him before taking the baby. "Nate! Come help Poppy with her bag and such."

Freya's husband jogged down the small hill toward them. Freya made introductions. Poppy reached for Nate's hand and said, "You put your woman's name first on your sign. Good on you."

Nate grinned. "She's the boss, ma'am."

"Call me Poppy."

He nodded. "I will. Now, where's your bag, Poppy?"

She nodded toward the car trunk. Lilly handed off Leo and lifted her own bag out, then pointed to Poppy's. Before he could step too far away from the vehicle, Poppy had corralled Nate with her arm tucked in his, and they chatted softly as Nate led her into the house.

Freya and Lilly exchanged a giggle.

"Nate has a way with little old ladies," Freya said.

"Charmer, that one." Lilly picked up her bag and closed the trunk. "And Poppy eats it up."

They wound their way on a garden path around the house to the side entrance. Freya let them down a long hall with tall ceilings and wood plank floors—dusty, but this was a farm, Lilly reminded herself —to two guest rooms across from each other. Poppy to the left, where Nate left her bag, and Lilly and Leo to the right.

"Check out your rooms and have a bit of a rest. The bathroom is just around the corner. I'll be in the kitchen—we passed it on our way in. We'll make sandwiches for lunch. Take your time. Come join me when you are ready." She turned to leave. "Oh, and if the breeze is too chilly, shut the windows. The mozzies are mostly gone now, so I like to air out the house in the afternoons when the weather is good."

Lilly watched her friend amble down the hallway and turn into the kitchen, then looked at Poppy. "I'm a bit knackered. If Leo goes down after I change his nappy and has a bottle, I might nap, too. Don't wait on me for lunch or to visit with Freya."

Poppy nodded. "Good on ya. Take some time to yourself. I'll let Freya know."

Lilly smiled and turned into the room, closing the bedroom door behind her.

Leo was cooperative, which surprised her. Tired from the ride, she supposed. After a nappy change, Lilly fed him, rocking him in a chair by the bed. Freya had placed a portable crib in the corner, away from the window, and Leo slept soundly there. She felt comfortable enough to lie back on the bed, let the cool breeze float over her, and maybe doze herself. There was something about country air that always lulled her to sleep—maybe it was more of a feeling, a sense of security—but no matter, she soon drifted off.

A stiffer breeze blew into the room, lifting the curtains from the windows, and she aimlessly reached for a coverlet at the foot of the bed, tugging it up around her.

There. Perfect.

With a deep sigh, her body, and her mind, slowly relaxed....

The pounding on the door wouldn't stop. Lilly rose from the bed and headed toward it, but it seemed she was walking in quicksand. Her feet were heavy, dragging against the sandy plank floors, and it was difficult to walk. The pounding reverberated through her skull.

My God, would it please just stop? *I'm coming!*

"Lilly! Let me in."

Max? He wants in? What is he doing here? No.

"Lilly! I want to see Leo."

No. No. I won't let him.

"Max, stop. You're waking the baby. Leave us alone." She glanced in the corner at the crib where Leo was sleeping. He was standing up in the crib, holding onto the side, looking at her.

Sit down, Leo! You can't stand yet. What are you doing?

"I will never leave you alone, Lilly. Get that through your skull. You have my son."

She whipped around, looking at the closed door. Yelling through it. "You don't deserve a child, Max. You're too self-centered."

"Don't tell me what I deserve. I'm the one who tells you."

"What a pig-headed ass you are!"

Mommy? Daddy.

Leo. She turned his way again, but now the crib was by the window. The breeze blew the curtains straight up until they almost touched the ceiling. The mosquitoes swept in, landing in droves on her arms and biting.

She batted at the pesky creatures.

Mommy!

Leo! Covered with mozzies! She tried to run to him. Her feet were stuck in the sand, sucking her back. *Leo!*

"Come on, baby. Come with me, Lilly. I'll take care of you, and you and Leo will never want for anything."

"But you still get to bloody fuck around. Right?"

"But you'll have everything you need. Leo too."

"You mean that really works on women?"

"Some women. Yes, it does. It worked on my ex."

No. No! "No. Not on me. Go away!"

The pounding stopped. Lilly quickly rotated toward the door and the absence of sound. Then back to the crib when she heard Leo call out.

Max was in the window, reaching for Leo. Leo reached for him. *Daddy!*

Max tugged him toward the window, smiling at her. "See, I always get my way."

"No!"

She reached for her legs, trying to pry her feet free, pounding her fists on her useless limbs. She was stuck. *Goddamn it!*

"Leo!"

Max pulled him all the way through the window. The wind and the mozzies carried them both away, tumbling with the twirling gale, like Almira Gulch carrying Toto off on her bicycle in the Wizard of Oz.

Lilly jolted up in bed and screamed. "No! Leo!"

Footsteps rushed down the hallway. "Lilly!" Poppy burst into the room with Freya on her heels. "What is it?"

She was breathing too hard, too fast. "Leo. Is he there?"

Freya went to the bed. "He's sleeping. I don't know how, but he is. Are you okay?"

Lilly tried to slow her breathing. She knew if she couldn't, she'd hyperventilate soon and get lightheaded. "Fine. Dream."

Poppy sat on the edge of the bed and put her arms around her. "Maybe a nightmare."

"Maybe." She laid her head on Poppy's shoulder.

Freya sat on the other side of the bed. "Don't mind saying you gave us a bit of a fright. What was that dream about?"

Lilly shook her head. "Maybe later."

"Alright."

She wound her arms around Poppy's thick waist. "Stay a minute?"

Poppy nodded against her, smoothing Lilly's hair with a free hand. "Always."

"NATE. TELL US ABOUT BALLYMORE," POPPY SAID LATER that evening, after they'd finished tea and kitchen cleanup. They'd settled in the O'Brien's casual family room, finishing their meal with cups of tea and conversation. The television was on in the background.

Freya turned down the sound. "We usually watch the evening news after tea, to stay up on the weather and other goings on in the area but let me turn that sound down for now."

"Whatever works for you, Freya. We don't want to interrupt your routine," Lilly said.

"But I *do* want to know about Ballymore, Nate," Poppy pointed out.

"Of course." Nate shifted in his seat. "It's a family station. We've been running cattle and sheep over this land for nearly one-hundred-and-fifty years. The O'Briens claimed it in the late 1800s, and we've been on the land ever since."

"How much land?" Poppy inquired.

"About eighteen-thousand square kilometers, give or take."

"Whew!" Poppy said. "That's a fair piece to muster up cattle and sheep on."

Freya smiled. "We manage."

"I bet there are stories here," Lilly said.

"Oh, for sure." Nate laughed. "Maybe we'll get into some of them later this week."

Freya turned to the television. "Oh, look. Mind if I turn this up? Looks like there is news about that chopper that went down in the Northern Territory a couple of days ago." She turned up the sound.

"No problem." Lilly fussed with Leo while she listened.

The television anchor droned on....

"We have an updated report on the missing helicopter that went down in the Northern Territory earlier in the week. After locating the crash scene by air this morning, a rescue and recovery team hiked into the ravine to search for survivors. One crew member and one passenger were on board the chopper, with both found deceased at the site of the wreckage."

"Oh no. Those chopper accidents are never good," Poppy said.

"Territory up there is rough." Nate scooted to the edge of his seat, listening. "They've been trying to find 'em for a few days."

Lilly bounced Leo on her knee, smiling at her boy.

The anchor continued. "The helicopter pilot, Jack Roberts, owned an adventure excursion company out of Melbourne. His passenger, a business partner from the states currently living in Brisbane, was Maxwell Oliver. Mr. Oliver leaves behind a wife and three children in North Carolina, U.S.A."

Lilly lifted her gaze and stared at the television set. "What?"

Poppy turned toward her, wide-eyed. "That your man?"

"Leo's dad?" Freya echoed.

"I... I think so. What was said, exactly?"

Freya moved across the room to sit next to Lilly. "He said the man's name was Maxwell Oliver. Is that your Max?"

"Yes. And, but no... What did he say about a wife and...."

Nate stood, letting go of a lengthy breath. "Let me see if I can find out more information." He left the room.

Poppy joined Lilly and Freya. "I heard what he said clearly," she told her. "He said that Max left behind a wife and three children in the states."

Lilly sat stunned, shaking her head—but to her surprise, remained calm. "That bloody mongrel."

Freya took her hand. "Oh, Lilly. I'm so sorry."

"He's dead?" The reality was sinking in. "I really should be more upset. Shouldn't I?"

Poppy took Leo, holding him on her lap. "He was a pig-headed arse. So, he's dead. Good on him. I don't feel sorry for you or Leo or his family. Instead, I feel better."

Just like Poppy to put it out there like she saw it.

"I don't understand," Freya said.

Lilly clasped her hand tighter. "The reason I wanted to visit is because I caught Max with another woman, and he was getting a little..." She wasn't sure what the word was she wanted to use.

"Mean and nasty." Poppy stared at Lilly. "Like bloody blokes do sometimes. I call it like it is. You're better off, and so is Leo."

Twenty-Three

It took ten days for Max's remains to get home from Australia and another three before they held his memorial. Maggie had him cremated before being shipped to the states, because of the condition of the body when he was found in the ravine—and frankly, she hadn't wanted to look at him one more time, anyway.

His parents were not pleased with her decision.

That's when she told them that everything else was on them. Memorialize him however they wanted. Bury him, or display him on their mantel, whatever they wanted to do. She wanted nothing to do with making the plans or footing the bill or keeping his goddamn ashes safe.

She was done with Maxwell Oliver, once and for all.

She figured they'd balk at the expense—to her surprise, they didn't.

Thank God.

She and the children stayed for the entire memorial at the funeral home, then went to the graveside service. Chloe was twitchy and anxious, but quiet. Jason and Carol were awkwardly silent, too. Both shed a few tears but, mostly, remained composed, holding their shit together.

She couldn't imagine how difficult it all was for them.

On second thought, she'd likely be the same upon her own mother's death.

How do I really feel? Am I sad? Relieved? Indifferent?

The emotions were elusive and ethereal.

Julia—*good friend that she is*—was at her side the entire time. As they were leaving the graveside, a man in a suit stepped up to them. "Maggie Oliver, I assume?"

"Yes?"

Julia intervened. "Maggie, this is Jonathan Murray, Max's attorney." She looked at him. "I didn't realize you would be here today."

He gave a quick nod. "I was hoping to speak with Ms. Oliver."

Maggie could tell Julia was uneasy. She looked at her, then glanced at the children. "Kids, why don't you all go on to the car? I'll be there in a minute."

"Sure, Mom." Carol put an arm around Chloe's shoulders and motioned to Jason. "Let's go."

She made sure they were a few feet away before she turned back. "Julia?"

Mr. Murray continued. "I just want a minute now, to see if you have time tomorrow morning to discuss Max's will. You know you are the executor of his estate. Correct?"

"No. I did not know that." Maggie stared at Julia. "Did you?"

"No." She turned to the lawyer. "Are you sure?"

"Quite positive. Max's former attorney drew the will up about ten years ago. He passed that information along to me a few days ago. Max's parents have made some moves toward contesting it and since he, the former attorney, is the Oliver family attorney, he thought it best to hand it off."

Puzzled, Maggie questioned that. "Wait. I don't understand."

"I think I do," Julia said. "In short, Max's parents may contest the will, and apparently, they and Max shared the same attorney. To avoid a conflict of interest, I'm guessing either Max's parents would have to get a new attorney, or someone new represents Max's wishes. In a semi-nutshell, I think."

"Close enough," Jonathan said. "Could we chat more thoroughly tomorrow morning at my office, say, around ten?"

"Yes. I can be there. Julia?"

"Of course."

"Here's my card." Mr. Murray handed a business card to Maggie. "I'll see you then."

He walked off toward a string of cars parked alongside the narrow cemetery road. As he approached a late model Lexus, Maggie's attention shifted to an older couple walking with purpose toward Max's parents. She did not remember seeing them at the memorial.

Julia noticed them, too. "Do you know those people?"

"No. But Max's parents seem surprised, maybe worried."

She watched the couple turn away and head toward their vehicle. The older man reached out toward Max's dad, saying something. Max's father spun around and shouted. "You have some nerve!"

The woman cried out. "See how it feels to lose a child? How do you feel right now?"

"Oh shit." Maggie turned to Julia. "Can you make sure the kids are in the car and away from this?"

"Sure. Why?"

"I think that's Caroline's parents."

"Oh, fuck. Are you certain?"

"I'm about to find out."

Julia glanced at the couple again. "I can take the kids on home. It's been a long day."

Maggie nodded. "That would be great. I'll be there soon." Good thing they drove separately.

"You're okay?"

"Yup. Gonna be." She headed toward the arguing couples, now in earshot of every word, and stopped just a few feet away.

Max's mother was livid. "How dare you come here in our time of grief? We just lost our son."

"I can't say I am sorry for your loss," the older man said. "We don't want to get in your way here. We just want you to know that we finally feel justice has been served."

"Justice!" Max's father roared. "What the hell are you talking about?"

"Your son took our daughter's life. Now he's gone too. Things come around," the woman said. "And it took its damn time coming, but as they say, karma is a bitch."

Max's father pointed his finger at the man's face. "We paid good money to keep your mouth shut. Keep that entire debacle quiet. The last thing either of us wants is this scandal brought to light again. Now, I suggest you keep your damn mouth closed, or I'll have to file for breach of contract."

"Try it," the man said.

His wife moved in closer to Max's parents. "You know he hit her. Right? He was mean to her. And that day? She was going to tell him she was leaving him. That's why he killed her."

Max's father's face turned red. "My son did not kill your daughter!"

"She was not leaving him," his mother added. "That's ridiculous. Why would anyone leave my son?" She spotted Maggie then, and though she appeared surprised, responded with a sneer. "Max was a handsome man, a hard worker, and a good provider...why would anyone even suggest leaving him?"

Maggie couldn't stand it any longer. "Because he was a nasty son-of-a-bitch? And yes, Mrs. Oliver, you are the bitch."

Max's mother grasped her husband's arm and fully faced Maggie. "And you, Maggie Oliver, are the tart who got knocked up only for his money."

"So that's what you've thought of me all these years."

"That's what he told us. I believed my son," Mrs. Oliver scoffed.

"That's a lie and you know it. I had money. I also worked hard. I had no choice but to take an unpaid leave of absence because of my pregnancy. He didn't have to stick around."

His father intervened. "But he did. The last thing we needed right then was you coming at us with a paternity lawsuit, too." He pointed at the McDowell's. "Those people were already leeching money from us hand over fist."

Maggie glanced at Caroline's parents. Good for them.

"Your son was a scoundrel. Of course you knew that. That's why you always covered for him. Right?"

"I covered for him because I could," Mr. Oliver said. "And because he was my son."

"And because he was sullying your long-standing, proper Southern family name, I imagine."

Mrs. Oliver pushed forward. "You know he never loved you. Or those kids. He wanted none of that, but because you trapped him, we had to do something."

Wait. We? Maggie's abdomen tightened. "What do you mean *we*."

"We!" she went on. "His father and I. You know *we* are the reason he married you. You should be grateful. We insisted."

Shut-the-fuck-up. "Go on."

Max's father pulled his mother back. "We're not getting into that today."

Maggie took two determined steps forward, closer to him. She spoke firmly and directly. "Oh, yes, we are. You are going to tell me what you did, because if you don't, I am going to make one helluva scene. Right here. Right now."

He stared at her, then at the McDowell's, and grumbled angrily. "Fine. If he didn't marry you, I was going to cut off his trust fund."

"Excuse me? What trust fund? Max told me you canceled that years ago."

"Oh, we threatened to several times when he'd come home whining about his lack of freedom. But the last time he did, about ten years ago, I told him if he came back again, I'd cut him out of the trust *and* the will for good."

"You should have."

His mother shook her head. "Not true. We always took care of him because..." She stopped talking.

"Because he always fucked things up. Right?"

"If he married you, and stayed married to you," his father went on, "he would continue to get the funds from the trust he'd been getting since he was eighteen. If anything, I wanted to make sure the grandchildren were taken care of, even if he wouldn't let me see them.

If he divorced you, however, the trust funds would stop." He glowered. "We don't do divorces in this family."

Just staged accidental killings?

Marital hostage taking?

All for money?

Maggie suddenly felt queasy and lightheaded. *Shit.* She took a moment, staring at the Olivers. "So you've been supporting us all these years?"

"Max's business was more of a hobby," his father said. "But it kept him busy."

"And away from home." She glanced away, seeing but not seeing groupings of people still hanging around the cemetery. "How perfect for him."

If Max Oliver was not already dead....

She looked back at them. "You know, of course, about Max's second family in Australia. Right? And his bonus child?"

Max's mother gasped. "You're lying."

"I'm not. He had a lover and a child. He wanted to keep both families intact. That's why I filed for a divorce. That and the fact that he beat the shit out of me several months ago, and he was hitting the kids. And this was your perfect son...the *piece-of-shit* you protected all these years."

"Well, I never!"

"Of course, you never. That's why you had a *piece-of-shit* son."

Mrs. Oliver squared her shoulders. "I always knew you would somehow make trouble for us."

Maggie narrowed her gaze. "Trouble followed your son. I regret every minute that I did the same."

"We're leaving." Mrs. Oliver tugged on her husband's arm. "Come on, Maxwell." They headed for the car.

Maggie followed. "Wait. Just one more thing, and I want to make this perfectly clear."

Mr. Oliver rotated quickly and roared. "What now!"

She stood tall, her shoulders back, her feet planted, and glowered. "You will do nothing to contest Max's will. Whatever he had in that will remain as is. If I get nothing, fine. If I get everything, fine. But you, and I, will abide by it, whatever it is. Because if you contest even one line item, if you try to take anything from my children, I will sully his name, and your family name, from here to the coast. I'll make it public knowledge—and I mean very public—about Max's family in Australia, about him putting me in the hospital last January, about how Caroline wanted to leave him before she was killed. About how he basically kept me prisoner these last damn twenty years—" she gasped, trying to hold back a sob, "just so he could keep squeezing the fucking dollars out of you!"

She exhaled hard—and realized she'd never felt better in her life.

"You want to avoid scandal? I suggest you back *the fuck* off. Got it?"

They stood there. Silent.

"He screwed us all. Didn't he, Mr. Oliver? Mrs. Oliver? Your goddamn perfect ass son? He screwed you, too."

They said nothing more. And she was finished.

Damn that felt good.

Mr. Oliver ushered his wife into the waiting town car, slamming the door shut. Maggie watched the vehicle slowly drive away. He stared at her through the window until she could no longer see him.

After a minute, she looked at the McDowell's, who still stood by in silence. They needed something more out of all of this, too. Didn't they? They damn well deserved it.

"You are Caroline's parents. Right?"

"Yes." They nodded. "We are."

"I'm sorry. I sort of circumvented your drama."

Mr. McDowell touched her arm. "No worries. We were winding up. And frankly, watching you was a little cathartic."

His wife moved closer. "We're sorry for all you've been through."

Her eyes were kind and still full of hurt—even after all these years. Maggie shook her head. "No. I'm sorry for what happened to you. I'm sure Max's death dredged up all kinds of emotions." She paused, looking away for a moment. "Caroline *was* poised to leave him, you know. You were right. And I can prove it."

"How?" Mrs. McDowell said. "What do you know?"

"If you have the time right now, there are some things I want to show you... Or rather, give you."

SHE GAVE THE MCDOWELL'S THE ADDRESS OF THE SELF-storage facility and asked them to follow her there. She called Julia on the way, sharing what had transpired with the Olivers, telling her where she was going and why, and assured her she wanted, and needed, to do this alone.

And could she please see if the children needed food, or anything? "I'll be there as soon as I take care of this."

Maggie knew she needed to bring closure to one more piece of Max's puzzling life.

She pulled up to the storage facility office. The McDowell's parked their pickup truck next to her. She asked them to wait there while she dealt with Louise.

Ah, Ms. Louise. You do not want to mess with me today.

She looked up as Maggie crossed the threshold into the office.

"Good afternoon, Louise. Remember me? Maggie Oliver. Max Oliver's wife. I'm here to get some of those things from Max's unit."

Louise blew out of breath. "I told you, Mr. Oliver said—"

"He's dead."

Louise's mouth clamped shut.

"If you need proof, I can get you a copy of a death certificate. But let's just cut through some of the shit and get on with it. Shall we? Max's credit card payment won't go through now. I'm the executor of his will, so everything will be cut off soon. You'll want the unit emptied and I want the stuff that's in there. Let's kill a few birds and get things rolling. Shall we?"

Louise stared at her, holding her breath. She reached for the envelope and pulled out the key. "Fine. Unit sixty-seven." She slapped the key down flat on the countertop.

Maggie placed her hand over it and slid it closer. "Great. I'll be back."

She left and asked the McDowell's to follow her to unit sixty-seven.

Once there, Maggie unlocked the padlock and opened the unit. Louise, or whoever, had placed all the totes and other items in basically the same position as before. She guided the McDowell's to the left side and turned to them.

"I found this storage unit a few weeks ago. Max never told me about it. I was looking for something we put in storage years ago and discovered all this." She pointed to the row of blue plastic boxes. "These containers are all Caroline's things, I believe. I don't know what is there, but I thought you might want them. There is another one at my house. I will ship the contents to you if you leave me your address. I took it because I wanted to find out more about who Max had been married to before me. I never knew about your daughter. He never told me."

She looked at Caroline's mother, who was in tears. Her father stood beside her, sniffling.

"I'm so sorry for what happened. I know that Max's anger and his drinking caused her death, whether or not he intended to kill her. And I'd already concluded that Caroline had planned to leave him, or why else would she have boxed things up and labeled them like this, and had them ready to move?"

Mrs. McDowell went to a tote at the end and laid her hand on it. "These things have been here for over twenty years?"

Maggie gave a nod. "Yes, apparently. Like I said, I just discovered them recently. Max had stored them away, with some other things I have yet to go through."

"We asked and asked for her things..." Mr. McDowell said. "He would never give them to us."

Maggie's heart went out to them.

Mrs. McDowell faced her. "He hurt you too, didn't he? I tried to warn you, you know."

She didn't know what the woman was talking about. "Excuse me?"

"The postcards. Did you get them? Every year on June 18? That was the day she died."

Suddenly, it all came together. The postcards were a warning from Caroline's mother? "Oh, my goodness. I got them, but I had no clue what they meant."

Caroline's mom grasped her hand. "I prayed you wouldn't suffer the same fate. And those beautiful children..." She glanced at her husband. "We always wanted grandchildren, but it wasn't to be."

Maggie sucked in a breath and released it slowly. "Thank you for your concern, Mrs. McDowell, and the warnings." She patted the back of her hand, then nodded toward the items in the unit. "I can help load these in your truck, if you like."

"That won't be necessary," Mr. McDowell told her. "If all the same to you, let us take our time loading and looking at things. We can padlock it back when finished." He reached in to give her a hug then. "Thank you," he mumbled.

"You're welcome. Take your time." Maggie gave him a quick squeeze back, then left them to their memories and their task.

THE NEXT MORNING AT TEN O'CLOCK, MAGGIE AND JULIA waited for Jonathan Murray. His administrative assistant led them to his office, and they sat in straight-back wooden chairs in front of his desk. Apparently, it was court day, and he was fitting them in between cases.

He breezed into the office after a few minutes. "My apologies. I've a full day in court, but wanted to meet with you as soon as possible. I knew I'd have a small window, so I'm glad you could meet now." He shook both of their hands and sat behind the desk.

"I'm eager to know about the will." Maggie shifted in the uncomfortable wooden chair and wondered if he had placed them there intentionally. She couldn't imagine lingering for a long time sitting there.

He made direct eye contact with her. "Well, things became simpler this morning. We should be able to take care of most things quickly, then get to probate, and settle."

Julia leaned in. "That sounds like there are no complications. Correct?"

He smiled. "The one complication I expected removed itself."

That made Maggie sit up straighter. "The Olivers?"

"I received a call from Maxwell Oliver before court. He and his wife are not contesting the will. We are moving forward with Max's wishes as they stand."

"Great." Maggie relaxed a little. She didn't care what the damn will said, she'd deal with it, but was just glad she could do so without complications.

He pulled out a large manilla folder and opened it on his desk. "Max's will was simple and to the point. Shall I go through the chief points now, then give you a copy to take with you? Then next time, we can go through executor duties."

"Sure. That's fine."

"Alright. You, Maggie, are the sole beneficiary and executor of his property and assets. Besides the house and the Escalade, Max owned very little property. The house is yours, transferrable upon death. No need to go through probate. We will get your name on the deed, and then you can do whatever you want with it, then. We will take care of that soon."

Maggie blinked and glanced at Julia, who smiled. "Okay."

"The Escalade is also yours, as well as any of his personal property in the home. There are no other personal property assets listed in the will."

Julia kept nodding, looking at Maggie, wearing a slight grin.

"Max had no savings, but had quite a bit of money in a checking account. Your name is not on the account, but he made you the beneficiary. He likely has some bills, credit cards, and the like, which will fall to you to see paid. All of this will eventually go through probate, and then you can access."

"I see." She paused for a moment, wondering if he was going to say anything else. "What about his business?"

He looked up. "Yes. Honestly, there are some unknowns there and you might need to do some research. Apparently, he had a home office, and I hope there are records there, and an office in Brisbane."

"He had a condo there, I believe. He worked out of it." She looked at Julia. "And we have the contents of his home office, files and such."

"Good." Jonathan nodded. "There are options, I suppose, but you will want to determine if the business had debt, pay that off, and then dissolve it. Of course, that is up to you."

Julia tapped her fingers on his desk. "So, you are saying he left the business to her as well?"

"Oh, yes. I guess I didn't say that."

"Just to be clear." Julia caught Maggie's eye.

She had no clue what to do about the business. Dissolving it sounded fine with her, but she'd consult Julia. Another day. "Is that all?"

He glanced at his watch, then shuffled through the file. "Just one thing, and I'll do this quickly." He hit the intercom button on his phone. "Pamela? I need two copies of the Max Oliver last will and testament, including the information on the Oliver trust. I don't see them here in my file. ASAP please."

Maggie glanced at Julia.

"The trust. You know Max received funds monthly from a family trust. His father is the grantor, and his attorney is the trustee. Max named his children as the beneficiaries. The money will accumulate until each child is twenty-one years old, and then they each will get a share of the funds. The details are in the document."

Maggie leaned closer. "Are the children specifically named in the trust?"

He glanced at the paperwork. "No. Apparently, Max wanted to leave that open-ended. In case he had more children, I suppose. It's not uncommon."

"I see."

Pamela walked in with the copies, handed them to him, and then pointed at her watch.

"Yes. The time. I am sorry to leave so quickly." He rose and gave them copies. "Look these over and I'll be in touch. We will get started on probate soon."

She supposed they would.

He stood, reached over the desk, and shook both their hands. "Make an appointment with Pamela for our next meeting." Then he was gone.

Maggie clutched Max's will in her hand and stood facing Julia, breathing a sigh of relief.

"Well, that's done."

Julia smiled. "Check."

Twenty-Four

Maggie laid her head back against the taxicab seat and closed her eyes. She wasn't sure when she'd been so tired.

"Mom. Don't go to sleep. We should be there soon."

She kept her eyes closed, half listening. "Wake me up if I doze." She could almost see Carol rolling her eyes behind her eyelids.

"Mom!"

She shot up and looked at her. "What?"

Carol leaned closer and whispered, "Don't leave me alone with this taxi driver. I don't know what to do."

Maggie didn't understand. "What? There is nothing to do. He knows where we are going. When he stops, we get out, get our luggage, and then I pay him. Just look out the window. Tell me what Brisbane looks like."

"Mom. Seriously? It's dark."

Oh. Right. "Sorry. Jet lag."

"It's five-thirty in the morning and it's colder here than I thought. I should have brought a jacket."

"It's winter. But not like our winter. Warmer. It's tropical winter, I think."

"Right, Mom. Whatever." Carol crossed her arms. "We should have gotten an Uber. I know how to do Uber."

"Well, I don't. You can show me next time."

"Great."

Maggie settled back into the seat, eyes closed again. Her daughter remained silent for a moment. Not long enough, though.

"Do you think we have enough Australian money?"

"I'm sure we are fine."

"Do you think the hotel where we are staying is a dump?"

"No. It's a Marriott, so.... I checked it out thoroughly online." *Please, my head is pounding. Twenty-seven hours since we left home, and I need a strong cup of coffee. Or three.* "Besides, it's within walking distance of your dad's condo."

"Do you think we will see a kangaroo or a koala bear? I hope so."

Maggie smiled. "That would be nice. If we get our tasks done quickly, then I hope we can explore a little."

Carol paused for a moment. "Do you think we are going to find anything weird at dad's condo?"

"Weird, like, what?"

"Like, you know, sex toys."

"Caroline Oliver!" Maggie sat up straight and glared. "What the hell?" She noticed the cab driver looking at them in the rearview mirror.

"Now you're awake." Carol smiled.

"Good gracious." She had not thought of finding anything like that at Max's condo, but what if they did? She was going to have to be mindful of where Carol was looking.

Maggie had decided the day Max died, thinking about Lilly and her child, that she had to go to Australia. She had questions, and not that she expected to get all the answers, she wondered if Lilly could fill in the blanks.

But it was the discussion about the trust in Jonathon Murray's office a couple of weeks later that confirmed her need to go. Someone had to deal with his condo and the business in Brisbane. She figured she and Carol could make quick work of packing up his shit and shipping it home.

Fortunately, they already had their passports, and she'd applied for tourist visas for Carol and herself the day after Max died. Those arrived within a couple of weeks. Max's death, and dealing with his estate, might have triggered a speedy approval, but she couldn't be sure. Cashing in on the two round-trip airfares Max had given Carol for her graduation present made the trip that much sweeter.

Her last dig at Max—hit him where it hurts. In his pockets.

"We're here," the cabbie said.

They pulled into the half-circle drive thru in front of the hotel. She paid the fare, and she and Carol gathered their things and exited the cab. A bellman approached at once, securing their luggage on a cart, and leading them into the hotel and the arrival desk.

He stood back. Maggie handed him some bills.

"If you need anything, please call down to the concierge," he said.

Nodding, Maggie turned and faced the desk clerk.

"Name please?"

"Oliver."

She typed in some things. "Party of two, staying for five days."

"Yes."

"May I use the card on file?"

"Yes, please." *That felt empowering.* She'd made sure she had a card in her name before they'd left. While her credit was wonky at best, she was slowly building it. The cash in Max's account, even though it was still in probate, helped convince the bank that she was credible. Maggie had to smile. Ms. Sandra Martindale, the bank manager, had been extremely helpful.

"Your room keys." The desk clerk handed them over. "We have twenty-four-hour room service, and our restaurant opens at six-thirty. There is a buffet."

"Thanks so much. Now, where's the coffee?"

The desk clerk leaned closer. "Just FYI, avoid the caffeine for a while if you can, drink lots of water, get a good meal, then sleep. Hopefully, the jet lag will be gone by tomorrow morning."

Maggie nodded and looked at Carol. "That sounds like a plan. What do you think?"

"Breakfast buffet sounds good."

"I'm thinking room service."

Carol eased out a slow grin. "In our jammies?"

"How else?"

THE WALK TO THE CONDO THE NEXT DAY TOOK ONLY TEN minutes. The weather was chilly, the sun bright overhead though, and the breeze was stiff.

"Goodness Mom," Carol said. "I'm freezing! I didn't expect this."

"I know. Me, either. Let's pick up the pace to warm up."

They arrived within minutes and headed up to the third-floor unit.

Maggie and Julia had had to dig deep into Max's business paperwork to locate the name and address of the condo, and the corporate management details and contact information. She'd finally reached the corporate manager several days earlier, explained the situation with Max's death, and discussed how she could access the unit.

They'd tentatively agreed to meet this week. Maggie was to call when she got to Brisbane.

She called that morning and scheduled a meeting for one o'clock that afternoon.

The condo manager let them in the unit, provided a key along with his business card, with instructions to let him know when they were ready to discuss the termination of the lease—which he also suggested might take some negotiation with the board, since there was approximately a year left on the two-year contract.

Maggie would not worry about that now. Today's priority was to clean out the condo and either toss, donate, or ship things back to North Carolina. She hoped the shipping would be minimal.

"You know, Carol?" She stood in the bedroom, looking at the piles of clothing they'd dumped on the bed. *Why did he need so many things here?* "I don't see much to ship back. Do you? Maybe someone over here could use these clothes."

"I wonder if Jason would want anything," Carol said. "Dad had a couple of cool casual jackets and some local T-shirts."

"Maybe. If you see something you think he might want, put it aside. You want anything?"

Carol scanned the piles, too. "Maybe a jacket, just because it's chilly here. If there is one small enough."

"Honey, we can buy you a jacket or a big sweater if you need one."

"Cool. Let's do that." She scanned the items on the bed again. "I hate to say it, though, but I'm with you. Let's donate."

"Great. One decision made." Maggie folded a few shirts and placed them on the bed. It was weird, but she felt nothing. No sadness, no melancholy, no grief. Perhaps the only thing she felt was a sense of finality. Closure. And that was a good thing.

She glanced at Carol, who was emptying a dresser drawer now, and wondered if she felt the same. "Sweetheart, are you okay?"

Carol turned back. "Why?"

"How do you feel? I mean, this was your dad's stuff. Does it make you sad? Weird?"

Carol exhaled sharply, scanning the items on the bed. "It's his stuff, but really, it's like it belongs to someone else. A different person. I honestly feel nothing right now."

"I know. Me too." Enough said on that topic.

"Let's organize these in like piles and get them ready to box up."

"Yep."

They went to work on the clothing. When finished there, Maggie stepped into the ensuite bathroom. "I'll clean out the things in here. Not much to do but toss the personal care items. We need to get some trash bags and boxes."

"And find out where to donate, if they will pick up, or do we have to drop off."

"Good thinking." Maggie glanced over the items on the counter-top. Aftershave, shaving cream, toothbrush and toothpaste, deodorant... He lived here. Max, her husband, had lived here. And still, she felt nothing. Nothing more to do but toss every single thing.

She poked her head into the bedroom, catching Carol's attention. "I bet there are garbage bags in the kitchen." She bypassed the bed and moved into the large living area.

Carol nodded and continued folding clothes.

After finding a box of trash bags, Maggie removed one, then set the box on a tall dresser. "Anything we're throwing away goes in these. I think I saw a garbage chute down the hallway when we came in." She moved into the bathroom and made quick work of the items there.

Before long, they had loaded up three garbage bags full of items to toss. Maggie lifted two. "Let's put these by the front door."

"Hey, Mom. I noticed a laptop in the kitchen, on the counter. I'll get online and see if there are places close by where we can donate the rest of this stuff."

"There's a laptop? Oh, good. Let's take that back to the hotel."

"Good idea. We can work on that tonight." Carol's face grew puzzled. If we can get into it. Password."

"Oh, yeah. Well, the sooner we are done with this, the sooner we can figure that out, and then we can play for a couple of days." Maggie opened the door and sat the bags partially in the hallway, propping the door open. Carol followed with the third bag and set it there, too.

"We'll take those down the hall in a few minutes. Let's check out those papers and files on the counter.

She stood and caught Carol's eye. "Mom?"

"Uh-huh?"

"Someone is here."

Maggie rotated back toward the door and saw a woman standing on the other side of the bags, looking in. She looked young, polished, and professional, dressed in a stylish black suit with a lavender low-cut blouse. She stood tall—taller than herself, Maggie imagined—and had long inky-black hair.

"Hi. May we help you?" Maggie said.

"Good day... Do you mind if I step in?" Her words were hesitant, as were her mannerisms.

"Of course not." Maggie rushed forward. "Let me move a bag. We were just doing some cleaning."

The woman took a few steps inside the door. "I noticed the door open. I'm... I'm the leasing agent for this unit."

Carol piped up. "Leasing agent?"

"I brokered the deal between the person who leased this condo and the corporation that owns the building. I just realized...."

"Yeah, he's dead," Carol said.

The woman blinked. Twice. And stood still, as if she didn't know how to respond.

Maggie stepped forward. "Yes, my husband leased this condo, so I suppose you knew him. Max Oliver? He is deceased now, so we are working with the condo manager to get everything tidied up so we can negotiate closing out the contract."

"Husband."

"Yes."

"I see." She gave a nod. "I can help with that. The lease, I mean. It's what I do."

"That would be wonderful," Maggie said. "Thank you so much."

"No problem." She reached into her bag, pulled out a business card, hesitated momentarily, and then handed it to her. "Call me when you are ready to talk."

"I will. Thanks again."

The leasing agent turned and left. Maggie glanced down at the card.

Lilly Colling, Real Estate and Corporate Leasing

"Lilly?" *Fuck.*

"Mom. What?"

"It's her."

Maggie sprinted out the door and spotted her down the hall, at the elevator. "Lilly. Wait. Please?"

Lilly turned and faced Maggie as she approached. As she grew closer, Maggie saw the tears in her eyes.

"Oh, shit. I'm sorry," she whispered.

Lilly shook her head. "No. I'm the one who is sorry."

Maggie angled closer and tried to focus. "I never expected to see you face-to-face."

"Nor did I." Lilly sniffed. "I thought you were the cleaning crew."

Carol jogged up to the women. "You're Lilly? I'm Carol. Do I have a baby brother or a sister?"

Maggie slowly turned toward her daughter. How long had she wondered that? Unexpectedly, Carol had narrowed things down to one simple question. She eased her gaze over to Lilly.

Lilly said nothing for a moment. Finally, she took a breath and exhaled, focusing on Carol. "You have a little brother," she said softly. "He's almost nine months old. Would you...?" She glanced at Maggie, then back again to Carol. "If your mother agrees, would you like to meet him?"

She looked at Maggie then. "I'll leave that up to you to decide."

Maggie lifted her chin. "Carol is eighteen and very much a young adult. She can decide." She focused on her daughter then, who peered back with questioning eyes.

"I would like to, Mom. Is that okay with you?"

Maggie nodded.

"Mrs. Oliver..." Lilly started.

"Maggie."

"Alright. Maggie. I am certain that I am the last person on earth you want to speak with, but I'm wondering if you would... I have questions, you see...and I have been concerned about you and the children. I know Max was not an easy man to be with and I...."

Maggie reached for Lilly's hand. "We have things to discuss."

"We do."

"We will be here for a few more days. Just let us know."

Lilly took a breath. "My address is on the card. Tomorrow afternoon? Say, two o'clock?" She looked at Carol. "Leo will be there."

"Leo?"

Lilly smiled. "My son. Your brother."

For the first time that day, Maggie actually felt something in her heart—if she could only pinpoint what that emotion truly was. "We'll be there."

Lilly held her gaze. "Take the passenger ferry over to Macleay Island, then it's about a twenty-minute walk. Where are you staying?"

"Marriott, downtown."

"I'm sure they can point you in the right direction."

"We will see you tomorrow."

The elevator dinged, and the door opened. Maggie and Carol watched Lilly disappear behind the closing doors.

"Well," Carol said. "That was unexpected."

"True," Maggie agreed, turning. "Are you okay with this?"

Carol met her gaze and held it. "I am if you are. I think we need to do this. We both need closure."

"Or maybe..." Maggie thought for a moment. "To open some doors."

———

At a little before two o'clock the next day, Carol and Maggie stood outside the door of the island home of Lilly Colling. Maggie knocked and also pushed the doorbell. Footsteps sounded behind the door and after a moment, it opened.

An older, plump, gray-haired woman stood there, looking back at them.

"G'day," she said. "You must be the family from the states. Well, come on in, then. We have tucker on the deck. Lilly's orders. But I think it's too cold out there." She turned and headed up the stairs.

Maggie glanced at Carol and grinned. Carol pursed her lips, holding back a giggle. They followed her to the second level, where they stepped into a large great room, the kitchen area to the right, and a living area on the left. The wide glass doors opened onto a sunny deck overlooking the bay.

"Wow," Carol whispered. "This is so pretty."

"Do you think it's too chilly to eat outside? The afternoon sun really warms the deck." Lilly stepped into the room, holding Leo. "Good day, Maggie and Carol. Please meet Leo. I'm glad you are here."

Maggie thought Lilly looked calmer, and a bit more put together, than she did the day before. After a night of mulling things over in her head, Maggie felt better about the entire situation, too.

Carol stepped toward Lilly, moving more quickly than Maggie. She felt like hanging back, letting her daughter take a minute to meet her new baby brother.

Fuck. That sounded weird. Reality can certainly take a turn, can't it?

"Oh, I would love to hold him," Carol said. "May I?"

"Of course. He's just been changed, so he's good to go." Lilly handed him over and Maggie watched as her girl smiled and lifted Leo into her arms.

"Hey there," she said, whispering. "You are a bit of a chunk, aren't you?" Smiling, she glanced at Maggie.

"I made sandwiches and salads," the older woman said. "On the deck."

Maggie turned and smiled. "Sounds lovely."

"It's all cold. Everything's cold."

Lilly laughed a little. "She thinks it's too cold to eat outside. Maggie, meet my nanny and long-time friend, Poppy. She took care of me growing up, and now she's helping me take care of Leo."

"Nice to meet you, Poppy."

"And you." She stared a minute, then said, "So, you were the one married to that nasty bloke. I feel for ya."

Maggie stifled a smile. "I had filed for divorce."

"Well, good on you. He was a piece of—"

Lilly intervened. "Poppy. How about you bring us a cuppa out to the deck? Maggie, come with me? Carol, you can stay here or come too, whatever you wish."

"Are those Leo's toys on the floor?"

"Oh, yes. He loves that ball. It's good for him to practice sitting up. He's such a plump sausage, and he rolls over a lot."

Carol laughed. "We'll be out in a few minutes."

They had no sooner seated themselves at the patio table when Lilly started talking.

"Maggie, I want you to know that when I met Max, he said he was divorced. I would never have entered a relationship had I known that was not the case."

Poppy brought the cups of tea and Maggie reached for hers.

"I also want you to know that I want nothing. I'm fine financially and can support Leo. Whatever assets Max had, those belong to you and your children. I do not want to cause trouble."

Maggie paused for a moment, thinking, swirling the tea in her cup. "Lilly, you've worried about all this, haven't you?"

"Oh, you don't know how much. That video call at Christmas? When Carol saw what she saw? I was confused and mortified. But by then, I was in it deep."

"And you had Leo."

"Yes. He was only a couple of months old."

Maggie thought back to that day. "Carol was shocked, of course. She told me the next day. Max told her not to tell me."

"Oh, that was a horrible thing to do to her."

"Yes, it was. But we got through it."

"Do your other children know?"

She thought about Jason and Chloe, and how they'd been oblivious for so long. She was grateful for Lia and Alice and Julia, who were taking care of them this week at the Gull. What would she have done without those women in her life?

Did Lilly have women in her life to support her as well? She supposed Poppy was a tremendous support.

"They didn't at first. They do now." Suddenly, she didn't want to belabor things. "But they are fine now, Lilly. I don't want you to be concerned. Max was never the father he should have been to them. I don't think he was capable. And I'm going to be honest when I say that little Leo is better off without him." She met and held Lilly's gaze. "And frankly, so are you."

Lilly's expression froze. "Did he ever hit you?"

She slowly nodded. "Yes. The last time he put me in the hospital."

Lilly's eyes closed. "I'm so sorry," she whispered. "He grabbed me once, hard. Yelled and said terrible things. Threatened me. Scared the bull crap out of me. Then I found him with another woman at the condo."

Maggie shook her head. "Lilly, that's who Max Oliver was. He was only out for himself. Commitments were easy to break. All he really cared about was money and women. Lots of women."

"I was so gullible," Lilly said.

"Not as gullible as me. I agreed to all kinds of things I never should have."

"How long were you together?"

"Twenty years."

Lilly sighed.

Maggie set her cup aside and reached for her hands, clasping them and holding them within hers. "Lilly, you are young. I dare say you are not much older than Carol, which honestly surprised me when I first saw you... But now that I think about it, it makes perfect sense. Max liked young and vulnerable. Maybe you were easy to manipulate. I don't know." She looked deeper into Lilly's eyes. "But I think you were stronger than he thought. Stronger than me at your age, I'm certain."

"You've endured a lot. I think that makes you pretty strong."

You have no idea the things I've endured... "Maybe so. I'm getting stronger."

"So, we're better off, eh?"

Maggie slowly nodded. "We *are* better off. And Lilly? As strange as this may sound, we share a bond. And I want you to know that I am here for you, anytime."

Tears formed in Lilly's eyes. "An unlikely friendship?"

Smiling, Maggie held her hands tighter. She glanced inside the glass doors to where Carol and Leo played on the floor. "In an even weirder way, perhaps an unlikely family."

They chatted for a while longer, sharing information, and then having sandwiches. Carol joined them after a while, and Poppy put Leo down for a nap. Before they finished lunch, Maggie pulled an envelope out of her bag.

"I have something for you."

Lilly looked surprised. "I can't imagine."

Maggie sighed. "Max left a trust fund for his children, and that includes Leo. I asked the attorney for a copy of the trust fund information so you could have it, and I gave him your name. I can put you in touch with him, if you like. The fund goes to Leo at age twenty-one. The children will each get one-fourth of the funds. It's one reason I wanted to come here, to give you this personally."

Lilly shook her head. "But I told you I want nothing."

"Exactly the reason you should take it. This is Leo's future. If Max could give him anything, this is the best thing possible.

"Take it, Lilly," Carol said. "Please?"

After a moment, Lilly gave them both a smile, and dipped her head in a nod. "Alright. Thank you."

Carol reached for her mother's hand, meeting her gaze. "Thanks, Mom," she whispered.

Twenty-Five

August, Tuckaway Bay
Beach Week

"*Oh. My. God.* I can't believe how much I missed this beach house!"

Alice hustled through the back door of Tequila Sunrise, carrying a cooler and set it down beside the refrigerator. "I have ice and..." She popped open the cooler lid and plucked out a bottle. "I have tequila on ice!"

"Yay! Margaritas!" Lia said.

"And Tequila Sunrises!" Maggie added.

Lia frowned. "Alice, you know the refrigerator works now, right? We really don't need the cooler."

"I like to plan for backup. Remember last time?" Alice popped open a bag of potato chips.

"But that was two years ago, and we got a new one."

Alice touched the hem of Lia's beach wrap. "I really like this. Is it new? The colors look good on you."

Maggie recognized Alice's M.O. of changing the subject. "It *is* a great wrap," she said to Lia. "But you look good in everything." She poked at her own bathing suit shoulder strap. "This feels tight. Have I gained weight? Am I fatter?"

Lia rolled her eyes and gave her a hug. "You are beautiful, my friend. Even if you've gained weight."

"Oh shit. So I *have* gained weight. Damn it!"

"I didn't say that, Maggie."

"But...."

"Ladies. Stop." Julia moved closer to the cooler and looked inside. "Great. We have margarita mix and grenadine and orange juice. Cool beans, Alice. I'll make my virgin versions of anything tequila."

"Well," said Maggie, "that will be the only thing virgin around here." She snorted.

"Good God, Maggie." Julia picked up the mix and wiped the water off with a paper towel. "We've had no virgins around here for a couple of decades."

"With the exceptions of our girls," Alice said. "I'm sure they are all still virgins." She opened the fridge and pulled out a cheese platter. "I guess we're doing snacks and drinks now?"

Lia coughed. "Excuse me? My daughter just had a baby out of wedlock. Virginity theory smashed on that one."

They all laughed.

"True." Alice dipped a chip.

"Wedlock," Julia said. "Is that even a word anymore?"

"No clue," Lia admitted. "Just came out of my mouth."

"Besides..." Maggie dug into a bowl of guacamole on the kitchen bar with a tortilla chip. "I'm betting Ella isn't still a virgin either, Alice."

Alice whipped around, giving Maggie a firm stare. "What? I'm sure she is."

"She's a freshman in college," Julia quipped. "Are you kidding me?"

Alice bristled. "Oh, she's still a virgin. Ella would tell me."

"Right." Lia rounded the bar. "Keep telling yourself that. Who is making the sunrises?"

"I will," Julia said.

They all stared at her.

"What? I can't drink them, but I'm still a good bartender."

Lia touched her arm. "You won't be tempted?"

"Hell no. I don't eat bacon, either, but that doesn't mean I fall off the bacon wagon when I cook it for Sam. I'm good. I promise. Besides, I like to concoct things."

"Well then, sister. Have at it," Maggie said.

"Time to par-ty!" yelled Alice.

"What about Carol, Maggie?" Lia poked a chip in her mouth. "You think she's sleeping with Logan?"

Maggie snorted. "She's on the pill. Definitely. And besides, she and Logan are staying at the Gull this week together, so there is that."

Alice whirled around. "You put her on the pill?"

Maggie laughed. "Seriously, Alice? Get with the century. She put herself on the pill and I bet Ella is too!"

Alice looked stunned, then plopped down onto a bar stool. "I'm still living in Pollyanna world."

"Well, you better get out of that soon because your life is about to flip. How's the divorce coming along?"

"Not."

"Really?"

Alice closed her eyes. "I don't want to talk about it. Maybe next year."

"Sure. Let's just drink then."

Their chatter halted for a few seconds, then Alice said, "Julia? What about Hannah? Do you think she's a virgin?"

Julia didn't miss a beat. "What kind of virgin? The boy–girl penetrating kind of virgin or lesbian virgin?"

Alice blinked several times. "I should know how to answer that, shouldn't I?"

Maggie burst out laughing. Lia joined her. Julia just smirked and pushed the button on the blender.

"Frozen margaritas coming up. Tequila sunrises are in the cups. Choose your poison, ladies."

Maggie reached for a sunrise. "I'll meet you chicks on the deck. Last one there gets the broken lounge chair."

"So, Maggie, tell us about Lilly." Alice took a drink of ice water.

They'd just finished dinner at a popular Carolina buffet, stuffing themselves silly with seafood and hushpuppies, and were contemplating cocktails.

"I'm so full I'm not sure I can even talk," Maggie said. "Let alone drink?"

"Oh, one margarita won't take up much room." Alice signaled the server. "A round of margaritas, please. Make one non-alcoholic." She pointed at Julia. "And make sure she gets that one."

The server smiled and nodded. "Got it."

Julia leaned across the table toward Maggie. "You don't have to talk if you don't want to, Mags."

Julia knew most everything that had transpired, anyway. She'd just not had the opportunity, yet, to talk much to Lia and Alice.

"No, it's fine. Lilly was awesome, actually. She got caught up in Max's shit just like me, but she's young and will survive. Little Leo, her son, is a stinker."

"Goodness," Lia interjected. "The way Chloe loves little Gracie, she will probably be obsessed when she finds out she has a baby brother. Belle and Zach said earlier that Chloe was stuck to Gracie like glue."

Maggie could easily imagine that. "I hope she's not making a pest of herself. I really do appreciate them taking on two more kids for the week."

Lia batted the air. "Oh, piece of cake. Belle's in her element." She stared for a moment. "Does Chloe know, though? About Leo."

"She knows there is a child." To be honest, that thought hadn't crossed Maggie's mind. "Interesting thought, though. Carol sure was taken with him. Maybe I should have her talk to Chloe."

"How did Jason react?" Julia plucked the last piece of shrimp from the cocktail appetizer and popped it in her mouth.

"With the same indifference he's reacting to everything else. Poor child. He wanted his dad's attention so bad—that is, until Max... Well, you know." She didn't want to dredge up that last day Max had popped into her kitchen.

Julia patted her hand. "No. Not going there. This is beach week."

"Do you think you will see her again? Lilly, I mean. And Leo?" Alice asked.

Maggie let her mind wander over that question. "You know, I actually want to see her again. I liked her. And Carol just completely fell in love with Leo." She thought for a moment. "And Brisbane was lovely. I want to go back and explore."

Alice grinned. "Hey, you should invite Lilly to beach week next year."

All the women stared at her.

"Not cool, Alice," Julia said.

Lia fiddled with her napkin. "Beach week is sacred. It's only for us. Right?"

Maggie agreed and nodded. "Lilly is not a beach week girl. Now, would I invite her to Tuckaway Bay for vacation? So she and Leo could meet Jason and Chloe, and spend more time with Carol and me? I'd definitely do that. But not beach week. No, ma'am."

"Of course, you all are right. Mouth engaging before brain." Alice met all their gazes. "So, Maggie, you're still glad you took Carol?"

"Definitely, Alice. We both needed the closure. Cleaning out Max's condo, and then spending time with Lilly and Leo, and her nanny Poppy, who is a hoot by the way, was something we both needed to do. Honestly, I feel good about the whole situation."

Alice looked thoughtful. "So, Julia told us about the scandal, by the way, while you were gone. I can't even believe we didn't know Max was married before you. And that investigation into his wife's death? I keep wondering why we didn't read about that in the papers?"

"Probably because it happened before I knew him," Maggie said. "None of us were exactly news junkies back then. Besides, we were young and busy."

"I guess you are right." Alice said. "Is the estate all settled now?"

"Geez, Alice." Lia punched Alice's arm. "You writing a gossip column or something?"

"No, why?"

"Kinda nosy?"

Alice looked shocked.

Maggie chuckled. "It's okay. We wrapped it up last week. The trust fund for the kids is all set. All four children are beneficiaries of Max's trust fund—yes, including Leo. Everything has cleared probate. I have the house, the Escalade, and the money he had in the bank. His bills are paid, and the business is dissolved. While I'm not sure what I'll do with the house, I'll probably sell the SUV soon and get Carol a car for school. I might consider selling and downsizing in a year or so. I want to let things settle first."

"I think that's smart." Julia's head bobbed in agreement.

Lia reached for Maggie's hand. "It sounds like most everything is resolved."

"Mostly. I still have Mommy issues but I'm sure I'll have those the rest of my life. I'm definitely handling things, though. Funny, though, how the Mommy issues were weirdly connected to the Max issues."

"But you are okay. How are you holding up? It's a lot." Lia gave her a concerned look.

"I'm good. I've had time to reflect, have learned a lot about myself, about Max, and about why I got caught up in his drama. The kids are good, too. Honestly, we're all still processing, and I'm sure we will continue to do that for some time. But right now, I couldn't feel better about my life, and where it's heading."

"And where is that?"

Maggie laughed and shrugged. "I honestly have no clue, and that's okay. I have some ideas, some things I want to do, but whatever happens, wherever the rest of my life leads me, I know I'm the one in control."

The margaritas came and Maggie took hers, tipping her glass to the girls. "Here's to the future. Our future, one and all."

———

A COUPLE OF HOURS LATER, THE WOMEN MEANDERED UP the back stairs of Tequila Sunrise and slowly rounded the deck toward the ocean side. They'd called an Uber to take them home because of a second round of drinks at the restaurant. Mostly, they were all tipsy.

Halfway around the house, Maggie abruptly stopped. "Do you smell that?"

Lia, Alice, and Julia paused, almost running into each other.

"What?" Julia said.

"Weed."

"Are you sure?"

"I am. Take a sniff."

They all did. Alice's eyes lit up. "You're right. Someone is smoking pot somewhere."

"Well, I want some," Maggie said.

Julia held her back, grasping her elbow. "Now hold on, Mags. You can't just go off...."

Lia had stepped ahead, still sniffing. "Wait. I think it's coming from our deck."

"No."

"Yes. Seriously. Someone is smoking weed on our deck."

They all froze for a moment, their eyes widened. Lia gasped. "It can't be."

In mass, they rushed around the corner.

Wren and Willow stood on the deck, facing them. "Surprise!"

"Shut. Up." Maggie stopped stone still.

"How...?" Lia shook her head. "I don't understand."

Julia dropped her sunglasses. "What the hell?"

"What *the fuck?*" Alice clutched at her chest. "You almost gave me a heart attack."

"Good God," Willow said, "it's beach week. Where the hell else would we be?"

"You brought weed?" Maggie gave Willow a smile.

"I found a weed man."

"I bet you did." Julia rushed forward and hugged Willow tight. "You bitch you! Where the fuck have you been? And Wren...? Seriously?"

"And what about the baby? Whose is it? *Where* is it?"

303

Willow grasped Lia's arms. "Slow down. The baby is with Spence. All is good. And yes, she's mine."

"We wondered if you were trying to trick us."

"So when you were sick...?"

"Some of that was pregnancy and some of it was some other health issues that are all taken care of now. I'm fine."

They all rushed together then, chattering and laughing. After a moment, they settled down and Lia asked, "But how? And where have you been? Can you tell us?"

Willow glanced at Wren. "We can tell you a little. Not much."

"See that guy over there?" Wren subtly pointed to a man sitting on the bench at the top of the dune walkway that led from Tequila Sunrise to the beach.

"Yes?" Lia said.

Julia clasped Wren's arm. "He's a cop. I can tell. Undercover."

Willow took a deep breath. "Yeah," she said softly. "We're in witness protection."

Alice's eyes flashed bigger. "Seriously? Like in the movies. Is he like, your handler or something?"

"Something like that. He's kind of our bodyguard for today, and he'll have to stay in the house tonight. Hope that's okay."

Alice waggled her brows a little. "Is he available?"

Wren laughed. "I thought you were married?"

Julia waved a hand and scoffed. "Yesterday's news."

"I'm getting a divorce," Alice said.

Willow laughed. "Alice, you tart you!"

Alice's cheeks pinked.

Julia snorted. "Tart? You have no idea. She is leaving George for a woman."

Wren's mouth dropped open.

Willow shouted, "Get the fuck out of town!"

"It's true." Alice sàid.

Willow put her arm around Wren's shoulders. "We've been gone too long, sister."

Maggie pushed forward. "Enough about Alice's old news. I want to know more about Mr. Undercover over there. Do either of you have dibs?"

"That, my dear," Wren said, "is outside of his job description. He's here to keep us safe."

"Say more."

The twins shared a glance. "We can't," Wren said. "Maybe one day, but not now."

"Can you stay all week?" Alice asked.

"Just tonight. We have to leave in the morning."

Julia stepped forward and hooked one arm in Willow's and the other in Wren's. "Well, come on in, then. Bring Mr. Undercover, too. We have a shit-ton of life to catch up on."

Maggie figured they had a shit-ton of beach week to cram into one night.

Thank God for Tuckaway Bay. And Tequila Sunrise.

Twenty-Six

SEPTEMBER

MAGGIE CHECKED THE WATERCOLOR CLASS SUPPLY LIST one more time, made her final selections, then paid for her purchases. As she headed to the back of the store where the classes were held, her tummy did a little dance of anticipation. To say she'd been looking forward to this day, this class, would be an understatement.

Andy Ryan was nowhere to be seen. Yet. Of course, he would be there, eventually. He was the instructor. She tried not to even think about him. Her reason for being there was to refresh her watercolor techniques—hone those skills again. Maybe even make some friends. She'd been working with acrylics all summer, and now she was ready to move on.

She smiled at that thought. She was, indeed, ready to move on.

In more ways than one.

Four women sat around a large table, arranging their table-top easels, prepping brushes and paints and cups of water—more or less placing things to their liking, she assumed. She spotted an empty chair at the end and made her way to it.

The women chatted, welcoming her.

"I'm Maggie," she told them.

"First time here, Maggie?" the woman to her left said. "I'm Kathy."

"Yes, it is." Maggie grinned. "Nice to meet you all."

"I'm Jan." The young woman waved from the end.

"Sally over here."

"Mavis." The woman to her right held out her hand. Maggie shook it. "We've all been coming for a while."

"Oh, then I have some catching up to do."

Mavis waved her off. "Naw. We're all learning. It's great to see a new face."

"I'll second that." The male voice came from behind her. Andy?

She turned. "Oh. Hello there."

Andy grinned that wide, happy smile of his. She'd occasionally thought of that smile over the summer. It was kind and warm and... welcoming. "Glad you could make it, Maggie."

"I'm glad you could fit me into this class."

Mavis giggled. Maggie wasn't quite sure why.

"Not a problem," he said. "Right, ladies? Always room for one more."

"Yes, of course." Jan gave Maggie a smile.

Kathy agreed. "Sure thing."

"We love getting to know new people," Sally added.

"Great." Maggie glanced around the group, suddenly feeling a little self-conscious. Andy still stood to her right, sort of semi-behind her. She reached for her bag and began lifting out brushes, water cup, paints....

Andy pulled up a chair and sat beside her, his voice a little softer. "How was your summer at the beach?"

How was my summer? Oh, the usual—death, scandal, possible murder... You wouldn't believe it if I told you. She met his gaze. "It was...eventful."

"Sounds like you have stories to tell."

"Perhaps." She grinned back, suddenly feeling a little shy. *Are we flirting?* "Honestly? I'm glad summer is over. I'm looking forward to a fresh start this fall."

He grinned again. "Fresh starts are *never* overrated."

"Unlike love at first sight, or so I've heard."

Tilting his head, Andy seemed to give that a thought, then chuckled. "Coffee later? After class?"

"That depends."

"On?"

"You feel up to listening to a story or two?"

His eyes widened, and he held her gaze. "I'm intrigued."

That's a good thing. Right? Okay, Maggie, go out on the limb. "You know of a hole-in-the-wall place with super-strong java? Because, that would be like, my kind of place."

He narrowed his gaze. "You mean the kind of place where third grade parents hang out to get to know each other?"

"Yeah." She grinned. "That kind of place."

"Fresh coffee, fresh start?"

She nodded. "I'm in."

Thank You

Thank you for reading *The Me I Left Behind*. While Maggie suffered through some incredibly terrible moments, I hope you connected with her growth and development over the course of the story, as well as her determined strength when dealing with her divorce, her children, her husband's death, and more.

If you would like to leave a review at your favorite bookstore, or at my website, I would be most appreciative. I look forward to, and thank you for, your honest opinion.

You can leave your review here: https://maddiejamesbooks.com/products/the-me-i-left-behind-maggies-story

More Tuckaway Bay

Beach Therapy: A Novel
The Space in Between: Julia's Story
The Christmas Storm
The Me I Left Behind: Maggie's Story
I Wish You Love: Alice's Story (August 2025)
Anywhere But Here: Wren & Willow (May 2026)
Before I Fell (For You): Belle's Story (2026)

...and more to come.

About Madeleine Jaimes

Maddie James (aka Madeleine Jaimes, M.L. Jameson) writes upmarket women's fiction and contemporary romance, both with emotional depth and relatable heroines. Her stories often explore love, loss, second chances, and starting over. She's the author of over 70 titles and the creator of the Tuckaway Bay series. Learn more at www.maddiejamesbooks.com.

Do you get my Insider News?

Be the first to get the latest news about Maddie James Books, no matter the pen name! Get new release news, free ebooks, sales and discounts, sneak peeks, and exclusive content! Just add your email address at this link, https://maddiejamesbooks.com/pages/newsletter and we'll take it from there!